I0600270

More than Fiction

Misty Springs Romance: Book One

Juniper Nicole

Copyright © 2025 Juniper Nicole

Cover Design by Shelly Congdon

Cover Edits by Jae Shadowlance

All Rights Reserved.

This is a work of fiction. Names, characters, places, and incidents are either the product of the author's imagination or are used fictitiously. The author acknowledges the trademark status and trademark owners of various products referred to in this work of fiction, which have been used without permission. The publication/use of these trademarks is not authorized, associated with, or sponsored by the trademark owners.

Dear reader,

I'm thrilled you picked up this book and are spending some of your precious time with my story. There are millions of words out there to read, but I'm grateful you chose mine.

Quick heads-up, there are themes of verbal abuse, physical altercations, drinking, death of parents, alcoholism, and car crashes.

Sometimes, life hurts. But we can't appreciate the good times without experiencing the bad.

Cheers,
Juniper

SCAN ME
Listen to the More than Fiction playlist on Spotify!

To new beginnings that come from failed endings.

Chapter 1

DOORMAT 101: AISLE SEAT ADDITION

SOPHIA

I was going to die single and broke.

Not with a bang, not even with so much as a crackle.

Single and broke.

Those two words resounded in my head like a depressing mantra as my plane tore through a patch of rough air.

I scanned the row of passengers around me—strangers I was nearly certain would be the last people I'd see before meeting my maker.

The noisy chip-eater in the window seat beside me—it was an annoying pleasure to sit by you.

The woman in the aisle seat who fell asleep almost instantly and stayed that way the entire flight—even now, as we meet our end, I'm genuinely impressed.

To the rest of you across the aisle—*Godspeed.*

Despite the existential spiral, I noted that none of my fellow air travelers seemed even remotely concerned.

There was a *slight* chance I was overreacting, and the bumps that felt like massive potholes in the sky were completely normal.

Perhaps I wouldn't die single, broke, and stuck working two dead-end jobs—I added that last one to the mantra for some additional self-deprecation.

If my sister Penny hadn't relentlessly nagged me to "stop wallowing, get off my ass, and visit her in Phoenix," insisting that I spend my 24th birthday with her, I would have stayed safely grounded in Misty Springs and avoided this incredibly long return flight home.

1

Penny made it impossible to say no when she bought the plane tickets and schemed with my friends to cover both of my jobs, though a couple weeks of missed tips and wages were going to sting a little.

Penny was the anti-me—five years older and wildly successful—married, kid, rewarding career, the whole shebang.

Meanwhile, I could barely afford my apartment, my only means of conveyance were my own two feet, and I struggled to remember the last time I washed this jacket.

I gave it an unsuspecting whiff as Potato Chip tilted the bag, tapping the remaining crumbs into his mouth and shaking out every last salty bit.

Sleeping Beauty still hadn't so much as twitched. I briefly wondered if I should check if she were still breathing.

We hit another bump, forcing me to refocus on the music in my earbuds to calm down. The song shifted to one of my favorites by The Used. Something about a screaming bridge and a screeching guitar helped me feel at ease.

My thoughts shifted to Luke, my nephew, and how his nose turned up when I let him listen to my "yelly music."

After critiquing my music at dinner a few nights ago, he leaned in at the table and whispered, "Momma says you need a new boyfriend. I think you should date Batman."

Mashed potatoes nearly shot out of my nose at the comment.

No doubt the dinner-table conversations between my sister and her husband, David, were stimulating enough that Luke overheard more about my love life—or lack thereof—than any four-year-old should.

While true, it hadn't been an easy few months for me. I wasn't miserable—I was too busy keeping my head above water to find time to be miserable.

Though treading water was getting exhausting, and some days, it felt like I was slipping under. Plus, the restaurant I worked at was bound to notice the ketchup packets I'd been pilfering sooner or later.

But I was adjusting to life after Landon. Struggling alone was better than struggling with him.

The woman in the aisle seat next to me was still snoozing away, and while I was impressed by her ability to sleep so soundly, I was also slightly aggravated. She had been my barrier to the tiny airplane bathroom and sweet relief.

Penny often called me a "toxic doormat."

I disagree. I think I'm just considerate.

But as I sat there—squirming, suffering, saying nothing—I started to wonder if Penny had a point.

I focused on the next song to distract me and took a slow, calming breath as my mind raced.

Has a bladder ever actually exploded from being too full?

Is it toxic to be considerate?

Is that why Landon cheated? Because I was a doormat?

Am I a big enough doormat that I'd eventually take him back?

A loud ding and the flickering of overhead lights pulled me from my disaster spiral—or, as my friends call it, my dizzy spell.

I often fell victim to those, a million thoughts rushing in at once, opening a barrage of floodgates where scenarios and regrets spilled out, leaving me drowning in "what-ifs" and "how-comes."

The noise also caused enough ruckus to rouse my sleeping neighbor. And when a flight attendant walked by, I saw my opportunity.

"Excuse me, miss." I interrupted the attendant mid-stride. "Do I have time to use the restroom before we land?" I asked, more as a way to avoid asking my row-mate to move.

Request by proxy—a technique I must have picked up in *Doormat 101*.

"Of course. Please make it quick, though, hun. We're preparing to land," the flight attendant offered as she moved down the aisle, picking up trash and asking people to put their tray tables up.

As planned, the lady in the aisle seat overheard my query and stood to let me through. I thanked her quickly and made it to the bathroom just in time.

After washing my hands, I checked my reflection in the harsh light of the tiny airplane bathroom. I tightened my low ponytail, the faint curls from last night's dinner with my sister still clinging to the ends of my hair. The bright sun and the chlorine from Penny's pool had lightened my caramel strands, giving them a few golden highlights. My skin had a soft glow from the long days of constant southwestern sunshine, and my blue eyes looked brighter and more rested.

Maybe Penny was right. I did need this trip.

***

After landing, I strolled through the terminal, my tennis shoes squeaking with every reluctant step across the polished floor.

My black leggings were comfortable this morning, but now they were begging to be peeled off. White proved to be a poor shirt choice—my tank hadn't recovered from the coffee incident mid-turbulence. The stains were mostly hidden under my jacket, which had taken an equal hit but was dark enough to fake clean.

Something teal caught my eye at a small stand—a vibrant book cover that showed a black dress crumpled beside a spilled martini glass. The author's name, Monica McKenzie, was embossed in gold letters across the bottom.

The cover screamed romance, a genre that lately felt more mocking than comforting, but I couldn't resist.

More focused on devouring words than food, I grabbed the first thing I could find from a tiny cooler inside the stand, along with a bottle of water.

I settled in at my gate, peeling back the plastic from my hastily chosen wrap, and I took a hesitant bite. The rubbery chicken fought back, but I pushed through, forcing down a timid swallow.

I regretted my decision—one of many regrettable decisions— as I hungrily took another questionable bite, allowing my gaze to drift to the bustling crowd moving through the terminal.

I couldn't wait to crack open my new book, but I didn't want to get whatever cloudy white sauce was leaking down my hand on it, so I turned to people-watching instead.

A man talking loudly on his phone caught my attention. He looked roughly in his mid-forties, wearing a tan trench coat, holding a briefcase, and pulling a tiny roller bag behind him.

I created a game in my mind, inventing a fake biography for him, where I decided he looked inconspicuous enough to be a master undercover spy. However, due to his inability to control the volume of his voice, he failed spy school and was now a traveling salesman.

Next, I watched a woman with glasses and a too-large hoodie taking slow, aimless steps, passing a group of flight attendants and a couple of pilots.

I imagined her feeling defeated after her canceled flight and hopelessly stuck in the airport. That is, until a chance encounter at Margaritaville outside gate 23 proved to be the meet-cute of a lifetime. Her story would eventually become a Hallmark movie called *Meet Cute at Gate 23*.

If only real life worked that way.

I turned my phone off airplane mode and quickly let Penny and David know I had made it to JFK. A flurry of texts buzzed through, but I found myself unable to focus on them, as a demanding figure caught my attention.

The newest character to enter my made-up game was pacing near a window, wearing a light gray suit, and talking on the phone like he was furiously trying to reason with a scammer.

The phone obscured half his face, but what I could see was... distracting. Broad shoulders, long legs, and a suit tailored so precisely it might've been sewn straight onto him. Every tense word he muttered made the fabric shift, flexing with muscles that clearly had no business being confined.

I tried to assign him a fake backstory like I'd done with the others—maybe a fed-up CEO, maybe a hitman with a heart of gold—but my brain changed course halfway through. Instead of a fake name or a dramatic past, all I could picture were very real, very *vivid* scenarios.

This dry spell was *really* starting to mess with me.

My eyes stayed locked on him as he continued to pace with a controlled urgency, like he was trying not to snap. His midnight-black hair towered above the crowd of travelers as they bounded through the terminal around him.

I finally remembered I had a chewy, gritty bite of chicken in my mouth and forced it down my throat, sighing at my own antics. Pining after a stranger wouldn't help me get my life back together. I needed something bigger—something cosmic—to get my derailed train back on track.

My sad excuse for dinner wasn't cutting it, so I turned my attention back to the only thing that might satisfy me—Gray Suit.

He turned, slowly, deliberately, as if he could feel the weight of my stare. His phone was gone now, no longer shielding him, and for the first time, I had a full view of his face.

But it was his eyes that captured my attention most—deep-set, piercing, and unmistakably amber, like whiskey through sunlight. Even from across the gate area, I could tell the color was vivid, almost otherworldly, like the cosmic missive I just asked the universe for was blazing across his irises.

And they were staring right into mine.

Chapter 2

PLOT TWIST FIRST CLASS

Sophia

I was caught, completely stunned and unable to think, unable to move, or even tear my eyes away. I felt my pulse everywhere, including places that made my cheeks heat.

The gorgeous stranger flashed me a tantalizing grin, eliciting a soft whimper from my lips.

"Excuse me, miss." An older gentleman stepped into my view, blocking the absurdly handsome stranger and breaking my trance.

Blood rushed to my head as my body re-learned how breathing worked. I turned my attention toward the interrupter.

"Y-yes?" my voice squeaked. I cleared my throat and tried again. "Yes?"

"Is this seat available?" he asked.

"Oh! Of course." I removed my belongings and watched as he and a woman shifted into the seats next to me.

The man was thin and leanly muscled, dressed in cream-colored linen pants and a collared white button-down shirt. The woman—his wife, I assumed—was petite, donning a "coastal chic" outfit with large pearl jewelry. The couple dressed like they were used to flying when air travel was a luxury, not the mass transit cattle herding it was today.

Their interruption hit me like an ice bath. I dared to look in the direction the mystery man was standing, but he was gone.

I couldn't tell if I was relieved or disappointed.

The elderly man who was now seated beside me asked a question, but I was still jumpy from my awkwardly sensual airport encounter, so I had to ask him to repeat himself.

"Business or pleasure?" he repeated louder and slower.

"Oh. Pleasure," I answered, and my face warmed, my mind still in the gutter using that word. "I was visiting my sister and her family in Phoenix."

"Phoenix. I spent a good amount of time down there. My wife and I are coming back from Montreal. I'm Dan, by the way." He smiled before gesturing to the woman beside him. "This is Ethel."

I introduced myself and continued chatting with Dan, while Ethel occasionally chimed in from behind her Kindle—mostly to fill in details Dan forgot or to gently smooth over the ones he missed. There was a quiet rhythm to the way they interacted, instinctively in sync, like only couples who've spent a lifetime together can be.

I welcomed the small talk, as it was doing wonders to tame my voyeuristic libido.

A crackling announcement blared overhead, informing us that the flight to Misty Springs would be boarding soon.

Just one more short flight, and I'd be home.

"Sophia, this is a long shot, but can I ask you what seat you're in?" Dan straightened in his seat and pulled his phone out of the inside pocket of his coat.

I glanced at my boarding pass to double-check. "Um… 23C it appears."

"Gee, I just knew it!" Dan slapped his knee. "Didn't I say it, Ethel? I knew she'd be the one."

"You called it, honey." Ethel raised an eyebrow, her eyes remaining locked on her screen.

I sat in silence with a puzzled smile on my face.

"After thirty years of travel, you get status on airlines. I was bumped to first class, but Ethel is stuck in the back, in 23D to be exact. I don't want to sit by a stranger on the plane. I want to sit by my wife." He turned to her lovingly before returning his attention to me. "Could I convince you to switch seats with me, Sophia?"

"First class?" I tried not to sound too excited. "Absolutely!"

"Great. See, Ethel? I knew everything would work out." He grabbed her hand and kissed the back of it.

My heart pattered at the genuine affection they shared.

I listened intently as Dan continued, "I'm going to board with first class to ensure I get overhead bin space for Ethel's bag. But I'll go to your seat instead—22C."

"23C," I corrected him.

"Right, 23C. I'll take your seat, and when you board, take my seat in 1B. If any flight attendants ask, just tell them you swapped seats with me. Trust me, they won't care. A couple of nice folks like us switching seats is the least of their worries."

"Wow! Thank you! Wait…" I paused, possibly finding a fatal flaw in Dan's plan. "Is 1B by the window?"

It didn't matter if it was first class or not, one thing I couldn't stand was being by the window. Flying made me nervous enough, but some illogical place in my head told me that if I sat away from the window, I wouldn't be sucked out of the plane if we all started careening toward the ground.

"No, it's the aisle. These tiny planes have one seat on one side and two on the other in the first class section," he assured me.

"Then that sounds great, Dan! Anything I should know about first class? Is there a secret handshake or something I should learn? Do they only speak Pig Latin up there?"

"Ouya etgay eefray inksdray," he fired back, not missing a beat.

"Free drinks?!" I exclaimed a little louder than I wanted to.

"Just one, but it's a short flight."

I smiled and thanked him, waving goodbye as he gathered his things and began boarding.

My face nearly hurt from smiling so hard—those muscles have been getting much-needed use these past few weeks. For the first time in a long time, it felt like things were finally looking up.

***

I took my seat at the very front of the plane. It felt strange up here. My legs had so much room, and the seat felt cushier—it was about as luxurious as things got for me.

"Hi there, do you care for a drink? Cocktail? Beer? Wine?" a beautiful flight attendant asked.

She had long, slick blonde hair and was donning the airline's trademark form-fitting blue dress.

"I'll take a gin and tonic," I replied with delight.

"Sure thing." She smiled, leaning in closer. "Dan in 23C already told us about your seat swap when he got on. He said to sneak you an extra bottle if I could. I'll see what I can do." She gave me a conspiratorial wink and turned to the front of the plane.

I was ecstatic. First class, free drinks, and it looked like whoever was supposed to sit next to me wouldn't make it.

I settled in, buckled up, and pulled out my phone—already grinning at the thought of sending the group chat with my friends a smug first-class selfie.

The flight attendant returned with my drink. She also slipped another bottle of gin into my palm from the pocket of her dress. She quickly tapped her finger to her lips, assuring me this was our little secret.

With a contented sigh, I leaned back in my seat and settled my newly purchased book on my lap.

I didn't even feel the need to drown out the noise with my music this time. I was ready to experience this entire flight with all my senses.

Chapter 3

SEAT THIEF IN 1B

Corbin

Commercial air travel. What kind of sick joke was this?

I'd spent the last thirty minutes on the phone trying to reason with Buzz, all while weaving through crowds, dodging rogue suitcases manned by distracted kids, and smashing the phone to my ear to hear him over the airport chatter.

But when my grandfather set his mind to something, there was no changing it. And for some reason, Buzz's mind was made up to task me with overseeing the new branch in the middle of nowhere to help ensure it got off the ground.

I was close—so close to becoming CEO. We both knew he was retiring, and we both knew I was the obvious choice to be his successor.

Why me? Why now?

"This is the final boarding call for Flight 2286 to Misty Springs. All ticketed and confirmed passengers should proceed to Gate 16. The boarding door is about to close," the gate agent's crackling message rang through the terminal.

Shit.

I'd better hurry.

I had become unaccustomed to the rigorous rules of commercial travel. I unfortunately waited too long—hoping to dodge this trip altogether—and someone else claimed the company jet.

That wouldn't happen again. New company policy: no one flies without my sign-off.

If I didn't get to my gate soon, they'd shut the door and wouldn't open it back up.

It didn't matter who I was.

But I needed to walk it off after duking it out with Buzz. A futile task—you didn't fight with Buzz—you could try, but you would lose.

Not to mention the fact that there was this knockout brunette practically eye-fucking me in the gate area.

I was feeling a little too keyed up to stand there idly waiting.

The boarding door was still open, and the gate agent gave me a tight-lipped smile.

"Thank you." I glanced into her eyes and gave her one of my trademark smiles, watching her cheeks tinge pink.

Women were easy. *Too* easy.

As I made my way down the jet bridge, I tried to erase the frustrating phone conversation with Buzz from my mind, but each step I took along the faded and stained carpet made me more and more infuriated.

I had given everything to our company.

I was a machine. No distractions. No slip-ups. A squeaky-clean reputation for the board.

I felt unstoppable.

Anyone who was anyone knew who my family was.

Being named one of Manhattan's *Top 30 Under 30* didn't hurt either—though one more year and I would have been too late for that designation.

Once I stepped over the threshold of the plane, I was greeted by a busty blonde flight attendant standing in the refreshment area.

"You're our missing Mr. Buescher, I suppose." Her hand slid to her hip.

"That's me," I replied smoothly.

"Can I get you a drink?"

"Whiskey, no ice."

"It would be my pleasure."

I cleared the aisle and paused. This was... unexpected.

The brunette from the gate—the one whose stare enraptured me right after my losing argument with Buzz—was on this flight.

But it wasn't just that she was on this plane, or in first class, that made my steps falter.

It was the fact that she was in the wrong seat.

Chapter 4

Emotionally Catfished

Sophia

I was texting my friends, filling them in on my trip as I gleefully sipped from my drink when a tap on my shoulder tore my attention upwards.

I internally screamed as I choked on my gin and tonic.

Quite literally choked—coughing embarrassingly loud, my lungs burned as gin infiltrated the wrong pipe. I inhaled instead of swallowing, and now I was slowly drowning in the asphyxiated drink as the man who'd caught me assaulting him with my eyes back at our gate was speaking unintelligible words at me.

"You're in my seat."

My coughing subsided enough to understand what he said—his words laced with a mix of irritation and amusement.

I swore Dan said I was supposed to be 1B.

"I'm quite sure this is my seat," I protested between coughs.

"Show me your boarding pass," he demanded.

My eyes narrowed at him.

What was the difference between 1B and 1C to this man anyway?

To me, it meant a relaxing ride in the aisle rather than a nerve-wracking, fear-inducing ride by the window.

"Show me yours," I challenged.

He rolled his eyes and turned his phone toward me.

Sure enough, it said 1B.

I was in his seat.

"Please take your seat, sir," a male flight attendant said with just the right amount of exasperation as he strode up the aisle.

"I was trying to, but this woman decided to steal it," he gestured toward me like I was a criminal on trial.

What a *nark*.

The flight attendant looked between the two of us, assessing the situation and deciding who'd be more difficult to deal with—tailored suit or several-day-old black jacket. "Ma'am, may I see your boarding pass?"

This guy clearly hadn't chatted with Dan, and since my boarding pass would reveal that I didn't belong in first class, the jig was up.

Resigned, I grabbed my drink and slinked over to 1C, quickly shutting the window shade.

"Glad we cleared that up," the flight attendant remarked with a healthy dose of sarcasm before moving on.

I tried not to watch the frustrating, stickler-for-the-rules man as he unbuttoned his suit coat and shrugged it off his shoulders.

The blonde flight attendant who snuck me extra liquor earlier was nearby with a hanger, ready to place his coat in the cabinet near the front.

He whispered something in her ear while his fingers grazed her arm.

She giggled and blushed slightly at *whatever* he said to her.

I rolled my eyes at their exchange.

1B fell into his seat, shaking the row slightly with his muscled frame. He unbuttoned his shirt at his wrist and rolled it toward his elbow. I tried not to be hyperaware of every move he made—tried not to stare.

But what else was there to look at?

I wasn't about to open the window shade, and there were only so many variations of off-white cabin decor I could pretend to study before I lost my mind.

Routine announcements crackled through the speakers as I stole tiny glances in his direction. His jawline was unfairly sharp, dusted with dark stubble that looked too perfect to be a five o'clock shadow. His lips were full—obnoxiously so—and I caught myself holding my breath as he ran his tongue across them.

What a mouth.

Too bad he used that same mouth to rat me out to the flight attendants.

The plane lights flickered, and my nerves kicked into overdrive. I downed the rest of my drink, tilting the plastic cup and tapping it to wring out every last drop of liquid courage, using my teeth to strain the ice. My very "non-first-class" behavior earned me a sideways glance from my new neighbor.

"Here is your whiskey, sir," the blonde flight attendant purred, handing him a plastic cup wrapped in a napkin.

I tried not to notice how the amber liquid mirrored the warm, rich tone of his eyes—the same eyes that had pinned me in place across the gate earlier.

She then slipped him an extra tiny alcohol bottle with a wink.

Guess Winky just doles out extra alcohol to anyone.

Needing a distraction, I turned my attention back to my phone, and since I was already in a terrible mood, I decided to read the texts I had been avoiding—my cheating ex-fiancé Landon's texts, to be precise.

Some of them were several days old. I had let them pile up, not bold enough to block him but unwilling to respond.

It had been several months since I called off our engagement. I thought it was all behind me.

But recently, he'd reemerged out of nowhere, popping back into my life like a weed.

Landon (3 days ago): Hey, babe, I miss you and am thinking of you. I heard you were in Phoenix.

Landon (2 days ago): I was thinking that you should keep the ring, it meant something to me, and it meant something to you. You should have it.

Landon (2 am this morning): Forget it, all of it, I hope you're happy. You've ruined my life. I'm pawning your ring tomorrow, along with the shit you left at my place.

Landon (5pm tonight): I'm sorry, babe. I didn't mean any of it. I just miss you so damn much. We need to talk.

Landon (8 pm tonight): Call me when you're home. I love you.

I suddenly felt the urge to break open my other bottle of gin before the boarding door even shut. I slid it from my jacket pocket and tried to open it quietly, but the seal cracked loudly as it broke.

1B overheard, and I caught him peering my way. His eyes darted toward my phone before lifting to my face.

I quickly closed out of my texts, switching it to airplane mode, and stuffing it in my jacket pocket—wishing it was that easy to shut Landon out in real life.

1B raised his plastic cup toward me with a grin. "Cheers," he said, his voice low and smooth.

It was unfair how it resonated somewhere deep inside me, swirling in my gut—or maybe that was the wrap from earlier.

"What are we cheersing to?" I asked.

"To new adventures. It's my first time visiting Misty Springs."

I watched his sinful lips as he articulated every syllable. Each word that fell off his tongue was polished and refined.

I couldn't help but feel inferior. The disparities between us felt glaring. I didn't belong in first class, and I didn't belong in a conversation with someone as disarming as him.

We clinked our drinks—my tiny gin bottle to his plastic cup—then sipped in silence as the flight attendants began the safety demonstration.

The routine instructions filled the space between us, as we both quietly sipped our drinks.

Once we started rolling toward takeoff, I glanced in his direction, searching for something—*anything*—to say. After all, I had technically stolen his seat—no reason to stay hostile.

"Are you traveling for business or pleasure?" After speaking with Dan, that felt like a casual air traveler thing to ask.

"Pleasure?" he asked with a huffed laugh. "What kind of person visits a crap town like Misty Springs for pleasure?"

"*Crap town?*" I repeated, incredulous.

"I did some research. Population not quite hitting 20,000. Entertainment options include a handful of bars that close at midnight and a few greasy-spoon restaurants. Seems *real* charming."

His arrogant assessment made my blood boil. "That's awfully judgmental for someone who's never been there."

"Just an observation," he drawled, clearly unbothered by my tone.

"Yeah, well… some people like small-town life."

"Sure. People who are too close-minded to go anywhere else." His eyes stared at mine with a challenge.

"Or maybe people have been elsewhere and realized some places are full of arrogant jerks." Not my finest comeback. The gin might've dulled my filter—and my ability to deliver a proper zinger.

"There are *arrogant jerks* everywhere," he shot back, smirking.

"That we can agree on." I let my gaze drag over him from head to toe, making it clear who I was referring to as the arrogant jerk in this scenario.

We snapped our heads forward, neither seeming to want to continue this unnecessarily hostile exchange. At least our squabble distracted me from takeoff—my least favorite part of flying. Landing was a close second, but at least when you land, the flight is over.

I dug around in my purse for my earbuds, internally screaming at how catastrophically wrong my attraction meter was.

It felt like I'd been catfished—but in reverse. Instead of falling for someone's fake photo only to discover they were balding and beer-bellied, I was drawn to the muscled frame, the tailored suit, and the smoldering confidence, only to find out that, beneath it all, he was just an…

"*Asshole,*" I muttered quietly, or at least I thought I did. The way his head whipped toward me, I couldn't be sure.

I popped in my tiny white earbuds, turned on my favorite angsty playlist, cranking the volume, and buried myself in my book.

Who knows? Maybe I'd get lucky, and we'd both get sucked out of this window.

Chapter 5

Dickish Raincloud

Corbin

I must have really pissed her off. I didn't mean to.

No, actually, I did. I was bitter and angry about my situation—I guess I wanted to spread it to others and let them drown in my misery alongside me.

Besides, once I glanced at her phone screen and saw she had some guy who couldn't wait for her to get home, anger flared in my chest. I wonder how he would feel if he knew his girl was fawning over some stranger at an airport.

Still, I didn't realize poking fun at Misty Springs would trigger her so quickly.

I assumed she was from the tiny town, as we were on an inbound flight there. I'd observed women get pissed off about their shoes getting ruined or another woman wearing the same dress as them. I've never witnessed a woman get so defensive about a town, even if it was a crap town.

The woman in 1C had turned her music up so loud to block me out that I was genuinely concerned for her hearing.

If she weren't so clearly angry with me, and if I were the type to enjoy small talk on a plane, I might have told her that the book she was reading, by Monica McKenzie, was one of ours. The publishing arm of the Buescher Enterprises empire—Buescher-Jones Publishing—signed her almost a decade ago.

I'd met Monica a handful of times. She was a bit high-maintenance, but her books raked in a fortune thanks to thirsty women worldwide.

I connected to Wi-Fi when we hit ten thousand feet, and a flurry of emails from Andi, my assistant, rolled in.

With this new project came a promotion for Andi, and a promise from me that she'd take over the branch as soon as possible. She'd been handling everything from scouting the location to setting up the offices and recruiting for some of the lower-level roles.

From: **Young, Andi**
Subject: Job Positions and Postings
To: **Buescher, Corbin**
   C,
   Your picks from corporate arrived this week. Ned Spriggs and Susan Rhett. I'll be honest, Susan seems great, but I'm not sure why you picked Ned because he is a total twat waffle.
   When you read this, you will probably be on the plane to lovely Misty Springs. I'm sorry, I'll miss seeing the reaction on your face when you first arrive.
   I have your room booked at the only hotel in town. I already asked, they don't have a fancy boy espresso machine. No worries, there is a lovely coffee shop nearby. I'll bring you an americano in the morning as soon as I get back into town.
   Believe it or not, Misty Springs has a taxi service. Your driver will be picking you up at the airport. I don't have to tell you where he'll be, the airport is so small, you cannot miss him.
   Attached are a few lower-level positions that I will post on job sites tonight. Review them if you must. It's a waste of your time, though. You know they are perfect.
   Don't go Googling twat waffle,
   A

Twat waffle... I'd never heard such *bold* language to describe someone. Then again, bold seemed like a good way to describe Andi.

Andi was young, sharp as a tack, and completely unfiltered. Her outfits were as colorful as her personality—vibrant colors and patterns that popped against her dark skin.

She's probably the only one brave enough to call me on my shit, too—besides Buzz—and now I could add the 1C to that very short list.

I chuckled, thinking about how cute 1C looked when she called me an asshole—the little V that formed between her eyebrows, the scrunch of her nose—and I wasn't the kind of guy who found things cute.

I closed my emails and switched to reading my text messages.

Davis: I'll keep your chair warm while you're gone.

Sullivan: Yo, on a scale of 1 - 10, how crazy is Cindy? I hope 10.

Gram: I hope you find Misty Springs as magical as I did growing up there. It is a wonderful place, with wonderful people. I wish I could visit you there. Send pictures.

Gram, the "Jones" name in the Buescher-Jones legacy, grew up in Misty Springs. I suddenly felt a twinge of guilt for calling her hometown a *crap town*.

She met my grandfather when she was twenty on a vacation to upstate New York. They fell in love, and the rest is history.

I took a doleful breath and closed my eyes, letting my head rest gently on the seat. My conscience prickled. I needed to lose my pissy attitude and focus on the task at hand.

This was a very personal challenge and one that would surely earn Buzz's approval. It's why he sent *me* to oversee things—it meant too much to him, to Gram.

Me: I'll see what I can do Gram, love you too.

Hers was the only text I responded to—Davis and Sullivan knew better than to expect a reply.

I sipped the cheap commercial airplane whiskey, its harsh flavor dragging me back to the nights spent at that crummy dive bar, Theo's, when I attended Cornell. I could almost hear the busted jukebox that only played Nirvana when you kicked it—or maybe that was just the music bleeding from my angry neighbor's earbuds.

Either way, this flight felt like a grim metaphor for all the downgrades my life was currently enduring.

The sun had begun to set, casting orange light into the cabin through the other passengers' open window shades. I glanced toward the nearest one, remembering my view had disappeared the moment my seatmate huffed and slammed the shade closed.

But with my gaze in her direction, I found myself caught up in the gentle slope of her nose, the way her cheekbone caught the last of the sun's warmth, and the curve of her lips that held my attention for longer than I'd like to admit.

Before I could stop myself, I turned my head to get a better look.

Her eyes were buried in the pages of her book, and I was hopeful she was distracted enough by whatever cutesy character Monica curated to notice my staring.

My gaze traveled down her body, drawn to the tight white tank top hidden beneath her black jacket—the way it kept teasing me with glimpses of the smooth skin of her waist.

Her long legs were crossed, with her hand wedged between them. Her thighs tensed subtly, and her lips curved into a grin that teetered between sweet and sinful.

I had read enough of Monica's novels to guess what kind of scene she was reading—the sensual images that were likely swirling in her head.

She caught her bottom lip beneath her teeth, a move that sent a rush of blood through me.

I let out a breath and turned back to face the front of the plane, letting my head fall back with a thud on the firm cushion of the headrest.

I couldn't afford to lose my focus. I had a mission: get this branch off the ground, keep Andi busy enough to handle most of it, and spend as little time in the tiny town as possible.

Then I could focus on what actually mattered—becoming CEO—and never setting foot in Misty Springs again.

Chapter 6

WHITE AND NERDY

Sophia

This flight was sponsored by alcohol, screaming loud music, steamy romance novels, and the comforting anonymity of a closed window shade.

After landing at Misty Springs Regional Airport, there was a very brief taxi to the gate. I popped out my earbuds, my ears ringing slightly at the sudden absence of yelly music.

My muscles ached, and I gingerly stretched out my arms in front of me and rolled my neck.

The plane stopped, and the seatbelt light turned off with a loud ding as the cabin sprang to life.

I didn't plan to see 1B again, but I knew the chances of running into him in a town like Misty Springs—especially if he stayed the night—were fairly high. There was only one hotel in town, and I just happened to work there.

Maybe it wasn't fair for me to call him an asshole. In my defense, I'd been flying all day, and the only food I had eaten was currently colliding with my stomach acid in what I assumed was about to be an epic battle.

Still, it wasn't in my nature to be rude to people, especially people I didn't know. I could try to be just a little nicer.

I shifted toward 1B and gave him a "bless your heart" smile. "Good luck with the *business* you have in Misty Springs."

He stared at me, mouth slightly open like he wanted to say something but didn't know what. I preferred his silence, so it was the perfect goodbye.

I eyed the flight attendant as she moved toward the boarding door.

Excellent timing.

I quickly formulated an escape plan—one that hinged on the fact that, thanks the turbulence, he still hadn't received his jacket from the flight attendant.

But before exiting, I couldn't resist adding one last remark as I stood and lifted my bag onto my shoulder.

I met his gaze head-on. "For the record, Misty Springs is pretty *damn* charming once you give it a chance."

With that, I trotted off the plane and rushed up the jet bridge, heading straight for the nearest ladies' room. If I timed this right, I could avoid crossing paths with 1B altogether.

It felt a little absurd—I didn't have a solid reason to steer clear of him, except for the strange mix of attraction and irritation he managed to spark.

After washing my hands, I turned my phone off airplane mode, and a single text flashed on the screen.

Devyn: Here! Outside door #2. Trunk is open.

I planned to pay Hank, our town's only taxi driver, for a ride, but Devyn insisted on picking me up.

At 5'3", Devyn was a tiny, terrifying force to be reckoned with—tough-as-nails on the outside, with a heart of gold. She had a fierce edge, but once you were in her circle, you had a protector for life.

After wrangling my overstuffed suitcase from baggage claim, I walked outside to a crisp autumn evening. The sun was drooping low in the sky, and off in the distance, the rich woodline of trees beamed with red, yellow, and orange leaves. As good as it was to see Penny and her family, I missed the colorful forest scenery and the chilly fall air while I was away.

I missed *home*.

As I took in the sights and smells around me, a pair of cheery horn bursts snapped me out of my thoughts, pulling my gaze to Devyn's little black car.

"You look tired," Devyn stated matter-of-factly as she helped me drop my suitcase into her trunk.

"I can always count on you to keep me humble, Dev," I replied with a smile, bringing her in for a tight hug.

"In the mood for a drink? The night is young, and I missed celebrating your birthday with you."

"I would, but I'm beat. Plus, I have to be at Elijah's early," I told her over the top of the tiny car.

"Boo. I missed you, and I've got some serious Theresa drama to share."

Theresa—Devyn and my boss at Boomer's, and the woman I'd seen entirely too much of the day I walked in on her writhing underneath my fiancé.

The familiar scent of the cherry car air freshener and tiny hula dancer on Devyn's dash greeted me with a nostalgic embrace as we plopped into her Corolla.

"Well, we've got five minutes until we get to my place. Can you spill it on the way there?" I was intrigued, but my exhaustion crept in, pulling me toward the edge of sleep.

"Alright, alright. Let's just say she's moved on. Quickly and often."

She shifted the car into drive, and we eased away from the airport curb.

"Oh boy. Who's the unlucky guy now? Is he engaged? Married?" I assumed since it seemed like *taken* was Theresa's type.

"A couple of out-of-towners first, then—wait for it—she locked in on Fredrick friggin' James."

Devyn rarely cussed, but when she was angry enough to, it was always in Spanish. And if it reached that point, you'd better tuck and run.

"Fredrick?! My daddy owns a Jaguar dealership, Fredrick?"

"Guess Landon got the axe," Devyn continued.

"And I guess that explains the uptick in the late-night texts to me lately."

Maybe Landon didn't understand how small-town gossip worked. I knew he was still with Theresa after our split, and now I understand why he was trying so hard to suddenly get me back.

Poor, lonely Landon got a taste of his own medicine.

"He's texting you?" Devyn asked, anger seeping into her tone.

I waved a hand in dismissal. "It's nothing you need to worry about. He'll get bored of trying and move on."

She side-eyed me, her lips in a tight line.

"What?" I asked, despite knowing full well what that look on her face meant.

"You need to tell him off. Guys like him will never get the message from your *kind rejection*. He needs to hear it loud and clear." Her smile turned devious. "And if that doesn't work. I know some people who could take out his kneecaps for us."

Devyn was so animated. Anytime she spoke, her whole body spoke with her.

I chuckled, knowing… well, hoping she was joking. Sometimes, when it came to her, I couldn't be sure.

"I'll keep you posted," I said with a laugh. "I think I just need to move on. Maybe he'll get the message if he sees me with someone else."

"Goody! Then you'll be happy to know that Cassie, Lana, and I have created the perfect Tinder profile for you as a birthday present." She dug out her phone and veered a little off the shoulderless road we were on.

"Devyn! Give me that!" I snagged the phone out of her hand so she could focus on driving, trying not to wince at the fact that the girls were scheming behind my back.

Cassie and I had been thick as thieves since we were kids, spending summers running barefoot down the gravel roads, daring each other to jump into the creek no matter how cold the water was.

Devyn found us our freshman year of high school, bold and bright, crashing into our lives like a firework. She won us over when she snuck extra cupcakes from the cafeteria into study hall.

Lana came along senior year, shy and wide-eyed after her family moved to Misty Springs. We won her over with friendship bracelets and late-night talks about everything and nothing.

Since then, it's been the four of us—stitched together by a thousand little memories, still holding tight.

"I created it on my phone. Open up the app. Sam was initially concerned, but I showed him it was for you. He and the guys helped me curate the perfect profile that would captivate the male audience."

Sam was Devyn's boyfriend. They were the perfect contrast—like fire and ice. Devyn, feisty, short-tempered, and fiercely passionate, was perfectly balanced by the tall, calm, easygoing Sam.

"I dunno," I whined.

"You need to get out there, Soph! Don't you know the best way to show someone you're over them is to reverse-cowgirl somebody else."

"I don't think that's how the expression goes."

"It does in my book," she said with a wink before returning her eyes to the road.

I opened the app with nervous tension. Saying I was ready to put myself out there and actually doing it were two different things.

An image popped up of me behind the bar at Boomer's, one of my two jobs, shaking a cocktail shaker. I looked carefree and happy, and my makeup was pretty on point, too. Come to think of it, that was the day Lana, Devyn, and Cassie had hijacked me, forced a makeover on me, and took me to dinner before my shift. An act I now suspect was based on ulterior motives.

There were two other photos. One showed me sitting in Lana's coffee shop by the large front window, iced coffee in hand, with "Sophia" scrawled on the cup in front of me. I couldn't remember when it was taken—one of the girls must have snuck the shot while I was distracted.

These little deviants must have been planning this for a while.

The last photo was of Cassie, Lana, Devyn, and me, taken by our friend Trevor. I remember laughing when he yelled for us to kiss right before he snapped it.

It was my favorite picture of us. I had it framed on a wall in my apartment. Even looking at it now, my heart fluttered.

These girls were my everything, and this picture? It was perfect.

"So I'm okay with the pictures," I relented, as the screen turned blurry through my misted eyes.

"Yes! See! Okay, now read the bio."

I followed her orders and scrolled down.

Sophia 24 - Misty Springs

Loves:
Coffee
Bar Food
Gin
Music
Tall, dark, and mysterious men

Three songs to describe me:
With a Little Help from My Friends - The Beatles
Beautiful Day - U2
White and Nerdy - "Weird Al" Yankovic

"Okay… where do I even begin?" I said, still staring at the screen, a little dumbfounded. "Let's start with tall, dark, and mysterious… and end with White and Nerdy?"

"Well, we figured Landon was blonde and not that tall, plus an obvious tool. We were going for an opposites thing."

"Sure. But *White and Nerdy*? The other two songs are great choices, but c'mon!"

"It highlights your love of music and shows how funny you are at the same time. Besides, you always have your nose buried in books—total nerd material. You're like Princess Belle, hot and well-read. We just need to find you a hot beast of a man to rub—"

"Okay, Dev. I get it. I get it," I said through a laugh.

She'd never stop if I let her keep going. Devyn was always ready to share her opinion, whether good or bad. The plus side? I always knew exactly where I stood with her.

On the other hand, Penny and I danced around serious topics, only scratching the surface of how we truly felt. I think we both closed ourselves off after my parents' accident, and neither of us has been quite the same since.

Devyn pulled into my apartment complex and threw the car in park. She turned to me, her bronze skin glowing despite the darkening evening light, her face serious. "We just want you to be happy, and you said it yourself: you need to move on from Landon."

"I don't *hate* it. I love you guys so much for doing this for me. I just—"

27

"Say no more." She gave me a wink, exaggerated by her long lashes and large honey-colored eyes.

She jumped out and helped me wrestle my bag from her trunk, the car squeaking in protest as we tugged it free.

"I missed you." She wrapped her arms around me, squeezing my waist. "Boomer's wasn't the same without my P.I.C. working alongside me."

"I missed you, too," I replied, pulling away from her. "And I am back to being your partner in crime tomorrow night."

I made my way up my apartment's stairs while Devyn watched from her car. Once I wrangled the lock and opened the door, I gave her a wave.

She tooted her horn a few times—lighthearted, like a salute.

I smiled as she pulled away, the sound of her engine fading into the distance.

I loved her. I loved all my friends.

With people like this in my life, being single, broke, stuck working two dead-end jobs, *and* nerdy didn't feel so bad.

Chapter 7

Maverick's Mach II Meatball Sub

Corbin

As Andi promised, finding my taxi driver was easy enough—an overly talkative, balding, middle-aged man named Hank.

From the moment I climbed into the back seat, I was treated to a history lesson of Misty Springs I hadn't asked for but seemed destined to endure.

Hank rambled on, his words spilling out faster than I could keep up with, turning what should've been a short ride into an eternity.

Finally, after what felt like hours of listening to Hank's life story and town trivia, we arrived at my destination: the only hotel in Misty Springs.

Elijah's weathered sign shone in the darkening evening light, casting a faint glow on the otherwise quiet street. The hotel was a modest, two-story building with rooms with exterior entrances.

Exterior entrances? What was this, a Motel 6?

I shivered as I considered what the interior would look like, exactly how many stains my mattress would have, and what part of the body those stains came from.

I walked into the lobby, still skeptical but pleasantly surprised. The decor was modern, and everything was bright and clean.

My eyes skimmed past the empty front desk, landing on a set of open double doors. Flickering lights and the rattling booms of what sounded like an action-packed movie echoed through the quiet lobby.

Curiosity piqued, I walked toward the commotion, and the smell of something rich and savory clung to my nose as I approached.

I peered inside the open doorway, spotting groups of people sitting at tables, eating and laughing, while the movie *Top Gun* played in the background.

The place was packed. Based on the number of people, the entire hotel might be inside. I couldn't recall ever staying at a hotel where guests watched movies together in a dining room. The situation was *strange*.

I lingered near the entrance. The iconic volleyball scene was just wrapping up when a whiteboard hung on the wall next to the door caught my eye.

I read what appeared to be a themed menu written in elegant, colorful handwriting.

Maverick's Mach II Meatball Sub: A turbocharged meatball sub served on a long, toasted hoagie roll

Iceman's Chill - made with blue curaçao, lemonade, and a hint of mint to cool down the heat

A movie and a themed dinner? Just as I was about to chuckle at the absurdity of it all, I felt a tap on my shoulder.

Turning, I was met by a woman with piercing green eyes and copper red hair. She was almost as stunning as the woman in 1C, almost.

"Mr. Buescher?" she asked, her tone light and curious.

"Yes. You know who I am?" I suppose it would make sense for someone to have heard about me here. Maybe some page-six news had gone viral enough to reach sleepy towns like this one.

"Yeah, well, you're our last guest checking in tonight, and your luggage—and the confused look on your face—kind of gave it away," she replied, her tone flat, turning to walk toward the front desk without even asking me to follow her.

Oh. Fair enough.

I followed her over to the front desk, dragging my feet more out of bruised ego than fatigue.

She moved through the check-in process like she was on autopilot—efficient, detached, and entirely unimpressed.

Not by my usual lines. Not by the casual flash of my watch. Not even by my tabloid-quoted "panty-dropping" smile.

It was… humbling.

The rest of our exchange was a well-rehearsed information dump—meal hours, gym access (there wasn't one), and how to reach the front desk for assistance (though it was unmanned from 12 a.m. to 6 a.m.).

She handed me my room key—an actual, physical key, the kind you insert into a lock and turn. The weight of the key in my hand felt almost foreign, as if I'd just stepped into a time capsule disguised as a hotel.

Without much more interaction, the woman—Cassie, according to her nametag, not that she bothered to introduce herself—plastered on a clearly fake smile and told me to enjoy my evening.

I grumbled, sauntering outside and up the stairs toward my room. Sliding the key into the lock felt strange—unfamiliar, but oddly nostalgic. And once inside, I was proven wrong about this place all over again.

The room had light-colored walls with a simple wallpaper, a sleek gray and black bedspread, a large flatscreen, and a small black recliner chair in the corner.

It wasn't much, but it was pretty *damn charming*.

I smirked as I recalled the woman on the plane's parting words to me.

1C had my full attention when she gave a little stretch, arching her back, her chest jutting forward just enough to make me wonder if it was intentional. When she flashed me that smile, it had an edge to it—something playful, maybe even a little dangerous.

I couldn't tell if I should be scared or turned on.

I think I was both.

As soon as she vanished, I found myself scanning the terminal, my gaze drifting toward the luggage carousel, hoping to spot her again.

Though she lingered in my mind, I wasn't going to read into it, or the fact the entire interaction left me feeling… off.

I was in a new place, surrounded by new faces.

Tomorrow, I'd be back home in New York, in my element, free from the haze of this town and its maddening inhabitants.

Chapter 8

BUT FIRST, COFFEE

Sophia

Five a.m. came way too soon. Dry shampoo was my friend this morning.

I spritzed my roots and threw my hair in a messy knot on the top of my head, pulling a few strands to frame my face. I grabbed my tinted moisturizer and toothbrush out of my suitcase, not having the energy to unpack yet.

Last night, I only managed to change into my *Sublime* t-shirt, shuck my leggings off, and pass out.

I needed to be at Elijah's by six, so I quickly washed my body, dressed, and packed my gym clothes in a duffel bag.

Cassie and I planned to work out after my shift was over and before I started my second job at Boomer's.

I studied my reflection. The days spent in Phoenix—away from the countless hours and struggle to make ends meet—were a much-needed reprieve. My skin looked clearer, my eyes were less puffy, and my nerves were less shot from the constant rush from one job to another.

I didn't realize how much stress had been piling up until I left it all behind. I'd gotten so good at dancing around the piles, I hadn't realized how high they were stacked.

As I faced yet another double shift in a long week of them, I felt everything start to teeter.

With a sigh, I stepped back from the mirror, giving myself a quick once-over—black slacks, a black polo with "Elijah's" embroidered on the lapel, and tennis shoes.

Yep. I was the epitome of glamor.

I rolled my eyes at my reflection, trying to shake off the feeling that I was settling into a routine that didn't quite match the life I'd envisioned for myself.

But I wasn't here for visions—just for the money.

I had bills to pay after all.

I grabbed my bag, tucked the book I'd picked up at the airport under my arm, and strolled out the door.

My first stop was Grounded, my friend Lana's coffee shop. It was a couple of blocks away from my apartment and a daily morning stop for me. Coffee shops in Phoenix were lovely, but none of them could compare to Lana's.

My apartment was a little pricey, but living in the bustling downtown area of Misty Springs had its perks. I was within walking distance of Grounded, Elijah's, a small grocery store owned by Devyn's family, and many other boutiques and local shops.

Which was a must since a vehicle was another luxury I walked away from months ago. Landon had held the RAV4 he'd bought me over my head for a while—first using it as leverage to force me to stay with him, then threatening to sell it, then threatening to trash it.

I hadn't saved up enough for a down payment for my own car yet—I was barely covering my rent and general living expenses as it was.

I opened the black glass door to full tables and a line of people waiting to place orders. Grounded was busy, and the sight of it warmed my heart. Lana opened it a couple of years ago, and watching it thrive felt like watching her dream unfold before me.

The smell of freshly brewed coffee hit me as soon as I walked in—rich, earthy, with a hint of sweetness from the pastries Lana had been perfecting.

The espresso machine hissed and steamed in the background, its sound merging with the melodious chatter of the patrons inside.

Lana, always effortlessly chic with her long dark hair perfectly in place and crisp black apron, was behind the counter, a face of calm during the rush. She was pouring a latte for one customer while gesturing with a free hand to another table.

I made my way into the crowded shop and stood in line. Lana noticed me, giving me an enthusiastic wave.

I waved back, right as my purse vibrated on my hip. I pulled out my cell while my eyes watched an adorable little girl in front of me—her face pressed eagerly against the glass display of cake pops, cinnamon rolls, and all kinds of sweet treats.

Her mom had just finished ordering when the girl threw her hands up in delight, spotting a butterfly-shaped cookie.

In her excitement, the little girl knocked my hand, sending my phone soaring into the air.

Panic surged as I scrambled to catch it, praying it wouldn't shatter when it hit the ground. I didn't see the woman walking by, holding two large cups of coffee, until it was too late.

My hand shot out instinctively, right into her path, and before I knew it, her drinks flew—one of them landing with a splash in the same instant my phone hit the floor with a wet, sloppy thud.

The woman looked at me, stunned, through her neon orange glasses. Her bright purple jumpsuit was miraculously dry, save for a little spot on her left shoulder where the coffee had splashed. The rest of her outfit—vibrant as ever—seemed untouched by the disaster.

She blinked a few times, processing the situation, before letting out a small, incredulous laugh. "Well, that was… unfortunate," she said, her voice full of playful disbelief.

"I am *so* sorry," I blurted, my words stumbling over each other. "I didn't see you, and I tried to catch my phone, and—I just… I'm really sorry."

"It's fine." She waved dismissively. "I think I'm in better shape than your phone, though."

"Please, let me get you a replacement drink. It's my turn to order. What did you get?"

"Don't worry, Soph, I saw the whole thing. I've got you ladies covered!" Lana called from behind the steaming espresso machine.

One of Lana's employees acted without question, grabbing a mop and heading straight for the mess. I winced a little, embarrassed by the scene I had caused and the extra work I put on Lana's shop during their hectic morning rush.

I bent to retrieve my phone from the puddle and sighed as I dabbed the black screen with a napkin by the pickup area, watching the coffee spread in messy, blotchy streaks across the screen. A new cell phone was not on the list of expenses I could cover this month.

"I'm Andi, by the way," the girl in the vivid clothes stated as she stood beside me, waiting for her replacement drinks.

I studied her briefly. Although she looked young, her voice carried the steady confidence of someone much older.

"Sophia," I replied. "And sorry again, I'm just glad it didn't get you too bad."

"No worries." She smiled, her gleaming white teeth contrasting against her dark skin. Then she glanced at the book still tucked under my arm. "Whatcha reading?"

"Oh." I pulled the book out from under my arm and turned it over in my hand. "It's called *Stirred Martini* by Monica McKenzie. She's one of my favorite authors."

"You're a fan of hers?"

I nodded.

I could talk about books forever, but I was sure this stranger didn't want to hear me ramble on and on.

"What do you like about her work?" she pressed, leaning in a little, eyes bright with interest.

Or maybe she did want to hear me ramble.

"Well… I like how she develops the side characters, almost as if they feel like friends of mine too. She gives her main characters real depth—flaws, edges, things that resonate with you, and make them feel alive. Everyone's layered in a way that keeps you gleefully pulling back each layer chapter by chapter."

"Anything else?"

I shrugged. "I love how, in the end, you aren't just rooting for the main characters to get together. You're left feeling like destiny was a word invented because of those two. You recall every shared experience they had as a way to believe in clandestine events, like fate. And if the two of them don't end up together, you're ready to put on war paint and go into battle to fight for their love."

A wistful smile spread across my face as I recounted the numerous beautifully written stories I read and how each made me feel butterflies and believe that love is real—even if it didn't feel very real to me right now.

"Plus, she knows how to write a hell of a steamy sex scene. More than just coming up with words for vagina or penis in different, clever ways."

Andi gave me a wicked-looking smile.

"Oh gosh." I smacked my forehead. "I just said vagina and penis in front of a minor, didn't I?"

Andi was full-on laughing at me. "I'm 21, you're safe."

Her laugh was so wild and untamed, it pulled one from my lungs as well.

I wondered if she was visiting Misty Springs or just passing through. Maybe she was new here?

Andi reached into her starburst-orange purse and handed me a business card as Lana set our new drinks in front of us with a wink.

"We could use someone like you around the office. Call me if you're interested." She reached for her two drinks, then turned and walked out.

I watched her leave, and my eyes jumped to the large clock that hung above the door, giving me a mini heart attack. I was going to be late. I tucked the card hastily in my bag, and while Lana's back was turned, I dropped a five-dollar bill in the tip jar and bolted out the door.

"Thanks, Lana!" I yelled over my shoulder on my way out.

Yep, vacation was over, and reality had come crashing back with a vengeance. The serene rhythm of sunlit days had been swapped for the frenzied chaos of my everyday life—constant shuffling, jumping from place to place, and a pace that left little room to breathe.

And whether I liked it or not, this was the life I'd somehow created for myself—forever dancing around piles of stress, hoping I wouldn't slip, and it would all come crashing down.

Chapter 9

EVANDER HOLYFIELD

Corbin

This morning, my driver, Hank, was once again in a chatty mood as he drove me from the hotel to the Misty Springs office. He blabbered incessantly, despite my very obvious lack of enthusiasm, and my attention focused solely on checking emails on my phone.

Dull driver choices aside, I had to hand it to Andi. She picked a hell of an office space.

The building was an unassuming two-story structure with a weathered brick exterior, standing tall against the sleepy town's nature-rich skyline. The layout was divided into two distinct office spaces, one on each floor, with a polished, black staircase running down the center.

The first floor of the building was vacant, a perfect opportunity to generate revenue as a commercial rental space—Andi was always thinking one step ahead.

Upstairs, where our offices resided, had a rich, industrial feel—tall ceilings, exposed brick walls, and rustic, well-built furniture made the scene feel like a combination of a cigar lounge with a brightly accented feminine touch.

It was clear Andi had her hands in it—her vibrant, larger-than-life personality bled into every corner. A neon yellow rug beneath a vintage leather chair, mismatched pillows scattered across a deep purple velvet sofa, and wall art were pieces just as bold as her.

She achieved a lot, with minimal oversight from me. A flicker of hope spurred in my chest—maybe I wouldn't have to be here as much as I initially thought.

Andi and I had discussed this being a "trial run" for her. Ned may put up a fight when I announce her being the manager here—he'd be reporting to someone much younger than him. But I barely knew Ned and felt more than confident in Andi's ability to take over this branch. Besides, Gram's sentimental attachment to this place would make it impossible for me to hand it over to a stranger.

After giving myself a tour of the space, I claimed the larger of the furnished offices to start chipping away at my inbox.

I had just set my bag on the oversized desk when the loud clang of the heavy steel entry door echoed through the space. I stepped out of my new office just in time to see a man—roughly my age and about the size of a Mack truck—walk in, his view of me obscured by a set of rolled-up blueprints.

He dropped the prints onto the large table in the common area, then jolted slightly when he noticed me.

"Shit, sorry. Oh, shit, I didn't mean to say shit." He heaved a large breath appearing to regain his composure. "Andi asked me to drop these off. She said no one would be here this early," he said as he motioned toward the rolled-up blueprints.

He brushed his hand against his jeans to dust them off, though the denim appeared dustier than I imagined his hand was. He closed the distance between us in a few long strides.

"I'm Brent," he introduced himself, stretching his hand. His smile barely visible beneath the thick bristle of red facial hair.

"Corbin," I replied as we shook, still unsure who this massive stranger was.

Brent let go of my hand, lifted the brim of his royal blue ballcap with faded letters that read *Chase Construction*, and ran a hand through his shaggy rust-colored hair before fitting it back on.

"I'm your contractor. I've been working with Andi on the remodel. I was dropping off plans for the ground floor."

"Ah, I see. Well, the place looks great, Brent. I look forward to seeing what you do with the rest."

"Thanks. Andi's been great to work with, though she's got my entire crew like putty in her hands. Plus, she's terrifying to negotiate with. She's whittled every change order down to nothing. I don't think I've ever seen my dad back down from a disagreement so quickly." He crossed his arms, making his domineering presence even larger, but something about him didn't come off as threatening despite his size.

"She is a force to be reckoned with," I agreed, knowing all too well what it was like to be on the receiving end of Andi's determination.

"We've had a great time and appreciate the opportunity to work on the next phase. It's nice to... change things up."

Something in his tone hinted at an underlying meaning, but I didn't care enough to read too much into it. My phone buzzed in my pocket—the relentless monster demanding my attention.

I pulled it out and glanced at the unread messages assaulting my inbox.

"You're busy. I should get going." Brent shook my hand again, flashing another semi-hidden but genuine smile, his green eyes crinkling in the corners. "Nice to meet you."

"You too, Brent."

I turned on my heels, head down, facing my phone, ready to face the chaos waiting for me.

I hung my navy suit jacket on the funky-shaped yellow coat rack in the corner, unbuttoned the sleeves of my white shirt, and rolled them up my arms.

Buzz always told me to dress the part, so I'd keep dressing like a COO presenting at a board meeting, even if I was only a glorified babysitter in a dead-end town, meeting with an angsty but brilliant twenty-one-year-old.

I had just opened my laptop when I heard the heavy steel door slam shut again, followed by the unmistakable tap-tap-tap of heels hitting the hardwood floor.

I could only imagine they belonged to some wildly intricate shoes that were as loud as the woman wearing them.

"Oh, good. The plans are here," Andi started talking before clearing the threshold to my office, as if she had some tracking beacon to know I was in here. She walked directly inside, not bothering to knock, and placed a tall brown paper cup on the dark wood desk.

"Americano for you," she announced as she tapped a straw open.

"Iced vanilla latte for me." She slammed the straw into the cup with an exaggerated flourish, taking a long, deliberate sip. Her eyes narrowed slightly as though tasting it wasn't just an act but a performance.

"Brent, the contractor, just dropped them off," I told her, my eyes locked on my computer screen.

"His dad is scared of me. You should see how red his face gets." She giggled mischievously.

My eyes flicked to her as she paused and took another sip—tilting her head in confusion before going in for another uncertain sip.

I shook my head at her before going back to my emails.

Despite it being the weekend, there were hundreds of them. Work didn't take a break at my level just because the calendar said Saturday.

My americano—though nothing extravagant—was surprisingly good. Smooth and bold and exactly what I needed after a restless night tossing and turning over dreams of a stunning brunette who couldn't stand me.

I wasn't the kind of guy to overanalyze dreams—or care about them for that matter—but the fact that the woman in 1C invaded mine was an annoyance I couldn't quite shake.

"Okay, what in the Evander Holyfield punch to the mouth is this concoction?" Andi asked incredulously.

My eyes lifted to her, eyebrows raising in question.

"This drink... It's not a vanilla latte. It's something else."

"Is it good?" I asked, not caring much about the response.

"It's *really* good."

"Then shut up and drink it."

"Oh no, my boss is being mean to me. Help HR, help." She sucked on her drink again.

I glared at her, and she smiled, holding the straw between her bright white, toothy grin.

"Your cup says Sophia. It looks like you stole some lady's drink." I pointed out before once again trying to tune Andi out.

"Sophia?" She spun the cup around, finding the little name written in black marker. "Oh, Sophia!"

I wasn't taking her diversion bait—I had too much to do. I stared at my screen, hoping she'd take the hint and leave.

Andi was silent for all of ten glorious seconds before interrupting me again.

"Aren't you going to ask me who Sophia is?"

"If I do, will you leave?" My patience was wearing thin, not that Andi cared.

"*Sophia* is the hopefully, possibly, probably, maybe, new Assistant Editor I'm going to hire."

"Great, can't wait to meet her," I said sarcastically. "Now. You. GO." I flicked my hand toward the door.

"Oh, boss man, you need to get laid something fierce," Andi said, strolling out of the office, loudly slurping the tiny remnants of her drink.

I snorted at that comment.

She's annoying when she's right.

Chapter 10

CLITORATI

Sophia

Cassie and I sat on two mismatched folding chairs in a small room behind the front desk of Elijah's. We had asked Julio, the hotel's master chef, to make our favorite salad, a bed of crispy greens, roasted vegetables, grilled chicken, cheese, and nuts. He also made a tangy vinaigrette dressing, blending the salad with savory, salty, and slightly sweet notes.

It was my second favorite food after the ribs at Boomer's.

Cassie was my oldest friend and the manager at Elijah's. She offered me a job working the front desk after the tornadic destruction Landon left behind.

"What's the theme for tonight?" I asked Cassie with a mouthful of salad.

"Jurassic Park."

My eyebrows lifted in amusement. "Who came up with that one?"

"Elijah, of course. The drink is yellow Jell-O shots with little gummy bugs in the middle. You know, to look like the frozen bug thingy that scientist guy found."

I snorted, almost sending salad flying out of my mouth. "Julio must be having a heyday with that one."

Elijah, the namesake behind Misty Springs' infamous hotel, was as eccentric as he was temperamental. He stayed away most of the time, only emailing Cassie to check in occasionally, or if he had an idea for a theme night he wanted to feature.

Every Friday and Saturday night, the hotel came alive with carefully crafted menus, specialty drinks, and desserts that matched the movie's theme.

Elijah wanted to create a place where residents and guests could connect, making Misty Springs feel more like a second home than just a place to pass through.

The theme nights were so popular that people traveled from miles around, bypassing chain hotels, just to spend a night in this quirky gem.

Julio, the chef, had a knack for crafting food and drinks that perfectly matched Elijah's theme, making the experience even more immersive. The flavors were always bold and intricate, with each dish showcasing his true talent.

We often commented that Julio's culinary skills were wasted in a small town like Misty Springs, but Julio laughed it off. He's a lifer here, always saying he wouldn't dream of living elsewhere.

Another amazing person who helped make this town so damn charming.

Take that, Mister Judgmental Fancy Pants, Better-Than-Everyone 1B.

"You look pissed. What's going on?" Cassie asked, interrupting my thoughts.

"Oh, it's… nothing. I'm just tired. The flight home kind of wore me out."

I wasn't sure why I didn't mention the gorgeous jerk from the plane. Maybe because I'd tried—and failed—to stop thinking about him all last night, and saying anything out loud would only make it worse.

"You still want to work out with me, right?"

I nodded as I pulled out my phone to check the workout for the day, thankful that the ancient device seemed to have survived the spilled coffee incident. The tiny envelope notification at the top reminded me I was just about to check my email in the coffee shop before I made a fool of myself.

The email preview's subject line caught my attention—a job alert. Odd, considering the only alerts I'd signed up for were publishing jobs within ten miles of Misty Springs. And let's be real—nothing ever happened within ten miles of Misty Springs.

Two job postings appeared for Buescher-Jones Publishing, triggering something in my mind from earlier.

"Oh my gosh! I completely forgot!"

"Whadja forget?" Cassie asked as she pressed her Diet Coke to her lips.

"I was handed a business card today from an extraordinarily dressed woman who I thought was a teenager. This was right after I spilled her coffee everywhere, and Lana had to make replacements for her."

As I continued, I dug around my bag, looking for the card left behind by the mysterious and flashy woman.

"And while we waited for said new drinks, I may have brought up penises and vaginas, maybe even some clitorises slipped out. Wait, is that right? Clitori? Clitoras?"

"Clitorati," Cassie stated matter-of-factly.

I barked a laugh. "No, it's not that. Clitorati sounds like a secret society for female erotica."

She shrugged. "So what's the story here? After you ranted about genitalia to this teenager, I'm going to see you on *To Catch a Predator*?"

"No, that's not the story. The girl—who was not underage, by the way." I pulled out the tiny white card and started reading from it. "Andi Young, Executive Assistant at, gasp!"

"Did you just say the word *gasp*?"

"I did and I'm going to do it again because, gasp! She works at Buescher-Jones Publishing."

"Buescher-who-what?" Cassie took another bite of salad. "And why does that name sound familiar?"

"Buescher-Jones Publishing is like… my dream company. They published my favorite authors! They published this!"

I held up my most recent Monica McKenzie book.

"And they just posted two job openings in Misty Springs!" I set down my phone and lifted my chin. "But they are in New York, not here. Are they here now?"

I'm not qualified to work there.

I didn't finish school.

Surely, they'd toss me aside once they learn that factoid.

"Dizzy spell. Take a breath." Cassie placed her hand on my shoulder and audibly breathed in and out a few times until my breathing steadied with hers. She dropped her hand and leaned back in her seat.

"I know this Andi person. She's been staying here. Are you going to reach out to her?" Cassie asked.

"I don't know." I started nervously bouncing my knee. "I'm not qualified. I don't even have a degree."

"Yeah, but you took a million English courses and aced every one. You're the most well-read person I know, and you already have an in with Andi. You *have to* go for it."

"Cassie!" A breathless Pam rushed in on us. "Jamie called in again. I'm not even halfway through the rooms yet. Do you think you can help me out?"

Cassie was one of those people who rolled up her sleeves to help anyone with any job throughout the hotel. She started working here during our freshman year of high school, cleaning rooms, and since then has held almost every position. She was also one of the few people who could handle Elijah and his unpredictable behavior.

"Sure thing, Pam. I'm just finishing up," Cassie said as she shoved a final forkful of salad into her mouth.

"You're the best!" Pam backed out of the door and then flung it back open, poking her head in once more. "And hi, Sophia, you look tan." She disappeared again before I had a chance to respond.

Cassie and I stood up, but before we left the break room, she grabbed both of my arms and locked eyes with me, her emerald green gaze intense. "You are amazing, Sophia Jane Carlson, and you can do anything you put your mind to. You are too talented to be the front desk clerk at Elijah's, and you need to pursue this."

I started to object, but she cut me off.

"Ah ah ah, nope. No more words. No more dizzy spells. That's it. Those are the facts." Cassie grabbed my empty salad bowl, stacking it in hers to return to the kitchen. "I'll meet you at the front desk at three. We can't be late this time, or the coach will make us do burpees."

I gave her a silent salute since I was banned from talking. She hated it when I did that, but she smiled anyway, and together, we walked out of the breakroom.

I tried not to get my hopes up, but a tiny voice in the back of my mind was already doing backflips, whispering that this might be exactly what I needed to turn my upside-down life right-side up.

Chapter 11

ANDY KNOTERBOY

Corbin

"Hey, boss man. Come look at the local talent," Andi yelled from the large common area outside my office.

I stood and stretched, rubbing my strained eyeballs. I felt behind—and the fact that I was hundreds of miles away from the main office made me feel restless. I walked out to find her scrolling on her phone with her elbows on the table next to a pizza box.

"What are you talking about?" I asked, pulling a slice out and slapping it on a paper plate. "And did you confirm my flight back to JFK this evening?"

I just needed to take a look at the space and get a brief lay of the land for now. I'd return to Misty Springs in a week or two to dig into things further and connect with the New York office transfers, Susan, and Ned. For now, I was itching to get out of this town.

"Just look. And yes." She turned her phone to me.

"Who is Andy Knoterboy?" I asked, reading a Tinder profile of a 25-year-old tanned, shirtless man with blonde curly hair and aviator sunglasses. "And why are you checking him out on Tinder? I thought you found men *repulsive*."

"Andy Knoterboy is me. Get it? Not-a-boy."

I stared at her with a confused look as I took a bite of the greasy pizza.

"Glad you asked. So, if you're a woman seeking women, you only see a small sampling of what's out there. Not that I'm trying to turn anyone, but I like seeing the whole pool, not just the shallow end. So, I created two profiles, one for Andi and one for *Andy*. You know what I'm saying?"

"No. I literally have no idea what you are saying. I rarely do." I grabbed another pizza slice, piled it on my plate, and turned back to my office, sucking my greasy finger into my mouth. I would have to run a few extra miles to burn this lunch off.

Andi skipped to my side, following me like she didn't recognize that my leaving was the end of this conversation.

"What I'm saying is…" She uninvitingly plopped down in the chair across from my desk and continued to prattle on. "I just click here. And I can scout all the single females in the area from the comfort of my phone."

She slid her phone across the desk to me, and I glanced down at a smiling 23-year-old blonde named Rachel, who was ten miles away.

"You sound like a stalker. A lying stalker," I said, turning my focus back to my increasingly growing to-do list.

She pulled her phone back and continued, ignoring my comment. "This is one of many eligible women in a 20-mile radius who are looking for love, hookups, dirty DMs, or just good, clean fun with a man. I created alter-Andi to see all the women in the area and increase my sample size. But here, you can tread these waters for a bit. Jump on in, the water's fine."

"Yeah, I'm not doing that." I pinched the bridge of my nose. "And stop with the pool analogies. I have to finish these projections. Can you please just go… elsewhere?"

"Oh, come on! It'll be fun!"

She was like a gnat that hovered in your vision—no matter how many times you swat at it, you just can't get it to leave.

"So, I'll pretend I'm you, looking for a nice woman to spend time with. Not her, not her, nope, not her."

An irritated breath shot out of me before I tore into another slice of pizza.

I didn't need an app to find a woman. I was just about to tell Andi to stop wasting her—and my—time when she suddenly shot out of her chair.

"This is her! Sophia!" She looked at me as if I was supposed to know who she was talking about.

I chewed on my pizza, knowing I didn't need to comment—Andi would keep going on her own.

"Coffee shop, Sophia? The one whose delicious drink I stole?"

"Oh, great. You can ask her what flavor of drink you stole and catfish her simultaneously," I deadpanned while trying to get back to work for the hundredth time. "Are we done with this now?"

Apparently, we weren't because she was still talking and pacing in front of my desk.

"The one I gave my card to? The one I want to hire? Aren't you even a little bit curious about her?" She asked, sliding her phone across the desk once more.

I groaned, but my curiosity got the better of me. I looked down at the profile, barely ready for what I was about to see.

I froze mid-chew.

A jolt of recognition surged through me, and my pulse quickened, and I leaned closer, as if doing so would change the reality of what I was looking at.

The woman who clashed with me on the airplane and then invaded my dreams.

1C. *Sophia.*

I hastily swallowed before I began scrolling through the photos—again and again, unable to look away.

There was no denying she'd caught my eye the moment I saw her—but my fight with Buzz had left me in a fog, too distracted to really take her in.

Now that I could look at her, I mean *truly* look at her, I was captivated. Unable to look away.

She wasn't just beautiful—she held the kind of beauty that stole the air from your lungs. As I let out a quiet, shaky breath, I realized she almost stole mine.

In one picture, she stood behind a bar, her face lit with a smile so wide it tugged one out of me without even trying.

In the next, she was gazing out a window, thoughtful. Her eyes were a calm, ocean-blue—and I couldn't help but wonder what was circling behind those waves.

Another showed her with friends, laughing—casual, effortless. But all I saw was her. The warmth in her smile, the way she lit up the frame.

"Well?" Andi's voice snapped me out of my daze. I had forgotten she was still standing there, watching me.

I cleared my throat. "You think hiring someone based on their dating profile is a good idea?"

I slid the phone back across the desk, locking my composure back into place.

Andi rolled her eyes dramatically, letting out an exaggerated huff. "I don't want to hire her because of this. I want to hire her because I think she'd be a good fit. Her observations on Monica's books were spot on. Plus, she seems to have a great personality, which is seriously lacking around here. I think you'd like her."

"What makes you think that?" My tone came out sharper than intended. Catching myself, I added with a smirk, "Since when have I liked anyone?"

She grinned, shaking her head. "Fair point. I just have a good feeling about her, that's all."

I leaned back in my chair, trying to appear nonchalant. "Well, we can't hire someone based on your *feelings*. Despite being exiled here, we have protocols and a human resources department to go through."

My brief encounter with Sophia had been enough of a distraction. The last thing I needed was her walking through those doors every day. I didn't plan on being here much, but I wasn't taking any risks, not with the vote for CEO so near on the horizon.

Andi waved off my comment like it was inconsequential, her confidence as solid as ever. "We'll see."

My jaw tightened as I once again focused on my laptop. I knew precisely how Andi operated—once she locked in on something, it was only a matter of time before she made it happen.

But that wouldn't be the case here, I'd see to that. Plenty of other candidates would be in the mix—it didn't need to be *her*.

Eventually, Andi took the hint that our conversation was over and walked out without saying another word.

I attempted to refocus, but the words on the screen might as well have been hieroglyphics for how little I was absorbing. My mind was nowhere near where I needed it to be.

My thoughts kept drifting off to 1C—*Sophia*.

Our encounter on the plane and the texts I probably shouldn't have but definitely did read.

Why would she be on Tinder if she had a boyfriend?

And *White and Nerdy* by Weird Al? Who was this woman?

Chapter 12

Jurassic Pork

Sophia

My shift at Elijah's ended and I changed into my gym clothes, waiting for Cassie. With a few minutes to kill, I decided to stop in the kitchen to see what my favorite chef was up to.

The second I pushed through the swinging door, the aroma of fragrant cumin and lime hit me.

Julio stood at the center island, chopping cilantro with rapid-fire precision. His white chef's jacket was somehow spotless, though his apron bore the evidence of a day's worth of culinary artistry.

He grinned as he saw me, pausing to slam the knife down and spread his arms wide like he was about to perform.

"Sophia! You are turning heads today. Que se ve muy *hermosa!*" he hollered with his trademark flair. His energy was contagious, a perfect match for the vibrant chaos of the kitchen.

I barely understood Spanish—most of what I did know came courtesy of the eccentric chef currently grinning at me. Still, I managed to pick out "miss" and "beautiful" from his playful greeting.

"Gracias, Julio," I replied, my tone laced with amusement.

He responded with an exaggerated bow. "De nada, mi reina," he said with a wink before returning to his cilantro.

"Jurassic Pork tacos, eh?" I asked, reading the blackboard and swiping a few bites of the tomatoes Julio had cut up already.

Julio smiled as he placed the cilantro in a metal tub in his prep station. This was his pet project, making the cuisine to accompany Elijah's theme movie nights, and he'd come up with some wild ideas.

Last month, he created an entire *Breaking Bad* menu featuring Walter White Russians, blue rock candy "meth" cupcakes—an arguably questionable choice—and "Pollos Hermanos" chicken sliders.

"¡Ah, cierto! I saved some shots for you and your amigas." He handed me a small paper bag of Jell-O shots he had extracted from the fridge.

"Julio, you really know the way to a woman's heart." I clutched the paper bag to my chest.

"Sí. And you know how to make the men swoon for you. You walk around like that, you'll find a man for sure. El Hombre!"

I snorted a laugh. "Based on my luck with men, I will have no *el hombre* anytime soon."

Cassie stormed through the door, exasperated. "There you are!" She made a beeline for me and started pulling me out of the kitchen.

"Hi Julio, bye Julio!" she yelled over our shoulders.

"¡Adiós, señoras!" Julio yelled back.

"Sophia, we have thirty minutes before we have to leave, and I still have a ton to do. I need your help!" She paused to look me up and down. "You look smoking hot girl!"

Thanks to the fiery redhead before me, I'd been hitting the gym with renewed dedication.

Hard enough that I finally felt brave enough to wear the olive-green shorty shorts I'd impulsively bought months ago but never dared to put on.

They clung to the tops of my thighs, a bold departure from my usual wardrobe. Paired with the black tank top with thin crisscross straps in the back, I revealed more than a fair share of skin.

I felt lighter and stronger—not just physically but emotionally. It had been a long road to reclaiming my confidence after shedding 180 pounds of deadweight, otherwise known as Landon.

"Reporting for duty." I stood ramrod straight and stomped my feet together. "What do you need?"

"First thing, I said it a million times, I am so tired of the drill sergeant routine. Find something new," she scolded.

"Sir, yes, sir!" I fired back.

She glared at me before continuing, "Second, I have a room that needs turndown service. It's the Davidsons' room, you know them, it won't be bad. In. Clean. Out. Done."

"Yes, drill sergeant!" I started to walk away, but Cassie grabbed my arm and pulled me back in front of her.

"*Third*, I have a room that needs a full clean. The next guest is here to check in already. You likely won't get it all done. Start in the bathroom, get as far as you can, and Pam will be in to finish it off before it's time to leave. She's already working OT. I'm just trying to make it easier on her."

"I got this, no worries," I assured her.

"Room 110 is turndown, 213 is a full clean. Here is the master key. Pam already has a cart outside their rooms. Be ninja stealthy so no one thinks a rando in booty shorts is in their room!"

The phone rang at the front desk, beckoning Cassie to answer. I saluted her, and she rolled her eyes before rushing off to answer it.

The turndown was a cinch. I made the bed, grabbed the used towels, emptied the trash, cleaned the toothpaste off their sink, and, for my own personal flair—just for regulars that I adore—I folded the towel into a cute little design and placed it on their bed.

Next was the full clean. I knocked twice to make sure no one was inside.

"Housekeeping!" I called, giving the door a couple more raps for good measure.

Nothing.

I inserted the master key in the lock, grumbling inwardly about the antiquated system. We all hated those clunky keys, but Elijah insisted they added to the inn's nostalgic charm.

"Housekeeping," I called again, cautiously opening the door.

The room was still and silent, neat as a pin. Whoever had stayed here was either a clean freak or hadn't been here long enough to do anything besides sleep.

"It's go time," I said to myself, setting my bag of Jell-O shots down on the desk. I popped in my earbuds and started walk-dancing into the bathroom.

The loud buzz of music filled my ears, and as much as I wanted to grumble about the extra work, there was something oddly zen about cleaning. Plus, I would always be there to help one of my friends, just like they'd been there for me—a silent promise we'd kept through the years.

That and the promise of downing one or two of those Jell-O shots from Julio later kept me moving.

Chapter 13

Booty Shorts

Corbin

"You sure you need it now? Can't you just call the hotel and ask them to hold onto it until you're back next week?" Andi asked as she floored the accelerator of her car—a canary yellow Chevrolet Corvette Stingray.

Of course, Andi would buy the most obnoxiously flashy option available.

"Yes, I need it now. It's important. I don't want to risk it getting lost." My stomach twisted with disbelief. I never forget things. Yet here I was, an idiot who'd left behind the one item I never traveled without.

"You still haven't told me what *it* is." Andi's curious tone bordered on annoyance as she turned briefly to face me.

"*It* is personal," I replied curtly, unwilling to elaborate.

The compass wasn't just an object—it was a lifeline, a relic of a memory I hadn't shared with anyone—not even Andi.

A gift from my grandmother when I was fifteen, given to me at a particularly difficult time in my life. It had quietly become my anchor over the years. Whenever I doubted my direction—literally or figuratively—it helped me find my way.

"I really admire your ability to open up and share with me," Andi muttered, but she didn't push further. "At least we've got time. The Misty Springs Airport probably has five people in it, and let's face it, I drive much faster than Hank. You're lucky to have me, you know."

I leaned back against the seat, the engine vibrating beneath me. "Remind me to thank you later."

"You could thank me by learning how to drive."

"I *can* drive," I countered, though it had been a while since I did.

"Sure you can." Her voice dripped with sarcasm.

The car's sleek design felt comically out of place as we wound through the quiet streets of downtown Misty Springs. The shops, their colorful facades picturesque, lined the cobblestone streets. Sunlight reflected off the river that ran parallel to the main road, where locals jogged, biked, and walked their dogs along a scenic path.

We turned onto the incline leading to the inn, its stately architecture perched on the hillside overlooking the river. In the early afternoon light, it looked almost regal, framed by lush evergreens and brilliantly colored mature trees.

Andi threw the car in park in front of the lobby. "I'm heading in to scope out the theme for tonight."

"I noticed that when I arrived. What the hell is that about?"

"On the weekends, they serve themed food and drinks paired with movies or shows in the dining room. You should try staying here for a full weekend sometime. It's fun, and the food is to die for."

I recalled the sandy volleyball scene and the delightful aroma that rivaled that of my favorite Italian restaurant back home. I shook my head. "*Food to die for.* At a hotel in the middle of nowhere? Doubtful."

She shrugged and pushed the door open with a theatrical groan.

As I stepped out of the car, my eyes flicked to the second floor, where my room was, and my heart dropped.

The door was ajar.

Damn it.

Maybe housekeeping was in there. I needed to move fast, hoping they wouldn't take it—or worse—mistake it for trash. I climbed the stairs two at a time, cautiously nudging the door open.

"Hello?" My question was met with silence.

The room looked empty. It appeared housekeeping had started cleaning but hadn't finished. My gaze immediately landed on the compass, still sitting on the end table where I'd left it. Relief flooded through me as I crossed the room, reaching for the tarnished metal.

Its weight was familiar and grounding. The slight crack in the glass served as a testament to its journey with me.

My thumb brushed over the inscription etched on the back: *Home is where the heart leads you.*

I slipped it into my pocket, exhaling deeply. It was time to leave this damn charming little crap town behind—for a few days at least.

As I turned to leave, my attention was caught by an unsuspecting paper sack sitting on the desk. I was sure it wasn't mine. Lifting it, I gingerly peeked inside to find little plastic cups of gummy bugs in yellow Jell-O.

What the hell?

I chuckled at how strange this hotel was, assuming it had something to do with the "theme" Andi mentioned earlier, when I heard a soft thump sound from the bathroom.

I set down the bag full of strange cups of goo and investigated the noise.

"Anyone in here?" I asked.

Silence answered.

I inched closer and caught a glimpse of something in the bathroom mirror—a reflection.

The realization hit me like a truck.

1C. Sophia.

In my room.

I watched her in silence for a moment as I tried to process seeing her here, in the flesh, as if my constant thoughts of her last night manifested her here—just a few hours later than I would have liked.

I moved closer, angling myself to see her reflection more clearly in the mirror. She was focused on scrubbing the shower walls, her movements methodical but energetic. A messy pile of hair swayed slightly atop her head, bobbing in rhythm to her too-loud music. But what really caught my attention was the miles of exposed skin peeking out from a crisscross pattern of thin fabric across her back.

And then my gaze slipped lower.

Her tiny shorts hugged her curves in molded perfection.

Mesmerized, I watched her body sway back and forth as she wiped the tile. My pulse thundered in my ears as my mind raced.

I *should* just grab my compass and go. Andi was probably already in her car, tapping her fingers impatiently on the steering wheel. That's what my rational mind was screaming at me.

But my feet? My feet had other plans.

Each step felt like an act of defiance against every ounce of common sense I prided myself on having.

And yet, here I was, moving closer—drawn by something intangible, something magnetic. Like the compass in my pocket pulling the needle North, forcing me forward.

I leaned into the doorway. If she turned her head just a fraction, she would see me standing there.

But she didn't, her attention drawn to her task.

I cleared my throat loudly, and the sound made her jump, letting out an adorable little squeak.

"Oh my gosh, you scared the hell out of me!" she yelled, ripping her earbuds out, the faint crackle of music still audible. Her eyes were wide, her chest rising and falling as she glared at me. "What are *you* doing here?"

"I feel like I should be asking *you* that question," I countered, slowly scanning her from head to toe.

She caught me doing it, her brow arching.

"This is my room," I clarified.

"Not as of eleven a.m., it isn't. Now, if you'll excuse me, I need to get this ready for the next guest." She shoved past me, brushing my arm as she did.

The contact was brief, but it set my nerves alight, leaving me wanting more.

"You work here?" I asked as I crossed my arms and leaned against the bathroom doorframe.

"No, I do this for fun," she shot back over her shoulder, her sarcasm sharp enough to cut.

"Is that your uniform?" I cocked my head to the side.

She turned to face me without missing a beat. "Standard issue."

With an exaggerated flourish, she gestured down her body.

My eyes followed, slow, deliberate, taking her in—the curve of her hips, the way her shorts clung to her thighs. When my gaze finally returned to her face, her cheeks were flushed, a rosy hue that crept to the tips of her ears.

She swallowed hard, her lips parted slightly as if to say something, but no words came.

In her silence, the air in the room shifted, charged with an electric energy that crackled between us.

And judging by the way her breath hitched, I wasn't the only one who felt it.

"What are you doing here, *1B*?" she asked, her voice cracking slightly.

"Forgot something, can't remember what now." I shoved off the doorframe and stepped towards her.

"No. I mean, what are you doing here, here? In Misty Springs?" She took a step back.

"Business, not pleasure, remember?" Another step closer.

"What kind of *business*?" She took another step back, meeting the wall of the small room.

Her eyes never left mine—two deep blue pools, calling me closer, drawing me in, and washing away any sense of logic or reason why this could be a bad idea.

I stepped closer, nearly closing the gap between us but keeping a slight distance, despite my body's plea to press up against her.

Her breath caught as my hand slid behind her, slow and deliberate.

My fingers skimmed the hem of her tight tank top at the small of her back. I braced my other hand against the wall. Our lips hovering inches from each other, breath mingling in the tiny hotel room.

Blood coursed through me, hot and steady as my fingers explored lower, trailing along the top of her shorts and gently sweeping across the exposed skin of her back.

"What are you... what are you doing?" she whispered, her words dancing across my lips.

My tongue darted out to taste them—and for a second, I swore I did. Sweet, warm, and entirely addictive.

She inhaled sharply as my arm jerked, snapping off a tag I'd zeroed in on earlier while very intently staring at her ass.

I smirked as I ran the tag along the waist of her tiny shorts, bringing it between our bodies.

"New shorts?" I asked, my voice dry.

She glanced down at the tiny white paper in my hand, then lifted her gaze—pausing at my lips before meeting my eyes again.

Every instinct screamed at me to kiss her, to lay her down on the bed where I'd spent the night tossing and turning with thoughts of her.

"Thanks for covering, Soph," came a voice I didn't recognize as the door swung open—spilling bright sunlight into the room and jolting us both.

Sophia shoved me back, her wide eyes darting to the intruder.

"Oh! Sorry, I didn't realize, um…" the woman stammered, clearly mortified by what she'd walked in on.

Her gaze darted between us as she shuffled awkwardly. "Actually, wouldn't you know it? I forgot my favorite dust cloth. Silly me, I'll, uh, go grab it now!" She turned and disappeared out the door as quickly as she'd arrived.

"Oh no," Sophia groaned, burying her face in her hands.

"Friend of yours?" I nodded toward the door where the woman had bolted.

Sophia let out a frustrated sigh. "Coworker—and a very gossipy one at that."

I raised a brow, letting a smirk curve my lips, though the twinge of something bitter gnawed at me deep inside.

"I see. Don't want the boyfriend to find out about your little secret? Eye-fucking strangers at airports. Looking for tall, dark, and mysterious men on Tinder. Hooking up with strangers in hotel rooms."

Her head snapped up, her expression conflicted—part indignation, part something else I couldn't quite read.

"I don't—" she started, stumbling over her words. "I'm not—" She took a deep breath, her shoulders dropping as if trying to ground herself. "I don't know what you think you know about me, but you're mistaken."

"Mmhmm," I replied, my tone deliberately nonchalant, though I could feel anger welling inside me.

Despite my having no right to be angry. What did her boyfriend or dating profile matter to me?

I glanced at my watch. "I have a flight to catch out of this *charming* little town anyway."

The haze Sophia had wrapped around me moments ago lifted, and clarity hit me like a cold splash of water. The intoxicating pull of her—the siren's lure that had almost dragged me under—was gone, leaving behind the stark reminder of my reality.

I had a plane to catch and a life waiting for me that didn't involve getting tangled up in… whatever this was.

Andi was sorely mistaken if she thought this woman would ever work for my company.

"You really are an asshole," Sophia said defiantly as she stormed out of the room.

I shrugged—she wasn't wrong.

For good measure, I stole the paper bag of Jell-O shots to make my hellish commercial flight home a little more bearable.

Chapter 14

SCIENCE SAVES LIVES

Sophia

Embarrassed. Angry. Still frustratingly turned on.

I let the steam curl around me as the warm water beat against my skin in my shower.

1B slipped into my thoughts with maddening ease, stealing focus from my workout, my walk home—everything.

The way the hotel room came alive under his gaze, how the air seemed to charge when he looked at me—it clung to me now.

The way he unraveled me with the faintest touch.

I've felt attraction before—the jolt that tightens your core, the heat that rises beneath your skin like a fever.

But this?

This wasn't just a jolt—it was untamable lightning. Not just heat—it was magma, still burning inside me long after I pushed him away.

I tried to clear my head, but the dizzy spell I was caught in wasn't just spiraling—it was ricocheting.

And as it ricocheted, the heat he ignited—every emotion sparked by 1B lit a fuse inside me, bounced around like wildfire—burning everything it touched.

I needed to pull myself together, though. Devyn would be here soon to pick me up for our shift at Boomer's.

I turned off the water and wrapped my body in a towel. I stared at myself in the mirror, fogged around the edges from the steam of my hot-as-my-apartment-allowed shower.

It was Saturday night, the busiest night of the week, and Boomer's wasn't just the largest bar and restaurant in town.

It was *the* spot.

This time of year always brought an influx of tourists, a lot of repeat visitors, and a few retirees searching for that off-the-beaten-path kind of vacation.

Misty Springs was tailor-made for autumn, with its vibrant cascade of fall leaves, charming local shops offering unique trinkets and boutique clothing, and cozy coffee houses and restaurants that served surprisingly indulgent food and drinks. We were a quiet little gem, a well-kept secret that drew in those curious enough to explore beyond the usual destinations.

Despite my best efforts, my mind drifted back to Mr. Business-Not-Pleasure-Asshat, AKA 1B.

Thankfully, I caught up with Pam before she found anyone to share her suspicions with and convinced her that whatever she thought she saw was nothing.

It was nothing, right?

The way my emotions were colliding with each other right now, I couldn't be sure.

My phone dinged.

Devyn: Be there in ten.

I dressed quickly in one of my obnoxious Boomer's slogan V-necks. A small Boomer's logo was scribbled near my chest, but the back read in large block letters, *"Ask me about Boomer's sauce—it's explosive."*

I pulled on my jeans and gathered my towel-dried hair in a high ponytail.

Devyn and I had tested it before—the high pony earned us the most tips. I tended to go a bit heavier on the makeup—a little blush, mascara, and eyeliner to make my eyes pop, and I was ready to go.

Two quick horn blasts sounded from outside. Recognizing Devyn's trademark *"I'm here"* beeps, I grabbed my black jacket, making a mental note to finally wash the damn thing tomorrow, and headed outside to Devyn's waiting car.

"Hey, you!" Devyn greeted me as I sank into the passenger seat.

I had a bone to pick with Devyn—with all my friends. "Hey."

"Oh no, who did it? Who do I need to stab?" she asked, obviously picking up on my deflated tone.

I ignored her usual flair for dramatic threats and pushed forward. I'd rehearsed this in between thoughts of 1B—but now that I was face to face with her, my stomach turned.

I hated confrontation. Even with Dev. Especially with Dev. With anyone, really.

"I have to ask... Did you post that Tinder profile?" I tried to sound calm, but 1B's accusations were still echoing in my ears.

Devyn's face turned guilty, and she winced as she looked at me. "Well, I actually had kina sorta... already done it before you even saw it."

"Devyn!" I threw my head back in my seat.

"I'm sorry! I thought I would find you a nice guy to date before you even got back from Phoenix. Then, you wouldn't even have a chance to be mad about it because it already worked out for you!"

I sighed, but my mouth pulled up at the corners. My friends could be intrusive, but they always meant well. Whether I needed rides, consoling, or a job to make ends meet, they've had to rearrange their lives—just because I couldn't keep mine on track.

"Well? Did you find me a date?" I turned my head to look at her, opening one eye.

She shook her head. "No. I only got a few disturbing messages and a lot of dick pics. Like an obscene amount. Sam was mad at first, then we made a game out of it."

I chuckled, shaking my head back and forth. "I don't even want to know."

"Sorry, Soph. I'll take it down. I was just trying to help you get back on the horse. You know, reverse-cowgirl," she said as she put the car in drive.

I let out a sharp laugh. "Thanks, Dev. I know you all were just trying to help."

Despite my friend's best intentions, a new guy was not the solution to my problems. What I needed was to get my life back on track—a track I'd already derailed from before Landon even entered the picture.

The first deviation from my course happened when I lost my parents. The devastation of their abrupt passing consumed me, distracting me to the point where I dropped out of Brown with just one semester left of my literary arts degree—my heart and my dreams both shattering into tiny pieces.

Landon popped into my life soon after.

The timing of his family's move to Misty Springs and our chance encounter during my shift at Boomer's felt like kismet, as if fate were pulling us together.

My heart was too weak, my soul too desperate for something good, that I mistook coincidence for fate, and manipulation for love.

We moved fast—the pieces of my broken heart fitting too easily in his grasp.

His parents offered me a job at their real estate firm, allowing me to cut back on my hours at Boomer's.

He bought a house and asked me to move in with him.

I thought he was mending my broken pieces and stitching them together one by one.

But I didn't notice how, with every stitch, he wasn't repairing me—he was reshaping me. Little by little, he morphed me into the version he thought I should be until I didn't recognize who I was anymore.

It wasn't until he delivered the crushing blow—feeding me pretty lies about love and forever, all while cheating behind my back—that I finally admitted to myself what an epic mistake Landon Norwood was.

"How long has it been since you, uh, you know?" Devyn whistled and swirled a finger above my lap, breaking my silent thoughts.

"Dev!" I playfully batted her hand away. She alternated between staring at the road and me, her face set in anticipation.

I rolled my eyes. "Too long. Since Landon," I admitted.

"I am not talking about sex, obviously. I know that you haven't had sex. You would be in serious trouble if you got laid and didn't tell me." She navigated into a tiny parking spot in the gravel lot behind Boomer's. "I mean, taking *care* of yourself."

"Oh my—Devyn, come on." My cheeks heated as I recalled how close I was to *taking care of myself* minutes earlier in my shower.

"What? I'm advocating for your health here. How are you supposed to move on if you're carrying around all that... tension? It's like science or something."

I threw my bag over my shoulder and climbed out of her car.

Devyn quickly jumped out and skipped beside me.

I slung my arm around her shoulder, pulling her close. "You're ridiculous, but I love you."

I love you too, chica," she replied, wrapping her arm around my waist, squeezing briefly before letting out a long, knowing sigh.

The hum of laughter and clinking glasses seeped through the propped-open doors, and the sight of the crowded lot out front confirmed it—this was going to be one of those nights.

One of those nights where the hours blurred together, the bar never seemed stocked enough, and you found yourself running purely on adrenaline, laughter, and a dash of chaos. But for now, the moment was ours—a small, unspoken comfort in the arms of someone who always had my back, no matter what.

***

The night was going great. The perfect flow of patrons left me pleasantly busy, but not so busy that I felt flustered. I already had enough tip money to pay my electric and phone bills.

I was filling a beer glass from the tap, bopping my head to the music playing overhead, letting it drown out my thoughts, when my gaze flicked to a new customer who had sidled up to the bar.

My body froze.

There he was, in the flesh—no longer a painful memory or a simple text I could ignore.

Landon Norwood.

For a moment, the clamor of Boomer's dulled to a distant hum, my vision tunneling.

He was leaning casually against the bar, that same disarming smile on his lips—the one that used to make me feel safe but now only made my stomach churn.

His gaze zeroed in on me.

Cold beer dribbled down my hand as the cup I was filling overflowed with my distraction. I flung it off, wiping the rest on the apron tied around my waist.

The man who ordered the beer looked disgruntled when I set the too-full glass in front of him. He must have seen something in my face because he said nothing as he carefully lifted it to his lips.

Gripping the bar's edge to steady myself, I tried to summon the walls I thought I'd already built between Landon and me. But they wavered, threatening to collapse entirely under the weight of his presence.

"Hey, babe." His voice somehow carried over the noise. Smooth and familiar, like a hand curling around my wrist, tugging me back to a place I swore I'd never return.

"You've been ignoring me."

Chapter 15

HOWDY PARTNER

Corbin

My flight to New York arrived early enough that I decided to have my driver, Eddie—who was blissfully quieter than Hank—take me to the office.

Buescher Enterprises occupied two sprawling levels of a high-rise in Midtown, with an unencumbered view of the city that never slept—always moving, always flashing, always demanding.

I liked coming in on the weekend. The usually frantic space—the constant hum of phones, the chorus of conversation spilling over cubicle walls—was silent, unlike the vibrant city below.

During the workweek, it was chaos, various pop-ins from department heads who seemed more concerned with posturing than with actual business-critical items. My associates—loosely labeled as friends—Davis and Sullivan, never failed to interrupt me with stories of weekend conquests or cleverly hurled jabs.

But on weekends? The space was mine.

No distractions. No interruptions.

Just me and the silence, a blank slate to focus.

Or at least, that's how it was supposed to be.

I sat at my desk, fingers poised over my keyboard, staring out the massive window as the sun sank lower on the horizon. Instead of diving into emails or strategies, my mind jumped between thoughts of antiquated keys, weird themed dishes, Tinder profiles, and a gossipy taxi driver winding through picturesque streets.

But the truly invasive thoughts, the ones that kept coming back, no matter how many times I tried to forget them, were of tight shorts, eyes that lured me in, and lips I ached to taste.

I forced myself to refocus, pulling up the latest quarterly reports.

Numbers. Projections. Market trends.

Things I could control.

But even as I clicked through the spreadsheets, her voice, her lips, and the desire swimming in her deep blue eyes played on a loop in my mind.

"What are you doing here?" a voice boomed, shattering the silent air and stilling my thoughts.

I looked up to find Davis leaning casually against the doorframe. Arms crossed, one eyebrow arched in silent challenge. Gone was his usual Tom Ford suit, replaced by something deceptively unassuming—black slacks and a gray pullover. But nothing about Davis was casual. Even dressed down, everything about him was deliberate, an opportunity to flaunt his status.

I leaned back in my chair, feigning ease despite his presence, which felt both a relief and a challenge. "I should ask you the same thing."

"Well, considering you just left yesterday for your new *assignment*," he drawled, "I'm going to lob that question back to you."

Most things with Davis were a test, a constant chess game of calculation. Just because I'd known him for years and called him a friend didn't mean I could give him any ammunition.

"I just needed to lay eyes on the space. I don't expect it to take long to launch, this isn't my first rodeo. Besides, I couldn't stay in that crap town all weekend."

A damn charming crap town. I thought bitterly to myself.

Davis chuckled as he eased off the doorframe, rubbing a hand over the close buzz of his dark hair. No frills, no fluff—just sharp.

"Speaking of rodeo, I half expected you to be wearing a cowboy hat and chaps, saying howdy when you returned."

"You think all small towns are synonymous with cowboy culture?" I asked, grabbing a nearby pen and tapping it softly on my desk.

"I reckon." Davis fake-tipped an invisible hat. "Since you're here, are you coming to *The Loft* tonight?"

The Loft was owned by Emilia Augustin, an effortlessly glamorous second-generation Austrian jeweler whose wealth was the stuff of urban legend. She had purchased the entire top floor of a mid-rise apartment building off Fifth Avenue, converting it into a sprawling expanse of opulence designed for entertaining. The place was part luxury penthouse, part exclusive club. Every Saturday, like clockwork, she hosted extravagant soirées that rivaled the best events in the city.

Davis leaned against my polished desk, and I considered the night ahead. The fatigue from a restless and sleepless night tugged at me, but a part of me still felt disarmed from my excursion to Misty Springs. Maybe a night out at The Loft was precisely what I needed.

"Sure," I said reluctantly, rubbing the back of my neck. "I'm in. I've got dinner with Buzz and Toni first, though. Meet you there?"

"Deal." Davis nodded, a flicker of a smile crossing his face as he turned to leave.

He turned back halfway, his dark eyes appearing soft with concern, a look he didn't wear often. "How is your grandmother? I haven't heard anything in a while. Buzz never talks about it."

I swallowed hard, the question hitting me like a sucker punch. "She's... not doing great. Doctors think it'll be less than a year."

The words tasted bitter.

Toni—or Antoinette Jones-Buescher, as the world knew her, was diagnosed with cancer just over a year ago. It was inoperable, and she'd refused chemo—claiming it wasn't worth the fight.

The treatment would've wrecked her body, made her miserable, and bought her, at best, a few extra months. She'd chosen quality over quantity—a decision I respected but hated at the same time.

The last time I visited her, she looked so different—frail. Her once-vibrant presence seemed faded. It was a gutting contrast to the woman who had tamed a rowdy, self-made businessman like Buzz Buescher and turned him into a devoted husband—the strong, commanding matriarch who stepped in and raised me.

Davis nodded solemnly. For all his posturing, seeing Gram's illness was hard on him, too.

Buzz may run this place with an iron fist, but Toni was the heart of this company—the maternal figure whose nurturing presence had touched everyone within these walls.

"I'll see you tonight, then." Davis left abruptly, his footsteps fading down the hallway, leaving me drowning in more thoughts than I'd started with.

I stared at the door, as if waiting for answers that weren't coming, then shook my head to clear the fog. I glanced at my watch—one hour before my driver would be here to pick me up.

Cracking my knuckles, I returned to my laptop, focusing on the familiar.

Work. Numbers. Strategy. The comforting, methodical rhythm of checking off my to-do list.

This was what I knew. This was where I thrived.

Women? New surroundings? Love? Loss?

Those were chaotic, messy things, full of unknowns and pitfalls. But this?

This, I could control.

Chapter 16

LANDON SHAPED FOOTPRINT

Sophia

"I'll take a rum and coke, gorgeous."
Landon's voice cut through the noisy bar and slithered into my ears, sending an unwelcome shiver down my spine.

"I have to um… help that person first," I lied, my voice steady despite the shake building in my nerves.

I turned away quickly, scanning the far side of the bar for any excuse to put space between us. I spotted a woman lingering near the taps, her expectant gaze fixed on me. Whether she truly needed something or not didn't matter—she became my lifeline.

With purposeful strides, I crossed to the other end of the bar, giving myself precious seconds to calm the tremor in my hands.

She asked for a draft, and I was grateful for the easy order, since my mind had lost the ability to mix a proper drink.

As I filled the woman's beer, I let my eyes sweep across the room, searching for Devyn.

She was weaving through the crowd, her tray expertly balanced as she navigated the chaos of a packed Saturday night crowd. I hadn't had a chance to speak to her since we walked through the doors together, but knowing she was here grounded me slightly.

Drink delivered—full of foam due to my distracted brain—my reprieve ran out. My feet dragged reluctantly as I returned to Landon.

I planted my hands on the bar in front of him, keeping a deliberate distance.

"You know, Theresa is working tomorrow night," I said tightly, forcing my lips into a smile that felt more like a grimace. "You should come back then. I'm sure she'd *gladly* service you."

"I don't want Theresa."

He leaned in, his voice low, his steel blue eyes locking onto mine with a sickly-sweet intensity. "I want you."

My lip snarled instinctively.

"When are you going to forgive me and come home?"

Landon's voice was soft, almost pleading, as he reached for my hand.

I yanked it away, crossing my arms over my chest like a protective barrier.

Home.

The word stung more than it should have.

Not because I thought of the builder-grade, cookie-cutter ranch in the new subdivision outside of town—the one Landon asked me to move into with him. I had tried to make it feel like my own by decorating it and pouring myself into it. But it was never truly mine.

No, when I thought of home, it was the house I grew up in— the one my parents owned. The one I lost years ago, thanks to Landon's clever plan to help me "get out of debt quickly."

His parents were quick to agree that it was the best time to sell, and my sister Penny couldn't wait to cross one more responsibility off her list—she was tired of worrying about insurance and taxes.

I poured Landon's drink, my hand trembling just enough to make me furious with myself for allowing him to crawl under my skin.

Slamming the glass on the bar between us, I felt the weight of all my frustrations coming down with it.

"You have to stop texting me, Landon. I told you I don't want the ring back. I don't want anything back." My voice shook despite my effort to sound strong.

Landon smirked, tilting his head in that familiar, condescending way that always made me feel two inches tall. "Babe, don't be dramatic."

Before I could muster a response, Devyn appeared behind the bar, carrying an empty water cup.

She bumped her hip against mine in greeting, followed my line of sight, and sighed—a heavy, impatient sound that carried her anger loudly over the chorus of patrons.

"Look what the cat barfed up." Her tone was sharp enough to cut steel.

She set the cup on the counter and planted one hand on her hip, fixing Landon with a withering glare.

Landon took a slow sip of his drink as though her insult didn't faze him. "Good to see you too, Devyn."

Devyn's eyes flicked to me. Her expression shifted, softening for a brief moment before hardening into fury.

I could see it in her face—she'd caught the helpless, terrified look I couldn't hide, no matter how much I wanted to. My emotions were an open book, painfully easy for anyone, especially my friends, to read.

She stepped closer to the bar, leaning in so she was practically nose-to-nose with Landon. Her voice was low but loaded with venom. "Landon, what don't you get? It is *so* over. Stop trying. You look pathetic."

His smirk widened. "I see you're still too bossy to let Sophia speak for herself."

Devyn let out a short laugh—cold and humorless. "I'm just saying what she's too scared to say herself. You cheated. You manipulated. You were never good enough for her. Trust that she realizes that now."

My heart pounded as I stood in silence, torn between gratitude for Devyn's boldness and shame for needing her to defend me.

I wasn't *scared*. I felt like I had been very clear with Landon after walking out of his life completely.

Landon's smirk faltered for a split second, but he quickly recovered. "This doesn't even concern you, Devyn."

"Oh, but it does. Because I'm not gonna sit here and watch you try to worm your way back into her life. She's done with you, Landon."

Landon slammed a twenty-dollar bill on the bar, leaving it alongside his half-sipped cocktail.

"We'll talk when your guard dog isn't around to yip at me." He yanked on his jacket and turned to leave.

I watched him retreat, my nerves settling now that I wasn't held by the scrutiny of his stare.

"Don't let him goad you like that, Soph," Devyn scolded as she picked up the water she had come to refill. "You need to stand up for yourself."

I wanted to say something—to tell her I can't very well stand up for myself when she doesn't let me. But the words stuck in my throat, blocked by years of conditioning that told me not to make waves, not to upset people.

A part of me wondered if I even *could* tell Landon off. Like Penny said, I was a doormat. Doormats don't confront you—they lie there, welcoming you in and let you stomp all over them.

I stared down at the twenty, my fists curling at my sides.

One day, I promised myself. One day, I'll stand my ground. One day, I wouldn't need to rely on my friends to hold up my frail sensibilities.

One day—but today wasn't that day.

Chapter 17

DEMONS IN THE DINING ROOM

Corbin

I stopped at a curbside flower shop before Eddie pulled up to meet me.

I tilted the pink peonies—Gram's favorite—as I glanced at my watch. It was nearly seven. I worried I was going to be late. Nothing angered Buzz more than tardiness.

Eddie wove expertly through the congested grid of traffic before pulling to the curb in front of a series of brownstones.

He and I had developed the ideal driver-rider rapport over the years. Eddie didn't use a nav system, relying on his keen knowledge of the city and its intricate inner workings to get me where I needed to go when I needed to get there. I hadn't thrown a task at him that he didn't navigate flawlessly and punctually.

I stepped out into the chilly evening air, climbing up the worn stoop, the cracked concrete serving as a reminder of how nothing escapes the ravages of time. Striding through the large ornate front door, the faint aroma of roasted herbs and something rich and buttery wafted from the dining room.

I took a breath and walked further inside, grappling with the knowledge that my time with Toni was ticking away faster than any of us wanted to admit, worried about how this place would feel without her presence in it.

"Corbin, you made it! Give me your coat. Come on inside," Louise exclaimed, her voice brimming with warmth as she bustled toward me. Her Italian accent was still as thick as ever, even after forty years in New York.

Without waiting for me to comply, she began easing my long coat from my shoulders, shaking her head at some unseen wrinkle before hanging it neatly in the hall closet.

She patted my cheek affectionately.

"It smells wonderful in here, Louise," I said, bending slightly to kiss both her cheeks.

She smiled, emphasizing the lines in her cheeks and around her eyes as she tucked her arm through mine.

"Well, of course it does. I made your favorite." She led me down the marble-lined hallway toward the dining room.

Louise had been a cornerstone of this family for as long as I could remember. Hired as a maid back when Gram was overwhelmed by the size of the opulent penthouse Buzz insisted on buying. She quickly proved herself to be indispensable.

Louise was the one who made sure my favorite snacks were waiting after school, the one who taught me just because she was here didn't mean I could let my room get messy, and the one who never let me skip my vegetables—no matter how much I begged. She cooked, cleaned, baked, and helped raise me after I moved in with Gram and Buzz.

She wasn't staff—she was family.

As we neared the dining room, I could hear the faint clinking of dishes and the low hum of my grandfather's voice.

Louise gave my arm a little squeeze. "Give me those. I'll put them in water for you," she said as she grabbed the bouquet of peonies from me.

"About time you made it, Corbin," Buzz's deep voice boomed across the dining room upon my entry, echoing off the expansive windows that framed the Manhattan skyline.

"Be easy on him, Johnny. He just got back to the city," my grandmother interjected gently, patting Buzz's arm with a knowing smile.

She was the only person who dared call him Johnny instead of the nickname that had stuck with him since his Air Force days.

Buzz had earned the name during a tour overseas. It started as "Buzzard," a nod to his sharp instincts and relentless nature during high-stakes missions—his commanding officers had joked that he could sniff out trouble like a bird circling prey. Over time, the nickname was shortened to Buzz, and it followed him back to civilian life.

Now, sitting at the head of the grand dining table, his silver hair neatly combed and his sharp suit perfectly tailored, Buzz still looked every inch the formidable man who once piloted fighter jets. Even at his age, he hadn't lost the commanding presence that could fill a room.

I kissed Gram on the cheek, and she patted my arm. Despite the frailty in her touch, her smile hadn't lost its glow.

I pulled out my chair and took my seat at Buzz's other side. The three of us gathered on one end of the expansive mahogany dining table, its polished surface reflecting the golden light of the chandelier above.

"How was Misty Springs, Corbin? Did you enjoy your visit?" Gram asked.

My mind betrayed me instantly. It went straight to *her.*

I cleared my throat, trying to push Sophia from my thoughts. "It was... charming." I tried not to choke on the word, "...in its own way. The office was impressive, and the people were... spirited."

Buzz chuckled deeply, reaching for his glass of wine. "Spirited? That's one way to put it. I've seen the type of women that town churns out."

"Oh, stop it, you." Gram gingerly lifted her arm to slap at him, the effort appearing more taxing than it should have been. She turned her attention back to me. "It sounds like Misty Springs left quite the impression."

I forced a polite smile, picking up my glass of water to avoid meeting her eyes. "It's a far cry from New York, that's for sure."

Louise emerged from the kitchen carrying a crystal vase filled with peonies. She gently placed them in the center of the table, and Gram's face lit up as she took in the flowers.

"From you, Corbin?"

I nodded, wishing I could do more to help her in this losing battle besides occasionally giving her something to smile about.

Buzz nodded approvingly before his cell phone rang out. The noise made Gram jump, and she gave Buzz a stern look of disapproval.

Buzz pulled the phone from his pocket and quickly silenced the call. He placed the device face down on the table and waved his hands in the air in an apologetic surrender.

"Tell me everything, Corbin. Did you visit the library? I read they just had the centennial celebration. Didn't you love the downtown area?" Gram's eyes lit up as they peered into mine.

Guilt tugged at my chest. "I didn't have a chance. There wasn't much time."

"Corbin was there to launch the branch, Toni. He has a lot of work to do." Buzz added, glancing at me from the corner of his eye.

"Well, maybe after the *work* is done, you can enjoy the town," Gram said, grabbing a cloth napkin and placing it on her lap.

My lips formed a straight line. The only thing I'd enjoy about the town is leaving it for good. But I wasn't going to voice that out loud.

Louise returned moments later, balancing plates of osso buco served over a velvety saffron risotto. On the side, she brought roasted asparagus spears and freshly baked focaccia.

"Louise, this looks incredible," I said, eyeing the spread before me. Though I never expected anything less, her meals were never simple.

Louise took her spot beside Gram. The conversation drifted between questions about whether buildings were still the same in Misty Springs and the occasional affectionate ribbing from Buzz— Gram didn't like business talk at the table—she deftly kept him in check.

When the meal ended, I helped Louise clear the table, stacking plates and gathering silverware.

As I carried the dishes into the kitchen, the faint hum of conversation from the dining room followed me.

When I returned to grab another stack of dishes, the atmosphere had shifted, heavy with a tension that made me pause just outside the door.

Gram's voice, tinged with panic, cut through the quiet. "Johnny, you're working James too hard. He needs to rest. His heart hasn't been the same since she left. It's going to catch up to him."

The words hit me hard in the chest and digging in.

Buzz sat stiffly at the table, his large hands resting on its edge. His face was pained with a helpless sort of sorrow and silence on his lips, for this was a conversation in futility.

A side effect of the cancer, her memories shuffled, and her sense of time ebbed and flowed. Right now, she was stuck in the past, dredging up ghosts that I preferred stay buried.

James. My father. Dead for nearly fifteen years.

Gram's words hung in the air, pulling me back to a time I tried not to revisit.

My mother walking out when I was ten. My father's descent into the dark comfort of alcohol and overworking. The sixteen-hour days he threw himself into as if trying to outrun his grief. The nights he drowned himself in bottles, leaving me to fend for myself.

I was an afterthought, a fleeting concern in a life consumed by loss and self-destruction. By the time he died, I had long since detached, already living with Gram and Buzz as if I were their son instead of his.

My father was on a path to take over the company—until his vices gutted his reputation and took his future with them. I'd seen firsthand how quickly a legacy could unravel, how one man's weakness could poison everything he built.

From my first day at Buescher Enterprises, I vowed that no one would ever have reason to draw a line between my father and me. Every move I made was measured—every decision calculated.

I shaped myself into the kind of man the board could trust without question—disciplined, dependable, unshakable.

My reputation wasn't just important. It was everything.

I stepped back into the kitchen, unwilling to face the demons in the dining room.

I forced a smile, asking Louise, my voice steady despite the swirl of emotions. "What can I do to help with dessert?"

Chapter 18

BLOODY MARY SUNDAY

Sophia

Sunday morning arrived, and I was feeling excited and anxious. I was going to email Andi my resume today after I polished it up a bit and received some feedback from the girls at Sunday brunch.

"Hey," I greeted as I squeezed into the little red booth next to Cassie.

Devyn sat across from me, our little squabble from last night already forgotten. She gave me a smile and a soft nudge of her foot that I returned.

"You're late," Cassie stated firmly.

"We texted you," Lana said almost immediately after, giving me a soft but concerned look.

"We thought you got kidnapped," Devyn said with a grin.

"Kidnapped? In this town? Whatever would make you guys think that?" I tilted my head, brow furrowing.

"Devyn told us about your run-in with Landon. We all got each other worried." Cassie sipped her coffee, her face puckering and shaking slightly. "Plus, we all started drinking Irish coffees, and I think the whiskey is affecting the rational part of our brain."

Our waitress appeared and asked what I was having to drink.

"I'll have what they're having." I motioned at the mugs surrounding the table.

"Another for me, too," Cassie tagged on.

"And me." Devyn raised her empty glass.

"Might as well," Lana added with a resigned sigh.

I sipped on the water that was waiting for me—the condensation indicating they ordered it for me a while ago. The girls eyed me expectantly.

"Nothing happened last night between Landon and me," I replied to their silent accusations. "You guys have nothing to worry about. Landon's the least of my concerns."

"Don't be so sure. He's deceivingly dangerous. Like those little blue-ringed octopuses," Devyn said with a hiccup. "Floating around. Seemingly harmless. But you get too close and BAM!" She slammed her hand on the table, eliciting stares from some surrounding patrons.

Cassie nodded in agreement. "He fills you with venom, and ya dead."

I rolled my eyes at their coordinated dramatics.

"We just want to make sure you're okay. We know what he put you through." Lana softly touched my hand from across the table.

The waitress returned with our drinks, and my friends simultaneously took eager sips.

I took advantage of their distraction to change the subject. "Ok, lushes. Before you get too drunk on a Sunday morning, can I please ask you for a favor?"

I pulled out my laptop and opened my resume.

"You're leaving me?!" Cassie gasped.

"You won't quit Boomer's, will you? I can't survive a night without my P.I.C., my partner in crime, the whiskey to my coke, the gin to my tonic, the 7 to my 7," Devyn recited our favorite nicknames to each other.

"I may not be going anywhere. Look how terrible this thing is. My education and experience are lacking big time. I need some pointers, or I won't even get my foot in the door for an interview."

"It can't be that bad," Lana assured me.

It turns out it was that bad. After switching from Irish coffees to Bloody Marys, we blew up and reassembled my resume into an actual, respectable-looking document.

"Make sure you look up their mission statement before the interview. Corporations like stuff like that," Lana suggested.

"Missionary? Seems a little vanilla, Soph, maybe try something different," Devyn said a little too loudly in the busy restaurant.

We all giggled and chugged water while waiting for the waitress to close our tab.

Sam, Devyn's boyfriend, was coming to pick the girls up to take them back home since the only thing as routine as Sunday brunch was getting drunk at Sunday brunch.

I hugged the girls as they loaded into Sam's small SUV. I leaned in the passenger window to say goodbye again, as goodbyes tended to take hours with us.

"You sure you don't need a ride, Soph?" Sam asked from the driver's seat as Devyn pulled and let go of his seatbelt repeatedly, letting it snap back on his chest.

"I'm good. I want to get some steps in."

"Bye, Soph! Don't forget to do missionary!" Devyn yelled out of the window as Sam pulled away.

I adjusted the worn straps of my backpack—my laptop nestled securely inside. The short walk to my apartment was a welcome reprieve, giving me time to gather my thoughts. The cool mid-afternoon air worked its magic, sobering me up just enough.

As soon as I stepped through the door, I dropped my bag and pulled out my laptop. Heart pounding, I composed an email to Andi, re-reading it a million times to ensure it was perfect and attaching my resume.

"There. Done," I said to my tiny, empty apartment.

Lana's advice popped into my head—mission statement. Then I chuckled to myself—*missionary*.

I Googled Buescher-Jones Publishing and clicked over to their website. Their homepage was sleek and professional, and I found myself diving headfirst into their mission statement and core values, jotting them down in my notebook.

As I clicked through, I uncovered that Buescher-Jones was a piece of a much larger empire, a subsidiary under the umbrella of Buescher Enterprises. The parent company had its hands in multiple industries and a heavy real estate presence.

I scrolled through press releases. Each one had a thumbnail, the tiny images serving as previews of articles about the company—skimming through a few without much thought—until one froze me in my tracks.

Corbin Buescher Named One of Manhattan's Top 30 Under 30

My breath hitched as my gaze locked on the accompanying photo. The thumbnail was small, but there was no mistaking the confident smirk, the piercing eyes, and the infuriatingly perfect jawline.

"No freaking way," I murmured, my voice cracking with disbelief.

Clicking the article brought up a larger version of the photo, confirming what I already knew but desperately hoped I'd misread.

There he was—1B in all his tailored-suit glory.

Brash. Arrogant. Unnervingly sexy. And apparently, the COO of Buescher Enterprises.

I leaned back in my chair, staring at the screen as my heart raced. What the hell was the COO of a major corporation doing in Misty Springs? It didn't make any sense. Surely, running a business empire would be more pressing than a new branch opening here.

I did a Google search of Corbin Buescher. I found various articles regarding his company, but I found it hard to pay much attention when the photos of him with drop-dead gorgeous women were in my face.

Stunning pictures of lavish venues, with Corbin in tailored tuxes, standing alongside high-profile people and model-worthy women.

I studied his features, my eyes lingering on the sharp angles of his face and the curve of his lips in those perfectly captured smiles.

Here, on my screen, I could study him without the fear of being caught—free from those knowing, intense eyes that seemed to see right through me.

My fingers hovered over the keyboard, itching to dig deeper, to find some clue that would explain his presence in my little corner of the world.

Maybe it was just a ceremonial visit, a brief pop-in to bless the office and then return to the glittery concrete jungle where someone like him belonged.

After all, he said he had a flight to catch right after he lit my nerve endings on fire, accused me of hoeing around behind some fictitious boyfriend's back, and then stole my delicious Jell-O shots—I noticed they were suddenly missing when I went back for them.

My pulse quickened as I imagined the possibility of seeing him again, of the way my body hummed when he stalked toward me inside his hotel room.

I slammed my laptop shut.

"Not today, brain," I muttered, rising to my feet. I had no time to entertain wild fantasies, especially not the ones threatening to pull me into Devyn's well-meaning but highly unhelpful advice.

I chuckled to myself—*science or something.*

I headed to the kitchen and began pulling out my cutting board and ingredients to prep meals for the week. The rhythmic chop of the knife and the structure of the task grounded me, pushing thoughts of Corbin Buescher into the recesses of my mind.

I slowly stirred my soup and called Penny. She put Luke on, and he proceeded to tell me that I should look for a man named Bruce Wayne—whispering that he was actually Batman and he'd make a great uncle.

I told him I'd do my best before saying goodbye with a huge grin. My nephew had a knack for bringing a smile to my face.

A knock at the door broke me away from the rolling boil of my soup. I quickly wiped my hands on my apron.

Peeking through the peephole, my stomach dropped as I saw none other than Landon Norwood standing outside my door. I groaned when I noticed the red roses in his hand and a large white box tucked under his arm.

After the initial end of our relationship—once his begging stopped and he was tired of dangling the roof over my head and the car I needed to get around like bait—he became a ghost.

No calls, no texts, just a haunted memory of a dark path not followed.

I had thought we had officially closed the chapter on our story.

But lately, he'd been relentlessly trying to contact me. I'd dodged every call and ignored every text, thinking silence would speak louder than anything I could say.

Rejection by omission, right?

Seeing him at the bar left an unsettling feeling in my gut, one that followed me around all weekend. At least I had Devyn there and a room full of patrons to be a buffer.

I wasn't ready to face him, not now, not alone.

"Sophia, I know you're in there. I can smell your chicken tortilla soup from out here." Landon's voice boomed through the thin door.

God, I hated this apartment.

A heavy sigh escaped me as I unfastened the lock. My fingers trembled, and I pulled the door open, bracing myself for whatever ploy Landon had in store for me.

Chapter 19

Obligations Are Like Assholes

Sophia

"What are you doing here, Landon?" I stood in the doorway of my apartment, my arms pebbling in the cool evening air. I wasn't about to invite him in, no matter how much my parents had raised me always to be polite.

He wasn't entitled to that anymore.

"I came bearing gifts," he said with a soft, innocent smile I knew better than to trust.

We stood in tense silence, his arms outstretched, flowers and a large white box dangling from his hands.

After a long beat, he let his arms fall to his sides. The smile faltered, his features contorting into a flash of anger that made my stomach tighten.

It was gone as quickly as it had appeared—Landon swiftly masking it with a calm, patient expression, but I saw it.

Looking back, I think I always saw it—I just wanted to deny it. The monster that prowled just beneath the surface, ready to strike when he didn't get what he wanted.

I channeled my inner Devyn and straightened, forcing myself to stand tall—though Landon had a couple of inches on me—my resolve settled like steel in my chest. "I'll ask again, what are you doing here, Landon?"

Though I felt like I already knew the answer.

He wanted what people like him always wanted from people like me—to control me, to make me feel small.

Landon had broken me down slowly when we were together, hurting me in ways that were almost invisible at first—backhanded comments, little jabs that didn't seem to matter as they landed.

Over time, they stacked up, heavy enough to crush me. They dug into my confidence, planting seeds of doubt until I couldn't even recognize the person staring back at me in the mirror.

"I just wanted to give you these and to talk." His tone was soft, inviting, deceivingly dangerous—*like a blue-ringed octopus.*

I stared at him, my arms crossed, my expression unwavering. "You can leave, Landon. I don't want your gifts." My voice was surprisingly firm as I stepped back, pushing the door closed on him.

But his foot shot out, jamming between the thin wood door and the frame before I could shut him outside.

My heart thudded as I tried to push back, but with a casual strength I was no match for, he shoved the door open with his broad shoulder, sending me stumbling backward into my apartment.

"You need to leave, Landon," I hissed, but the words felt weak.

He stalked inside, kicking the door shut behind him, the sound echoing in the small space.

In an instant, it was just the two of us, standing in the quiet tension of the room, alone. The weight of it pressed in, suffocating.

Landon had never physically hurt me. He had always kept that line unbroken, knowing his power over me didn't need force to be felt. It was in the words, the insults, the manipulations. But even now, with no raised fist, something dangerous was hovering between us.

"Will you please just listen to me, babe?" he asked, his words polite, but heavy with malice as they passed through his clenched teeth.

"Out with it. So you can leave." I crossed my arms, the weight of them across my chest offering a small sense of control.

It was clear from the tightness in his jaw that he expected a softer version of me.

"I came to make sure you follow through with your obligations." His voice was low, almost too calm, too practiced.

"What obligations?" I spat, shaking my head. "I thought I made it clear that any *obligations* I had to you were over the second I threw that ring at your head."

"Not obligations to me. Obligations to my parents." He placed the flowers on my coffee table before handing me the large white box.

Reluctantly, I took it from him, the weight of the box surprising me.

A large gold bow gleamed on top, and a small envelope was taped to the front.

My fingers trembled slightly as I walked over to the kitchen bar and set the box down. My eyes continuously flicked to Landon, ensuring he stayed put, as I peeled off the envelope and opened it.

The contents inside made my stomach churn. A cold sweat spread across my skin as the reminder hit me.

Before everything—the heartbreak, the betrayal—I had been a part of Landon's life in a way that felt like a future, a certainty. His mother, Alicia, had bought tickets to a gala in New York, including plane tickets for both of us. I had excitedly agreed to go, thinking it was just another step in the life we were building together.

I had forgotten entirely—until now.

The tickets felt like lead in my hand, along with the note from Alicia asking me to come despite everything that had transpired between Landon and me.

I doubted Landon had told her the *real* story of what happened between us. Even if he had, I knew his parents would never believe their *golden* child could do anything wrong.

"Alicia would be crushed if you didn't come," Landon added, his voice fully loaded with both contrition and intimidation.

Alicia—as Landon informally referred to her. Not *Mom*. Cold. Detached. Just like how he called his father *Perry*.

But still, the mention of her gave me pause—Alicia was not the type of woman you said no to.

The Norwood family, despite being in Misty Springs for only a short while, had branded this town with their iron will.

When I worked for them, I had watched as their influence seeped into every corner, their power more insidious than overt.

Reputations crumbled in their wake. Whispers turned into storms that stripped people of their standing, their businesses, and their livelihoods. One wrong move, one misstep against them, and suddenly, you weren't just an outsider—you were nothing.

It was part of why I found my diplomatic—some might say doormat—approach to handling our breakup necessary. I never wanted to be in his family's crosshairs, and even more so, I worried about my friends.

Norwood Realty owned the space Lana rented for her coffee shop. They had just purchased the building that housed Devyn's parents' grocery store. And Cassie and Brent's family? Chase Construction practically survived on Norwood-funded projects.

One wrong step, one reason to turn on me—on us—and everything my friends had built could come crashing down.

Landon seemed to notice my internal deliberation and used it as an opening. "You told her you'd come, remember? After all, you were supposed to be part of the family."

I hated the way he baited me—and hated the way it was working.

"And whose fault is it that I'm no longer going to be a part of the family, Landon?"

He took two bounding strides toward me, my body recoiling instinctively. "I've been trying to make it up to you. You're the one being stubborn!"

I wasn't properly equipped with the fight response. I couldn't yell, scream, or even find it in myself to lash out.

Instead, I shut down—my mind and body locked up tight.

Landon stepped back, his hands raised in a wavering retreat. "Look, babe, you're mad at me. I get it. But please, be reasonable."

I knew I wasn't being *unreasonable*. He was the one who destroyed us—not me. But I also knew how his brain worked and how fragile his mother's ego was.

I knew it would be seen as an uneven scale if I skipped out on this. He'd hold this over me and use it as a way to try to manipulate me into believing I owed him, and she'd take it as a personal slight against her.

Perhaps there was a way I could make this work to my advantage.

"If I go, this has to be it. I owe you and your family *nothing*. You have to agree to stop trying to get me back. This makes us completely over."

He scoffed, his eyes narrowing at me once more. He shook his head back and forth, inhaling deeply.

"The flight leaves this Saturday. I'll pick you up at one. Bring what's in the box." He turned on his heel, his confidence unshaken.

Then he was gone. His response was neither a confirmation nor a denial of our agreement.

My mind reeled as I considered how my friends would react to me going to New York with Landon. But they didn't know the Norwood family like I did, didn't know the level of petty, deceitful torment they could inflict.

I would do this if it would protect my friends' livelihoods. I would do this if it meant finally ridding myself of Landon completely.

This gala would be the final nail in our coffin, and I planned to hammer it in with high heels and a ball gown.

Chapter 20

Vodka Luge

Corbin

I peered through the tiny window of the corporate jet as it bounced lightly through the air on a cloudy Monday morning. I mulled silently over the events that set my course back to Misty Springs—sooner than I'd originally planned.

After leaving dinner with my grandparents on Saturday, I went to The Loft and instantly wondered why I had shown up in the first place.

I recall standing there, drink in hand, scanning the crowd of glitzy, overconfident faces, unable to muster the energy or the desire to make small talk with anyone. Not like my silence mattered—I had learned long ago that the finer the event, the easier it was to disappear into it.

The centerpiece of the party—a vodka luge carved from a massive block of ice, with frozen rivers of liquor cascading down its channels into waiting shot glasses—served as a colossal tribute to the grandstanding I'd become all too accustomed to.

It was all so… vapid.

Davis and Sullivan arrived together, clearly in rare form—likely the result of a pre-game session of their own.

I hovered nearby them as they worked the room, their charming discourse giving me an excuse to quietly nod along as I fought to drown out the thoughts in my head.

The alcohol burned, but it didn't numb. The night dragged on, an endless swirl of laughter, clinking glasses, and superficial conversations. Somewhere between the music and the meaningless exchanges, I realized that the party, the people, the effort to chase away the lingering ghosts of my past had been an exercise in futility.

Sunday morning, with my head pounding and my mouth feeling like it had a dozen cotton balls stuffed inside, I called the corporate travel agent and booked the jet for Monday.

The draw of something quiet, slower paced, pulling me in. As I thought of returning to Misty Springs, the weight pressing down on me—so subtle I hadn't fully noticed it—lifted slightly.

It wasn't relief exactly, but something close.

I wasn't letting myself read too much into it. Buzz tasked me with opening the branch, and I was going to make it the best damn opening Buescher-Jones Publishing had ever seen. That was my motivation for coming back so soon. *That* was what placed me on this jet today.

I let my gaze drift out the window as the clouds broke, revealing the vast stretches of land below, and the downtown area of Misty Springs came into view. It was quaint and compact, nestled along the river's edge like a scene straight from a postcard.

Part of me recognized why Gram wanted me to see it, and why she held on to so many memories here.

I let my eyes linger on the landscape as the plane descended.

Beautiful, yes—but I wasn't here for the view.

After I deplaned, a sleek black Infiniti Q50 was waiting for me. A sharp blast of wind carrying an icy chill stabbed through my suit as it tumbled dead leaves across the tarmac.

The man who delivered my car walked me through the features as he loaded my bags in the trunk.

I rushed him along and sat down in the sleek interior. The car was idling, the heated leather seats were warm underneath me—the relief instantly soaked into my skin.

I unintentionally peeled out of the parking lot, watching the concern on the rental car guy's face as I did so.

It certainly had been a while since I had driven, and this car had some power. Despite this being a "one-horse town," as Davis and Sullivan described, I needed to use my GPS to find the office. My driving skills were not expert-level like Eddie's—or Hank's, I suppose.

I looked around, familiarizing myself with the sleepy town, and was surprised at the amount of architecture to admire.

The simplistic but intricate craftsmanship of the brick homes— many with side-gabled roofs, segmental-arched windows, and stone foundations—stood proudly amongst the sprawling downtown blocks. Massive trees with diminishing but still brightly colored leaves were everywhere, some towering over the homes, fighting for space on their plots of land.

It was a quiet town, especially on a dreary Monday morning, yet it felt alive. The streets were calm but far from lifeless. Shops lining the main strip were open, their window displays bright and inviting, while the occasional pedestrian strolled by, bundled against the cool weather.

A handwritten sign propped on the sidewalk caught my eye as I drove past: HOUSE-MADE SYRUPS. A simple coffee mug sign with the word *Grounded* scrawled across it hung overhead.

Coffee sounded like the perfect way to shake off the dreariness of my travel. I pulled off into one of the empty parking spaces along the front of the shop.

Once inside, my eyes landed on a woman behind the counter with long black hair and a friendly smile. Her dark eyes were focused on the cup she was crafting, her hands deftly swirling foam into an intricate design.

"What can I get you?" she asked me, her eyes never drifting from her task.

I started to speak, then hesitated. An americano was my usual choice—a reliable classic—but the *house-made syrups* sign intrigued me.

Decisiveness and routine were my cornerstones.

Every morning, I ate the same thing: one egg, two egg whites, wheat toast, and berries. I ordered the same dishes from the same restaurants, bought the same brands, and stuck to what worked.

End of story.

But here I stood, like a confused puppy trying to make sense of these new sights and smells before me.

"You look conflicted," she stated, now having handed her mug to a customer and her full attention focused on me.

"Conflicted about what to order or conflicted about my life?" I startled myself with my questions. I didn't make a habit of small talk, especially not with strangers.

"Both, perhaps." She leaned on the counter, resting her forearms on the dark wood surface. "I can help you with one of those things."

Her presence was warm and inviting, her stare was penetrating, like she could see through any armor I wore. She seemed achingly familiar, though I couldn't place where I'd ever seen her before.

"What do you typically drink?" she asked.

"Whiskey."

She gave me a slight eye roll.

"Americano. Black," I admitted.

"But you want something different today." Her tone was both a question and a statement.

I nodded.

"I have just the thing for you." She picked up a Sharpie. "Name?"

"Corbin."

She quickly introduced herself as Lana as she worked the register and started on my drink. Her warm smile held firm throughout every mundane task she performed, as if she genuinely loved what she was doing.

After a few short minutes, a gentle plunk of a paper cup sounded where I waited off to the side.

"Half sweet maple-bourbon cappuccino," Lana stated.

I turned to face her as she dropped a paper bag on the counter next to my coffee. "Plus a scone. On the house since you're a first-timer."

"How do you know I haven't been in here before?" I asked, reaching for my items.

"I know everyone who comes in here, and I never forget a face." She wiped her hands on her apron before adding with another genuine smile, "Welcome to Misty Springs."

I dropped a twenty in the tip jar on the counter and thanked her before heading out into the chilly air. Shaken by the hospitality, I felt oddly nostalgic as I hopped into my still-warm car.

Once I arrived at my office in the Misty Springs branch, I paused in the doorway, eyeing the intruder sitting in my seat.

"Oh, I am sorry, here I thought this was my office."

Andi's head shot up. "What are you doing here? I thought you weren't coming back until next week."

I stepped inside and dropped my briefcase on the desk. "Yeah, well, I decided to come back early, so…" I flicked my hand toward the door.

Andi leaned back in the chair and scrunched her face. "What if we rock, paper, scissors-ed for it?"

"Out," I barked.

"Fine, fine. Thanks for getting me something, by the way." She nodded toward my coffee cup, grabbed her lime green jacket from the coat rack in the corner, and sighed with the dramatic flair of an ER doctor who just lost a patient.

***

Andi scheduled a brief introduction meeting for the afternoon—"for optics," she claimed, since I hadn't been formally introduced to Susan or Ned yet.

Andi introduced me to Susan, who looked like someone I'd expect to see in a Buescher boardroom—young, polished, and sharp. Why she chose the small-town life in Misty Springs was a mystery.

"And this ray of mediocrity," Andi said with a tight smile, "is Ned."

Ned ignored Andi's gibe and stood to shake my hand with too much enthusiasm. "Pleasure, sir. We've all been looking forward to your leadership."

"Appreciate that," I responded with as much enthusiasm as I could muster. "We've got quite the team here. With all of your efforts, this branch will be on its feet in no time."

My comments were more for my relief, not theirs. I couldn't wait for this branch to be up and running, so I could get the hell out of here.

Around five, Andi left with a remark about seeing me around Elijah's, and something pulled at my chest at the thought of returning to the landmark hotel.

When I booked my flight and car, I searched for other accommodations outside of Misty Springs. I only found a Hampton Inn about twenty miles away—not too far, but not ideal.

Elijah's stately exterior stirred nervous energy in my gut as I drove up the steep drive.

I took a deep breath to steady myself.

Nerves are reserved for signing million-dollar deals and meeting high-profile clients—not colliding with angry brunettes with short shorts in my hotel room.

A combination of relief and disappointment hit me when the *oh-so-charming* redhead I had met when I first checked in stood behind the counter.

"Hello again, Mr. Buescher," she said with a strained tone and a plastered-on smile. "Are you needing a room for the night?"

"Yes, I am, Cassie," I answered, scanning her nametag again.

I handed her my credit card, watched her swipe it, and stood quietly as she began typing away at her keyboard.

For a moment, the silence felt almost comforting. My nerves started to settle, relieved that maybe I was getting off easy—no Sophia, no awkward confrontation, just a quiet check-in and a room key.

"And do you plan on accosting any of my employees during this stay?" Her tone was as innocuous as asking me if I needed extra towels, but her words were sharp as blades.

So much for easy.

The only response I could give her was me choking on air.

She smirked like she'd just cornered my king in a chess match as she placed my credit card back on the counter.

As she turned toward the rack of keys, I worked to regain my composure. Cassie's words surprised me, but something deeper cut at my core.

Women bragged about being with me before—looking for clout, attention, validation—I hadn't pegged Sophia for that type.

Cassie turned back with my key, and despite my insides twisting, I set my face into that neutral, unbothered expression I'd perfected over the years in boardrooms and hostile acquisitions.

I tilted my head slightly, letting just enough smugness edge into my voice. "So what, you two are friends? She tell you we hooked up?"

Cassie made a face like I'd just offered her sour milk. "Ew. No. Pam told me," She bit back. "You seriously need to get over yourself."

That knocked a bit of the satisfaction from my smirk.

"I didn't bring it up to anyone, especially not Sophia," she added, her tone softening a touch. "She's a little... raw right now."

Cassie crossed her arms and straightened her stance, her voice tightening. "Look. I'm not one to overstep, but when it comes to people I care about, I'd do almost anything. Sophia is smart.

Talented. Has a future if she wants it. I just don't want her to tie herself to someone who could snap that thread without a second thought." I thought I heard her mumble, "*not again.*"

I forced a smile. "I'm not one to mix business with pleasure."

The last thing I needed was small-town gossip about a relationship that wasn't even happening.

Cassie nodded as a breath of relief escaped her.

The thought hit me—sudden and unwelcome. Who or what happened to Sophia to make her feel *raw?*

But I collapsed that tunnel of thought immediately. Sophia wasn't my responsibility. Her feelings weren't my problem.

"How late is the bar open tonight?" I asked, forcing the change in subject.

"Oh, sorry. Bar's closed on Mondays," she said back, without a hint of apology in her tone.

"Thanks—as usual—for your hospitality," I muttered, grabbing the key.

I *really* needed that drink.

Chapter 21

Your Friendly Neighborhood Dealer

Sophia

Monday nights were a toss-up. Sometimes, we were so busy that it was all hands on deck. Others were painfully slow. Tonight was one of the slow nights.

Devyn wanted to get cut. Sam asked her to see his nephew's preschool play, which would undeniably be a chaotic but adorable train wreck.

She offered to drive me home after we closed, but I didn't want to interrupt her night.

I told her I'd get a ride from Terry, one of our cooks. My apartment was on his way home, I just had to deal with his obnoxious advances, and hope we weren't so slow that he tried to leave early.

"Thanks, Sophia. Take care," Pete, one of my regulars, mumbled as he laid down a twenty and slid off the bar stool.

He slipped on his tweed coat, which may have once fit his swollen frame but now clung to him uncomfortably, and adjusted his glasses, pushing them up his red-flushed nose.

Being a bartender sometimes felt like juggling a dozen different jobs at once. Some nights, I was a therapist, guiding someone through the chaos of a messy break-up. Other times, I played a mother, calling Hank to give a young, freshly twenty-one-year-old a ride home after his friends abandoned him—leaving him passed out on one of my barstools.

But then there were the darker moments—when I felt more like a dealer. Serving someone another drink, fully aware it was feeding their worst habits. Knowing it was hurting them, but taking their money anyway.

It left me torn between enabling their escape and denying them what little solace they seemed to find in the bottom of a glass.

"Is Hank giving you a ride?" I asked Pete.

He nodded and shuffled his feet toward the door.

I slid his crumpled-up twenty off the bar and closed his tab.

Pete always came in on two-dollar well night, always drank Jim Beam straight, always had the same total—eighteen dollars—and always left me the same two-dollar tip. His tip brought my grand total tonight to a whopping… twenty-eight dollars.

I sighed as I dropped the two one-dollar bills in my apron. Considering we were nearing the end of the night, I didn't expect much more to come my way.

Terry strutted through the swinging door to the kitchen. He threw a towel over his shoulder and tightened the knot on the back of the black bandana that clung to his head.

Grabbing a plastic soda cup, he filled it from the fountain machine behind the bar and scanned the nearly empty room.

"Slow night," he commented, letting out an obnoxiously loud belch after taking a long sip.

"Very," I replied with a polite smile.

I hesitated, weighing my options. I hated bumming rides, but the thought of walking home alone after midnight wasn't exactly thrilling.

"Hey, Terry, do you think you could give me a ride home tonight? I know it's slow, but if you're hanging around?"

"What do I get out of it?" He raised his eyebrows in an exaggerated waggle.

"Never mind," I muttered, heading toward the only occupied table.

A group of three guys had closed out their tabs and finished watching the game twenty minutes ago. Now, they were just nursing the last sips of their beers.

"Wait, wait." Terry laughed, jogging a few steps after me and grabbing my arm lightly. "I'm kidding, c'mon."

I crossed my arms and faced him. His gaze dipped—too obviously—before snapping back up to my face.

"It's no big deal. I can walk." I turned away again.

"Stop, I'm sorry!" He blocked my path. "Seriously, sorry. It's just… when you cross your arms like that, your, uh… your…" He waved vaguely at my chest. "They were looking at me, is all."

"Terry," I groaned, more weary than angry.

"I know, I know! Look, I'll give you a ride home. I was only joking, I'll stop."

I gave him a tight-lipped smile. "Thank you."

I slipped past him, heading for the table I knew didn't need anything, but needing a reason to walk away.

I couldn't wait to have my own car again. Another crappy night of tips and yet another reminder that I was stuck begging for rides made me long for a sign—anything from the universe to tell me things were going to get better.

The universe must have finally decided to get off its ass because before I reached the edge of the bar, the front door opened, and in walked the last person I expected to see.

Mr. 1B, himself.

COO of Buescher Enterprises. Manhattan's Top 30 Under 30.

Star of way too many of my recent—and very vivid—dreams.

Corbin Buescher.

Corbin walked like a man with purpose—his long strides oozed confidence like he'd been commanding rooms since birth.

His dark coat hung over a navy suit, one I was sure clung to him just right, tailored to perfection down every decadent inch of him.

I forced myself to blink, breathe, and swallow—to remember how to function like a normal human being. Every muscle in my body was tense, every nerve alive with the awareness of him.

Whatever task I was set out to perform instantly vanished, and I turned awkwardly in a few half circles as I tried to nonchalantly look busy. I picked up an already-cleaned pint glass and casually wiped it with a towel, giving every ounce of my attention and energy to the extraneous task.

I watched him in my periphery as he shrugged out of his coat and perched himself on a barstool. Even with the glass in my hand as my main focus, I could make out the muscles in his frame, the sharp lines of his face, and his ridiculously perfect black-as-night hair.

He's just some guy, I told myself.

Some obnoxiously handsome guy who could hold the fate of your future in his hands.

But still, he's just some guy.

"That uniform looks more appropriate than your other one." His voice carried across the nearly empty barroom like a low rumble of thunder, sending an involuntary thrill over my skin.

I cleared my throat, ignoring his comment and the memories it spurred. "Can I get you a drink?"

He stared at me for a beat, his expression unreadable, before shifting his gaze past me to the rows of bottles lining the wall.

"WhistlePig Ten Year. Neat." His eyes found mine as he placed his order. "Please."

My eyes dipped to his lips, and I swallowed hard before quickly turning to reach for the bottle. Even with my back turned, I *felt* his presence, my body burning under his stare.

I steadied my shaking hand as I poured his drink, trying not to form a list of why someone like me should feel inadequate around someone like him.

Add in the fact that he practically owned the company I was desperate to work for—and that I'd called him an asshole a couple of times—and I was a bundle of nerves threatening to unravel.

And beneath all of that? I was still angry. Angry about what he'd said in the hotel room. About the accusations he'd made that I was sneaking around behind some fictitious boyfriend's back. The way he looked at me like I was just another girl playing games.

I slid the glass toward him, swallowing the words I really wanted to say.

This wasn't about setting the record straight—not right now.

"Look. About what I said before."

His brow arched, amusement flickering across his face as he silently waited for me to continue.

"When I called you an asshole, I mean. I shouldn't have said that. It was uncalled for."

"Which time?" He took a slow sip of his drink, setting the glass down, his large hands slowly spinning it on the bar top.

"I guess both." I bit my lip, trying not to smile despite myself. "I didn't realize you heard me on the plane."

He gave a sly smile, his eyes crinkling in the corners. His expression shifted from a teasing playfulness to a mask of humility. "You weren't wrong."

I blinked, surprised by his candor. "Well, be that as it may." I grinned. "I'm still sorry."

"And I'm sorry for being one. I can be… difficult. It tends to run in my family."

The tension in the air eased slightly, the untouchable man before me becoming more corporeal with his admission. "So… what brings you in tonight?"

He shrugged, glancing around the dimly lit bar. "I hoped to find a place with a decent alcohol selection to admire."

"And how did we do?" I asked, showcasing the display behind me.

"Not much to admire up there, but this place has its charm." His eyes settled on my face with a kind of intensity that made my core tighten.

Was he flirting?

The scuffed and polished wooden bar acted as both a barrier and a bridge between us, and my thoughts churned as I debated my next move.

Just as I opened my mouth, Terry burst out of the kitchen, pulling on his jacket and keeping his eyes trained on his phone as he rotated it between the hands he shoved inside his sleeves.

"Soph, it's so dead. I'm leaving," he announced casually.

I frowned and gave Corbin a "one-moment" gesture as I pulled Terry to the side.

"But you were gonna give me a ride home," I reminded him, trying to keep my voice low.

"Oh, shit. That's right. I forgot." Terry scratched the back of his head, feigning guilt. "Um…" he trailed off, looking for an excuse he didn't seem interested in making.

I should have known better. Terry was not exactly reliable. He'd either called in or simply not shown up to work so many times, I was surprised Theresa hadn't fired him years ago.

"Don't worry about it." I waved him off, after all, it wasn't Terry's fault I didn't have a car.

The thought of cutting into my meager tips to pay Hank for a ride wasn't appealing, maybe it wasn't too cold for the long walk home.

"Great! See ya," Terry said cheerfully, vanishing out the door without a backward glance.

I watched the kitchen door as it swayed back and forth, then began pacing behind the bar, muttering under my breath.

"I could give you a ride home." Corbin's voice cut through my tiny tantrum.

I turned to him, slightly embarrassed that he heard the exchange. "Oh, no. That's okay. I've still got about an hour before I close up. It'll be a late night."

He raised his glass. "I've got time."

As he said that, my last table stood up, shooting me a quick wave goodbye, leaving Corbin and me alone in the quiet solitude of the dimly lit bar.

"Okay. Thanks," I said, feeling a flutter of excitement low in my belly.

The next hour passed in a blur of motions I'd done a hundred times before—wiping down the bar, balancing the register, restocking napkins—but tonight, every task felt magnified.

Because I wasn't alone.

Because I could feel him watching me.

Corbin sat quietly at the far end, nursing his whiskey, his phone in hand but barely touched.

The air buzzed with a charged sort of quiet, like the seconds before a summer storm.

Each time I glanced in his direction, his gaze darted elsewhere—toward his screen, the floor, his glass. But not before I caught that flicker. That unmistakable awareness.

So, I let myself lean into it.

Just a little.

I straightened my posture the way Penny always nagged me to, lifted my chin, smoothed a loose piece of hair behind my ear. I bent to reach under the bar more gracefully than usual, careful not to smack my head like I typically would, and tried not to smirk when I felt his gaze slide right back to me.

When I finally turned off the last light behind the bar, I looked straight at him.

He was already watching.

This time, neither of us looked away.

His mouth curved slowly. Not quite a smirk, not quite a smile—something sultrier, more persuasive.

My heart thudded once, hard.

"You ready?" he asked, voice low.

I nodded, grabbed my bag, and stepped outside with him into the crisp night air toward a sleek black car.

"Nice car," I commented as I rubbed my arms, cursing myself for leaving my coat at home.

He slid his dark coat off his arms and draped it over my shoulders, the chivalrous move warming me more than the soft material did. Then he opened the passenger door for me.

"It's just a rental." He shrugged.

The interior was pristine, the leather seats buttery soft and warmed by the car's heating system. Corbin had pressed a button and started it before we even left the building.

I tried not to let my awe show as I settled in. After seeing those photos of Corbin, a car like this was probably as mundane as Devyn's Corolla.

The fabric of his wool coat was soft to the touch, with a rich texture that screamed wealth and luxury. Its scent was intoxicating—cedar and citrus—blurring my other senses as I tried to savor every note.

As Corbin turned onto the quiet streets, I twisted my hands in my lap, reaching for something to say to the intimidating force of a man beside me.

Before I could get a word out, Corbin's deep voice broke through the dark cab.

"So," he began, glancing over at me briefly, "I noticed you reading on the plane. Do you have a favorite author?"

I swallowed my unsaid words down—lucky for me, books were my favorite subject.

I smiled, relaxing into the seat. "That's tough. Right now? Probably Monica McKenzie. I know it's cliché. The romance genre can be so derivative, but I love a good love story."

He nodded appreciatively. "Not going to fight you on that one. She's very successful. Anyone else?"

I paused, realizing he didn't mention that his company had published Monica's stories. Perhaps he wasn't that close to the publishing side of the company?

It was also doubtful that somebody at his level would get involved in the hiring process for my position.

Maybe I shouldn't even bring up my desire to work there. Maybe it would only hurt my chances.

Instead, I relished in sharing a few of my other favorites—the classics I've read a million times over and the novels that shaped my view of the world, of love, of life.

The conversation continued in between my turn-by-turn directions. We flowed through genres, favorite characters, and literary pet peeves, each exchange laced with light teasing and the occasional shared laugh.

Before I knew it, he was placing the car in park in the lot outside my apartment.

"It's been a while since I talked books with someone who shares so many of the same interests as me," he said, turning to me, his expression unreadable.

I felt a blush creep up my neck as my gaze locked with his. "Yeah, me too."

We both turned away from each other, our silence grew heavy as the cab of the car brimmed with unspoken tension.

"Well, thank you. For the ride." I unbuckled and startled slightly when his seatbelt snapped open as well.

"I'll walk you to your door." His offer was genuine, but his tone had an indistinguishable edge.

Corbin walked close beside me, his shoulder at my eye-level, our footsteps soft against the pavement. The air was cold, and the parking lot was quiet—like the rest of the town at this hour.

He didn't say anything as we reached the stairs, just followed close, the steps creaking under our weight. I could feel the heat of him behind me, his presence pressing against the cold air.

Halfway up, I glanced back—he looked up at me, and didn't look away.

His eyes looked like he was fighting some internal battle, but I didn't ask. I just continued my silent ascent to my apartment.

At the top, I fumbled with my keys—my fingers shaky from the chilly air and his magnetic, confounding presence. When the lock clicked, I pushed open the door and flicked on the interior light.

I turned and watched as Corbin's eyes dropped to my mouth before peering over my shoulder into my apartment.

Before I could overthink it, the words spilled out, sharp and sudden. "Looking for someone?"

He shrugged, cool and unbothered.

"I live alone. Despite what you may have heard, I don't have a boyfriend," I clarified, slipping his coat off and holding it between us.

He stepped closer, and unlike our moment in the hotel room, I didn't back away.

His hand reached for his coat, and my nerve endings sprang to life when his fingers brushed across my skin.

It started as a flutter, isolated where he touched me before ricocheting through my body, skimming just below my skin before settling between my legs.

His eyes snapped up as if reading my mind—they bore into me and mined out every salacious thought.

I watched his face as he took a deep, contemplative breath before he skimmed his fingertips slowly up my arm, leaving a trail of scorched skin in their wake.

Every hair on my arm stood on end, a shiver coursing through me as two fronts collided—the inferno burning inside me clashing with the cold air outside.

Once his hand reached my neck, he cupped the side of it, and my core became molten as his tongue darted out to wet his lips.

Fire burned in his amber eyes, partially covered by the dark hair that spilled down his forehead.

He leaned in, slow and deliberate, giving me time to stop him.

But I didn't want to.

His lips gently touched mine in a soft press.

His kiss was chaste, but once his lips came into contact with mine, I lost every ounce of restraint.

I kissed him back—hungrily, without hesitation. My mouth opened for him as white hot need coursed through me.

His coat fell to the ground between us as our bodies crashed together.

The tender beginning of our kiss descended into an unrestrained clashing of teeth and tongue.

I moaned, and he echoed with one of his own, the noise vibrating through my lips and shuddering through me all the way down to my toes.

His hand wrapped around to the back of my neck and fisted in my hair, his other low on my back, pulling my body hard into his.

My hands raked through his dark roots, grabbing onto the thick tendrils of his hair.

I shifted my hips forward and moaned again as I felt the rigid outline of him.

Suddenly, he pulled back, releasing his grip on me one finger at a time, like he had to force each muscle to move one by one.

His forehead pressed against mine, his words tight and hoarse. "I have to stop."

He stepped back, bending over to pick up the discarded coat. He brushed his hand over the material, as if wiping away some unseen dirt. His brow furrowed before smoothing out as his eyes met mine once more, the inferno snuffed out and replaced with a soft glow.

"Good night, 1C," he said softly.

I didn't have time to respond before he bounded down the stairs, his long legs taking two at a time. He didn't look back.

Confusion and embarrassment clung to me. I backed into my apartment and quickly shut the door, throwing the deadbolt and the chain lock closed for good measure.

I peered out of my window, unable to identify more than his outline as he sat in the dim light of his car. After a few minutes of sitting in the dark, he drove off, his taillights glowing in the late-night hour.

My fingers traced my swollen lips as my mind raced—dizzy spell running rampant.

What was that?

Did he regret it?

Did I misread everything?

Exhaustion settled deep in my bones as the chaotic whirlwind of the last couple of days weighed on me.

Later that night, despite my fatigue, restlessness clung to me as I lay in bed, my lips lingering with phantom brushes of Corbin's tongue.

After an hour of tossing and turning and in a desperate need to ward off dizzy spells, I adhered to Devyn's sage advice—*science or something.*

And Corbin Buescher became the inspiration for relieving some of my pent-up tension.

Chapter 22

THE SOPHIA

Sophia

It had been five days since I submitted my resume to Buescher-Jones Publishing and four days since I kissed the COO of the parent company that owned them.

Corbin hadn't returned to Boomer's any other nights I worked, and I would only occasionally get heart-rate-inducing, pulse-pounding glimpses of him at Elijah's.

Since our lobby was really only for those checking in and out or for anyone who wanted to partake in the breakfast buffet or theme nights, I wouldn't see Corbin unless he needed something from the staff.

I found myself hoping he would need extra towels or have a clogged drain in his shower to complain about, just so I could have a reason to talk to him again.

It was a rare Friday when I had the day off from Elijah's. I had a shift at Boomer's later, but that wasn't until six. My mind was on the verge of a dizzy spell every thirty seconds.

I glanced at my phone for the thirtieth time today—hoping for an email that wasn't junk mail—as I walked to Lana's coffee shop.

"I have good news for you." Lana grinned wide as I approached the counter, already reaching for a plastic cup to make my favorite drink.

My friends and I played a game with Lana. She refused to take our money for drinks, but we wanted to support her, so we had to find clever ways to pay her. Sometimes, it was as easy as throwing cash in the tip jar, but I didn't see it at the moment.

"Good. I need good news," I whined.

"Andi was in here this morning," she shouted over the grinding of beans, her wall of inky dark hair facing me.

"Andi, Andi? The woman who holds the fate of my life in her hands, Andi?" I shouted back, embarrassed when the grinding stopped, but my voice was still loud, disturbing the handful of patrons trying to enjoy an early lunch in the shop.

Lana giggled. "Yes, that Andi. She ordered a *Sophia* to drink."

I stood there quietly, waiting to understand what that meant. *Curious* news, I thought. *Interesting* news, yes, but not *good* news.

"What is a *Sophia*?"

She gestured to the cup in her hand. "I must have made two of your favorite drinks that day you ran into each other. She said she'll never want anything besides *The Sophia*."

"I am not sure how that is good news. Besides reaffirming my amazing taste in beverages and your incredible barista skills." I didn't even know what was in my favorite drink. I just knew I liked it.

"You're on her mind," Lana said matter-of-factly. "Even if subconsciously, you'll get the interview and go in with an advantage because she already associates you with something good."

"Maybe." I shrugged, wishing I could share Lana's unfounded optimism.

Seriously, where is that damn jar?

"I think it's a sign—a good sign. Today is going to be a good day for you. I can feel it." Lana set my drink down, and my name was signed with a four-leaf clover over the "i."

I smiled at the sentiment. "I hope you're right. Love you." I said with force as I reached across the counter and shoved a five-dollar bill into her apron. Then I turned and bolted out of there before she could return it.

"I love you too, and I'm giving this back to you!" she shouted at my back.

I returned to my apartment and tried to fill myself with Lana's positivity with every sip of my coffee. Pretending each swallow ingested was a liquid punch of damn sunshine to my gut.

Around 2 p.m., my phone pinged. I jolted up from my couch and wiped a little drool off my mouth. I must have fallen asleep.

Real productive day for me.

An email with Andi's name appeared on my screen, apologizing for the last-minute request but asking if I could come in for an interview at four today. It went on to say she'd call me to provide details.

I kicked my feet in the air and squealed.

Then quickly proceeded to freak out and frantically started pacing.

What should I wear?

How should I do my hair?

Will Corbin be there?

I stopped pacing and squashed that thought immediately.

Who cares if he is there?

This job is about me. This is for me.

The last few encounters I've had with him, I was unprepared. He got the jump on me like a sexy ninja. This time, I will be prepared—prepared to see him, his face, his body.

Squash the thoughts. Squash!

My phone rang, and I screamed, an actual audible scream at the noise. I shook off the embarrassment and answered the New York area code number that flashed on my screen.

This could be it, my big break.

***

I showed up at the address Andi gave me, the old Monroe building on the East side of Misty Springs. Since it was too far to walk, I had to call Hank for a ride.

I would definitely need a car if I got this job. Maybe I could afford a car if I got this job.

Hank dished about the latest town gossip while I sat in the backseat, answering imaginary interview questions in my head. I didn't hear who he was talking about—just that they still had their carved pumpkins out despite it being mid-November.

"I've been driving to this address a few times. The guy's real uptight," Hank muttered as he parked outside the brick building.

I chuckled, knowing exactly which uptight guy he was referring to. "Thanks for the ride, Hank."

"Good luck, kid. You look the part, that's for sure," he said while looking at me in his rearview mirror. "No one else needs me right now, so I won't run the meter while I wait."

"Thanks, Hank." I climbed out of the car, hoping he was right about me looking the part.

I was wearing one of my only businessy outfits. It was a gray pencil skirt with a small slit in the back, a white button-down, and a matching gray blazer.

Landon's mom bought it for me when I worked for the Norwood family business. She thought it made me look more *professional*—or, in her words, "less like some aimless cocktail waitress playing office dress-up."

I took a deep breath to steady myself. The last thing I needed right now was to be thinking about my ex and his psychotic mother. My nerves were a wreck already.

I turned the handle to the suite and entered Buescher-Jones Publishing's offices.

The office was an eclectic mix of old world and new, with funky accessories and pops of color everywhere.

I stood in the open air for just a second, admiring the scene around me, imagining myself getting to show up here to work every day. In my periphery, I noticed a man exiting his office to my left.

I startled, expecting to see Corbin.

Instead, he was a middle-aged man with salt-and-pepper slicked-back hair. He was wearing dark blue pants and a gray plaid button-down shirt that was loose around his chest and tight around his midsection.

"Hello there. Who might you be?" he asked as he approached me with his hand out.

"Hi, I'm Sophia. I'm here to meet with Andi." I held my hand to him.

He shook it and placed his other hand over mine, holding it a little too long and settling in closer as he repeated my name.

He had a symmetrical face, but something about his smile looked fake. After years of bartending, I had gotten pretty good at reading people. You see the worst in people when their inhibitions are lowered. If he showed up at Boomer's, I'd expect a low tip and for him to ask me for my phone number.

"Ned, back off. She's not interested." Andi's voice came booming from a back office.

She emerged looking like a runway model in bright pink pants and a matching jacket. Her neon yellow heels matched her earrings and chunky necklace. With each strut of her long legs, her heel clicks echoed in the space.

Ned dropped my hand and took a few menacing, long strides toward her, his height barely making him eye-level with her. "When Mr. Buescher gets back next week, you can believe we'll be discussing your disrespect toward me," he said quietly, but not quietly enough that I couldn't hear.

I tried not to react to Corbin's name and used every ounce of muscle control not to do a mini fist pump.

Back next week—I would not have any Corbin distractions hanging over me during my interview.

"Please do. *Mr. Buescher* loves discussing trivial matters of employee squabbles," Andi flung back.

Ned turned and angrily walked to his office, not giving me a second thought.

"Right this way," Andi said with a smile of bright white teeth and a wave of her hand as if the exchange didn't phase her in the slightest.

I followed her into the office she emerged from. The room was big and bright, with an oversized desk and large windows overlooking the river that wound through the heart of Misty Springs.

"I'm sorry. Ned is a creep," Andi began.

"Oh, um, he seemed nice." I stumbled through my words, not wanting to offend any potential coworkers.

"Don't defend him. I know that's always the go-to. Be nice. Smile. Be polite. Say, thank you. Say please. Don't offend. Be a lady." She puppeted her hands as she said each nicety that was drilled in my head from birth. "Some people don't deserve your nice. Plain and simple. Ned is one of those people. Besides, we have a strict no-relationship policy here. If he tries anything with you, I will gladly get him fired."

"I think I love you, Andi."

"The straight ones always fall for me." She smiled before both of us fell into a fit of laughter.

That broke the tension and made the rest of the interview proceed smoothly.

Andi asked excellent questions, challenging at times, but I felt good about every reply. I was focused and ready, my mind only wandered to Corbin three—maybe four times.

"I'm so glad you were able to come in, but I feel I need to be transparent with you," Andi said, leaning back in her chair.

I braced for the bad news. I knew this was too good to be true.

"I haven't gotten the go-ahead from my human resources department yet, and in this company, there is a lot of... red tape sometimes to navigate around, and I lose patience. I didn't want you to keep waiting to hear from me, and after our last conversation, I was anxious to talk to you again."

I nodded, unsure what this meant for me.

"What I'm trying to say is, I have a good feeling about you, Sophia, so I'm admittedly going about this a little backward."

She plopped down what appeared to be a draft of a novel—a binder-clipped pile of printed pages with no name and no title.

"I need you to read this. I'll give you a couple of weeks. Hopefully, by then, HR will get their shit together enough to green-light the interview process. Then I would like you to come back in and give me your notes on it." She pushed the large stack of papers toward me. "Do you think this manuscript has something? What kind of direction do you think it needs? Anything jump out at you? Anything missing?"

"Yes, I can do that, absolutely." I wanted to crack it open now. If this was what I needed to do to prove myself, I would make it happen.

"Great. Let me pull up my calendar to see when you could come back." She opened her laptop, the glow of the screen reflecting off her thick yellow glasses.

I heard the door click open behind me.

Andi glanced up, head tilted, eyes gleaming like she'd just swiped the last cookie off the tray and was daring someone to call her out.

"I thought you had already left for New York," she said over my head.

I knew who he was before he spoke a word, his scent hitting me before the rich timbre of his voice did.

"My flight was pushed out to seven. My original pilot got food poisoning, waiting on a replacement."

I felt his stare at my back, pinpricks dancing along my neck where I felt his eyes linger.

"Gross. Well, while you're here, meet Sophia Carlson." Andi stood to provide the introduction. "Sophia, Corbin Buescher, COO. Mr. Buescher, Sophia." She gestured to both of us, unaware we'd already met... more than met.

I stood and brushed my hands on my skirt, trying to delay the inevitable of looking into those damn bourbon eyes of his and losing myself in them.

Oh God, I was just touching myself to images of him last night.

My body reacted instinctively, betraying me with a flush of warmth.

I turned, my mouth going dry as my eyes landed on Corbin. My heart pounded in my chest, nearly drowning out every word of Andi's introduction.

I scrambled to regain control.

I wanted this job. I *needed* this job.

Corbin's eyes flicked to mine as he stepped into the room. His casual air was unnerving, but then I caught the subtle tick of his jaw—the only hint that my presence was affecting him, too.

That small tell gave me the confidence I needed. I straightened my shoulders and took a step forward. His gaze didn't falter as I extended my hand.

"Nice to meet you, Mr. Buescher."

His hand wrapped around mine, warm and firm.

The same hand that was snaked in my hair while his tongue danced with mine. The same hand that I pretended to be touching me instead of my own, after he had left me in a heated mess on my front porch.

"Likewise." The way his fingers released mine felt almost teasing, and I couldn't help but notice Andi beaming between us, oblivious to the undercurrent of tension.

"I was just looking for a time for Sophia to come back for a second interview. Do you want to sit in on it?" Andi walked around the desk to look at the calendar she had pulled up on her screen.

"Seems a little premature, don't you think?" Corbin's voice came out sharp, slicing through any hope building in my chest that I had this job secured. "I haven't seen anything come through from HR yet."

Andi straightened and crossed her arms, her face shifting into a scowl. "Well, we both know how slow those asshats can be. I was helping speed things along."

Corbin's eyes narrowed at her, and I suddenly felt caught in the middle of something I shouldn't be privy to—like when you're a child watching your parents fight about matters you don't understand.

"Don't you think you should let me take things over here like we agreed?" Andi pressed.

"Don't you think we should talk about this later?" Corbin said through semi-clenched teeth.

That felt like my cue to get out of there. One thing a doormat hated was being caught in the middle of a raging stampede.

"Andi, you can email me once you have a date secured. Thank you for letting me come in to speak with you today." I turned my attention to Corbin, his expression unreadable. "Nice meeting you, Mr. Buescher."

"I'll walk you out," Andi said, in my direction, though her eyes were still narrowed at Corbin.

Andi and I strolled down the hallway toward the lobby.

"Don't worry about him," she said, her voice low but fierce. "He's been like that all week. I'll email you some available times for your second interview. Read that manuscript and send me your notes in a couple of weeks."

Her dark eyes burned with certainty—the kind that made it hard to doubt myself, even when I wanted to.

"Thanks, Andi." I hoped my voice carried even a fraction of the gratitude I felt. "Really… this opportunity means a lot to me."

Outside, Hank's car waited at the curb like a lifeline. I climbed in without looking back.

Chapter 23

THESE MEET CUTES ARE GETTING OLD

Corbin

Sophia. She was everywhere. The hotel. The bar. In my damn head, every time I closed my eyes.

And now, in my office.

Self-discipline was a cornerstone of who I was, something I'd built brick by brick after watching my father burn every bridge he ever crossed. Restraint wasn't just a virtue—it was a survival tactic.

And yet, Sophia unraveled it with nothing more than a look. She slipped past the walls I'd spent years reinforcing and lit fires in places I thought I'd turned to stone.

I never planned to kiss her when I drove her home earlier this week. In fact, I'd set a very clear boundary in my head that I wouldn't so much as touch her.

But the drive passed too quickly, our conversation filling the cab with the easy swell of shared interests and soft laughter. I offered to walk her to the door—not because she needed me to, but because I wasn't ready for the night to end—desperate to stretch every moment I could with her.

And when she stood in the warm glow of her apartment light, soft and stunning—after a night spent watching her from a distance—wanting her in a way I had no right to.

I broke.

Even today, seeing her inside my office with Andi, it tilted my axis in ways I didn't expect. When my fingers grazed along her smooth palm, I felt something dangerous, forbidden, thrilling.

I will not be my father.

The majority of the board members at Buescher Enterprises had a front-row seat to my father's downfall. As whispers of quid pro quo deals, sexual harassment allegations, and inappropriate relationships mounted, the legal department scrambled to contain the fallout. By the time the first formal lawsuit was filed, the board moved swiftly to implement a strict no-relationship policy—one that served as both a legal safeguard and a not-so-subtle response to the chaos he'd left in his wake.

And it wasn't just a rule—it was a guillotine. I'd seen men and women, even those perched high on the corporate ladder, lose everything because of it, and I wouldn't be exempt just because my name was on the building.

Any relationship with a subordinate would instantly draw a line between me and him in a way I couldn't afford.

"What the hell? Why were you so rude just now?" Andi's raised voice interrupted my thoughts as she stormed back into my office after walking Sophia out.

"What? There is no way HR came back already, she just submitted her resume," I stated, my voice rougher than intended.

HR felt like a good scapegoat—I needed a buffer, some excuse to deny her that wasn't *me*. There were a million companies where Sophia could work—why did it have to be *mine*?

"Who gives a shit about HR? She'd be perfect for us," Andi pressed, shoving her resume in my hand.

"She doesn't have the right education." I tossed out the first objection I could find as I skimmed over Sophia's resume.

Andi scoffed, rolling her eyes. "Education? You and I both know how overrated that is."

My lips twitched in annoyance. "Look at this experience—Boomer's? That dingy hotel, Elijah's? And Norwood Realty. Wait, Norwood Realty... why does that sound familiar?"

Andi shrugged. "Probably because they have billboards plastered on every corner of this city. Mom, Dad, and their spokesperson for WASP-looking son—they're everywhere."

Andi stomped a heel and let out a huff of air. "Look, none of that matters. You took a chance on me when I was... when I had a not-so-stellar background. You saw something more in me. I see something more in Sophia. I know I'm right about this."

The truth was, I knew she was right, too. Driving Sophia home earlier this week, I could tell she was sharp, with a keen eye for literary prose. I didn't care about degrees or formal education—

what mattered to me was work ethic, personality, and knowing your craft.

But I had to protect myself.

I stared at Andi, trying to come up with something else, but she wasn't budging. I could feel the heat rolling off her, practically daring me to argue further. She had instincts, damn good ones, and we both knew it.

"Keep looking, Andi. She's not the right fit." I handed the resume back to her. "HR won't approve it. It'll never get past the screening phase. You're wasting everyone's time."

Her nostrils flared, her arms crossing over her chest as she glared at me. But she didn't say a word. Instead, she spun on her heel and stormed out, slamming the door behind her.

I am an asshole.

I exhaled heavily, dragging a hand down my face. This was the only way. Sophia was too much of a risk.

The fact that she was still stuck in my head was infuriating. I'd barely slept all week, spending my mornings navigating Elijah's front lobby like a minefield—doing anything to avoid running into her.

The hotel bar had become my go-to, even though their whiskey selection was garbage—something I was trying to convince Cassie to fix.

But the thought of Sophia here?

Steps from my office. Her scent lingering in the air. Catching me off guard with every breath. Knowing she was close, yet completely off-limits?

It would be impossible.

And I would not repeat my father's mistakes.

Chapter 24

Girl Fight

Sophia

"**It was going great.** Until the COO showed up," I told Devyn as we closed up after another busy Friday night at Boomer's.

"He sounds like a jerk," Devyn declared, flipping the dining room chairs on the tabletops.

I let out a sharp laugh and considered her words.

I started mentally weighing each interaction on some invisible scale. Our incredible car conversation and mind-blowing kiss had nearly offset the balance of our airplane and hotel encounter toward *not jerk*.

But he bolted after said mind-blowing kiss. And the way he acted during my interview? The scale didn't just tip back—it flung itself violently in the other direction.

A loud howling wind rumbled outside, sending some object thumping against the thick windowless walls of the bar. I jumped, letting out a little gasp.

"You're jumpy tonight," Devyn jested as she marched toward the bar to start wiping it down.

I shrugged it off. I still didn't have the guts to tell her—or anyone else—about Landon, and the fact that I agreed to go with him to New York tomorrow. He'd been texting me all week, reminding me.

The box Landon left behind contained a gorgeous gold ballgown and the engagement ring I lobbed at his head. I shoved the ring in my sock drawer, hidden beneath the unmatched ones and ones with holes in them that I couldn't seem to throw away, its resting place oddly metaphorical.

"I'll go lock up," Devyn said as she flung a damp rag on the bar top.

I was focused on putting away the last of the glasses when I heard the bell ring, signaling the door opening. I assumed it was Devyn checking something outside until I heard her voice.

"What the hell are *you* doing here?"

I barely looked up before my stomach sank. Landon walked right past Devyn like she wasn't even there, eyes locked on me.

"Can we have some privacy?" Landon asked me, his tone teetering on the edge of impatience.

I glanced briefly at a disgruntled, wide-eyed Devyn before sighing and motioning for Landon to follow me to the other side of the bar.

Devyn gave me an exasperated look in return, and I watched her stare at us in disbelief before she turned to the utility closet, her long curls bouncing with each angry step.

"What do you want, Landon?"

"Did you get your ring?"

"Yes, I pawned it," I lied.

"You didn't. I know you better than that."

He did, and I hated that he did.

"I don't want the ring, Landon. You bought it, you keep it."

"Look, I didn't come here about the ring." He raked his fingers angrily through his dirty blonde hair. "I came because you've been ignoring my texts."

I didn't *ignore* his texts. I just… didn't respond. Every text merely asked me what I was up to while laced with pet names for me and the familiarity of someone who lost that privilege. I had already agreed to go on this trip with him. That was where my commitment to him ended.

His tone softened, leaning in close. "I wanted to make sure you wouldn't flake on me. This is a big deal, babe. You know how Alicia can be."

I took an instinctual step back.

My mind drifted to my friends and how easily Alicia could crush them under her heel without a second thought, just to make a point.

"I'm not flaking on you, Landon. But *you* never acknowledged *my* end of the agreement. I need your word. After this, I owe you and Alicia nothing. I don't want you to text me anymore, no more showing up at the bar, no more expectations that I will get over this and get back together with you. You have to agree to fully let me go."

I spied Devyn inching closer, holding a broom and dustpan. Her fake brushes on the broom, not even touching the floor as she eavesdropped.

He tapped his fingers on the bar and hesitated. A flash of anger hit his face and then disappeared instantly. "This is the last time I'll bother you," he finally agreed.

"Then I'll see you tomorrow." A sinking feeling settled in my gut.

His face lit up in victory, like he wasn't taking the rest of my words seriously. I meant them, though. This was going to be it. There was nothing left for him to hang over my head once this was done.

He turned to leave, and I quickly followed to lock the door behind him.

"And Landon," I said as he stepped through the doorway into the cold late-night air.

He turned to me curiously.

"Stop calling me babe. I'm not your babe anymore."

I shut the door in his face and turned the lock.

I wanted to scream at the fact that I could never seem to free myself from Landon. It was like a script I couldn't stop reading from, and I hated that I couldn't find the courage to flip the page.

And now Devyn was standing there, arms crossed, ready to hurl her opinion at me like *everyone* always did. Like, I didn't know how bad this situation was. Like, I couldn't see the cracks in every decision I made.

"You're not seriously going with him, are you?" Devyn's voice cut through my spiraling thoughts.

I bristled at the accusation in her tone, my nerves in overdrive after dealing with Landon.

"I don't know, Devyn. This isn't just about him. It's his family, too." My words felt defensive, shaky.

Her expression darkened, and she stepped closer. "He's been blowing up your phone for weeks, showing up here randomly to torment you—and now you're letting him drag you to New York?"

"You don't understand. He came to my apartment last weekend, Devyn. He won't stop. This is how I end things with him. He just said..."

"You already ended things with him! You don't owe him anything," she interrupted.

She didn't understand. She doesn't know the Norwood family like I do. Their behavior was borderline insane. They acted like they were some sort of Misty Springs mafia. I knew she wouldn't believe the lengths they would go if I tried to explain it to her—or worse, she'd try to intervene.

Her jaw tightened, and her eyes flared with anger as she continued. "And he came to your apartment? And you didn't tell us? Why? Why would you keep something like that to yourself?"

"I didn't want to burden you," I said softly, my gaze falling to the scuffed floorboards.

"*Burden us?* We're your friends, Sophia! This is why we're here—for you. We care about what you're going through. But you *always* shut us out. You never told us when you quit Brown. You never talked to us after your parents died. And you sure as hell never told us how bad Landon was treating you! We had to watch you nearly wither away from afar. You shut us out." Her words were caring, but her tone was bristling.

The weight of her words slammed into me, each jab loosening a stitch I haphazardly placed over the pains of my past. Pain that I never wanted to spread to anyone else, so I tucked it away instead.

But as I stood there, Devyn's words still hanging in the air, I felt my pain twist into anger—anger at her for not understanding and at myself for always being the one to bend, to concede, to play the role of doormat.

"Why does every decision I make have to go through you like you're some kind of jury for my life?" I snapped, the tone in my voice surprising both of us. "I can make my own decisions!"

"Maybe your decisions are terrible. *La mierda*," Devyn shot back, her tone cutting like a blade.

"Maybe I'm okay with my *shit* decisions," I snapped, my voice rising.

"Maybe you shouldn't be!"

Devyn and I locked eyes. This was the first real fight I could remember since junior year. When we both swore the pair of jeans we kept swapping back and forth were originally ours.

I broke first, my voice quieter but still hard-edged. "Maybe you should let me close up by myself, and you can leave and take your judgment with you."

The bitterness of the words hit me the moment they escaped, regret settling in their wake. I hadn't meant any of it, but I couldn't take it back now. My anger may be misplaced, but it was loose and untamed.

Devyn's expression flickered—hurt, disbelief, and rage flashing all at once—before she turned and stormed out.

Looks like I was in for a cold walk home. I've been on such a roll lately. What's one more disappointment?

Chapter 25

PARTY OF SEVEN

Sophia

It was early Saturday afternoon when a knock sounded at my door. I peered through the peephole, not sure who to expect, since Landon wasn't arriving for a few more hours.

My heart swelled when I saw Devyn standing outside with her boyfriend, Sam.

I opened the door slowly, feeling like I wanted to bury my head in the ground like an ostrich. Devyn didn't deserve my anger. I wasn't even angry at her. I was angry at Landon and myself—at this whole situation I found myself in.

We stood silent for half a second before we both started crying, and hugging, and apologizing. Her head nuzzled into my shoulder, and her arms wrapped around my waist as we walked inside my apartment, talking almost simultaneously through our tears.

Sam followed behind, holding a black duffel bag and huffing a laugh. "Wow, I don't know how you ladies even understand what each other is saying right now."

We both looked at him, batting our eyes.

"It's girl frequency. It's too delicate a sound for male ears to pick up on." Devyn sniffled as she walked over and pulled the duffel bag from his hand, turning to me. "I hate that you are going with him, but I trust you, and if you think this is the best way to get him out of your life completely, I support you. I brought a peace offering."

Devyn lobbed the bag onto my kitchen bar.

"Oh! The treasure trove." I ogled, searching through the bag.

Devyn's aunt worked as a makeup artist for celebrities, and she always ended up with the most luxurious samples or partially used products that she handed down to Devyn.

"I'll be fine, Dev," I promised, swirling a bright red lipstick tube. "Just a few hours of misery. We're taking a red-eye back to Misty Springs tonight. And then, I'll be completely rid of Landon Norwood."

A knock sounded, followed by Cassie and Lana strolling into my apartment, with Trevor and Brent lagging behind them.

Cassie hauled drink carriers with coffee, and Lana had a small pink box of pastries from her shop. They set their things down on my kitchen counter and smothered me with hugs.

"What are you all doing here?" I asked.

Brent punched me lightly on the arm, his hulking frame making the delicate gesture seem near impossible. He wasn't just Cassie's older brother—after all the years we spent growing up together, he felt like mine, too.

"Devyn said you needed an intervention." He scratched at his beard, overgrown and rough around the edges.

"What?" I crossed my arms and gave Devyn a piercing glance.

She shrugged innocently.

"Cassie, Devyn, and Lana are all talking about how you lost your mind and are taking Landon back," Trevor weighed in, squeezing past me directly to my fridge.

"That's not true," Cassie yelled.

"Shut up, Trevor," Devyn snapped.

"That's not exactly what we said," Lana added.

All three of their voices overlapped.

Trevor just shrugged as he grabbed one of my sodas and popped it open without asking. His hazel eyes widened as he loudly sipped the soda with his pinky in the air.

"Okay, let's hear it then," I told the group as I made a come-at-me motion.

"We just want to make sure that you are sure about this. And that it isn't opening the door for Landon to come back into your life," Lana started, her soft tone calming the room.

"Yeah, he's a manipulative jerk who will say anything to get back with you," Cassie added, elevating the room back up a notch with her fire.

"Guys, please, listen to me." I held my three fingers up in a salute, just like Cassie and I used to when we were little girls in Girl Scouts together. "I, Sophia Carlson, vow to never have a romantic entanglement with Landon Norwood ever again for as long as I live."

"Scouts honor?" Cassie asked.

"Scouts honor. Now, if we really want to have an intervention, can we focus on Brent and his Duck Dynasty-audition beard?" I said, trying to steer their attention away from me.

Brent stopped a scone midway to his mouth. "What? You guys don't like the beard?"

"Dude. That isn't a beard. It's a burning bush on your face," Sam chimed, squinting slightly as he scratched at the back of his chocolate-brown hair.

"Yeah, man, what started as a ginger mane has now become a full-fledged forest fire," Trevor added.

Brent's eyes flickered with doubt as he looked at all the nodding faces in the room. His eyes lingered on Lana's face, the one we all turned to for the sagest of wisdom.

She shrugged. "Sorry, Brent, it's gotta go."

My plan to divert attention away from me seemed to be working.

"Great, with Landongate behind us and Operation Red Beard finally executed, we can move on," Devyn said, turning to me. "So can we talk about this Hottie McHottie, who Terry said was all over you Monday?" She grabbed a cheese danish from the pink box of pastries, handing it to me like she was passing me a grenade.

So much for diverting attention.

I hadn't shared anything about Corbin with my friends. He was confounding—even to me—and I didn't even know where to start.

Was he the handsome stranger I accosted with my eyes at the airport and then stole his seat?

The guy who gave me a ride home earlier this week and gave me one of the most stimulating and enjoyable conversations—followed by the most earth-shattering, mind-altering kiss?

My, *hopefully*, future boss?

Something clicked at that last thought—I remembered what Andi said in passing about Ned: "Besides, we have a strict no-relationship policy here, so if he tries anything with you, I will gladly get him fired."

This job could be everything for me. It could be a turning point in my previously rudderless life. And if I got it, Corbin and I couldn't be anything other than the COO of Buescher Enterprises and Associate Editor at Buescher-Jones Publishing.

"That guy was most definitely not all over me on Monday night. Terry was mistaken. His name is Corbin Buescher, and he's... an executive at the company I'm applying for. That's it." I took a bite of my danish to stop me from saying anything more as my thoughts continued to swirl.

"Oh damn. I didn't realize he was an executive," Cassie remarked. "Guess I should've figured with all the suit-wearing. I'll take it a little easier on him. It's been a little too much fun to torment his arrogant ass at Elijah's."

"Aw, Cass, I thought you saved all your evil schemes for me," Trevor quipped, jutting his lip out.

He spun his Chase Construction baseball cap backward—identical to the one Brent wore—his butterscotch-colored tresses rustling with the movement.

I chuckled, thinking of all the clever ways Cassie had no doubt found to irritate Corbin. She was a master at reading people and exploiting weaknesses. She had a gift for finding ways to get under anyone's skin.

"So we're definitely sure she's not going back to Landon?" Sam asked, snagging a bite of Devyn's pastry.

She protested immediately.

Cassie scoffed from her new perch by the window. "Of course, she's not getting back with Landon. She just scouts honored us. We live and die by the Girl Scout code."

Brent crossed his arms, inflating his already overgrown muscles. "But you're still going to New York with him?" he asked in a big brother tone.

"I have to."

All six of them groaned in unison.

I couldn't help but laugh.

None of my friends were quiet about their dislike for Landon. I thought they just hadn't gotten the chance to know him yet. And according to Landon, it was hard for an "outsider" to fit in with our tight-knit group.

I thought maybe they just didn't see the real him, or didn't give him enough of a chance. It turns out they saw exactly who he was the whole time, and it was me who didn't see him clearly.

A knock sounded at the door again.

We all looked at each other, confused, like we were all counting and realizing that no one else should be showing up.

Sam walked to the door, peering through the peephole before letting out an exasperated sigh. "Speak of the devil."

"Landon is here?" Cassie hissed.

"Good," Brent said as he cracked his knuckles.

Landon was early.

I took a steadying breath and moved through my crowded apartment, opening the door as Sam stood aside.

Landon stood on my welcome mat, holding two cups of coffee and a self-assured smirk. He nudged a cup of coffee toward me. "I thought you might need a pick-me-up before the flight."

"She already had her coffee, thanks," Devyn announced from inside.

Landon's smirk wavered slightly as he glanced over my shoulder into the apartment, his gaze landing on the group. "Oh *good*, you're all here."

Brent gave a malicious wave while Trevor winked at him.

Landon stepped back, giving himself some additional distance from the group that he insisted never gave him a chance.

"We should go. We've got a tight schedule," Landon said, impatience seeping through his tone.

"Let me just get my bag." I backed into my apartment and motioned for my suitcase. The gown Landon gifted me earlier this week was carefully folded inside, along with a few new products from Devyn.

"I'll wait for you in the car," Landon announced before turning on his heels, not giving anyone inside a second glance.

"Let me help you with that," Brent offered as he grabbed my suitcase, not missing the opportunity to face off in front of Landon outside.

The rest of my friends hugged me and wished me luck.

"We'll lock up, Soph!" Lana called out as I walked away.

Brent walked out with me, carrying my bag down the stairs of my apartment complex.

He pulled me in for a hug, eyeing Landon as he stood near the open trunk of his town car. "Don't you dare get back with that loser," he not-so-quietly said in my ear.

"Never," I promised as I hugged him back.

Chapter 26

MINDFUCKARY PIMPAGE

Corbin

As expected, the Grand Ballroom of The Plaza Hotel was a masterpiece of wealth and excess. Everything from the polished floors to the silk-draped tables reeked of meticulous planning, the kind only a hefty donation could buy.

It was all so… predictable.

Sullivan called me earlier—interrupting my Saturday morning jog with an animated reminder of tonight's event.

"So… you bringing arm candy to the gala this year?" he asked.

"No." I replied, my voice shaky from my run.

"Stag? I like that. Wait—you don't already have some little piece you picked up in that dumpy town, do you?"

Typical Sullivan—his radar for detecting things I'd rather keep hidden annoyingly accurate.

I left his question unanswered, focusing on the sound of my feet hitting pavement while he continued to ramble about tux choices and how Davis was banned from tequila after last year's incident.

The Haitian Housing Gala always pulled a big crowd from the real estate world. Last year, I sealed the military post-expansion deal I'd been chasing for months—a few cocktails and a stogie on the balcony closed it in just a couple of hours.

Of course, this annual event inevitably devolved into something resembling a frat party, where wild stories became fresh fodder for blackmail and collateral in our little circle.

Tonight was no exception. The ballroom buzzed with champagne flutes and performative laughter, every corner packed with expensive labels and strategic networking.

Guests floated between tables, their designer gowns swishing and suits perfectly tailored. Waitstaff carried silver trays of canapés that looked more decorative than edible, while the scent of floral arrangements and aftershave thickened the air.

Fundraising was the secondary objective here—the primary being to whip it out and measure it against the competition. It also served as the premier gossip mill, finding the next hot lead or learning who was tanking and prime for being gobbled up.

After engaging in droll conversation and grinding my teeth through a few sneering jabs about my father—not to mention feigned concern about my grandmother's health or whispered questions about my grandfather's mental state, more about collecting intel than offering sympathy—I needed a drink.

As if he read my mind, Davis sidled beside me, two whiskeys in hand.

He passed one to me.

"If I never wear another tux again, it will be too soon."

"I'll cheers to that. Maybe we could all wear assless chaps next time," I gibed as I clinked our glasses together.

"I'm glad to see you've accepted your new persona with aplomb. Bravo." Davis smiled as he sipped the amber liquid.

Tonight, he opted for a deep blue tux, a trendy take on the traditional black-and-white garb the rest of us penguins wore. Then again, Davis was always one to push the envelope.

"She's here!" Sullivan exclaimed, stepping between Davis and me, throwing his arms around our shoulders.

Both of us nearly spilled our drinks.

"Who?" I asked, annoyed that my mind spent half a second jumping to Sophia.

"Cindy. She's been blowing me off. I'm gonna go shoot my shot. Wish me luck," Sullivan beamed.

Davis and I watched as he practically skipped toward Cindy.

"I don't know why he's so stuck on her," I muttered to Davis. "She's not the kind of girl you bring home to mom. She's going to break his little labrador heart."

Cindy was someone you needed to be careful around—a lesson I had unfortunately already learned. She wielded secrets like weapons, using men only to keep herself well-armed. I'd warned Sullivan to be careful, but he didn't seem to be heeding my advice.

Sullivan was tall and broad, not someone I'd ever try to pick a fight with in a bar, but he was mushy as a marshmallow inside.

"You sound like you've gone soft, Corbin. Misty Springs, melting your ice heart a little?" Davis jested.

I grew up alongside Sullivan and Davis. We went from the same prep school to different Ivy League campuses, but our social circles always overlapped. They were the closest thing I had to friends.

Of course, friendship never stopped us from competing at everything.

With Sullivan, it was always playful, a sport for bragging rights.

But Davis? He made it a war game, turning every challenge into a battle he had to win.

I scanned the crowd, checking if Buzz had made his arrival yet. Ever since the dinner that warranted an exorcism the other night, he'd gone radio silent.

A tiny flicker of unease wormed its way into my mind. My life was beginning to shift in ways I couldn't control.

Gram, my rock, my unwavering source of support, was sick. Buzz was teetering between being non-existent, or behaving erratically—his decisions veering toward the impulsive.

The constants in my life, the pillars I'd built everything around after my previous foundation had crumbled, were becoming variables.

Timon Griggs, a recently elected City Councilman, approached Davis and me, engaging in small talk and inquiring about our latest development near Brooklyn.

I was half listening when something across the room briefly caught my eye. I honed in on the movement.

Time seemed to slow down, voices muted, as I tried to process what I was seeing, or rather—who I was seeing.

Sophia.

Not in Misty Springs.

Here, in New York.

Shining like a damn goddess in a shimmering gold gown.

My mouth went dry, and I casually brought my whiskey glass to my lips, attempting to feign indifference while racking my brain with explanations of why she was here.

She turned her back to me, the cut of her dress exposing sleek muscle and smooth skin.

My eyes followed the fabric of her gown spilling to the floor, slowly drinking in every perfect detail of her. My scanning stopped the second a hand settled on the exposed skin, dangerously close to her ass.

I choked on my drink, eliciting concerned looks from both Davis and dipshit Griggs.

Davis jokingly patted my back.

I shoved his hand away.

"Excuse me," my voice cracked as I dismissed them both.

I prowled toward Sophia, eyes locked on the man whose hand was about to be forcibly removed from her.

He turned his head, and recognition sparked.

Landon Norwood. And sure enough, hovering nearby, were his parents, Alicia and Perry.

The Norwoods were bottom feeders. I hadn't seen them since the Maddingly job—the one we won, despite their smear campaign, forged documents, and leaks to the press.

The crowd made it hard to move fast, but I kept pushing forward, fueled by one thought—get Landon's damn hand off her.

I'd figure out the rest later.

The Norwoods didn't fight fair either. Hell, they didn't even pretend to.

Masters of speculative buying, they crept in like a virus—parcel by parcel—until entire communities were backed into a corner. Property owners bullied. Permits mysteriously delayed.

Then came the big announcement: a highway, a corporate HQ. Their cheap land flipped overnight.

What followed? Shoebox apartments. Vanishing families. Fractured neighborhoods.

They didn't build communities.

They gutted them.

Landon broke off from the group just as I hit the halfway mark, veering toward the bathroom and turning his head to ogle a leggy blonde in a skin-tight cocktail dress.

I felt the tension in my chest ease slightly now that he wasn't touching Sophia, but my mission hadn't changed—I needed to talk to her, to get some answers to why she was here… with them.

On the plane, I remembered a text popping up on Sophia's phone—an "L" name. Landon? And there was "Norwood Realty" on her résumé. Was she some kind of plant? A spy?

I shoved the thought aside. Every assumption I'd made about Sophia so far had turned out wrong, but still, I wanted some damn answers.

I stopped behind a large pillar—close enough to overhear, but out of sight as Alicia's voice carried over the crowd, grating and impossible to miss.

I could play spy, too.

"All I'm saying is it's been long enough, don't you think? You got what you wanted. Landon is sorry. He's doting all over you like you want him to. Stop stringing him along already."

Ugh. That voice could pierce steel.

"Mrs. Norwood." Sophia's tone was tight and angry. "All due respect, I'm not stringing your son along. He said *you* wanted me to come here—that's why I came. I don't want anything from him or you. We're here as friends." Her voice caught on that last word.

"Oh, nonsense. You accepted the ring back, did you not?" Alicia asked, smug and ignorant.

Ring? What the hell? Sophia was engaged? To Landon fucking Norwood?

"I didn't take it back. I don't wan—"

"And you're here tonight," Alicia interrupted, "on the airfare we paid for, in the dress we bought, eating the food from the ticket we gave you."

"The only reason I'm here is because Landon told me he'd leave me alone after this," Sophia rapped back, her voice cracking.

"Oh darling, you're not fooling anyone. Like some bartending hotel maid could do better than my son. You have nothing without him. You'd do well to remember that."

"Excuse me," Sophia murmured, and I caught the moment she turned to walk away.

My eyes followed her as she slipped through the crowd—a golden swan in a sea of vultures. Just before she disappeared into the bathroom, I saw her swipe a tear from her cheek.

I remained locked in place as Alicia turned to her sniveling husband.

"Our assistant booked the suite for them." Her voice sliced through my eardrums like nails on a chalkboard. "She and Landon can work everything out tonight. If he's going to be stuck in that damn town, he might as well have the woman he wants to keep him occupied."

Something snapped inside me.

Everything began to fall into place. Of course, the Norwoods had manipulated Sophia—just like everyone else.

They were sinking their teeth into Misty Springs, slowly sucking the town dry, along with the people in it.

No fucking way.

I wasn't about to let that family ruin another town. Not one that meant so much to Gram. And not one that meant so much to Sophia.

I was going to dig up whatever intel they were chasing and beat them to it.

But first—I had to get Sophia away from them.

Chapter 27

Couture 'For the Kids'

Corbin

I waded through the crowd, following Sophia's path toward the enclave near the restrooms. I was nearly there when Cindy stopped me dead in my tracks. I glanced around for Sullivan—nowhere in sight.

She wore a bright red gown, fitting for the she-devil herself. The neckline plunged low between her breasts, the "girls" perched high like a Venus flytrap with oversized fake tits. Her jet-black hair was piled high on her head, a few long, spiraling strands framing her heavily painted face.

I tried to sidestep her, but she slapped a hand to my chest, physically halting me. Her blood-red nails were long and sharp like claws—sharp enough to shred the tux off my body. And by the look in her eyes, she wanted to.

"Why have you been ignoring me, handsome?" she purred.

"Not ignoring, just busy," I said aggressively.

I didn't have time for her shit right now. I stepped around her—anxious to get to Sophia before she rejoined the Norwood cult.

"Fine. I guess you don't want to hear the rumor about your grandfather, then." Her words reeled me back in—just as I broke free of her succubus spell.

I grabbed her arm and turned her around, her eyes lighting up like this was some sort of twisted foreplay.

"Talk. Now," I demanded, briefly turning toward the restroom again to see if I could spot Sophia.

There was no sign of her yet, but I glanced over Cindy's shoulder to see that Landon had made his way back to his parents.

The three of them having what appeared to be a heated conversation.

"And what do I get out of it?" Cindy asked, pulling my focus back toward her as she drew little lines with her pointer finger across my chest and licked her crimson lips.

"Depends on how good it is. Now spill."

She pouted but started talking. "Rumor has it, your legacy is about to be sold to the highest bidder. Buzz is priming the company to be bought. Bye, bye CEO Corbin."

"You're lying. I would know about that."

Wouldn't I?

Is that why Buzz shipped me off to Misty Springs? To keep me distant, out of the loop?

She shrugged. "Guess you'll just have to wait and see. Now... what's my reward for being a good girl? Should I stop by tonight?"

She opened her hand and laid her palm on my chest, then slowly dropped it down my abs.

I grabbed her wrist, making her eyes spark with desire.

Until I turned her hand over and dropped a fifty-dollar bill in it.

She snarled her lip and looked up at me.

It wasn't money she was after. Information was what she craved, and she had her own way of siphoning it from men. Information was power, and the amount of *siphoning* she'd done, she had more power than half of the people in here.

"What the fuck, Corbin?" She crumpled the bill in her hand but made no move to give it back to me.

I turned and left her to stew while I scanned the crowd once more, searching for Sophia. But I was too late to grab her. She was already back with the family of leeches.

Shit.

As I drew nearer to the Norwood cult again, Alicia was making introductions to a couple I didn't recognize. As she gestured toward Sophia, I approached.

"And this is Sophia, our soon-to-be executive assistant to our company."

Seeing Alicia straight on was almost frightening. She looked like someone had stretched a flesh-colored balloon over a skeleton, slapped some paint on it, and then put it in a puffy fur gown.

Sophia didn't say a word in response, instead taking a huge drink from her champagne glass.

This was my opportunity to strike.

I stepped in between Landon and Sophia, forcing him to step away from her. His glare flickered in my peripheral vision as he tried to figure out who I was.

"You wouldn't be trying to poach my new employee now, would you, Alicia?" I asked with the charm of a cobra, coiled and primed.

Sophia spit her drink back in her glass and started coughing.

"Corbin Buescher. What a pleasure to see you again," Alicia responded, her tone full of apprehension and whatever I assume a horde of wasps would sound like.

Landon scowled at me, fucker had to look up to do so. Perry just looked bored.

The strangers I didn't recognize earlier seemed to take advantage of my interruption to retreat away from the Norwood family, perhaps smelling the approaching storm I planned to conjure.

I reached out to shake Perry's hand firmly but quickly, Alicia's was ice cold and lingered a little longer than awkward, and I took the opportunity to crush Landon's hand in mine, just a little.

"You'll have to excuse me, Corbin, dear." The word *dear* coming out like an insult. "I don't think I heard you right. Did you say Sophia works for you now?"

"Yes. Sophia just accepted a job with us… *today,* actually." I flashed a smile at Sophia.

Sophia was still for a moment, looking at me with disbelief, her eyes unblinking as she searched mine for answers.

My smile turned more devious, and she caught on—her ocean-blue eyes sparking with mischief—she was quick, I had to give her that.

"That's right," Sophia said, as she cleared the champagne from her throat. "Sorry, I hadn't had a chance to mention it before. It's all so new." Her face lit up with a huge, genuine smile.

I beamed, thrilled with myself for being the one to make her light up that way. The sight of her nearly stole my breath.

"Yes. That information would have been pertinent." Alicia sneered at me through gritted teeth. "But you should know, we also have an offer on the table for her. One she should thoughtfully consider."

"I have considered it, Mrs. Norwood, and my answer is no. Not now, not ever. Thank you, but no." Sophia's head shook back and forth with every rejection.

"Actually," I placed my hand on Sophia's elbow, the small contact igniting the flickering flame inside me, "if you all will excuse us, I need to take Sophia around to meet some people. Got to represent Buescher Enterprises. You know how these things go."

Perry finally reacted, glaring daggers at me. Having a pretty young thing to parade around with you is like chumming the waters. I just stole his family's shiny gold lure.

Sophia gently grabbed my arm, and I felt a jolt rock through my system. The way she looked at me—in that dress—dragged every sinful desire I had right to the surface.

"Thank you," she whispered as soon as we got far enough away from the Norwoods' prying ears.

She pulled away from me, now that we were a safe distance away, but I dragged her right back to my side.

"Don't thank me, thank Andi. She was very convincing that you were the one."

I stopped walking as I finished my sentence, looking into her eyes, hoping that I would feel something shift. That something in my brain would switch on that she was untouchable, throw up some guardrail to protect me from veering off this cliff.

She looked like she was about to add something more, just as music erupted and dancing started around us.

It appeared the waltzing portion of the evening was underway. I hated dance lessons as a kid, and the fact that these events have any dancing at all is absurd. More antiquated practices brought on by crusty old event planners.

"I can't dance." Sophia's eyebrows lifted as she started to turn away.

I grabbed hold of her, gently stopping her retreat.

For the first time I could ever remember, I *wanted* to dance. I wanted to hold someone close to me. To show Landon, Alicia, and everyone else in this damn room who Sophia belonged with. Strictly, professionally speaking, of course. And since it is technically a company function, and such a charitable cause, I could do it all without breaking company fraternization rules.

"Think of the children we're helping by dancing." I pulled her hand to my back.

My fingers trailed down her arm to hold her delicate hand.

She laughed, and the sound nuzzled in my chest. I wanted to hear it again, and I wanted to be the one who made her do it.

She scraped her bottom lip under her teeth as she considered my offer. "If it's for the children…"

"It is. We wear thirty-thousand-dollar couture and eat pounds of caviar—all to save lives." We smiled together at the absurdity of the evening's extravagance.

My other hand rested on the smooth skin of her back, imagining that each swipe of my hand removed any trace Landon's touch may have left behind.

"I'll lead, you follow," I whispered in her ear.

Her pink lips parted, and her breath came out in a sharp huff.

Pulling her close, I breathed her in, finally getting more than just the faint trace she'd left in my coat. The real thing—fresh and close—caused settled something in me I didn't realize had been restless.

Sophia was intoxicating and beautiful, and for the next few minutes at least—she was all mine.

Chapter 28

BARTENDER BABYSITTER

Sophia

I was dancing with Corbin Buescher.

He was holding me in his arms, his hand sending delightful shivers down my body at each soft stroke. With every breath in my hair, every flex of his arm that pulled me into him inch by inch, he eroded the imaginary wall he built after kissing me on my stoop.

"So, Landon Norwood?" Corbin's warm breath hit my ear, and my spine stiffened at the mention of Landon's name.

"It's a long story…"

"Well, I have time," he murmured, pulling me closer. "And you don't have an escape route."

I grinned, feeling more charmed than trapped by his ensnarement—an all too willing participant in this game of cat and mouse.

"What can I say? We dated for a year—shortly after he and his parents moved to Misty Springs. I was… not in a good place when we met." It didn't feel like the time or the place to bring up my parents' death, my spiral depression, my dropping out of school, and my decision to cut my own bangs. "A few months ago, I walked in on him cheating on me with my boss."

"You caught him, like walked *in* on?"

"Like walked in on. I chucked the ring at his head and stormed out."

Corbin twirled me away from his body before pulling me back in, and I surprised myself by not tripping over my own two feet in the strappy heels I wore.

My smile beamed at him as we settled back into position, my heart dancing along with the sway of our bodies.

"I think I always knew we weren't meant to be. But once he cheated, a lens opened to who he truly was. Every memory, every interaction, was darkened by a screen of black, like looking through cheap sunglasses. I realized I was never happy with Landon, not truly."

Our bodies swayed in unison for a couple more shaky heartbeats.

"I can't believe I'm airing all my dirty laundry to my new boss."

"Technically, I'm your boss's... boss's... boss's... boss," he corrected. "And the good news about me is, I will never sleep with Landon."

I threw my head back and laughed. I felt Corbin's deep chuckle beneath my hand as it rested on his chest between our bodies.

"Despite the initial shock, I can now look back and be glad it ended before we made vows of forever."

"I'm glad you ended it, too." His hand dropped lower on my back, skittering along the edge of my dress.

We spun in silence for a few seconds, our bodies slowly pressing in tighter with each shuffle of our feet.

Every time I glanced his way, he was already looking at me—his gaze a mix of longing and restraint—sending a shiver of excitement down my spine.

The push and pull between us was both maddening and titillating. Corbin had drawn some invisible line somewhere between us, one that I wasn't sure where it started or ended, but I was desperate to poke and prod until I found the edges of that line.

I pulled him closer.

He pulled me even tighter.

I smiled—soft, uncertain.

He smiled back like it hurt a little.

The space between us diminished, yet the line we couldn't cross still separated us.

I dared to keep testing, and my hips pushed forward, pressing me into him deeper, and I felt him harden under the gentle sway of my body.

His breath came out short and hot in my hair. His hand flexed against my bare skin before dropping lower, cupping my ass through the silky material of my dress and pushing me harder against him.

I turned my head, my heels placed me at the perfect height to press my lips gently against the soft scruff of his neck, just below his ear.

"Sophia," he whispered like a warning into my hair.

His hips slowly thrust forward, rubbing his hard length against my core.

The friction set my veins on fire, a living flame in a sea of pretentious bodies, all too self-absorbed to notice me burning alive in the darkened corner of the dance floor.

More. I needed more.

Instead of giving me what I craved, he slowly released my hand.

A twinge of panic set in, worried that I had pushed too far until I realized the room was quieting and the song had wound down.

My body protested at the loss of his touch. And just like the night he drove me home, it felt like we didn't have enough time. These fleeting moments coiled me up tight, leaving my pulse pounding and my body dripping with need.

My aversion to dancing was completely eradicated—now that was all I wanted to do—to hold him against me, to push and feel around for the edges of Corbin's boundaries.

But I knew better than to expect it to last. Corbin had more important things to do than spend the entire evening with me, and I couldn't expect otherwise.

This is why, when he tipped my chin up to meet his gaze and asked, "Care for a drink?" I almost had to pinch myself.

"Definitely," I answered.

On our way to the bar, Corbin was stopped constantly, introducing me every time as his new Assistant Editor to their Misty Springs branch. People didn't care to meet me—they only gave me attention because Corbin directed them to.

We had just wrapped up a conversation with another over-posturing couple when a deep voice sounded behind me.

"Who is this lovely lady you've seemed to entrap tonight, Corbin?"

I turned to a man in a navy suit that fit him impeccably well. His tan skin was smooth, his chiseled features framed by a perfectly trimmed beard that made him look like he'd just stepped out of a luxury cologne ad. His coffee-brown hair was cropped short, creating an effortlessly polished look.

"Davis." Corbin's tone shifted to an undercurrent of tension. "This is Sophia."

"Sophia," Davis repeated, his lips curving into an easy grin as he extended a hand.

I slid my hand into his large grip. "A pleasure."

"Sophia is the new Assistant Editor at our Misty Springs branch." Corbin cut through our exchange.

"I wasn't aware that any other Buescher employees were coming to tonight's event," Davis said, his eyes bouncing between us.

Corbin feigned indifference. "She was initially invited through another firm. This was long before we finalized the details of her employment. But what luck, she agreed to join our company instead."

"Luck indeed." Davis's eyes scanned me subtly.

His presence set off an alert in my brain—absurdly handsome, undeniably charming, but something lurked beneath the surface. Perhaps it was nothing, or perhaps after everything I went through with Landon, I had gotten better at detecting monsters.

Corbin came up with some excuse to move on from Davis, but the brief interaction had changed something in the air. The weight that pushed around us, driving us together, thinned—forcing us to move asynchronously.

Corbin no longer extended his arm for me, instead keeping a small but safe distance.

We approached a large oak bar, and Corbin waved at the bartender to come over as we hovered near two barstools.

"What's your name?" Corbin asked as he slid a fifty across the bar to the man.

"Brandon, sir," he replied, picking up the money and leaning casually over the bar top.

"Brandon, you'll get another one of these when I return. Keep an eye on her, don't let anyone near her, and get me a whiskey, neat," Corbin commanded.

"Um, wow, ok, first of all, you are my boss's... boss's... whatever at *work*, not in my personal life. Second of all, where are you going? Third of all, can I have a gin martini, please?" The first two were directed at Corbin, the last at Brandon.

Brandon looked at Corbin as if for permission.

He nodded.

I scoffed.

Corbin put his hands on my arms, the smallest amount of contact driving out my anger and reigniting my desire.

Damn, my traitorous body.

"I need to look for my grandfather—it's important. And I don't want you to get kidnapped by Landon, murdered by Perry, or eaten by Alicia while I'm gone."

I let out a breathy laugh and fell onto the barstool.

"Fine. But only because my feet are killing me in these heels, and all the people-ing I've had to do with you has been exhausting."

"Just give me five minutes, ten tops." Corbin grabbed his drink and spun away, not sparing me a second glance.

The bartender shook the martini shaker that housed my drink as a woman came up with a full glass of wine. "I asked for a chardonnay. How hard is it to pour a proper glass of wine?"

"My mistake, ma'am. I'll get you another right away." He took her glass and poured it out, then quickly plucked the chardonnay bottle from its icy scabbard, showing her the label before pouring a fresh glass.

The woman huffed and turned away, muttering how hard it was to find good help.

"How do you stand these people, Brandon?" I asked him as he placed my drink in front of me.

Brandon grinned as he leaned on the bar, one elbow resting casually on the polished wood. His sandy blonde hair curled slightly at the ends, a little too long to be considered neat, but it suited him. His warm hazel eyes, framed by thick lashes most women would kill for, sparkled with mischief as he gave me an exaggerated shrug.

"They're not so bad." He shrugged, his voice light with amusement. "Keeps me on my toes, you know? One minute, someone's asking for a vodka soda. The next, they want an *essence of artisanal elderflower in a glass misted with unicorn tears.*" He tilted his head, pretending to consider. "You'd be surprised how often I have unicorn tears on hand."

I laughed, unable to help myself. "Sounds exhausting."

"Eh. Pays the bills. Plus, I get to meet interesting people."

Fine, let Corbin wander off all he wants. The people at this gala were vapid, terrifying monsters. But bartenders? They have a natural rapport with other bartenders, and this one just so happened to be just as fun to talk to as he was to look at.

Chapter 29

OPERATION NORWOOD EVICTION

Corbin

The excuse to step away from Sophia was supposed to clear my head and sober me from the lust clouding my judgment.

The second my hand touched the smooth skin of her back, I knew I'd only end up wanting more. I guided us through the crowd to a quiet corner, needing her closer, like she was my life raft in a churning, shark-infested ocean.

I got that much.

But every time I acted against the invisible rules I'd set for myself, I pushed the boundaries further.

Don't stroke her smooth skin.

Don't pull her too close.

Don't press her soft body into mine.

But I did all of it.

The ache to taste her lips again was unbearable. I had pulled us toward a darkened alcove—we were nearly alone. And I almost pressed too far.

The song ended just in time, saving me from losing the last of my resolve.

But when we ran into Davis, and I saw the way he watched her—his eyes calculating, like he was assessing more than just the moment—it reminded me where we were.

People would be watching, scrutinizing.

I forced my mind to be distracted by a new mission: find Buzz. After a couple of laps, I deemed my mission unsuccessful, though I did run into Davis again.

His expression was neutral, but his words sounded acidic. "Oh, didn't I mention it? Buzz told me weeks ago he wasn't planning to show. Guess it must've just... slipped through the cracks."

He threw a glance toward Sophia at the bar before winking at me and wishing me a good evening. The exchange made my skin crawl, a pressure blooming behind my temples like a warning.

Buzz never misses these events, and the fact that he didn't even think to inform me of his planned absence was another strange act to add to the increasingly long list.

I looked at my phone again to make sure I had service. Sure enough, it had full bars and no messages from Buzz.

Glancing back over to the bar, I noticed the bartender, Brandon, was leaning toward Sophia. He said something that made her laugh. She threw her head back and throatily bellowed. It was completely unladylike and crass, making a few women sneer in her direction.

I enjoyed being the one to earn those laughs, and I didn't like seeing someone else doing it.

Come to think of it, the two of them were looking awfully chummy right now.

Each step toward the bar sent a jolt of anger down my spine. Buzz, Davis, the entire Norwood family, Brandon the fucking bartender, every damn guest here—all contributing to the tension that had been building in my shoulders since I walked into this stuffy event.

When I walked up to the bar, Brandon saw me and instantly straightened.

"Welcome back, sir. No one talked to her, no one kidnapped her, no one ate her," he reported.

Sophia giggled at his joke, which was *my* joke first.

"Yeah, you seem to be doing a great job at keeping her company," I said, not even attempting to hide the bite in my voice.

I leveled him with a look, and when he didn't throw a snide comment back—and I caught a bit of worry in his eyes—I slid another fifty across the bar.

"You can go now," I told him.

He left abruptly, not acknowledging Sophia again.

"You could be a little nicer, you know. He and I were just sharing some awful bartending stories," she chuckled and hiccupped.

I leaned my arms against the smooth top of the bar and took a deep breath. Each day, the crumbling pillars of my life were getting harder and harder to shoulder.

"Do you want to talk about it?" Sophia asked, breaking my thoughts.

"Talk about what?"

"Whatever is making your face look like that?" She drained the last of her martini.

"And what does my face look like?"

"Like someone kicked your puppy and then lit your Beanie Baby collection on fire."

I chuckled, my throat felt raw, but Sophia was already brightening my dark mood. "That sounds like a personal story of yours."

"They are very flammable... Beanie Babies, not puppies."

This time, I couldn't help it, I laughed—a throaty, authentic laugh. It snuck up on me—the noise and the sensation were almost foreign after years of practiced restraint.

I didn't share my feelings with anyone—it felt like exposing a weakness, and I couldn't afford to be weak. But something about the way she looked at me—the sincerity in her eyes, the mounting stress that was pressing on my chest like a lead vest—opened something within me.

"It's my grandfather," I sighed as I sank into the barstool next to her, "and a slew of other things I don't have time to dig into."

"Well, I have time." She placed her hands on each side of my barstool, trapping my legs with her arms, unintentionally giving me a great view down her dress. "And you don't have an escape route," she added, eliciting yet another genuine laugh from me.

In our quiet corner of the bustling gala, I shared my concerns about Buzz. It felt good to get it off my chest with someone who—despite only knowing a short time—felt like a vault to store all of my troubles in.

Her hands found my shoulders somewhere in the middle of one of my rants. With practiced fingers, she dug in deep, working loose a knot I swear had been buried for years.

"Is this okay? Not crossing any lines?" she whispered in my ear—and I felt those words travel straight through me.

This woman didn't just chip away at my defenses—she dismantled them, piece by piece.

She listened intently, asking me deeper questions to get beneath the surface answers I would always initially give people.

Usually, I hated these stuffy events—putting on the mask, playing the part. But with her, it felt... easy. Good, even. Like I could finally exhale.

I didn't even know how much time had passed when I noticed a figure standing in my peripheral.

I turned, my face morphing into anger, when I noticed it was Landon. His parents were lingering behind him like tiny, pathetic bodyguards.

"It's time for us to leave." Landon nodded toward Sophia.

Sophia stood up, straightening her dress before looking at me. Her face was calm, but I saw the unease beneath the surface. "Thanks for the opportunity, Mr. Buescher. I look forward to working with you."

They started to walk away together, and bile rose in my throat. Sophia probably didn't realize Alicia was forcing her and Landon to shack up together tonight.

I needed a reason to make her stay. One that wouldn't raise suspicion or cause a scene.

"Actually," my voice boomed as I stood from the bar stool, buttoning my jacket as I strode toward them.

Landon and Sophia turned, her eyes curious, his murderous.

"I need Ms. Carlson to stay here for a while longer. There are a few more people I need to introduce her to."

Sophia's eyes went wide with excitement, and she took an eager step in my direction.

My body thrummed with victory. This was too easy.

Instead of letting her go, Landon grabbed her arm, pulling her back like a spoiled boy on the playground who didn't want to share his toy.

"She's not staying here," Landon said with a scowl.

Sophia's face winced in pain, and I saw red. I closed the gap between us in two hurried steps. My fists clenched at my side.

Perry stepped quickly between Landon and me, whispering forcefully to his son. "This is not the time nor the place. Let her go."

Landon looked at his father and then at Sophia, his face teetering on the edge of rage and loss.

"Let. Me. Go. Landon," Sophia bit out.

Her words were laced with double meaning, and I don't think I was the only one who heard it.

A small crowd of onlookers started to gather around us, undoubtedly storing this in their flour sack heads to be ground up later at the rumor mill.

So much for not causing a scene.

Landon clenched his teeth, but slowly uncurled his fingers from Sophia's bicep. He gave me one last parting sneer and then turned briskly away, following Alicia out. Perry kept his hand on Landon's back the whole way, preventing him from coming back and making a stupid decision.

I *wished* he would make that stupid decision.

My focus shifted to Sophia, the expression on her face dissolving my rage.

"Are you okay?" I stepped toward her, fighting between needing to scoop her up in my arms and wanting to keep a low profile.

She nodded, but the onlookers continued their not-so-covert observations. We needed to leave quickly before anyone else took notice.

"Come with me." I led Sophia toward the coat check, winding through the massive ballroom, carefully keeping my hands off her.

We made it to the small coat check line. I reached into my pocket and fished my ticket out, anxious to get the hell out of here.

"We're not staying?" Sophia asked.

"No, we're done here," I answered my voice low and abrupt.

"Well… how does one get a new plane ticket to Misty Springs when theirs just walked out the door?" Sophia asked, as we waited.

Her question reignited the simmering anger I'd been trying to bury. The Norwood family and their manipulations were poison— and she'd fallen right into their trap.

I clenched my jaw, forcing my voice to stay level. "You never had a ticket home tonight."

"What? What do you mean? Of course, I did. We were supposed to take the red-eye back to Misty Springs," she insisted, confusion clouding her expression.

I didn't bother softening the blow. She needed to know the truth, and we didn't have time to sit here and dissect the many levels of fucked-up-ness the Norwood family encompassed.

"There is no red-eye to Misty Springs. There never was. Alicia set this up. She wanted you stranded, so you'd end up staying with Landon tonight. It's a power play—to humiliate you into crawling back to her pathetic son." The absurdity of it all only fueled my rage.

I handed the claim slip to a coat-check kid dressed in suspenders and a bow tie.

"What?" Her wide eyes reflected disbelief and innocence that made my chest tighten. "I knew they could be cruel, but that's… that's diabolical. Who does that?"

She had no idea how twisted people like the Norwood family could be.

"Your ex-future in-laws, that's who."

Her voice wavered. "How can I get home if there is no flight? What am I going to do?"

"You can stay with me tonight. We'll figure out the rest tomorrow." The words slipped out before I could reel them back in.

The thought of Sophia in my apartment stirred something primal. The flash of her dress pooled in the corner on the floor— the idea of her, barefoot and padding across my floor, curled up on my couch.

Too intimate. I blinked the thought away.

Her eyes found mine, wide and uncertain, while her fingers twisted at her side.

The crowd started to thin, and my gaze locked on Cindy, prowling behind a group of guests sipping a cocktail like a Bond villain. Sophia and I needed to slip out of here now, before we drew more attention to ourselves.

"I've got a spare bedroom—plenty of space. You're not getting a hotel tonight, not in this city." I held her gaze. "So it's either come with me, call up Alicia and let her know you're ready to be pimped out to her son, or find yourself a nice park bench."

I shrugged on my coat and walked toward the exit, my pulse hammering.

No time to debate. No room for hesitation.

Negotiation tactics didn't only work in the boardroom—sometimes, survival demanded clarity, as harsh as that may be.

She didn't deserve my impatience. But I was tapped out for the evening.

I only hoped I still had enough of a defensive line to avoid doing something stupid once I got her alone in my apartment.

Chapter 30

LONELY GIRL, SEEKING DRESS REMOVAL SERVICES

Sophia

The thought of spending the night with Corbin triggered a flurry of activity in my body.

Flurries that started with my head. A jolt to my insides, a rush of excitement at seeing more of Corbin's world, of peeling back another layer. The coil spooling inside my body somehow twisted tighter.

Sometime during my internal discourse, Corbin pulled a power move and stormed off, leaving me no opportunity to think things through and forcing me to decide quickly.

I glanced at the coat-check teenager. He was too bored to eavesdrop, scrolling through his phone.

I didn't want to deal with toting around my clutch all night, and it's not like dresses like this have pockets, so I had to rely on Newton's Third Law here and allow the force of my boobs to push tight against the fabric of my dress to keep hold of my coat check ticket.

I fished around for it, which—embarrassingly—now caught the young man's attention.

He grinned and wiggled his eyebrows as I finally found the ticket and handed it over. He disappeared behind the rows of expensive shawls and coats, quickly returning with my clutch—I didn't have a nice enough coat to wear to something like this.

I turned away from the still-grinning coat-check boy to stare at Corbin's retreating back.

This was it—decision time.

I either went with Corbin or was stuck with Landon tonight—though honestly, the park bench was more appealing than the latter choice.

What was I even pretending to debate here?

I caught up to Corbin at the exit just as he pushed open the golden-trimmed doors. A blast of cold air bit at my skin, but Corbin quickly opened the rear door to an idling, sleek black car. The inside was warm as I slid in, my dress gliding across the buttery leather.

Corbin slipped in next to me, his citrus and pine scent overtaking the new car smell, forcing my libido to start doing backflips.

We rode in silence, the air of the quiet car thick with tension.

I spent much of the ride playing through the near-miss scenario I had just avoided. Landon and his family were worse than I realized, and I feared this evening might start a domino effect—one that I was too small and weak to stop from crushing me and my friends as the pieces toppled down on us.

To calm my racing thoughts, I turned my focus to the world outside the car windows. The city buzzed past us—street performers, late-night crowds, and storefronts were bursting with life.

I don't know how much time had passed when the car stopped before a tall brownstone with black-trimmed windows and a tidy iron fence. Sparse trees clung to dying leaves near a pair of benches.

Corbin exited without a word.

"Thank you," I said to the driver, who smiled and nodded in the review mirror.

I reached for my door handle, but Corbin beat me to it, pulling the door away from me.

He helped me out of the car, dropping my hand as we entered a lobby that radiated quiet wealth—black marble floors, low-hanging lights, and a dramatic orchid arrangement perfuming the air.

Behind the reception desk, a sharply dressed concierge glanced up and gave me a polite, short nod—the kind that said, "You're only welcome here because of him."

Corbin led us to a private elevator with one button: *PENTHOUSE.*

He scanned his key, and we soared upward. In no time, the elevator doors opened directly into his apartment.

I stepped in and paused, heels sinking into the plush rug.

Warm oak floors stretched into an open space lined with glass walls showcasing the Manhattan skyline. Everything gleamed—leather furniture, a marble fireplace, platinum accents. To the left, a pristine kitchen glinted under soft light. A staircase spiraled upward, its glass and steel railing catching the glow of a chandelier so luminous. The whole apartment felt like stepping into a dream.

After taking it all in, I turned to Corbin—his eyes watching me closely. Guarded but vulnerable, lustful but reserved.

He unbuttoned his jacket, pulled at his tie, and unfastened the top button of his shirt—revealing the beginning of a carved ridge of muscle that hinted at a body built for more than business.

Down girl.

"I'll show you where you'll be staying," Corbin rasped as he stepped toward the stairs.

Stairs I knew I'd break my neck on if I tried to climb them in these shoes.

"One sec." I held a finger to him as I stepped toward one of the leather accent chairs in his living area.

I plopped down and reached for the clasp of my heels, finagling with the buckle until my feet were refreshingly horizontal. The plush area rug felt unearthly soft against my aching arches. And I was suddenly curious what kind of access money gave you to the softest textiles known to man.

"Okay, ready," I said, heels hanging in my hand.

Corbin stood still as a statue with his hands tucked casually into his pockets. His gaze flicked to my bare feet for a moment, then back to my face. He wasn't quite smiling, but there was a softness there like he was amused or... something else entirely.

He motioned with his head for me to follow, and I let him lead me to the second floor. He opened the dark, charcoal-gray door at the top of the stairs, and my jaw nearly dropped at the room I found myself in.

This was his spare bedroom?

The room was larger than my entire apartment. The king-size bed was adorned with a light gray bedspread. A minimalist art piece was hanging above the headboard, and a smooth side table with a chrome lamp stood next to it.

My hand pressed into the plush mattress, a mattress I tried not to imagine myself sinking into with my body pinned beneath Corbin's. Tried not to picture me fisting a handful of the comforter as he sent me over the edge. I swallowed deeply, and my cheeks blushed as I caught his gaze.

My friends always said I was an open book. My face told an entire story on its own. And if the way Corbin's gaze was darkening was any indication, he could read every salacious word I was crafting.

"I'll get you something more comfortable to sleep in," he said, clearing his throat before quickly leaving the room.

I slapped my palm on my forehead and took a deep breath. I needed to find a way to block Corbin's effect on me. If only there were some sort of appetite suppressant for sexual desire. Now, *that* would be a great product.

I stared at myself in the bathroom mirror, giving my reflection a silent pep talk as I pulled bobby pins from my hair one by one. The tension eased from my head, and I gently rubbed my aching scalp with my fingertips. It felt so good that I closed my eyes, exhaling a soft moan.

When I opened them again, I clutched my chest, catching Corbin's reflection behind me. "Geez! Give a girl some warning!" I yelped.

"Sorry," he murmured, placing a pair of boxers and a white t-shirt on the marble countertop. The corner of his mouth turned upward as he added, "Maybe you blew out your eardrums with your deafening music."

I rolled my eyes. But I couldn't help the small smile that pulled at my lips. Just knowing he was paying attention to me—noticed a habit of mine—made me feel warm inside.

Our eyes met in the mirror, and the look we exchanged was heavy. The room pressed in all around us, catching my breath in my lungs. His body was inches from mine, not quite touching, but I could feel the heat rolling off of him.

If this were a Monica McKenzie novel, this would be the moment we lost control, tore each other's clothes off, and finally gave in.

"I'll leave you to it," he said as he stepped away, gently closing the door as he exited.

I sighed and turned on the water, the hiss of the shower masking my disappointment.

This wasn't some fictional romance novel. This was real life— and in real life, there are lines and rules and exes and reasons why we can't be… *more*.

Steam filled the room, and I sniffed at tiny spare shampoo bottles that were sitting on a shelf. It smelled heavenly. Everything was luxurious, the bathroom was all sleek marble and platinum fixtures—far beyond any elegance I was used to.

Though I loved the golden gown, I hated that it was bought with the Norwood's money. The design was both elegant and sexy, making me feel—if only for a moment—that I belonged in the same spaces that someone like Corbin did.

Slim straps crossed at the middle of my back, fastening with a delicate, intricate clasp. A clasp so annoyingly tricky that I'd been forced to ask Landon to help secure it earlier, the memory of his clammy hands on me making me gag.

I tried—and failed—several times to release the clasp. Whoever designed this dress clearly assumed the wearer wouldn't be single.

Well, they sure didn't anticipate Sophia Carlson, did they?

My arms ached from stretching at impossible angles, and I let out a strangled growl in my frustration.

This was it—death by dress.

Maybe this wasn't such a bad way to go. Surrounded by the warm steam of the shower in an opulent room, with a gorgeous dress on.

Somewhere around the eighth attempt, I came up with a name for my sexual appetite suppressant.

I'd call it *libido-away.*

Chapter 31

THUMPER

Corbin

I poured myself a drink from the wet bar downstairs, too pent up to sleep. I convinced myself I could handle this.

Twenty-two stairs separated me from Sophia. I stared at the spiraling steps that would serve as an emblematic barricade for tonight.

I took a small sip, letting the whiskey burn as I thought about this evening. The way she made me feel, her laugh, her quiet understanding as I shared pieces of my life with her.

Another sip. And I thought about how she looked in that dress and how her body felt underneath it as I held her on the dance floor. She was a golden goddess who could drive a saint to sin.

I drained the glass. My sole focus on one thought, one image: Sophia—upstairs, her shimmering dress on the floor, her body wet and slick from the shower.

Fuck.

I uncorked the decanter and poured more into my glass.

A loud *thump* came from above my head.

What was she doing up there?

Not that I was going to go find out—twenty-two stairs—I needed that separation.

My mind went blank earlier when she unclasped the delicate strap from her ankle, removing her heels. The slit in her dress revealed her smooth thigh, her hands gliding down her leg as she found the buckle—the angle of her dress falling low enough I could see straight down it.

And when she slipped the pointed heel off her arched foot, her eyes rolled back in something that looked like pure ecstasy.

I drained another glass.

My fingers pulled at my hair. I felt like a madman. Shrugging off my suit coat, I tossed it on the couch, desperately trying to find an escape from my torment of want.

Another *thump* sounded from above, followed by a muted curse.

I yanked my tie over my head and tossed it by the discarded coat.

Another *thump* and my legs were on autopilot.

I ascended the stairs quickly—a new record for me, I believe.

Quietly, I opened the door to the bedroom and stood outside the bathroom. With my ear pressed to the door, I listened to see if I could detect what Sophia was doing up here.

I felt like a deranged stalker.

What was this woman doing to me?

Chapter 32

Almost Exactly How I Pictured It

Sophia

After trying to break the clasp or rip the seams of the straps, I came to the mortifying realization I was going to need Corbin to help me.

A light rap sounded at the door before I could work up the courage to seek him out. "Are you okay in there?" Corbin's muffled voice asked.

Oh. My. God.

I probably sounded like a confused baby elephant up here.

I was mortified.

I promise I'm a good hire. I really am smart. I just can't figure out basic human life skills like getting undressed.

I opened the door, which caused him to practically fall into the bathroom. He quickly straightened himself, fixing his sleeves nervously.

"I can't get the clasp undone," I admitted. "Could you help me?" I turned so he could see the trap I was in.

It was embarrassing enough to deal with your certifiably crazy ex and his insane family in front of your new boss's boss, whatever. I might as well end on the high note of needing his help disrobing me in his spare bathroom.

"Oh." His voice squeaked slightly.

I moved my hair to the side, my body tense, and I swallowed hard as I felt his fingers on my skin, feather-light and gentle.

His touch bloomed from my spine right to my core—the slightest contact from him nearly euphoric, lighting up my body in a way that made me force back a moan.

I felt the pull of the straps as he twisted the clasp. They loosened over my shoulders as he unfastened it in one swift movement.

I released a shaky breath of relief, or maybe nervous energy. I couldn't be sure.

The dress began to fall, and I quickly placed my hands on my chest to hold it.

If I let go, it wouldn't necessarily fall down, but the top would be loose enough that he'd definitely get a healthy dose of side boob—and forget about wearing a bra with this dress—or underwear, for that matter.

His task was complete, but he didn't move.

My back tingled at his proximity, my skin aching for more of his touch.

Silence stretched between us, the only noise coming from the hot water that continued to cascade from the shower head, enveloping us in a cloudy mist of steam. The mirror had fogged over, every surface slick with soft water droplets from the damp air.

"Thank you," I whispered with a soft glance over my shoulder.

I met his stare.

His whiskey eyes were smoldering, and unlike before, the reservation was gone, replaced only by a fervent hunger. He took a deep, shuddering breath, his exhaled "you're welcome" warming my neck, sending a wave of shivers down my body.

My voice was silent, but my mind was reeling—a chaotic storm of desire.

All thoughts evaporated the moment his fingers gently traced up my exposed spine, leaving goosebumps in their wake.

His touch lit me up everywhere—my nerves firing off all over my body, celebrating, screaming: *finally.*

He stepped closer, his firm body pressing against my back, lips brushing the nape of my neck.

"You don't know how hard it's been for me to keep my hands off you tonight." His words tingled against my skin. They hummed beneath the surface, tingling every nerve ending.

My pulse throbbed—swelling in my chest, my head, in between my legs.

Once his fingertips reached the top of my back, he edged them along my shoulder until they met the strap of my dress. His other hand grazed the opposite strap, slowly pushing them simultaneously off my shoulders. He slid them fully down my arms, baring my chest—the rest of my dress clinging low on my hips.

My body was eager to feel his next touch, ready to accept anything he'd give me as he tiptoed across the line he placed between us. After spending so many nights wrapping myself up in blissful thoughts of him, I wanted it hot and fast—and *now*.

But Corbin had other plans.

His moves were slow and methodical. Calculated and precise.

"You're stunning, Sophia." He stepped around me, slowly circling me like a predator stalking his prey.

Except this prey was pent-up and ready to pounce back.

My fingers twitched at the desire to touch him, to fulfill every fantasy I'd been dredging up in my head since first laying eyes on him. But I was too intrigued, eager to watch him work, to stand still and allow Corbin Buescher to show me exactly what he wanted.

He reached out with his thumb to trace my bottom lip as his fingers gently nudged beneath my chin, forcing my eyes away from the defined lines of his chest peeking out from his open shirt, to meet his gaze.

His eyes turned molten when my tongue darted out to trace the pad of his thumb. Whatever self-control he was still clinging to unraveled.

He pressed in closer, and his hand grazed my cheek before his fingers dug into my hair, pulling my head back before crushing his lips to mine.

This wasn't like the kiss outside of my apartment. One that felt like regret and apprehension. This kiss felt like a promise—a promise I was desperate for him to keep.

He tasted like whiskey and mint and fulfilled fantasies. His trademark smell of cedar and citrus filled every breath of my lungs. My hands ran along the smooth fabric of his designer shirt, feeling his solid body beneath.

He groaned as my hand danced along his abs, and the sound sparked a blazing color to burst behind my closed eyes.

Corbin effectively infiltrated every one of my senses—his smell, the feel of his muscles, the taste of his mouth, the sound of his heavy breathing, the blazing color behind my eyelids.

I couldn't take the space between us any longer. I pushed my body into his. The smooth texture of his shirt felt luxurious against my bare chest.

I shifted my hips forward and felt the hard outline of him rub against me, the bottom half of my dress preventing me from getting the friction I desperately wanted.

I whimpered into his mouth, relishing how that made him lose more of his careful control.

He turned us around and pressed me against the wall, lifting my leg, the motion ripping the slit of my dress.

Good riddance.

Corbin pushed himself into me—the friction hitting me exactly where my body was craving.

I couldn't stop the moan that escaped me. I released it into his mouth, and he echoed one of his own into mine.

There was no ex, no corporate policies. There were no reasons why this was a bad idea. There was only this moment.

Only *us.*

Consequences be damned.

His hand ran up my thigh, reaching my hip, and when he felt that I didn't have underwear on, he pulled his lips away from mine, his lips twisting into a wicked grin.

"It's a good thing I didn't know you weren't wearing anything underneath this dress while we were on that dance floor. I don't think I would have been able to stop myself." He ground his hips into me again, causing my head to lean back in ecstasy. "We would have really given those stuffy pinheads something to talk about," he drawled as his fingers trailed to the inside of my thigh.

His touch inched higher, testing, teasing, as his eyes watched mine intently. He brushed his fingers against me, exhaling sharply as he whispered into my ear, "You're so wet for me, Sophia."

His finger danced along my most sensitive area, applying just enough pressure to drive my hips forward, begging for more.

When his expert fingers plunged into me, I let out a ragged breath.

This. Him.

I needed his touch like I needed the air in my lungs.

He trailed kisses from my chin down my neck and along my collarbone as he continued to pulse in and out of me in a heady rhythm.

His mouth found my nipple, and he sucked as my fingers threaded through his thick hair.

He used his thumb to swirl around my clit. Each move, each drive into me, coiled my body tighter and tighter.

I rocked into his hand, my body greedily taking what it wanted from him.

His kisses trailed back up my chest, sucking along the way, until he nipped his teeth along my collarbone.

I cried out in a wild release, riding his hand as I came undone. The months of pent-up tension released a tremor that rocked through my entire body. If Corbin hadn't been holding me up, I would have slid down the wall in a messy, satisfied heap on the floor.

Corbin pressed his head against mine, our breaths mingling in the humid air.

"Should we go in the bedroom?" I asked in a breathy whisper.

Then, like a sign, a punishment, or a bad omen, a low buzzing sounded from his pocket.

He pulled back, his eyes not leaving mine as he reached into his bulging pants. He quickly glanced at the number on the screen, and I watched as the blazing inferno in his eyes extinguished.

Anger welled up inside me that a call could distract him so quickly. But then I remembered who he was—an important man, with an important role, at an important company.

His face said it all—a flash of concern, followed by an apologetic "one-second" finger in the air before he turned to answer the call.

He stepped out of the bathroom as I strained to pry on his conversation. It was difficult to make out exactly what he was saying with the shower still running in the background.

"What's wrong?" I heard him ask, irritation flickering beneath the layer of concern in his voice.

"… Buzz?"

"Why didn't… call me earlier?"

Then he heaved a heavy sigh and gave a tortured glance over his shoulder at me, and I heard his next words loud and clear.

166

"I'll be there in fifteen."

He was leaving?

The realization sobered up my post-orgasm buzz, and the immediate sting of rejection settled on my skin.

He looked at me, his breath still slightly ragged. "I have to go."

I nodded, my focus dropping to the dark gray grout lining the marble slabs of the floor. I watched him out of the corner of my eye as he fastened the top buttons of his shirt.

"I don't want to. God, I can't even begin to tell you how much I don't want to." He strode over to me and gently lifted my chin, allowing me to read the regret in his eyes. "I wouldn't leave if I didn't have to. It's... important."

I nodded again, this time keeping eye contact, hopeful the mask I wore was that of an understanding, cool girl—instead of a wreck of emotional turmoil.

"I'll fill you in as soon as I'm back. Please, don't leave. Promise me you'll stay. That you'll be here when I get back." His voice was pleading, and it was impossible not to see the sincerity in his face.

"I'll be here."

Like I had a choice.

He took a relieved-sounding breath as his hand raked through his dark hair.

"Good," he huffed, quickly turning away and striding out of the room.

The absence of his incredibly tempting face and body cleared my head. This was a mistake. We both knew this couldn't happen— though neither of us had discussed the no-relationship policy openly.

Perhaps whatever force just interrupted us was right, and the feelings I'd been developing for Corbin were wrong.

The cell phone ring acted like a Pavlovian de-lusting response. Perhaps libido-away could be a sound trigger, like a hypnosis technique.

Regardless, as I watched him leave, the door closing on one of my most epic fantasies playing out—one thing was for certain—my life just got a lot more complicated.

Chapter 33

INTERVENTION FROM THE CORPORATE GODS

Corbin

She was off limits. A fleeting moment of weakness. Discipline was a cornerstone I built myself on, and Sophia had rattled my foundation to its core with one glance over her shoulder.

That was a mistake, one that could cost me everything.

At least it didn't go any further.

I wanted it to go further.

So. Much. Further.

I sealed my fate with Sophia when I offered her the job in front of Landon's family. Davis met her—lots of people met her—her employment was out in the open.

Unclasping her dress and watching it nearly fall off her sent me into a frenzy, one that eliminated all sense of reason and left me operating purely on instinct and want.

Then, like a cruel intervention from the corporate gods—or maybe God himself, because I didn't deserve a happy ending—my phone rang, shattering the moment just as the last of my resolve slipped.

It was Louise. She'd called 911. Gram had fallen. She was heading to the hospital. The entire conversation ended any possibility of Sophia and me finishing what we started in an instant.

And, of course, Buzz was nowhere to be found.

What was he up to?

Eddie arrived immediately outside my building, and I slid into the back of the town car, speeding toward Mount Sinai Hospital. The late-night hour got us there relatively quickly, and I hurried inside, the cold air cutting through my thin white shirt. I didn't even grab a coat in my rush out the door.

I was juggling too many flaming bowling pins—the new branch in Misty Springs, my future position as CEO, the fate of the company itself, the fate of Misty Springs at the hands of the Norwood family, Buzz, Gram, Sophia—I feared that one wrong move would send everything careening to the ground, setting my life up in flames.

The nurse, dressed in a soft pink uniform, greeted me as I crossed the threshold into Gram's room with a reassuring smile.

"She's stable," the nurse said. "Nothing broken, just some minor swelling and bruising. She'll be okay."

Relief washed over me, though it barely loosened the knot in my chest. Gram was dressed in a mint-colored gown that looked impossibly soft, her small frame nearly swallowed by the hospital bed. An IV was taped to her thin arm, and the steady rhythm of beeping machines filled the room.

The sound sent me back to a different time, frozen in the sterile doorway of a different hospital, staring at the frail figure of my father. Machines surrounded him, too, but there was no softness there—just the stark reality of a man brought to the edge by his own choices.

The doctors called it a heart attack, the inevitable conclusion of cirrhosis eating him alive from the inside out. Stress, overwork, and a bottle that never left his hand—they were his business partners, his family, his crutches, his escape. He spiraled, taking everything with him, leaving me with only a bruised and tarnished reputation.

I blinked, forcing myself back to the present. Gram's chest rose and fell steadily, her face serene even under the pale hospital light.

I tried to call Buzz half a dozen times, but my calls went straight to voicemail each time. Avoiding me was one thing. This was the last straw—the least he could do was be here for his wife.

"James?" Gram asked in a weak, groggy voice.

My father's name—correction—my dead father's name. She was having another one of her episodes. My heart cracked as I faced this version of her alone.

"It's me, Gram. Corbin," I replied gently.

I scooted closer to her bed, softly placing my hand on hers.

"James," she said with effort, "you're going to lose them."

"Gram, you're at Mount Sinai. You fell."

"That boy adores you. You're all he has left. Don't toss him aside like you did with Mary. He needs you." Her eyes were closed, but her hand gripped mine tightly as she spoke to me like a memory. Like these words were rehearsed and repeated in the past, an echo of a conversation already spoken.

In an instant, I was ten, begging my mom not to leave us. She went with tears in her eyes and a Chanel suitcase in her hand.

I was thirteen, picking up empty bottles from the living room floor to hide my father's shame from the cleaning lady and snuffing out a lit cigarette as he lay passed out on the couch.

I was fifteen, watching my father succumb to his poor decisions, without enough energy in his body to even say goodbye.

"Don't leave me alone. I don't like the beeps," Gram's soft voice murmured. This time, her eyes were on my face, studying me.

"I'm not going anywhere." I forced a smile, though I was filled with dread.

Seconds passed, and Gram's jumbled memories gave way to her soft, rhythmic breathing. I didn't know what time it was when my eyes grew too heavy to keep open, but when the door to Gram's room creaked open, and Buzz walked in, my anger snapped me awake—a living, breathing thing clawing at my chest.

I leaped out of my chair, quickly pushing him into the hallway, careful not to wake Gram.

"Hey," he protested angrily as I shut the door to the room behind us. "I came to see my wife."

"Yeah, it's about fucking time you show up." My voice was jarringly loud in the quiet hallway of the hospital. "Where have you been?" I asked, lowering my voice to a sharp whisper.

Buzz didn't flinch. "I had some important meetings to take care of." His tone was flat, dismissive.

"At…" I checked my watch, trying to keep my disbelief from boiling over. "Five a.m.? On a Sunday?"

"You wouldn't understand," Buzz deflected, his tired eyes skimming the floor.

That stopped me. Buzz had never backed down from a confrontation before, not with me, not with anyone. He lived for conflict and thrived on dominance, yet here he was, folding in on himself like an overburdened structure.

It wasn't just the late hour. Something in him had changed, something subtle but unmistakable. His face, once chiseled and sharp, was lined with fatigue. His shoulders slumped, and his usual commanding presence had shrunk, his hair thinning into a shadow of its former fullness.

For the first time, Buzz didn't seem larger than life. He seemed *small*.

"You're shutting me out, Buzz," I said, softer this time. "You've been shutting me out for months. It's like you want nothing to do with me anymore."

"This has everything to do with you!" he snapped, his voice cracking, raw and unrestrained.

The words hung in the air before something even more jarring happened—a tear broke free and slid down his cheek.

Every muscle in me tensed.

Buzz Buescher didn't cry. Not when his son died, not when his wife was diagnosed—never.

But there it was—a glimmering line cutting down his face, catching the sterile fluorescent light like a damning piece of evidence.

I felt unmoored, unsure of how to respond to this man, this vulnerable stranger, standing before me. Watching him felt like a jagged piece of my foundation broke loose, something integral that would alter my structure indefinitely.

"I have to go," I muttered, retreating a step. "If you want to do something for me, take care of her." I nodded toward Gram's room before storming off.

I didn't want to be here. I couldn't be here.

I couldn't face the scene unfolding before me or reconcile this broken version of Buzz with the indomitable force I'd known my entire life.

I needed space, an escape—my apartment beckoned like a safe harbor in a storm. But it wasn't the four walls I was seeking.

It was Sophia.

Chapter 34

HOW THE OTHER HALF LIVES

Sophia

I jolted awake, disoriented. For a moment, my brain scrambled to process where I was. All I knew was that this definitely wasn't my apartment.

Then, like puzzle pieces falling into place, it all came rushing back. The gala. Landon's awful mother. Corbin offering me the job. The dance. The lies Landon told me unfolding. My dress getting stuck. The feel of Corbin's body against mine—and the crushing disappointment when he left so abruptly.

The bed beneath me was impossibly soft, the kind you sink into like a cloud. The sheets were silky smooth, and the duvet was perfectly weighted, cocooning me in luxurious comfort.

The room was pitch black. I fumbled for my phone on the nightstand, remembering I'd placed the dead thing on a wireless charger before collapsing into bed.

Thankfully, I texted my friends before it died to let them know I wasn't coming back home last night.

My hand grasped the tiny rectangle, and I tapped the power button. The ancient thing flickered to life, dim and pale in the darkness, and I saw that it was already morning.

A steady hum of vibrations came through our group text as their undoubtedly curious responses trickled in.

Devyn: Sorry, what?! Not coming home. Please don't tell me you're staying with that creep!
Lana: Sophia wouldn't do that. Right?
Brent: I just looked it up, there wasn't a single flight coming from JFK to Misty Springs. I think he tricked you.

Trevor: What if Soph is actually hogtied in the back of Landon's trunk somewhere in Mexico and we're texting Landon right now? Soph, if it's really you, send a pic. Preferably a shirtless one!

I chuckled and stretched my arms above my head. My movement must have triggered something, because a low hum filled the room, and the windows began to reveal themselves as the dark gray shades slowly lifted.

Sunlight poured in, flooding the room with warm, orange light. I squinted against it, taking in my surroundings.

I glanced down at myself. A baggy white shirt hung loose off one shoulder, paired with boxer shorts that sagged low on my hips.

My mind went to Corbin.

Was he gone all night?

Or did he come back and choose to sleep alone?

I wasn't sure which one of those scenarios sat more comfortably with me.

After calming my friends down, letting them know I was safe in New York and not hog-tied in the back of Landon's trunk—the details of where or who I stayed with kept vague—I decided to forage for some caffeine and hopefully food in this strange and extravagant land.

I tiptoed down the stairs, the soft pads of my feet barely making a sound. As soon as I stepped into the main living area, the shades began their slow, deliberate ascent—just like upstairs. Sunlight spilled into the room, painting Corbin's magnificent apartment in warm hues.

So much for sneaking around in the dark.

I found a glass and filled it with water, downing it in one long, greedy gulp before refilling it.

Hydration, step one.

I opened the refrigerator, sighing when I saw only a leftover Chinese food container and various bottled drinks—not a single scrap of edible food in sight.

I went in search of coffee instead. My temples were already starting to ache from caffeine withdrawals. I found a contraption that looked more like the control panel of a spaceship than a coffee maker—stainless steel, glowing buttons, and not a single word of guidance.

Seriously, what was wrong with Mr. Coffee? One button, that's it, and you're on your way to caffeinated bliss.

A loud ding from the elevator door echoed in the silent apartment.

My heart picked up speed, and I scrambled to adjust my shirt, trying to tame my wild hair—preparing myself to see Corbin again in the light of day.

Corbin stalked inside, his eyes immediately finding me. The look on his face tugged at my frantic heart. He looked defeated, tired, exhausted. Whatever situation he just left didn't look like it was easy on him.

Any resentment I'd been holding onto from him leaving last night dissipated as I studied him. His rimmed eyes, hunched shoulders, disheveled hair, and a look on his face told me he needed me.

Not someone to kiss, not an employee, not a one-night stand.

He needed a friend.

Chapter 35

A First for me

Corbin

"I had no clue how to work that thing," Sophia admitted as I loaded my espresso machine.

I smirked as I locked the portafilter into place, pressed a button, and the machine let out a familiar hum. A rich, slow, and syrupy shot of espresso began to pour.

"It's not as good as Lana's, but it'll wake you up." I handed her the tiny cup of caffeine as my mind whirled.

There was too much unsaid between us, and figuring out where to start felt impossible.

She took a sip, her eyes meeting mine over the rim. When she licked the foam from her top lip, I had to glance away before I did something reckless—like kiss her right there in my kitchen.

I needed to keep my head straight. But with her this close, with silence stretching between us, pulling taut—it was getting harder to separate what I wanted to do and say from all the things I shouldn't.

She set the cup down and rubbed her arms, my loose hanging shirt doing little to keep her warm in my cold apartment.

"Give me ten minutes," I said, already texting. "I'll have something here before your coffee's cold."

I messaged Eddie—he was used to my last-minute asks—and told him to grab a few options: pants, a couple of soft tops, maybe even a hoodie, and some sort of shoe—figuring she wasn't planning on squeezing back into the heels she immediately ripped off last night. I told him to cover the size range.

"You just have a guy who buys clothes for you on demand?" Sophia asked, one brow raised as she wrapped her hands around her coffee cup.

"I have a lot of people who do things for me on demand."

She didn't say anything to that—just watched me like she was trying to figure out what world she just stepped into.

I cleared my throat and nodded toward the couch. "Should we..."

"Yeah, we should talk."

I waited until she got comfortable on one end before grabbing the throw draped across the back and settling it over her legs.

More for my sake than hers—her bare legs were a distraction I knew I couldn't ignore for long.

"Thanks," she murmured, folding it closer around herself.

We sat on the couch, side by side, silently sipping our coffee. The smooth leather beneath me felt stiff and unfamiliar, as though it resented being used.

I stole a glance at her, her eyes fixed on some distant point across the room.

She was not prying, not pushing, just existing here with me, calm and beautiful, her presence like a sentry protecting my space.

In a life filled with noise and complications, her quiet companionship felt like the closest thing to peace I'd known in a long time.

Before I could decide where to start, my phone buzzed on my lap.

I pocketed the phone as Sophia looked at me.

I gave her a soft smile. "Clothes are downstairs when you want them."

She nodded but didn't move, her gaze still fixed on me.

I took a breath.

"Listen, about last night," I began, but the words faltered, stuck somewhere between my chest and throat.

I couldn't shake the image of Buzz's face, the lone tear trailing down his cheek. It cracked something inside me, a fault line I'd spent years ignoring. Suddenly, I felt it—the exhaustion, the rawness.

The dam I'd built, the one that kept it all locked away—grief, anger, regret—was starting to break. Despite years of shoving these feelings into the darkest corners of my mind, they came surging back with the force of a raging river.

Sophia touched my arm, and I looked into her eyes to see the careful emotion and empathy inside the deep blue well of her irises.

The dam broke.

I unleashed everything I held inside, the bright and happy, and the dark and twisted pieces of me. I recalled my trip to Italy with my mother back to her small village—with giant green hills and tiny cottages straight from a storybook.

I shared how hard it was the day she chose to leave my father and me, but also the combination of relief and guilt I felt at her taking the late-night arguments and crashing fights with her.

I unleashed the dark times spent with my father after my mother left—then came the glimmers of light that Gram carried.

First, there were the "sleepovers" with Gram, Buzz, and Louise that stretched into weeks.

Then came the quiet migration—one drawer, one backpack, one box at a time.

Until one day, I simply didn't go back home.

I told her about my career and my uphill battle to prove myself. The wars I waged against viewpoints of nepotism because of who my grandfather was, or judgment because of my father.

My warred past, my tumultuous present, and my uncertain future were splayed out before her like an open wound.

When I was done, she held every piece of me—a colorful array of fucked-up strands to weave the complete tapestry of my fucked-up life.

When she reached up to touch my face, I flinched—startled, not realizing she was wiping away tears. Hell, I didn't even know I had tears to wipe away.

I leaned back against the couch, letting my head sink into the plush cushion, bracing for what I thought would come next. Any second now, she'd get up, make some excuse, and tuck and run.

Who could blame her? She didn't sign up for this. She didn't sign up for me.

She'd been duped into coming to the city, tricked into this mess, and now she was tangled in someone else's wreckage. But instead of pulling away, she nestled her head against my chest, her warmth seeping into me like the coffee in my veins.

"You know," she began, her voice soft but steady, "it's not the tribulations in life that define you. It's how you continue to live your life in spite of them. You've carried more than your share of pain, but it hasn't consumed you. That says something, doesn't it?"

Her voice was a sweet relief, soothing the raw edges of my soul. I wrapped my arm around her shoulders, pulling her just a little closer.

It felt... right.

She was warm and soft, and for a fleeting moment, it felt like she belonged here with me.

I wanted to say more, to find the right words to capture how she made me feel. But nothing came out. Nothing could convey the complicated feelings I had for Sophia, feelings I'd never experienced before with anyone.

The weight of a sleepless night and everything I'd just unpacked pressed down on me. My vision blurred, and darkness tugged at the edges.

"I'm glad you're here," I managed, my voice strained.

The words hung in the air for only a moment before exhaustion pulled me under.

Chapter 36

HELLO, NEW YORK!

Sophia

I sat in the soft glow of the morning light, the sun spilling warmth through the towering windows.

Corbin had fallen asleep with his arm draped over me, holding on like I was the last tether keeping him grounded.

When he showed up this morning, it was clear he had the weight of the world pressing down on him.

As we sat here together, he gave me piece after piece of him. Each confession felt like a revelation, another word added to the enigmatic story of who Corbin was.

Now, in the stillness of the morning—his steady breathing the only sound in this silent oasis—I was left with more questions than answers.

Where did this leave us?

Co-workers didn't sound right. Corbin and I weren't friends either—last night had obliterated any semblance of that boundary. And yet, we couldn't be in a relationship. Something we both knew but neither had dared to discuss out loud yet.

I looked up at his sleeping face, peaceful in the release of the nightmares he had held inside to fight alone. The surface of the man who held me was a formidable presence—one that the world could see and knew to respect and admire.

But beneath all of it? Was someone even more astonishing, someone who captivated me more than I ever knew possible.

My phone vibrated against my leg. I had ignored its incessant buzzing until now, my mind far away from Misty Springs.

Cassie: Can we at least get a hint about where you even are? This is driving me crazy! And when will you be back? You're on the schedule for Monday.

Trevor: Guys, it's Landon, I'm telling you.

I quietly got up, careful not to disturb Corbin as he snoozed away on the couch. I felt a tug at my heart as I watched him.

A tug, I quickly reeled back in.

This couldn't happen. *We* couldn't happen.

There was no way any other publishing company would give me a chance without a degree or experience. This was my chance, my only chance.

And there was no way I would intertwine my life with his in hopes he would financially support me. It was a stupid mistake I already made once with Landon, and look where that got me.

I tiptoed to the kitchen and found a blank wall to stand in front of. I held up a middle finger and took a selfie.

I hit send.

Devyn: Oh that's original, like you don't have at least a dozen of those lewd selfies in your camera roll.

Sam: Yeah, I agree, not today Landon! Not today!

Lana: <Cry laughing emoji>

I giggled inside Corbin's pristine kitchen, my voice echoing slightly in the huge space. My eyes scanned the bright white cabinets, the polished white marble countertops, and the glistening grey and white floors. Everything looked new, untouched. I wondered if Corbin had ever cooked a meal in here.

My phone vibrated again, and skin prickled when I saw Landon's name flash across my screen.

Landon: Guess you're too busy screwing your new boss to pick up your shit. We left it with the front desk at the hotel. Here is the location. Have a nice life.

My gut twisted.

Not because of guilt—but because a part of me worried about retaliation. If this relationship policy was as strict as Andi mentioned, would Landon somehow sabotage my chances at Buescher-Jones Publishing?

I wouldn't put it past him—or his mother, especially after last night.

I checked the location on my phone—the hotel was only a couple of blocks away. Easily walkable.

I glanced down at what I was wearing. Definitely not street-ready. But then I remembered that some task-oriented driver had left new clothes for me downstairs.

I found a pen and notepad in a console drawer—the most organized junk drawer I'd ever seen—and wrote a note to Corbin in case he woke up. It occurred to me that I didn't even have his phone number to text him and let him know I was leaving.

My clutch was sitting on the entry table where I'd dropped it last night. Above it, hanging on a hook, was a black hoodie of Corbin's. I tugged it on over the tee and instantly felt less exposed.

I grabbed the wadded-up twenty-dollar bill I'd tucked into my clutch. Hopefully, it would be enough to grab a few things to eat while I was out—the food at last night's gala seemed more about presentation than sustenance.

I shoved the bill into the hoodie's front pocket, squared my shoulders, and headed for the door.

Watch out, New York—well, at least two blocks of you—here I come!

Chapter 37

I OWN A TOASTER?

Corbin

The first thing I noticed was how bright it was behind my eyelids. Strange, why weren't my shades closed?

Then, as the light filtered through my vision, my clarity filtered through as well.

I just shared every detail of my life with Sophia, and after what felt like exorcising a demon, fell promptly asleep.

I popped my eyes open to find my chest devoid of her head. I shot up and scanned my apartment. It was empty and quiet—a setting I was accustomed to—but instead of the comforting familiarity, it felt like a cold, hollow echo of what it had just been before I fell asleep. Something essential was missing, or more like someone.

I stood up, stretched my aching back, and rubbed my eyes. The hospital chair and my couch weren't exactly ideal sleeping positions for good-quality REM.

"Sophia?" I called, but there was nothing but quiet.

I darted up the stairs and gently nudged open the door to the guest room—*Sophia's room.*

The bed lay empty. The bathroom door was open, and the room was dark.

A lump formed in my throat.

I pulled my phone from my pocket and opened my contact list—raking my hands across my face.

I didn't even have her phone number.

My finger hovered over Andi's name. Perhaps she could stop by the office and pull it from her resume.

No. Then she'd ask questions, questions I wasn't prepared to answer. It was only a matter of time before she heard through the grapevine about the new hire I had shown around at the gala. She'd be suspicious enough.

I raced back down the stairs and paced the length of my living room, wearing a path into the plush black-and-white rug beneath my feet. I glanced down—I was still in my slacks and shirt from last night.

Maybe I should just accept it: I'd scared her off. After everything I dumped on her—years of buried trauma and a damn near breakdown—what reason did she have to stay?

It was probably for the best. We were doomed from the start. Destined to unravel before we even figured out what we were.

I quickly showered, attempting to scrub the tension from my skin. I threw on gray sweats and a white tee before my stomach let out a loud, hollow growl, reminding me that I hadn't eaten since whatever they thought passed for food was doled out last night.

I opened a delivery app and stared at the options before abruptly closing it to return to my pacing.

When the elevator dinged, my heart lurched, and I froze mid-step—my gaze snapping to the doors.

I stood there like a loyal dog waiting for its owner to come home, hopeful and eager, every nerve alight with the hope of seeing Sophia.

Disappointment rocked me when I saw Joseph, the concierge from downstairs, holding a brown paper bag and wearing a smile. A genuine smile, nothing like the tight-lipped one he'd given me for years when I walked through the lobby.

Sophia came into view behind him, rolling a suitcase with a black shopping bag piled on top and laughing.

Tension eased from my shoulders almost immediately.

"Just set this here?" Joseph asked Sophia.

"Yes, please. Thanks, Joey," she replied.

Joey?

"My pleasure, Ms. Carlson," Joseph—or Joey, I guess—said with a wink and a tip of his hat before turning to me. "Mr. Buescher, enjoy your afternoon."

He stepped into the waiting elevator and left me standing there like a confused third wheel.

"You're awake," Sophia said, her voice casual.

She started unpacking the brown paper bag my doorman set on the counter, pulling out a loaf of fresh bread, a couple of tomatoes, and something wrapped in butcher paper.

But I couldn't focus on any of it.

She wore the lounge pants my driver must've picked out—simple black joggers that clung just enough to make my thoughts drift somewhere they shouldn't—but it was the hoodie that caught me off guard.

My hoodie.

The one I'd hung by the door was now pulled over her head, the hem almost swallowing her hips. The sleeves were too long, and she kept pushing them up, leaving them bunched at her forearms. Seeing her in it did something to me. Some part of me liked the idea of her wrapped up in my clothes more than I probably should've.

"Yeah, sorry, I fell asleep." I stepped toward the kitchen. "It's strange to me. I don't nap. Ever," I admitted as I wiped at my tired eyes.

"Not really a nap when you didn't sleep the night before." She smiled, and the sight lit up my chest.

Already, the apartment felt in balance again. I felt in balance again, like when she was near me, all was right with the world.

Even if everything else in my life was fucked.

"What all do you have here?" I asked her curiously.

"Well, you have no food. And I, as a human, need food. So, I decided to make an early lunch." She began rifling through my cabinets.

"And the suitcase?"

"Mine. I picked it up from the hotel Landon stayed at," she said as she placed a pan on the stovetop.

"You saw Landon?" I tried and failed to hide the tension in my voice.

"No, thankfully, he had already left. I got it from the front desk. I left a note for you." She gestured toward a sheet of paper virtually undetectable against my kitchen's countertop.

She returned to the stovetop and attempted to click on the gas burner. Her brow furrowed as the little flame evaded her.

For all I knew, that stove didn't even work. I couldn't think of a single time I used it.

I watched Sophia struggle and stomp her foot in frustration. I grinned at the tiny fit she was throwing, her scrunched-up nose, the little V between her eyes—reminding me of her frustrated face when she called me an asshole weeks ago when she stole my seat on the plane.

I grabbed a lighter from my console table and walked up behind her, standing close, placing my hand on her hip to still her.

She froze in place, the air around us charged instantly, thick and heavy with all the things we still weren't saying to each other, all the things we weren't doing to each other.

"Turn it again," I murmured, my voice thick.

I thought it was the alcohol, the dress that made me lose my control last night—but it wasn't.

It was her.

She was a desire and temptation—it didn't matter if she had on a too-large hoodie or nothing at all. I wanted her with every fiber of my being.

She did as I asked, and I aimed the lighter under the burner, igniting the gas as fire encircled the coils. I stood there for a moment, wanting more, needing more.

"Thanks." She broke that need as she moved away from me to grab the ingredients.

I released a breath and stepped back, using the counter as a barrier. I had to adjust myself before I sat down, but that was nothing new around her.

I watched her move as she sprawled strips of bacon across the pan. I studied her as she searched through the cabinets for more essential cooking items.

I offered no help. I didn't even know I owned a pan or tongs. I just took in each sway of her hips, each bend of her waist, each toss of her hair with an avid intensity.

She adjusted a bracelet on her wrist for about the tenth time before turning her focus to me. "Are you really just going to sit there and stare at me the whole time?"

"I'm enjoying the show." I shrugged.

She adjusted her bracelet again. It was like a tick of hers, twisting it and moving it up her wrist, to let it settle back where it was.

"Nice bracelet," I commented.

"Oh, thanks." She paused for a moment, focusing on slicing a tomato before continuing. "It was my mother's."

"Where is she now?" I asked.

It occurred to me that I knew nothing about Sophia's family. I spent the morning unloading everything about mine, and it felt a little one-sided.

"She... died," Sophia said, then she swallowed hard, forcing down what seemed like more of a story.

"I'm sorry."

"It's okay. It was a few years ago." She twisted the bracelet again before returning to her task.

A look on her face indicated that it was not actually okay.

The bacon sizzled and crackled, wafting a delicious aroma. My stomach roared in response.

"And your dad?" I pried.

I just poured my guts out to this woman. She could give me a little more.

"Him too... car accident. They were both in the car."

"Wow, that's... I'm sorry. That had to have been difficult." I knew what it was like to lose your parents. Though the way I saw it, both of mine chose to leave me. I couldn't imagine losing parents who actually wanted to be in your life.

"It was." She hesitated like she shouldn't say more, then turned to me—her face shifting, like she'd made some internal decision. "It was why I dropped out of school. I had one semester left. I just... couldn't do it anymore. It felt like I was working toward this dream of mine, this goal. But why? What was the point? One day, you could be here, living your life, and the next..."

She pulled the bacon from the pan and set it on a paper towel, then retrieved a toaster from a bottom cabinet—another item I hadn't realized I owned.

Sophia stared longingly at the toaster, her face appearing to recall something unseen in this apartment.

"I felt like being across the country only pulled me farther away from them. If I could be in Misty Springs, I could at least be in the same place as they used to be, feel their presence on the paths Mom and I used to walk along. Visit the movie theater Dad loved to take me to. Just existing in the spaces they did—especially our home. But I quickly realized that I could barely afford their house. All I could find with my experience was a bartending job, which led me to Boomer's. Thankfully, Cassie helped me get a job at Elijah's. Those became all I had time for. Then, student loans came due, and I felt like I was drowning. Until... Landon."

"Ah," I replied with a sharp edge to my voice. It all made sense now. I wondered how someone like her could fall for someone as vile as Landon. That creep took advantage of a broken, beat-down Sophia.

"He convinced me to sell my parents' house," she said softly, her voice laced with a wistfulness that tugged at something deep in me. "It was gut-wrenching. I had so many memories tied up in that house. Losing them so abruptly... selling it felt like a betrayal, like any moment they'd return asking where they were supposed to sleep now."

"I can't take this bracelet off. It feels like... all I have left of them." Sophia's fingers traced the bracelet around her wrist, twisting it. "It probably seems silly to be so emotionally connected to a piece of metal."

I let out a sharp breath, recalling the tarnished piece of metal I raced back to retrieve from my hotel room weeks ago—the compass I inexplicably needed to bring when I first visited Misty Springs.

"It's not silly," I assured her.

We gazed quietly into each other's eyes for a moment, and inside my chest, another thread that linked me to Sophia pulled tighter.

"Landon was so helpful and attentive," she continued, slicing sandwiches into neat little triangles, her movements methodical, as if the routine steadied her emotions. "He was sweet, too—at first. When he offered me a job working for his parents, I could make more than I did at both jobs combined, so I jumped at the chance. All the money from the sale of my parents' house went to school debt, and I was struggling to make ends meet again, so—at the time—it felt like a lifeline." She placed the sandwich on a shiny black plate she had pulled from the bottom of a stack in a high cabinet.

My mind—previously solely focused on her, was distracted—curious about who Landon sold her parents' house to. If it was in the right location, it was a bullseye for the Norwood's schemes. I made a mental note to check the public records—if they had it wrapped up in one of their exploits, who knew what would become of it.

"The rest is history. After spending all that time together, we eventually became a couple. He asked me to move in with him. Asked me to marry him. It all happened so fast."

She placed the sandwich before me, the plate clinking on the counter.

"He showed me all the good sides of him for a year. My friends saw the truth, though—they couldn't stand him."

I took a bite of the BLT. It was delicious. It dawned on me that this may be my first home-cooked meal here. Sophia continued as I savored every bite.

"Cassie could see how unhappy I was. She's known me forever, and I swear she knows me better than I know myself. Devyn and Brent both took turns offering to beat him up after I'd told them about our fights. Trevor and Sam were lighthearted about it, mostly cracking jokes, but I could tell they couldn't stand him. They were never quite themselves when Landon was around. And Lana... Lana has the kindest ways to tell you that your life decisions are horse shit." Some of the names Sophia mentioned sparked a memory of people I'd encountered in Misty Springs.

Sophia's smile beamed as she continued to tell me how they helped her and rallied behind her through some of her darkest moments, even when she initially pushed them away.

"This is amazing, by the way," I raved as I took another bite.

"It's nothing special." She waved dismissively.

"So, then you caught Landon cheating and kicked him to the curb, and now here we are?"

"Pretty much," she said through a mouthful of food.

She swallowed it down, and I tracked the movement down the column of her throat. Everything about her was delicate—her slim hands, her soft features, everything except her iron will.

"You know," I started as her words from earlier rang in my head. "Someone wise once told me, it's not the tribulations in life that define you. It's how you continue to live your life in spite of them."

She snorted. "Oh sure, let's see, I have a broken engagement, two dead-end jobs, a crummy apartment... I'm really killing it here."

How was it possible that someone like her couldn't see how incredible she was?

I leaned across the counter, my voice dropping to a softer tone. "First of all, life isn't just about the material things you've acquired. You're a good person, Sophia. Your friends are a testament to that. The people who love you and stand by you—that's where your wealth lies."

I let the words linger between us, watching as she stopped chewing and blinked at me, the weight of my statement sinking in.

"Not everyone has that," I added quietly, leaning back in my chair. "Not everyone has people who would fight for them, who'd care enough to stand in their corner no matter how bad it gets. You may not realize it, but you're richer than most of the people in this city."

The words hung in the air, and I felt the weight of them settle uncomfortably in my chest. I felt like a hypocrite—my life's ambition had always been about accumulating money and power, clawing my way to the top of the corporate ladder at the expense of everything else. I'd spent years measuring success by bank accounts and titles, yet here I was, telling her the opposite.

But as I looked at Sophia—at her quiet strength, her resilience, the unshakable bond she shared with her friends—I couldn't see her as a failure. Not even close. She had something money couldn't buy, something I'd spent my whole life missing and didn't even realize was so valuable.

Her expression softened, her eyes misted, and the tip of her nose turned into a delicate shade of red.

So, this was what it was like to open up to someone and have them open up to you. This was what it was like to feel vulnerable.

It was terrifying and freeing all at the same time.

We hadn't slept together, but Sophia had seen more of me than any woman ever had. She held on to so many delicate pieces that I'd kept hidden away.

The question now was what she'd do with them.

Chapter 38

WAVERUNNER

Sophia

I stood there, caught in an awestruck, gooey puddle, as Corbin's words washed over me. Clearing my throat, I reached across the kitchen counter and grabbed his empty plate, busying myself to avoid the intensity of the moment.

The routine rhythm of washing dishes felt like a lifeline, grounding me as I filled the sink with warm, soapy water. I pushed the sleeves of Corbin's oversized hoodie up my arms.

My heart fluttered at the quiet care behind Corbin's actions in getting me clothes. He hadn't waited for me to ask—he'd just noticed I needed something warmer and acted. No questions, no commentary. Just... instinct—and the fact he was so decisive and demanding was pretty damn sexy.

His muscled arm brushed against mine, and the tiny hairs on my arm stretched on end like they were reaching out for him.

I glanced up and found him watching me—his gaze unflinching. There was a quiet intensity in it, but something in the way his eyes lingered made my pulse stir.

His fingers brushed lightly against my hip. That same crackling energy from earlier—when he'd helped me light the burner—roared back to life, stronger and more consuming than before.

We'd both broken ourselves open and allowed the other to see all the messy parts—the parts we kept locked away from the world—and somehow, despite all of that, the need for him was stronger than ever.

"I can help," he murmured, leaning down.

His voice was low and warm against my ear, and his breath skimmed my skin.

I closed my eyes, a shiver rippling through me. It was maddening how easily he unnerved me with the slightest touch, the faintest sound, the barest brush of his breath.

I did my best to bypass my hormones and shoved a towel into his chest. "I'll wash, you dry."

His rough hand grazed mine as he took the towel from me, his touch like a current, writhing up my arm and settling tight in my core.

How was everything he did so sexy?

We worked in silence, exchanging flirty smiles and lusty stares.

"Was there a second of all?" I asked, trying to break the silent tension.

"Hmm?"

"Earlier, you said, '*First of all, life isn't about the things you acquire.*' Which would imply there were more *of all's* to follow."

He turned to me, setting the dried dishes on the polished countertop in a neat little stack.

"I was just going to add that you no longer have two dead-end jobs. You are about to have a rewarding and prosperous career."

My heart lifted—and then splattered to bits in my ribcage.

True, I could now leave Elijah's and Boomer's behind for a career—a real career—in my dream industry with a publisher who worked with one of my favorite authors.

But that also meant closing the chapter on whatever was happening between Corbin and me.

His expression shifted into a quiet realization as if he'd just recognized that he'd unintentionally drawn attention to the elephant in the room.

"I know about Buescher-Jones' policy regarding workplace relationships," I admitted, begrudgingly pulling the metaphorical elephant out of the corner on a rope.

"Oh." He tossed the towel on the countertop.

"Andi told me when I showed up for the interview. It was an idle threat to get Ned fired, but still, I know."

He chuckled. "She hates that guy."

I studied his deep-set, whiskey-colored eyes—the same ones that had pulled me in the moment I spotted him across the chaos of the airport. Now they were shadowed, his dark hair falling into them as he looked down at me—not styled, air-dried after his shower, looking disheveled and impossibly sexy.

"This job… this career. I need this," I said softly.

I couldn't pin my hopes on Corbin—on the idea of *us*. I'd made that with Landon—wrapped my identity around a relationship until there was nothing left of me that didn't have his name on it.

And when it crumbled, so did I.

I couldn't go through that again. I couldn't lose myself so completely only to be left alone in the wreckage.

His lips twisted into a pained smile as if he knew everything I wasn't saying.

I wasn't going to choose him over this job.

A part of me wanted to ask why he couldn't just change the damn policy. But after he shared so much of his life with me, I felt I already knew the answer.

He wasn't just honoring a company guideline. He was creating a chasm between who he was and who his father had been.

I couldn't risk the job, and he couldn't risk his bid for CEO— not for something that hadn't even begun. Not for something as fragile and undefined as *this*.

The space between us was full of what-ifs, regrets, and unquenched desires. As my ever-present need to avoid uncomfortable situations flared, I silently grabbed the plates and moved toward the wall cabinet to put them away.

The shelf was high, and I stretched on my tiptoes to add them to the top of the stack, straining as I extended my body to the fullest. These damn things were easier to get down when I pulled them from the bottom.

Corbin's warm chest pressed against my back, his hands brushing mine gently as he took the plates from me. The mound of his biceps surrounded my head as he easily stacked the plates in place.

I turned in the cramped space between his firm body and the countertop.

We stood there, unmoving, eyes locked, teetering on the edge of a dangerous precipice.

My eyes dropped to his full lips, remembering how they felt on mine, how they felt trailing rough kisses on my neck, the way his stubble rubbed against my skin.

Any rational thought was melted away by the white-hot need coursing through me.

"I don't officially start for a couple of weeks, though," I breathed. My eyes shot back up to stare innocently into his. "Right?"

My words seemed to unleash something within him, and he wasted no time claiming my lips with his.

My back dug into the countertop at the force of his approach. His kiss alone was enough to ignite my body into nothing but molten need, craving more than what it was given last night.

He lifted me onto the counter, his warm hands crawling up the loose hoodie. His moan filled my mouth when he felt the absence of a bra.

He stepped back—eyes burning, hair wild—a confident smirk painted across his face. "As much as I want to take you right here in the kitchen, I have some things in mind that require you to be a bit more... horizontal."

Without warning, he grabbed me by the waist and effortlessly tossed me over his shoulder in one swift motion.

I yelped when he smacked my ass as he carried me toward one of the closed doors on the first level, reaching into his pocket and tossing his phone onto the sofa.

"No distractions this time," he promised, voice laced with sin.

I knew we were in his bedroom the moment his intoxicating scent surrounded me. It was a sleek sanctuary of masculine elegance. The oversized bed was covered in crisp white linens while floor-to-ceiling windows let in the city's golden glow.

He kicked the door shut, throwing me down on the plush bed.

I crawled backward, moving inch by inch toward the headboard.

Corbin stalked up the mattress on all fours, hovering over me, following me move for move.

His perfect lips found mine again. Our tongues danced, tasting, exploring. He settled in between my open legs, the length of him pressing hard against me through his soft sweatpants.

My body ached for more.

As if he read my mind, his hands found the base of the hoodie, gliding it up my torso. I lifted slightly so he could pull it over my head, pulling the soft tank his driver purchased for me along with it.

His mouth trailed kisses from under my ear, down my neck, until he reached my chest, and I felt his warm mouth suck on the hardened peak of my nipple. He kissed and sucked, while his other hand squeezed.

I pulled at his shirt, working it over his head.

When I walked into his apartment earlier, I thought I had stumbled into the wrong building. I'd never seen Corbin in something so casual. He was infuriatingly sexy dressed down like this. The man looked good in everything he put on his perfect body.

I let my fingertips wander over the corded muscle of his arm, tracing the peaks and valleys of his chest before gliding down his abs—caressing each defined ridge—then slipping my hand between us, down to his waistband.

My hand palmed the length of him through his sweatpants, and he moaned a breathy moan into my chest.

I tried—and failed—to pull down his waistband, desperate to explore more of him.

He pulled up from my chest, and his swollen lips gave me another sly smile.

"So impatient." His voice vibrated my skin as he peppered kisses down my stomach, his fingers caressing the elastic band of my pants. "But you'll have to wait. I want to take my time with you."

He shimmied my joggers down my legs, the cool air doing little to alleviate the flush burning across my skin.

Corbin was on his knees, hovering above me, his eyes raking up my body from my toes to the top of my head, the outline of his arousal straining against his pants.

I was completely bare to him, lying with anxious need. Too pent-up to feel self-conscious. Too turned on to feel uneasy.

A coiled spring just waiting to be sprung.

"I'd been mapping out your body from every stolen glance I've taken," he said, kissing the inside of my ankle.

"Turns out my imagination is shit." He kissed the inside of my knee next.

"You're fucking beautiful, Sophia." He pushed open my legs, and his final kiss landed exactly where I wanted it. Feeling exactly how I dreamed it would.

His mouth on me lit me up inside, stoking the raging flames to a near-unbearable degree. His expert tongue took a long, languid stroke, filling me before spiraling and flicking in a euphoric rhythm.

His rough stubble grazed my thigh, contrasting the sensitive strokes of his tongue in a beautiful balance between pain and pleasure.

My body was completely at his mercy. I was his to do anything with in this moment, and I would gleefully oblige as long as he didn't stop making me feel this good.

"I could savor you forever." His deep voice vibrated my core with every syllable.

He slid his fingers inside me, immediately putting glorious pressure where I needed it. He moved like a skilled musician, my body responding like a tightly wound guitar string, vibrating a beautiful melody with each pluck of his experienced hands.

I felt the pressure build inside me, growing more and more tense with each stroke of his tongue, each press of his fingers. My fingers wrapped into his hair, the image I conjured when I first saw him in the airport playing out in real life—better than my imagination.

So much better.

The tension built until every muscle was taut. I forgot my name. I forgot why this was against the rules. I forgot where I was. I forgot everything that wasn't the unrelenting pleasure that Corbin gave me.

Then, release hit me like a tidal wave.

Lights burst behind my eyelids, and I moaned in ecstasy as wave after wave of pleasure crashed over me.

Corbin rode the waves with me, ensuring he hung on until the very last one dissipated onto the shore.

After a few breathy moments, he looked up at me, his mouth glistening with my arousal. His tongue traced his lips with a satisfied slowness, savoring the lingering taste as a sinful smirk tugged at the corners of his mouth.

"I'm not done with you yet," he said as his hands moved to the waistline of his pants.

Those words from his masterful lips sent a clench-worthy shiver through my body. My muscles were blissfully languid, but I was primed and ready for more.

I watched him undress, his muscled physique highlighted by the vivid hues of the sunlight beaming through the windows.

My imagination could finally take a breather, no longer trying to paint his muscles with my mind. My eyes trailed lower, my breath catching as I watched him roll a condom over the swell of his hardened cock.

I smirked, considering how what Corbin carried around definitely contributed to his cocky attitude—pun very much intended.

His hand fisted the base as he looked at me with a heated intensity, filled with wicked promises.

My body was aching for him, legs open, body dripping, I was practically pulsing in anticipation to feel him inside me.

He kissed up my body, lingering on my throbbing clit and moving higher, swirling around my sensitive nipples. His mouth skimmed along my shoulder before landing on a sensitive patch below my ear.

He lined himself up with my entrance, my body tense with anticipation. My fingers pulled at his hips. The need for him to fill me was dire.

"So greedy, Sophia." His warm breath whispered in my ear as he kissed the column of my throat. His lips moved to mine, his tongue tangling with mine as I tasted my arousal along with the flavor that was so inexplicably his.

He finally answered my silent pleas and buried himself inside of me, filling me inch by inch with the length of him.

My breath shot out, and a moan slipped from my lips as my body adjusted to the stretch of him inside me, thick and unrelenting.

"Fuck," he breathed into my mouth.

He pushed himself up, his eyes looking worried, like they were searching my face for something—looking for pain, hesitation, or regret.

But I only felt the need to feel more—I *needed* more.

"Don't stop," I pleaded.

His mouth pulled in a sly grin as he slowly pulled out before pushing inside of me again—his eyes studying me with each slow churn of his hips.

The fullness had me clinging to him, my entire body coming alive around him. My breath loosened, and my core tightened as the thrust of his hips came harder and faster.

His lips crashed into mine again, this time more wild—hungry. He lowered his hard body onto mine, pinning me to the bed as he continued to drive inside of me.

I felt him everywhere, his lips sweet and devouring, his skin hot and smooth, his cock rigid and penetrating.

He lifted himself once more, moving to his knees. My body chilled as the air in the room merged with the lingering sweat on my skin.

He looked down at my glistening form, lifting my ass slightly, continuing to drive inside of me, the angle hitting a new spot deep inside—one that had never been reached before.

My body was wracked with pleasure, the tension building again in my already spent muscles. The buildup broke—white-hot and blinding.

I closed my eyes as another orgasm ripped through me. His name screamed from my lips as he sent me over the edge once more—my body vibrating as my walls pulsed around him.

He lowered his body to mine again, covering me with his warmth.

My muscles shook as my body quaked beneath him, still riding the edge of what I could handle. Each drive trembled through me like a welcome aftershock. I clung to him, utterly undone but still aching for more.

His rhythm slowed and deepened, his groan muffled into my shoulder as I felt the pulsing throb of his release.

We lay in silence for a few moments, breathing shallow breaths, covered in sweat and contented bliss—our bodies still joined together.

The haze of my feral nature lifted as realization set in.

I just had sex with my new boss.

Broke the no-relationship policy before I even started my first day.

And I was already dreaming about doing it again.

Chapter 39

Donald Ducking

Sophia

I knew sex with Corbin Buescher would be good. I had no idea it would be a mind-altering, life-changing, euphoric experience.

I lay in bed, my muscles languid and my body blissfully spent, stroking the strands of his thick hair as his head rested on my chest.

I thought about how unfair life could be.

Maybe somewhere out there, in another universe, there was a Sophia and a Corbin who got to do more together.

Who went on dates and learned each other's quirks. Who knew what their favorite foods, movies, and colors were. Who could name every favorite dish from every favorite restaurant, and always be able to order their regular takeout choice—without even asking.

The buzzing of two distinct ringtones sounded from the other side of Corbin's bedroom door. Both of our phones—our tether to the grim reality outside this room—hummed relentlessly in alternating succession, playing a melancholy soundtrack to our otherwise blissful scene.

I was being irresponsible, being here with Corbin and shutting out real life in Misty Springs.

Cassie was definitely one of those callers. I had never acknowledged that I would come in to work Monday after she texted me. This wasn't like me, Ms. Reliable. I never missed a shift. I rarely missed calls. I always texted her back.

I never shacked up with my new boss hundreds of miles away and shut out the world.

"We should probably see what they want," Corbin finally said, popping the bubble that held us in this blissful little world.

He sat up and eyed my body up and down once more with a heavy sigh. He watched me the entire time he pulled up his pants, angrily forcing each muscular leg inside the thick gray sweats.

I recalled how soft they were as they rubbed against my body. Did people with money to spare even know what it was like to wear itchy fabric? The kind that chafes your skin raw? Or was everything that surrounded them made from silky clouds?

"Can you hand me my clothes?" I pointed to the floor as I sat up in bed.

"Do I have to?" he teased, pulling his shirt overhead. "I am enjoying the view."

I raised my eyebrows and extended my arm, making a grabbing motion with my hand.

"Fine," he huffed. "But maybe we could compromise?" He held my new tank to his chest.

"I don't think that will fit you," I joked.

He tossed it to me with a grin. "How about just that little tank top and panties?"

"While you get to be fully dressed? No way."

He slowly paced in front of me, his finger tapping a coy smile on his lips. So far, I had met arrogant Corbin, decisive Corbin, broken Corbin, and now I was meeting playful Corbin—and he was, by far, my most favorite Corbin yet.

"Okay, bottoms only, nothing on top," he retorted.

"What if someone came up here? They'd open the elevator right into my tits," I said as I pulled the tank over my head.

"You realize now, every time I come up that elevator, I'm going to imagine that it'll open up to you topless."

I laughed, but a part of me felt delusionally elated enough to think that he may just do that. That when he was CEO at Buescher Enterprises, and I was tucked away working for the publishing branch in Misty Springs, I would exist somewhere in his mind—after this fleeting moment of us was over.

"By the way. You know I can lock the elevator? We can totally shut the world out."

Shutting the world out sounded heavenly. To hang on to this moment, to act like there was nothing else out there.

No crazy exes, no relationship policy, no sick loved ones.

Just us.

"Hmmm…" I said while dramatically tapping my chin, mimicking him. "How about you walk around with no bottoms and just a shirt—like Donald Duck— and *I* get fully dressed."

Ultimately, we settled on him in just his sweats, shirtless, and me in his hoodie, with nothing underneath, and panties.

We walked out of his bedroom and faced the realities of the world outside our happy little cocoon.

But first, he locked the elevator, just in case.

Chapter 40

ESPIONAGE? I'M FUCKING IN

Corbin

"Why the hell did I find out about you hiring Sophia from some random a-hole in accounting? What a horse-shit, egotistical, egocentric thing to do! You told me you didn't want to hire her, that I was 'wasting everyone's time'—now suddenly you do? Oh, and you brought her to New York to introduce her to other board members? What is going on in your head, man?" Andi's *charming* voice crackled the speaker in my ear.

I was grateful that Sophia was too wrapped up in her own phone conversation to hear Andi's maniacal rant.

Andi may have been a certified genius and made my life immensely easier by being so overwhelmingly good at her job, but she could be a loose cannon and threw the most horrendous fits. I'd learned it's best just to let her wear herself out—like a toddler.

"You done?" I asked after Andi's screaming finally reached its decrescendo.

"Yeah, think so," she sighed.

"Good. Look, things changed. She came to the gala with a competing offer, which made her more appealing. Simple as that." I wasn't proud of convincing Andi that hiring Sophia was due to little more than choking out the competition, but it was the reason that would rouse the least amount of suspicion.

"Who?" Andi asked.

"Norwood Corporation," I quickly answered, trying to sound indifferent.

"So, real estate? What does that have to do with publishing?"

"Nothing, but regardless, it changed my mind. Can we move on?"

"Touchy, touchy," she said.

Like she didn't just spend the last five minutes screaming every adjective she could conjure up for the words *egotistical asshole* at me.

"I'll get with HR tomorrow. They can draw up her official offer. I'm sure it'll have to go through some approval process since you're bypassing them completely. 'HR needs to screen her. We have processes, Andi," she added in a mocking, deep voice.

"Copy me in the email. I'll push it through."

She sighed but then let out a giddy giggle. "I'll send the papers to her address on her résumé. We'll get them overnighted. If things move quickly, she'll have them by Tuesday and can start as soon as Wednesday if she doesn't have to give notice. We need someone quick. I hope she can start ASAP."

I swallowed. Two days. How quickly things shifted from trying to convince Andi not to hire her to now expediting the process.

"Great," I choked out.

"See you in two weeks?" she asked.

After spending an entire week in Misty Springs, I told Andi I needed a break before I returned. Now, watching Sophia as she padded barefoot on my kitchen floor, something was tugging at me.

"Yeah. I dunno, maybe sooner." I passively avoided a firm answer and hung up. Andi and I never did goodbyes.

I strode over to the window to view the skyline. The Hudson River reflected the early evening sun as it sank behind the towering skyscrapers. The day was quickly fading into night, and though it felt like one of the longest days of my life, it also felt like it was coming to a screeching end.

The time Sophia and I had spent here—this apartment feeling like a sanctuary for the first time—was something I wasn't ready to let go of yet.

"Corbin?" Sophia asked hesitantly, breaking my thoughts. "It feels a little crazy that I hadn't brought this up yet—I think I was trying to avoid facing reality. But… how am I going to get back to Misty Springs? And when?"

"We'll take the jet. I'll call them and see if we can get out tonight," I said with a tight smile.

The corporate travel agent didn't have a flight out tonight, which was music to my ears. Instead, they booked the jet for Monday morning.

Sophia called Cassie to let her know she could still work at the hotel tomorrow afternoon.

I took advantage of her distraction to make my last call of the night.

"Yello," Sullivan's carefree voice sounded from the other line.

"Hey, I need you to do something for me," I spoke in a voice just above a whisper.

"Okay," Sullivan said, lowering his tone to match mine. "Does it involve espionage? Cause if so, I'm fucking in."

"No, no, it's just a bit of a… sensitive topic, so I'm speaking quietly."

"Where are you?"

"In my apartment," I answered, then quickly smacked my forehead at my oversight.

"Oh ho ho, with who? Whom is it you are keeping this *sensitive topic* from?" he asked, his voice animated.

"Don't worry about it, it's… just listen."

I asked him to keep his ear to the ground, check out every back alley source, and find out any news he could learn about something developing in Misty Springs and anything he could dig up on the Norwood family's recent dealings. I knew that if the Norwoods were sniffing around, they had to have a reason.

I needed to find out what it was and fast. If they'd already been working the town over for a year—whenever Sophia said Landon and his family moved to Misty Springs—their infested roots likely have already taken hold.

"Roger that, have fun with your *no one*, Corby," Sullivan jested before the line went dead.

"Done!" Sophia exclaimed as she plopped down on the couch next to me.

Her gorgeous bare legs stretched out to rest her foot on my coffee table, inching my hoodie up her thigh.

"I ensured everyone knew that I was alive, not kidnapped, not brainwashed, not Landon using a high-pitched voice, and that I would see them all tomorrow."

"Well done." I lifted my phone as I tried to multitask, pulling up the reservation app. "Now… I have good news and bad news."

"Okay, bad news first." She bounced beside me.

My eyes fell on her wiggling chest. Knowing what she looked like underneath those clothes made me feel like I'd won some sort of cosmic lottery.

"Bad news is, my favorite restaurant is booked for tonight. But my second favorite has one table left for seven p.m."

"Was that... the bad and good news combined?"

"No. Now ask me what the good news is." I grinned as I clicked to confirm our reservation.

"Okay. What's the good news?"

"The good news is, we have two hours to kill, and I know exactly how I want to spend that time."

Then, I pounced on her.

Chapter 41

I Quit

Sophia

I tapped my fingers aimlessly as I leaned on the front desk at Elijah's. The events of last night replayed in my head over and over again.

Corbin had decided that it would not only be efficient, but also environmentally conscientious, if we showered together before dinner.

His shower was massive, with jets that caressed our bodies in warm water and a waterfall feature cascading a steady stream from above.

We were very *efficient* with him pressed up against me, his warm, wet body trapping me between him and the cold marble wall. But with the amount of time we spent there, I don't think we saved many gallons of water.

I recalled how the suds trailed down his chest, bumping over the muscles of his stomach. I tracked them with my fingertips. Following the tiny bubbles lower and lower until I wrapped my hands around his...

"Earth to Sophia." Cassie slapped her hand on the desk.

The move knocked me out of my daydream. I straightened, pulling at the wrinkles on my Elijah's polo.

"You said you wanted to talk to me." She crossed her arms, reminding me of how Brent, her brother, always looks when trying to appear intimidating.

Though she's a fraction of his size, she's probably twice as mean.

All of my friends were upset with me. They still didn't know the details of where I stayed in New York, and despite their constant pressing, I didn't have an answer for them.

I couldn't tell them I was with Corbin, for more reasons than one. I didn't want them to think I was repeating the same Landon-shaped pattern again. Also, I feared for the small-town knowledge and rumors that could easily circulate regarding Corbin and me. I trusted my friends implicitly, but the fewer people who knew about us, the better.

Besides, Corbin and I agreed that everything between us would stay in New York. Though the decision tore at my heart in an uncomfortable way, it was how it had to be.

Cassie and I stepped into the backroom. It was a semi-unfinished area with a couple of vending machines, two round linoleum tables with a few mismatched chairs from different eras scattered around them, and a *Mr. Coffee* machine.

I looked at it longingly, recalling that I had never figured out how to use Corbin's spaceship coffee machine.

Cassie looked at me expectantly. "Out with it."

I took a deep breath. Here we go.

I hated disappointing my friends, and leaving Cassie was going to be tough. Working at Elijah's wasn't exactly a dream job, but I loved the people here—Julio, Pam, Cassie, and even Elijah, who, despite his unpredictable nature, was a great guy to work for.

Before I could start, she held up her hand. "But if you're not in here to tell me you got that new job of yours and you are quitting here ASAP to pursue your dream, then it better be something better—because the look on your face is killing me."

Tears sprang up in my eyes. Working with one of your best friends was a privilege, one I would forever be grateful for. I gave her a tight hug.

She wrapped her hands around my waist and hugged me back.

"I quit." I sobbed.

"I accept your resignation," she said smoothly. Cassie wasn't one to wear her emotions on her sleeve like me. "Are you quitting Boomer's too? Devyn will be so disappointed."

"I will eventually. I just haven't decided when yet. I have some financial catching up to do. I especially need to work through Thanksgiving. I can't pass up those Thanksgiving Eve tips."

"Oh, *shit!*" Cassie exclaimed as she threw her head back.

"What shit? What?"

"No, it's nothing. I just…" She looked at me and then looked away quickly.

"Tell meeeeee," I said as I shook her gently.

"Next week is Thanksgiving."

"Yeah," I confirmed, then recognition struck. "Oh."

Thanksgiving was one of the busiest times of the year for Elijah's, too. People came from all over the country to visit loved ones for the holiday in Misty Springs. Not to mention, most of the staff requested time off to spend with their families—most of them, except me.

With the holiday season approaching, the entire downtown looked like a Hallmark movie—with the soft glow of wreaths on every streetlamp and cozy shops with Christmas decor lining their windows.

Cassie had already started dazzling up the lobby with the elaborate decor Elijah insisted on every year.

"It's fine. We'll be fine. I can make it work." She started chewing on her thumbnail.

That move meant she was not fine, and she was not going to make it work.

"I'll stay," I told her, touching her shoulder. "The least I can do is give my current employer two weeks."

"Are you sure they won't care?"

"I haven't signed a thing yet. I haven't even told them a start date."

"Thanks, Soph." She wrapped me in another tight hug.

"Thank you, Cassie—for everything. I wouldn't have survived these last few months without you."

"I'm always here for you, Soph." She backed away, looking at her watch. "Now, go do your job. You're on the clock for another ten minutes."

We walked out of the backroom giggling. Cassie's arm was slung around me in a lazy embrace when I looked at the front desk—and stopped dead in my tracks.

Cassie found the words that were lodged in my throat. "Oh, it's the ever-charming Mr. Buescher, back to annoy us again."

Okay, maybe not the exact words I would have used.

"Ah, hello, Red. Nice to see my time away hasn't lessened your superb hospitality skills," Corbin quipped back.

He turned to me. My breath hitched as I drank in those eyes—my body priming at just the sight of him.

"Sophia," he said as he nodded in my direction, his throaty voice sending shockwaves through my system.

How was I going to work with this man? I could barely control myself when he was around.

"So... now you've taken to *poaching* my employees," Cassie remarked, crossing her arms and leaning across the front desk from him. "Hope you don't expect me to be nice to you just because you're one of my best friend's bosses."

"Actually," Corbin proclaimed as he leaned across the other side, "I'm not her boss. I'm her boss's boss's boss's boss."

"Not yet, you aren't," Cassie said, straightening and placing her hand on her hip.

"You're right, *not yet*." His voice dropped low as he looked at me, causing my thighs to squeeze involuntarily together. "I need to check in," he said as he rang the front desk bell that sat between us.

His eyes slid to mine, his full lips spreading into a "playful Corbin" grin that made my heart feel squishy.

Cassie's eyes bounced between Corbin and me before narrowing slightly. Of all my friends, Cassie had known me the longest—she could read me better than anyone, so I tried my best to school my features.

She glanced at her watch. "Shoot, I have to meet the delivery driver." She glared once more at Corbin. "You'll be happy to know that I ordered it."

Corbin's face lit up. "About time. Is it here?"

I stood curiously near Cassie, silently watching their exchange.

"I'll check today's truck and let you know. Elijah is going to kill me. It was like four hundred dollars."

"I'll buy every single glass from your bar. You can sell it for twenty bucks an ounce, and I'll gladly pay it. You'll easily make at least eighty percent off that bottle from me alone."

"Fine, but you're buying me some too."

"Fine."

It seemed like they must have encountered each other more than I realized.

"What is happening?" I finally chimed in.

Cassie turned to me, resting her arms on the end of the counter. "Mr. Bossy pants McNeedy over here has been begging me to order some Macallan whiskey."

Corbin rolled his eyes.

I couldn't hold in the elated chortle that escaped my throat.

Cassie's joking face shifted to her serious one, the two nearly indecipherable to the untrained eye.

"Treat her good, okay?" she said to Corbin, swallowing as if forcing down words she wanted to say but either couldn't or wouldn't. "She's my best employee."

"Of course." Corbin nodded, his face resolute.

Cassie disappeared behind the kitchen's swinging door, and I once again focused on this confoundedly perplexing man.

He was leaning over the counter again, his face level with mine, our mouths inches apart.

All my thoughts abandoned me, replaced instantly by nothing but a throbbing need. A need that followed me from New York. A need that was obviously not going to be defined by geography— though a part of me hoped it would.

"I need to check in," he reminded me again, his breath hitting my lips.

I reluctantly backed away from him and entered the prompts on the screen to get him checked in. What should've been an easy process was increasingly difficult with my shaky hands and coiling core.

I reached across the counter to hand him the key, his fingers grazed mine as he took it, sending a jolt through my body.

Would this ever subside?

Would my body ever stop kicking into overdrive every time he spoke to me, innocuously touched me, hell—even looked at me?

Corbin stepped back, picking up his leather duffel bag off the floor.

"Room 215, Mr. Buescher." I wet my lips, still partially dry from my earlier mouth-breathing daydreams of our time together in New York.

He tracked the movement, watching as my tongue darted out to meet my lips with a heated intensity.

"Will there be anything else?" I asked, a teasing edge to my voice.

"Yes, actually," he smirked, hoisting his small duffel bag on the counter between us. "I need help carrying my luggage to my room."

Chapter 42

More than Playful Banter and Jell-O Shots

Corbin

I unlocked the door to my room, cursing at the archaic manner in which I had to do so. My hand was shaking like an overexcited prom date who scored a hotel room for the night to get their cherry popped.

Sophia looked around nervously, muttering something about hoping Pam left on time today. I'm sure the flimsy excuse of helping me carry my luggage, one lightweight duffel bag with a change of clothes and a toothbrush, wouldn't hold much weight if we were caught.

I finally got the damn door open and pulled her quickly inside.

She let out a little excited squeak as I yanked her through the threshold.

I shut the door—the spring-loaded system preventing me from closing it as fast as I'd like—and pushed her up against it.

Here we were again, Sophia and I, in my hotel room. Except this time, I didn't have to imagine what she looked like underneath those clothes. I didn't have to dream about how her mouth tasted or wonder what sounds she made when she came undone.

My hands grabbed her hips and pulled her body into mine as my mouth found hers. Blackout curtains and the thick hotel door shut out the evening sun—and the world—from our endeavors.

When Sophia and I were together, it was easy to forget anything but her—easy to get lost in her touch, her moans, her taste—and forget the world burning around me.

Today was stressful. Andi was on edge, still angry with me for going behind her back and wary of the fact I surprised her like a "jackass-in-the-box" by coming into Misty Springs today.

I also learned from a colleague that Buzz had been meeting with an old accountant of Buescher Enterprises without my knowledge, one who retired years ago.

The flimsy rumor Cindy shared with me at the gala was starting to feel more solid.

My head was spinning, doubt was creeping in, and stress was attacking me from all angles.

We said we weren't doing this again, that this stayed behind in my Manhattan apartment.

But I needed this.

I needed her.

I broke our kiss as dread hit me. I had quickly packed this morning, not thinking about us having a chance to be together again.

I was unprepared.

"I don't have a condom," I admitted, defeated.

Sophia shrugged. "I've had the implant since Landon. And not to kill the mood, but I got tested after... just in case—not knowing who all he'd been with besides me. I'm clean."

"I'm clean, too," I said, not going into details, but it was something I kept up with.

I was always careful—never letting my guard down, not around some of the women in my world. I never had sex without a condom—ever. Some women almost made it a sport to find ways to squeeze money out of men like me. There were plenty of honest women, too—the problem was telling the difference.

But Sophia's honesty was bone deep—something about her burrowed beneath the surface of every doubt, every fear, every ache within me.

I kissed her again, deeper this time, my tongue meeting hers, relishing in the taste of my new favorite flavor.

Her hands dropped to my pants, working my belt loose. She was so greedy, so rushed.

I fucking loved it.

But I didn't want to rush with her, not when these fleeting moments would be over quickly—too quickly.

I pulled back, breaking our kiss, a smile spreading across my face. "Always so greedy."

"I don't have much time. I have to get to work," she whimpered.

"I thought you were done with work," I whispered each word between peppered kisses on her neck—pleasantly elated with myself as her body vibrated with pleasure.

"I'm done with *this* job. I have to get to Boomer's next. Devyn will be at my place to pick me up in like thirty minutes."

Thirty minutes? That's all I had?

There was likely an envelope with her official offer waiting on her doorstep. I was heading back tomorrow and then spending the next two weeks—through Thanksgiving, in New York.

This could be our last time together. The thought hit me harder than I thought it would. I waved those thoughts away, focusing on the task at hand.

"I can work with thirty minutes," I said as I pulled her tucked-in shirt from her pants and brushed my hands over her stomach.

"Try ten minutes." She winced. "I need to walk to my apartment first and get ready."

"What if I drive you?" I growled.

"That'll save us about eight minutes." Her soft hands glided under my shirt, causing every muscle to twitch with excitement under her touch.

"Eighteen minutes it is." I pulled her shirt over her head and crushed my lips to hers again.

I'd never been addicted to anything. I forced myself to be disciplined enough to fight against addiction, knowing I'd be prone to it. But as I kissed Sophia, my head felt light, my entire body thrummed, and I felt utterly and completely alive.

It felt like a high I wanted to chase forever.

She unbuttoned my shirt, our race against time rushing her movements. We moved in sync over to the bed, Sophia pushing into me until the back of my legs pressed against the plush mattress.

With a wicked grin that made my heart palpitate, she pulled at my belt in one swift motion. It clanged as she dropped it to the floor, her hands moving quickly to the button of my pants.

I liked control—craved control—but hot, greedy, forceful Sophia taking what she wanted from me was a new fantasy I hadn't thought to dream up.

I let my body relax and allowed her to push me down on the mattress. She stood over me and forcefully pulled my slacks and my boxers down to the floor, releasing every inch of me.

Her caramel hair cascaded down her shoulders over her lacy bra as she leaned over me with her hands on my thighs.

She bit her lower lip as she stared at me—hard and ready—always ready for her.

"I think I should return the favor from last night, don't you?" she asked with all the sweetness of a dominatrix.

She wet her lips and bent at her hips, her mouth inches from my cock. Her tongue darted out and licked my tip, and my brain short-circuited.

She wrapped her soft hand around the base and took me in her mouth. Her tongue swirled in a euphoric cyclone that made my eyes roll back in my head. She lowered her head, keeping her hand at the base, going deeper and deeper until I hit the back of her throat.

Yes, I'd give her control.

I'd give her anything.

I watched her intently, focusing on every detail and storing it in my brain. I wanted it there forever, kept on my hard drive like a lustful secret file, able to pull it open when she became nothing but a memory to me.

She looked up at me with a satisfied, lustful smile—her eyes watery, her lips swollen.

I quickly wondered how much time we had left, concerned that this may be the last time I could have her. I didn't want to stop her talented mouth, but I wanted to be buried inside of her more.

I sat up, grabbed her shoulders, and pushed her slightly back. She watched me with quiet anticipation, her eyes dancing with desire.

Her time of control was over.

It was my turn now.

I stood, towering over her delicate frame, and hastily unfastened her bra, dropping it to the floor. My hands made quick work of taking off her jeans, sliding them down her body along with her sexy little thong.

I tugged at my open shirt, letting it fall to the floor, and we stood there for a moment, both naked and primed, breathing in each other's air.

Seconds ticked by, and we both shared a look of desperation, realizing that we didn't have as much time as we wanted.

And not just now—not just before her next shift—not enough time to figure *us* out.

Simultaneously, we crashed into one another. Our kiss was a frantic barrage of teeth and tongue.

She bit my lip, and I lost the ability to think clearly.

I was unleashed. A primal hunger raged through me—there was nothing but her and pure, unfiltered need.

I threw her on the bed, her ass near the edge. The mattress was a perfect height for me to line up to her wet center.

I couldn't wait any longer, officially reaching the end of my restraint, and I buried myself inside of her.

The feel of her, wet and unrestricted, was incredible. Anything—anyone—before her was forgotten, wiped away with each thrust.

"Sophia, you *undo* me," I shuddered through my breath before pulling back and slamming into her again.

I looked down at where we connected. Watching as I drove into her over and over, how good she took every inch of me—another memory I would store forever in my brain.

This was not slow. This was not innocent. This was fast and heady, and sexy as hell.

She moaned my name as I felt her tightening around me, her walls closing in as she got closer and closer to release.

I held on, keeping mine at bay, though it was nearly impossible with how she felt around me.

I took my thumb in my mouth, moistening it before bringing it down to her clit. I pressed gently at first, before building up. Faster. Harder.

"Oh God!" she screamed as I felt her pulse around me, her walls contracting against my cock.

The feel of her release unraveled me, making me lose every last ounce of resolve before I erupted inside of her.

I fell on top of her, my feet still on the floor, our bodies on the plush mattress.

We lay there for a moment, lost in the aftermath of lust and need and broken agreements. I pushed up and looked down at her face, flush and lightly dewed with sweat.

She was breathtaking.

This beautiful, broken girl saw every jagged piece of me, every scar, every ache, and still looked at me like she was now—like I was her everything, like I was every bit a part of her as she was of me.

My mind wandered down a dangerous path, one that considered Sophia might decline the offer from Buescher-Jones Publishing—a path we could explore without me risking my bid for CEO.

But I learned long ago that you can't force people to choose you.

I pulled out of her, my entire body protesting at the loss of her warmth. If I thought these rooms were haunted by Sophia before, they were now completely possessed, a phantasmal experience I'd never escape during my stays at Elijah's.

We dressed in silence, me watching her, her watching me watch her.

Sophia peeked out the window, and an orange streak from the sinking sun beamed into the hotel room, illuminating tiny dust motes as they fluttered through the air.

"Coast is clear. Ready to run?" Sophia asked me with a grin.

I nodded, and she flung open the door. We darted toward my car like a couple of kids sneaking out past curfew, giggling and breathless.

We slid into the small BMW SUV.

Her cheeks tinged pink, whether from the cold, the excitement, or the mind-blowing sex we'd just had, I couldn't tell.

She looked radiant—glowing in a way that made my chest tighten. She was adorable, and that thought alone startled me. I wasn't the guy who found things *adorable*.

My hand reached for hers on instinct, our fingers entwining effortlessly.

I also didn't hold hands. I never had the desire to, and I couldn't remember ever acting on such an impulse. But with Sophia, it felt natural—like something I had to do.

When she wasn't near me, I wanted her. When she was, I needed to touch her, hold her—anything to keep her close.

The drive to her apartment was quick—too quick—the engine's hum filling the silence. My mind welled with too many thoughts, all of which were impossible to articulate.

When we pulled up to her building, I let her hand slip from mine reluctantly as I shifted the car into park.

She turned toward me, her eyes meeting mine—big, expressive, and impossible to read. She sucked her bottom lip between her teeth, a move so innocently sexy it sent a jolt through me.

I'd never get enough of her. The obtrusive and uninvited thought popped into my head.

"Cassie asked me to stay at Elijah's through Thanksgiving," she said to the dashboard after turning away from me. "But you'll be away until then, so I guess this is..."

She didn't finish. Didn't have to.

I turned my attention toward my hand as it tightened on the steering wheel, knuckles turning white.

This was goodbye. Goodbye to any attempt to see if we could be something more.

Boss and subordinate, that's it.

I nodded. The only part of me that moved. "Right." The word came out clipped—shallow—like I couldn't afford to let it dig any deeper.

"It's probably for the best—the time apart. Once I start... It's not like this could keep going." She gestured between us with a casual flick of her wrist.

I turned and searched her face, desperate for something—a flicker of hesitation, a sign that she was as torn up as I was. Anything to prove this wasn't as easy for her to switch *us* off as she made it sound.

"Sure," I said, my voice low, hands dropping into fists in my lap. "We'll be professionals."

"So we're aligned? It's totally over now."

Totally over.

Like we were nearing the end of a contract. No hard feelings—just business.

The finality in her words, the casual tone of her voice—they clashed hard against the memory of the woman who curled into me last night, soft and unguarded in my arms.

Maybe I misread it.

Maybe because I never let anyone in, the simple act of opening up made everything feel bigger—deeper—than it really was. Maybe I mistook my own vulnerability for something more.

"Yeah, agreed. We're aligned," I shot back, unable to stop myself. "I'll be back in New York most of the time anyway. We won't run into each other much. Not at all once the branch is off the ground."

Her expression faltered, just for a moment, but she recovered quickly, her walls going up so fast I barely had time to notice the crack—or maybe that was just me pretending she cared.

She grabbed her bag and opened the car door. "Goodbye, Corbin."

I silently let her go.

The shutting of her car door sounded jarring in the quiet cab, the air thick with my disappointment and her floral scent.

She walked away without looking back. I watched every step she took across the parking lot, every climb of her stairs until she slid behind her apartment door.

This was absurd—the tightening in my throat, the heavy stone I felt in my gut—this feeling of loss for a woman who was never even mine in the first place.

Throwing the car into reverse, I drove myself back to the office. I'd get more work done now that Andi wasn't there to glare at me.

This was why I didn't let myself get distracted. Letting someone in, even for a moment, threw everything off balance.

Things were off to a good start—no, a *great* start—for the Misty Springs branch. That was what I needed to focus on.

That was the goal. The plan. What I wanted.

Deviating from my life's goal for a woman I hardly knew was not the objective here.

So why did it feel like I was driving away from my dreams, not towards them?

Chapter 43

Hockey Team Soirée

Sophia

I told myself I wasn't falling for Corbin. That, whatever this feeling was, it couldn't be heartbreak—we hadn't even gotten far enough for that.

But the truth was there, painful and persistent, like a hangnail.

I wasn't falling for Corbin. I fell.

And even if I stopped myself before I hit the bottom, I didn't come away unscathed.

I tied more and more invisible threads tighter and tighter to him with every moment we shared—threads we just severed, cutting through them with our words in his car.

I was grateful for the clear divide between what we were and what we weren't. I needed to keep my head on straight. Focus on me, focus on my future.

I couldn't do this again.

I couldn't change my life's course for a guy—couldn't let my heart rule over my head.

Even if he was the most handsome man I think I'd ever seen in real life. Even if I found the pieces he shared with me endearing and wholesome, turning him from some untouchable Adonis to a beautifully imperfect man.

I wondered how many people knew the Corbin Buescher I knew? How his shattered past carved him from stone to this unyielding force. How beautiful his unguarded heart is. How gentle his rough hands could be.

I texted Devyn to let her know I'd be late meeting her and hurried to prepare for another long night.

219

A thick FedEx envelope was leaning against my apartment door after Corbin dropped me off. My heart fluttered in my chest before plunging into my stomach as I read through the offer from Buescher-Jones Publishing.

Salary, benefits, vacation days, holidays, sick days. Exactly the kind of career I had been dreaming of. But why did every high in my life seem to be met with a crashing low?

I shook my head, clearing my thoughts. Corbin and I might have ended before we had a real chance to begin, but a new chapter of my life was unfolding—one that was just for me.

I pulled on my black V-neck, the one with *"Boomer's, it's dynamite"* screen-printed across the back—and stared at my reflection, trying to convince myself that this was the beginning of something, not the end.

But no matter how hard I stared at the high-pony-tailed, soon-to-be-retired bartender in the mirror, I still ached for what almost was.

***

"You're crazy if you think we're missing out on five-dollar pitcher night. Besides, you need someone to drive you home." Brent slurped some of the foam directly from the pitcher I handed him.

It was a slow night, even for a Monday, but we never closed before midnight. Even if it meant just one person stayed to work alone. Boomer's was to remain a haven for anyone who wanted a late-night drink, no matter what. But not even the cheap draft special seemed to draw people in tonight.

Devyn had to catch an early flight and decided to spend the night at her parents' house. They had bought her a ticket to her grandparents' home in Puerto Rico. I told her to leave me tonight so she could finish packing and get some sleep before her long flight.

So, Sam, Brent, and Trevor decided to come and enjoy the cheap, stale beer from the weekend kegs that didn't sell like we thought they would.

"This one is on me."

"You don't have to do that," Brent attested.

"I insist," I cut him off.

I was about to officially stop being a burden on my friends. In a few weeks, I would start my new job, and stop forcing them to uproot their lives just because I was such a failure.

"I have a big girl job I'm about to start. It's about time I start repaying you guys," I said as I wiped my hands on my jeans.

"You know you don't owe us anything, Soph. We're practically family. Family is there for each other, no matter what." Brent smiled softly before tipping his pitcher at me. "But, thanks."

I watched him retreat behind a partitioned wall where Trevor, Sam, and the dartboards were. His features were so much like Cassie's, unchanging from our youth—authentic, real, familiar.

I couldn't help but smile despite the hole in my chest left from my conversation with Corbin earlier. Things were coming together for me—sure not in the love department—but I had the most incredible group of people to rally behind me and a shiny new career on the horizon.

I glanced around the barroom. There was a couple quietly chatting in the corner. They slowly sipped the cocktails I made for them twenty minutes ago—no rush for another drink—no rush to be anywhere besides the quiet company of each other.

It was sweet… it made me want to puke.

I walked into the kitchen to find Paul, the other cook at Boomer's, leaning against the prep station, his face lit by the dull glow of his phone. He was quiet, the kind of guy who mostly kept to himself. Married, with a kid—maybe two? Honestly, I wasn't sure. What I did know was that he'd already finished most of his closing duties, judging by the spotless counters and the mop leaning against the wall.

The kitchen officially closed at ten, and he'd be leaving soon. He didn't even look up when he spoke to me. "Slow night, huh?"

"Yep," I replied, popping the "p" with exaggerated enthusiasm.

Right then, the chime of the front door echoed through the bar. Once. Twice. Then again. Paul and I exchanged glances as the sound of heavy footsteps filled the space.

We pushed through the swinging door together and were met by a flood of guys, at least thirty—maybe even forty—in mismatched hockey jerseys. Some had damp hair, fresh from a shower; others were still glistening with dried sweat.

"You guys still open?" one of the men asked.

He stood at the front of the pack, about my age, with curly blonde hair, warm walnut eyes, and a dimple that should've come with a warning label.

"Yeah," I said, my voice a little unsure as I glanced at Paul.

"Great. We just finished a hockey tournament. Loser buys dinner for the winner, and this is the only place still open."

As he approached the bar, I shot Paul a pleading stare. Closing the kitchen early was one of life's greatest joys, and nothing was worse than having to undo hours of work to dirty it all up again.

I leaned toward him and whispered, "I'll give you forty percent of my tips."

Paul glanced at the horde, then back at me, shaking his head with a resigned sigh. "Deal. Bring me the tickets when you're ready." He sauntered back toward the kitchen with the slow, deliberate steps of a man whose peace had just been stolen.

I turned back to the dimpled blonde and his army of hungry teammates. "I'll grab you some menus," I said with a smile I planned to keep plastered on all night.

I hoped they were good tippers.

Behind me, I could practically hear Paul muttering under his breath before he entered the kitchen. I knew what he was thinking—I was thinking it, too.

So much for a slow night.

Chapter 44

CRICKET

Corbin

After finishing up at the office, I was too keyed up to lock myself in my hotel room for the evening. The crumpled comforter reminded me of my afternoon with Sophia and the bruise on my heart from the conversation that followed.

I wandered into the lobby, knowing I wouldn't find Sophia. Instead, I found Cassie, who insisted I start buying some of those "damn expensive whiskey drinks I forced her to order."

I spent over a hundred dollars on drinks. Only one was for me, the rest Cassie guzzled down after her shift ended.

I didn't know where she put them. She was small, maybe five foot five, and slender, but she drank more than I'd seen most men handle.

She and I had developed… not quite a friendship but more of a mutual understanding. After she caught me off guard with her comment about Sophia, I cleared the air with her. After that, we would occasionally talk during my stays at Elijah's—if you could call quips, backhanded comments, and the occasional roast "talking."

I found Cassie's company refreshingly easy. We could share silence without it ever feeling awkward. Through her, I picked up bits and pieces about Sophia—fragments of who she was, seen through the eyes of someone who clearly cared for her. Cassie spoke about Sophia with genuine admiration.

I also learned Cassie's dad owned the construction company working on our office space, and that her brother, Brent—the beast of a man who dropped off plans on my first day—was part of the crew.

The more time I spent here, the more I realized Misty Springs wasn't just a town—it was a web of people tightly woven together. So many stories overlapped, like books in a series.

Cassie even mentioned her grandmother used to know mine. They both used to volunteer at the town library before she moved away.

That small detail stuck with me more than I expected. No one mentioned my grandmother unless it concerned Buzz or the company. This piece of history was solely Gram's. It was like finding a thread from the past stitched straight into the present—and into this strange little town I hadn't meant to care about.

After the bar closed at Elijah's around ten, I found myself venturing out into the cool evening with another destination in mind—I was a glutton for punishment.

I pulled into Boomer's parking lot and was surprised by the number of cars still there this late on a Monday.

What was I even doing here?

I sat in the car, drumming my fingers on the steering wheel, steeling myself against the irrational urge to go inside. As I stared at the building, a couple walked out, the guy casually throwing his arm around the girl.

They moved together through the cold parking lot, their foggy breaths puffing into the night air. He leaned down and whispered something in her ear, and she laughed as she nestled into his chest.

The whole thing was disgusting.

I took a breath and, against my better judgment, walked through the door into Boomer's.

Sophia was busy, far too busy to even notice me walk in. Engrossed with jotting down orders amongst a sea of rather large, athletic-looking men.

The scene settled uneasily in my veins. The way those tight jeans hugged her ass, the way her hips swayed as she shimmied her way around the table, the low *V* of her shirt—the way they all noticed it, too.

I walked over to the bar, which held even more burly men.

What the hell was going on tonight that caused all of these guys to be here? Where did they come from? The whole scene was chaotic.

I was just about to admit defeat, turn around, and leave when I saw a flash of red in my periphery. With his trimmed beard, it took me a moment, but I eventually recognized Brent.

He strode behind the bar like he worked here, tossing an empty beer pitcher in the air before refilling it at the tap.

He glanced up at me, recognition filling his face. "Hey, fancy seeing you here."

I shrugged. "I needed a drink. Thought I'd stop in."

"It's a little louder than usual tonight." He glanced around, scowling at the crowded bar before turning back to me. "You like darts?"

"I do."

"Good, we need a fourth." He plucked a pint glass from behind him before stepping out from the bar. He cocked his head at me to follow.

Beer wasn't my first choice, but something told me I'd be waiting a while before Sophia could spare a moment to get me anything different. Assuming she could spare any of her attention tonight.

I felt slightly defeated as my planless plan to talk to Sophia failed as I followed Brent past a dividing wall. The scene back here was quieter, more relaxed.

"That's Sam." He pointed the pitcher toward a guy with mahogany-colored hair and a matching beard, who gave a quick wave. "This is Trevor," he added, nodding to a bright-eyed man with a few wild, light-colored tresses peeking out from under a backward baseball cap.

I nodded toward the group, but a sudden unease hit me in the lingering seconds that ticked by after our brief introduction.

I was used to crowds that buzzed with distraction—live music loud enough to fill any silence, champagne glasses constantly refilled before they were ever emptied, and conversations that barely skimmed the surface.

But here?

Here, there were no velvet ropes, no calculated small talk, no scripted pleasantries disguised as networking.

Just me and them.

I shifted my weight, suddenly hyperaware of how out of place I might seem. And for the first time in a long time, I wasn't sure how to blend in.

Thankfully, Brent didn't allow my anxiety to rise too high before he slapped me on my back, introducing me in return.

"Guys, this is Corbin, and he and I are about to mop the floor with you at Cricket."

Chapter 45

Back Alley Bad Decisions

Sophia

My feet were aching, and my back was killing me by the time the last hockey player left with a belly full of food and beer.

I glanced at my watch. We closed five minutes ago, but I had a few things to do before I could leave.

Muted laughter carried from the dartboard area, followed by a gleeful yell that sounded like Brent and a couple of painful moans from Trevor and Sam. The sound of their antics softened the tension knotted in my chest, bringing a small smile to my face. If they were stuck here because of me, at least they were having a good time.

The guys had come here so many times when we were swamped that we devised a system. For each pitcher they filled, they left a tally for Devyn or me, whoever was tending the bar. That way, they didn't distract us from customers, and we didn't prevent them from "getting their buzz on."

Paul left soon after his last dish was plated. I told him I'd make good on my promise to split my tips with him.

I counted the tips left by the last-minute swarm of guys and a phone number courtesy of Dimples.

I tossed the number, my life was way too complicated for that right now, and put Paul's share in an envelope I labeled with his name before sliding it into the register.

I walked through the swinging door into the empty kitchen. Paul had left it mostly pristine, but I spied a few large trash bags that didn't reach the dumpster. I couldn't blame him—he had a family waiting for him to get home.

The muscles in my arms protested as I dragged the heavy bags to the back door. I heaved it open with a grunt, wincing as a blast of frigid air tore through the threshold.

The back lot of Boomer's was shrouded in an eerie stillness, the creepy factor intensified by the hazy light of the nearly full moon casting long shadows across the pale gravel.

Propping the door open, I grabbed the first bag and struggled to hoist it into the dumpster. My fingers ached from the cold, but after a bit of effort, I managed to toss both bags in. Their clang echoed sharply, bouncing off the surrounding buildings and fading into the unsettling silence.

I paused, brushing my hands together to chase away the sting of the icy air. Something about the lot felt... off. My pulse quickened as a prickle of unease crawled over my skin. The lot was empty, but the sense of being watched wormed its way into my gut.

I shook it off, determined not to spook myself. With a brisk stride, I speed-walked back toward the propped-open door. Relief hovered just within reach, but as I crossed the threshold, a cold hand clamped around my arm.

My breath hitched, panic surging through my body as I was yanked backward into the freezing night air.

Chapter 46

SEEING RED

Corbin

I sipped on flat beer and leaned against a sticky table, the faint scent of spilled liquor and stale beer clinging to the wood.

I threw darts at a battered dartboard, its face missing a few numbers. Only faint impressions remained where the metal rungs used to be, still present enough to mark our targets.

I listened to stories about people I didn't know in a town I barely recognized.

And I had a surprisingly good time doing it.

Brent and I easily beat Trevor and Sam in the first game, but they caught on to something in the second. We had to play one more to break the tie, but Brent and I clinched it in the end when I threw a double bullseye.

As we sipped on the last of our beer, the noise from the bar area had grown quiet. Hopefully, the mass of guys had cleared out at this point.

I felt a twinge of jealousy at the images I conjured up of one or two of them lingering to flirt with the hot bartender.

"Good game, man," Brent said as he shook my hand firmly.

"Yeah, I'd ask you to join our Tuesday night league if you were going to stick around," Trevor added.

Brent had filled in the blank spaces of who I was for Trevor and Sam. They pressed me for a few personal questions, enough to scratch the surface. The news of Sophia's new job had already spread to them—and based on what I could tell, that was the only news that had spread to them—and they ribbed me about my newest employee.

Besides that, their stories and jokes flowed easily, carrying the conversation through the evening.

It was simple, lighthearted fun.

It struck me how different this was from nights with Davis and Sullivan back in New York. With them, there was always an edge to our conversations, a calculated undertone beneath the surface. Every laugh came with an agenda, every drink carried an unspoken barter. It wasn't just friendship—it was strategy, a constant game of chess where trust was just another piece to be played. I didn't fault them for it. It was my nature, too.

But sitting here, sharing aimless stories with Trevor, Brent, and Sam, I realized how rare it was to let my guard down. No stakes, no angles—just the fleeting simplicity of cheap beer and friendly competition.

I felt like this could also be my nature—two different worlds, two different lives, two different brands of fun.

"I'll make sure Soph got all these tallied up," Sam stated as he carried the empty pitcher with him toward the other side of the wall.

I started gathering the empty glasses and followed close behind, wanting to ensure I paid the bill. I figured it was the least I could do. These guys unknowingly turned a shitty night into a halfway decent one.

The bar was empty—no more burly men—but also no more Sophia.

"Soph!" Sam called out, his voice echoing in the space. The sound of the glass pitcher being set on the bar was almost noisy in the now quiet room.

"This is creepy," Sam remarked.

I set the glasses down, and a sinking feeling settled in my gut. I felt a cold gust of air prickling my skin as I walked to the end of the bar. I peered down a small corridor where a backdoor was propped open, leading to a dimly lit gravel lot.

I didn't think, just acted, and stormed outside into the biting cold. I let my eyes adjust to the darkness. The chill bit through my shirt, but I barely felt it.

My gaze darted frantically across the dimly lit parking lot, and my breath clouded the air.

"Sophia!" I shouted, my voice echoing into the stillness. No response. Just the eerie quiet of the empty lot. My pulse pounded as I quickened my pace, each step heavy with dread.

"Get off of me!" Sophia's voice cut through the silence, sharp and desperate, coming from behind the concrete wall near the dumpster.

Adrenaline surged like wildfire as I sprinted toward her voice, my veins fueled by alcohol, fear, and unrelenting rage.

When I rounded the corner, I saw him. Gripping her arm like she owed him something that he was intent on taking.

Sophia's face was flushed, her breath coming in harsh puffs, and her eyes were wide with fear.

His smug expression vanished the second he saw me.

Landon *fucking* Norwood.

I didn't hesitate. I slammed into him, shoving him back with all the force I could muster. He stumbled, his hand slipping from her arm as he caught himself against the wall.

His shock was evident—he hadn't expected me, especially not here.

"Corbin!" Sophia's voice wavered, a mix of relief and fear.

But I couldn't focus on her.

All I felt was anger, red-hot and relentless, coursing through me.

All I saw was Landon, and he was a fucking dead man.

Chapter 47

BIG BROTHER(S)

Sophia

I was frozen—frozen in fear, and just plain frozen.

One minute, Landon had me pinned against the wall, his vice-like grip on my arm making escape impossible. His voice was desperate, pleading, *begging* me to reconsider taking him back.

The stench of alcohol rolled off him, his bloodshot eyes wild and unfocused.

I tried to shove him off, but his grip was iron, his drunken strength fueled by some twisted determination to make me listen. My t-shirt did nothing to shield me from the cold, and a deep sense of dread hit me as I realized my friends couldn't hear me yell.

I braced myself, ready to knee him in the balls as a last resort, when suddenly, Corbin appeared. He came out of nowhere—a force of nature—and hurled Landon off me with a snarl that made even *me* flinch.

Landon staggered back, eyes wide with shock, clearly not expecting anyone to come to my rescue, least of all someone he never expected to see in Misty Springs.

Footsteps crunched behind me, fast and deliberate. My friends spilled out into the freezing night, taking in the scene: me shivering against the wall, Corbin looming over Landon like a storm on the verge of breaking.

Trevor was at my side in an instant, wrapping an arm around me to guide me back inside. I leaned into his warmth for a moment, but something in me resisted. I didn't want to leave. Not yet.

I didn't want Corbin to do something he'd regret.

The rage radiating from him was visceral, like a living, breathing thing. It was palpable, suffocating.

Landon wasn't worth it. *I* wasn't worth it.

Brent moved quickly, wrapping his arms around Corbin's chest, trying to pull him back. Sam hurriedly stepped between Corbin and Landon, arms outstretched like a referee in a boxing match about to turn dirty.

Corbin thrashed against Brent's grip, his fury untamed, his eyes fixed on Landon as if the guy was the sole source of everything wrong in the world.

"He's not worth it, Corbin," Brent said firmly, his voice steady as he shot a hard look at Landon. "Trust me."

Wait. Since when did *Brent* know Corbin?

"You stay the fuck away from her!" Corbin roared, shaking Brent off with a shove.

Sam stood as a silent barrier, but Landon still stumbled backward at Corbin's approach, his bravado crumbling as he took a few shaky steps away.

Landon looked at Corbin, and then at me—his eyes reflecting hurt and betrayal, followed by a hint of malice.

"Guess you'll just fuck anyone who hires you, huh, Sophia?" he spat, swaying slightly.

"Get the hell out of here before we all kick your ass, Landon. God knows it's been a long time coming," Trevor's voice roared with fury.

I'd never heard Trevor talk that way before—to anyone. He was always lighthearted and easygoing, but this was a side of him that had an edge I didn't realize existed.

Landon backed away, then retreated on swaying steps—unscathed—with the exception of his ego.

I watched Corbin, his chest heaving, his fists clenched at his sides as Landon disappeared into the night. His jaw was tight, the muscles flexing as though he was still fighting to hold back whatever was left of the storm raging inside of him.

This wasn't just about some business rivalry or lingering resentment. No, this was *different*.

The guys looked between Corbin and me, their faces painted with intrigue as they witnessed the same thing I was.

Corbin noticed the tension, the flames taming in his eyes as his usual tightly controlled sense of self returned.

He walked up to me, keeping a safe distance, but his face was full of concern. "Are you okay?"

I nodded, too quickly, taking in a shaky breath. "Yeah, I'm fine, he didn't hurt me."

"Good." He fixed the cuff of his sleeves nonchalantly before looking at the guys. "It's been a pleasure, gentlemen, but I have an early morning tomorrow."

He walked back inside, not sparing any of us a second glance.

I shut the lid to the dumpster, my brain unable to focus on anything besides closing, looking for a distraction, begging for a reprieve.

The guys silently followed me inside, Trevor coming in last, shutting and locking the back door behind him.

Two crisp hundred-dollar bills lay on the bar near four empty pint glasses and a pitcher.

I longingly picked them up, staring at the twin Ben Franklins like they had the answers to all the questions spinning through my head.

"Um, Soph," Trevor said my name like a question.

I turned to look at him, and all three men stood side by side. Their arms were crossed, their expressions a mix of concern and stern disapproval, the kind you'd get from protective brothers catching you sneaking in past curfew.

"Wanna tell us what the hell all that was about?" Brent demanded.

Chapter 48

GOING DOWN, DOWN

Corbin

It had been four days since I last saw Sophia.

Four days of no contact.

Four days of sticking to what we agreed to.

Totally over.

I flew back to New York the morning after nearly bashing Landon's face in. I felt like an ass for leaving Sophia after what he put her through. But I had to remind myself that I wasn't her boyfriend or even her friend, for that matter. I was grateful she had Brent, Sam, and Trevor looking out for her—I'm not sure I could keep my distance if that weren't the case.

Sophia left me feeling raw and emotional—so unlike myself. The lack of restraint when dealing with Landon proved that.

I buried myself in work and tried my best to think of anything besides the countdown to her start date. Andi informed me that Sophia had submitted her paperwork, and the process had begun to get her into the system.

The Monday following Thanksgiving, she'd be a Buescher-Jones Publishing employee.

That was ten days away.

My fingers drummed on the polished desk at Buescher Enterprises' Manhattan office. Things were quieting down quickly—like a silent alarm sounded right at five p.m., signaling everyone to exit immediately.

I didn't welcome the silence like I usually did. The noise and chaos were a welcome distraction from the girl who was hundreds of miles away—yet somehow everywhere.

I saw her face in unsuspecting coworkers, only for it to vanish when I blinked.

Her scent still clung to the fabrics in my apartment.

Her phantom moans still echoed in my ears when I lay my head down at night.

I was pathetic.

I picked up my phone for the hundredth time, fingers lingering on the contact, reading her name. The numbers we exchanged on the plane ride back to Misty Springs. The plane ride where we naively believed we were leaving *us* behind in New York.

I slammed my phone face down on my desk—a little harder than necessary and went back to work. I forced the complicated thoughts away of an unattainable girl with something attainable—CEO.

As if my mind wasn't preoccupied enough, Sullivan strolled in and plopped down in my office chair with an exasperated sigh.

I didn't look up, deep in schedules, pushing to finish this latest project.

He sighed once more, louder and more exaggerated than before.

"Can I help you?" I asked, finally looking up at his exasperated face.

"No," he said, lounging in my chair like he owned the place, one leg crossed casually over the other. He inspected his fingernails with the lazy indifference of a man with nothing better to do.

His tailored umber suit looked like it had been stitched directly onto him, and his sandy blonde hair was slicked back with precision. A manila envelope rested on his thigh, tucked under his hand.

He dropped his leg and leaned forward. "But I can help you." He flung the envelope on my desk with a thud.

"What's this?" I picked it up, prying open the metal closure.

"My Christmas list," he deadpanned. "What do you think it is? You asked me to use my sources to dig up what I could on that creepy little family and Misty Springs."

"And?" I asked.

"Just look in the damn folder, gosh." He crossed one arm across his torso, resting his opposite elbow on his hand. "You make the *worst* spy."

I did as he said, and the thrill of victory thrummed through my veins.

Photographs, transcripts, bank records. Even records of untraceable wire transfers between the Norwood family and a company I knew in my bones was a money laundering front—just a few phone calls to the right people would confirm that for me.

I wasn't sure how Sullivan got it, but there was a shady affidavit signed by a sheriff's deputy with the Norwood last name—like *that* wasn't a strange coincidence.

The documents were a web of deceit, everything I needed to bring them down. This wasn't just about bad business practices. This was bribery, money laundering, fraud—all tied to the Norwood family.

This was exactly what I needed to finally put an end to the splinter under my finger that was Landon Norwood. If this hit the press, it wouldn't just be their empire that fell—it would be their entire legacy. Jail time, lawsuits, criminal charges—they'd lose it all.

This was better than punching Landon's prickish face in. This hit the entire scummy family—harder than my fists could.

And the best part?

They'd never see it coming.

"This is perfect," I said to Sullivan with a grin. "I could kiss you!"

"Can we cuddle after?" he asked, jutting out his lower lip.

***

"Quiet, Landon!" Alicia snapped, her shrill voice slicing through the stifling tension in the back office of Norwood Realty.

"Yes, Landon. Quiet," I said, leaning back in the desk chair with a smirk. "The adults are speaking."

His jaw tightened, his face twisting into a sulk.

I was getting under his skin. Perfect.

"Here's how this is going to work," I said, my tone cool but firm. "You're going to leave Misty Springs. Quietly. No grand exits or desperate attempts to save face. You'll sell every single property you acquired illegally—at fair market value. And for the people you've already screwed over? You'll dissolve their contracts and let them buy back their properties under fair and legal terms."

The room was deathly silent.

Landon glared daggers at me, his lips twitching like he wanted to argue but didn't dare.

Alicia sat frozen, her expression unreadable beneath layers of Botox.

Perry, on the other hand, looked... *relieved*. His shoulders slumped, and there was something almost resigned in his eyes, as though he'd been waiting for someone to end this charade for years.

I leaned forward, steepling my fingers as if this were a boardroom negotiation instead of an ultimatum.

"And if you think that government contract is going to pan out, you're sadly mistaken." I paused for dramatic effect, though it was difficult. This next bit was the smoking gun, the reason that drew this sniveling family to Misty Springs in the first place.

"It turns out, we have some similar acquaintances, and when it came to the choice between building in Misty Springs or Wapakoneta—they chose Ohio. Fun fact: it's the birthplace of Neil Armstrong. Who knew?"

Their illegally acquired properties were useless without the government contract—they had nothing tethering them here now.

This was the only way out. If I had taken this evidence to the authorities, their properties would be tied up in legal battles for years. Misty Springs would suffer foreclosures and plummeting values. Maybe Buescher Enterprises could step in eventually, but that's a long road—messy and painful.

Perry sighed heavily, rubbing a hand over his face. "We'll do it," he said at last, his voice hoarse with fatigue.

"Smart choice." I straightened in my chair, dropping my voice, sharp as a blade. "But trust—if you try anything like this again, I'll find out. I'll come for you, and I'll finish what I started. I. Own. You."

Alicia's jaw tightened, and through gritted teeth, she hissed, "Fine."

I rose, buttoning my navy suit jacket and smoothing the sleeves. Sullivan had joked about me playing the spy, but right now? I felt like James Bond—if Bond were dismantling shitty wannabe empires instead of saving the world.

My polished leather shoes clicked as I turned toward the door. At the threshold, I paused, glancing back at the defeated trio.

"Oh, and Landon," I added, rapping my knuckles on the doorframe, my voice low and menacing. "If you ever go near Sophia again, I'll end you."

His face blanched, and I didn't wait for a response.

I stepped out, leaving the Norwood family stewing in their downfall.

***

"Tell me again what you said to them. What was it?" Sullivan's animated voice crackled through the speakers of my rental car. "I. Own. You," he mimicked, lowering his voice down a few octaves.

I laughed as I relished the victory, glad the Norwoods took option number one of tucking and running.

Sullivan and I had spent the weekend conspiring backup plans amongst backup plans—it was a relief having someone like him in my corner.

Actually, now that I thought about it, this might've been the first time I ever reached out and asked Sullivan for help.

And he came through. No hesitation. No questions.

Just showed up—and delivered in spades.

"Just like that," I told him. "Their faces were priceless. I think Alicia may have cried if her tear ducts weren't clogged with all the plastic she's injected into her face."

The jet needed minor maintenance, so I decided to stay in Misty Springs for the night. I turned down Main Street—the primary vein of downtown—where both my hotel and Boomer's were located, all while answering Sullivan's many inquiries.

Did they see it coming?

Did they like the pictures?

Did Landon cry?

I slowed past the drive leading to Elijah's and looked up at the building looming high on the hill. The luminescent glow of the streetlights cast shadows from the tall trees nearby.

"You make a pretty good spy, after all, Corby. I'm proud of you," Sullivan said.

"Thanks, I couldn't have done it without you." And I truly meant it.

With that, I ended the call.

I could turn now, pull into the hotel, check in, and call it a night.

Or… I could keep going and see if a certain bartender was working at Boomer's tonight.

Sophia and I hadn't talked in over a week. It gnawed at me for some stupid reason and left me feeling empty.

We knew this was ending. Hell, we hadn't even started. But something felt unfinished.

Fuck it.

I pushed my foot on the gas. I didn't know what I was going to do there, what I was going to say. All I knew is I felt too damn keyed up to head to Elijah's right now.

The parking lot seemed full for a Wednesday night. Then I remembered that today was the day before Thanksgiving—the biggest bar night of the year.

Hesitantly, I walked inside and was greeted with a roaring crowd. People were standing nearly three rows deep in front of the bar, and every table in the place occupied.

Maybe this was a bad idea. I almost turned to leave when I heard someone call my name.

I looked around the room before spotting Sam waving me over. His towering height made him easy to spot amongst the crowd.

He was standing around a bar-height table, surrounded by a few empty barstools with coats and purses. Trevor and Brent were there, too.

I shook their hands in greeting.

Several empty glasses and beers were scattered on the wooden tabletop, indicating they had been there a while.

Sam wordlessly handed me an icy beer from the bucket. I accepted and thanked him.

There was a timid silence, the guys each taking sips of their drinks and eyeing the ceiling, avoiding eye contact with me.

I took a swig of the cold liquid, watching their eyes shift to me as I did. I threw my head back and drank deeper, my nerves kicking in.

Just then, two ladies showed up, and I recognized them instantly—Cassie and the dark-haired coffee shop owner, Lana.

A curly-haired waitress bumped into me as she stood at our table—Devyn, I assumed, based on Sophia's description of her. "You guys have two seconds. What do you need?" she demanded more than asked.

"Bucket," Sam ordered.

"White wine, please," Lana answered with a smile.

"Another one of these," Cassie wiggled her empty glass. "And get one for Corbin, too."

I gave her a suspicious glare.

She shrugged. "What? You'll like it. Trust me."

Not that I had time to argue. Devyn had already spun away and left.

Sam handed the last few beers in the bucket to Brent and Trevor. The girls settled onto the barstools, pushing aside empty bottles and cups.

I didn't know what to do, what to say. The bar was loud, music played in the background, but I could barely hear the song through the chorus of voices all around us.

I just destroyed the real estate equivalent of a Bond villain. Earlier this week, I locked in a multi-million dollar government contract. Neither of those situations made me feel timid, nor did they make me feel nervous.

Not like this.

Sophia's friends exchanged looks with each other, none of their eyes falling on me—wordlessly having some sort of discussion I was not privy to.

Cassie nodded at her brother, and Brent's eyes fell to mine.

"So." Brent's deep voice broke through the noise, crossing his arms and inflating his biceps. "You and Sophia only know each other through work?"

I nodded, taking a longer pull from my beer bottle, trying to rush alcohol into my system.

"Wow, I think it's next-level leadership when a boss is willing to throw down on a shady ex in a back alley," Sam added before pressing a beer to his lips, keeping his eyes locked on me.

"Yeah, not to mention you seem *awfully* curious about Sophia's whereabouts every time you stay at Elijah's," Cassie piled on with a knowing smirk.

"Yeah, and he lives in New York," Trevor added, cocking his head to the side. "Say, gang, didn't Sophia just mysteriously vanish in New York for a couple of days with some unknown stranger?"

"And when she came back, she seemed all... flushed with excitement." Devyn startled me, sneaking back to the table with our drinks and responding like she'd been a part of the whole conversation.

I choked on my beer while all Sophia's friends exchanged giddy grins.

Chapter 49

ZOOLANDER

Corbin

After their accusations, followed by a back slap and a *we're just messing with you* dismissal from Brent, Sophia's friends gave me a reprieve.

Their curiosity shifted to other areas of interest—namely, drinking games. The raucous energy of their games—quarters, and some chaotic thing called fingers—filled the bar with laughter.

I joined in, Sophia's friends, and the game eased the tension in my chest.

It was nearing midnight, the crowd had barely begun to thin, and I still hadn't seen Sophia.

"Darts?" Trevor called out from behind Cassie, who gave an exaggerated eye roll.

"Let's go!" Sam grinned, tossing me an inviting glance.

Brent led the way as we wove our way through the crowd to the other side of the bar. Once we crossed the dividing wall, the atmosphere noticeably shifted—quieter, calmer, with a subdued energy that felt like a different world entirely.

Sam plucked the darts from their rack, tossing one lightly in the air and catching it effortlessly. Trevor fiddled with the tattered dry erase board that served as our scoreboard, his voice rising in a mock play-by-play as he narrated their imagined victory.

"Don't psych yourself up too much, champ." Brent smirked, grabbing a dart and eyeing the board with mock intensity. "Zoolander and I smoked you last time, and we'll do it again."

"Zoolander?" I asked, raising an eyebrow.

"Your nickname," Trevor said with a smirk. "Since you always dress like some damn model."

"And out of all the models in existence, *that's* who you went with? Zoolander?"

Sam nearly spit out his beer, laughing as he wiped at his mouth with the back of his hand, and Brent's grin widened into a toothy smile.

Trevor grinned as he lined up his shot, the four of us falling silent as he flung each dart at the board.

"So, what is your intention with our Sophia?" Trevor asked after his last shot landed.

"Shit, Trev. Lana said to have some tact about it," Brent chided.

"What the fuck is tact? We all want to know." Trevor rebounded.

"I have no *intention*," I said, lining up my shot. Then I dropped my hand at my side, turning to face them. "She's about to work for me. That's it."

The guys each found a different corner of the ceiling to avert their eyes to, quietly avoiding my attempt to convince them—and myself—that there was nothing more between us.

The guys' silence threw off my game. I missed every dart I threw.

"Trevor, will you shut the hell up when it's our turn to throw?" Brent grabbed the darts I handed him. "You keep messing Zoolander up."

"If a little distraction about Sophia is all it takes, I'll bring her up all evening," Trevor joked. "Right, Sammy?" Trevor nudged Sam's arm. "Sam! Why are you so quiet, man?"

"What? I'm not! Is it my turn?" Sam jolted out of his chair.

Sam lined up and threw, missing every one of his shots, too.

"What is with you guys tonight? My back hurts from carrying you. Focus Sammy. FOCUS!" Trevor made a two-finger *I'm watching you* gesture between him and Sam.

Brent lined up to throw next, easily hitting his targets as he spoke. "I'm just sorry I didn't let you punch Landon in his stupid fucking mouth. That guy needs a good ass-kicking."

I took a sip of the whiskey Cassie had ordered for me—she was right—it wasn't bad. "Landon won't be a problem for any of us anymore."

Trevor paused mid-throw and turned his head to me. "Okay, that was the most badass fucking thing I've ever heard someone say in real life." He walked over to me, his eyes wide as he excitedly turned his Chase Construction ballcap backward. "What'd you do?"

***

The bar was empty, with the exception of Sophia and her friends, by the time the guys and I emerged from the back room.

I'd filled the guys in on the high-level details of the Norwood family's sudden exit, and they all insisted they owed me a shot the next time we threw darts.

Next time.

The words stuck with me. A month ago, I would've considered this whole town a pit stop—just a rung on the ladder to CEO.

But things were shifting. I hadn't expected to enjoy the quiet camaraderie with the guys, the easy way Cassie called me out without blinking, or Lana's coffee.

I hadn't expected to feel anything at all.

And now, even with the Norwood family handled, even with Sophia and me off-limits, and no reason to come back once the branch took off… a part of me was already anticipating that next time.

And another part—one I didn't quite recognize—was surprised by how much I might actually miss this place, these people, this *feeling.*

I saw Sophia bussing glassware from tables near the bar. A deeply rooted sense of desire clung to me to protect what was mine, even if it wasn't.

She looked up at me, her face morphing into shock. She clumsily dropped the glass she was holding. The shattering sounds echoed off the empty walls of the bar.

"Shit," she cursed.

"I got it!" Trevor called, walking instinctively over to the broom and dustpan as if he'd cleaned the floors of this bar a hundred times.

Her friends were all performing some sort of job: Brent stacked chairs, Lana wiped tables, and Cassie wiped the bar top. Even in their slightly buzzed state and the fact they weren't getting paid a dime to work there, they all pitched in.

Sophia strode over to where I stood by a row of booths, grabbing a bucket with spare rags on her way. Her friends paused their tasks briefly to watch our exchange.

"What are you doing here?" she asked.

"I had some business to attend to in Misty Springs."

She crossed her arms as she looked at me.

"Really? We're doing this again?" Her face tinged slightly pink.

My eyebrows lifted as we both seemed to recall our conversation in the hotel room when I pulled the tag from her shorts.

She glanced back at her friends, who quickly resumed their labors, before lowering her voice. "What kind of *business?*" she asked with a coy grin, confirming my suspicions.

Looking into Sophia's deep blue eyes, I realized I didn't want to see them ache with talks about the Norwood family and their schemes—I definitely didn't want tonight spent with her thinking about her ex-fiancé and his family.

So I avoided the question altogether. "I'm heading back tomorrow morning to spend Thanksgiving with my grandparents."

I held out my hand, gesturing toward the bucket she brought over. She handed me a spare rag. I got to work wiping the neighboring booth.

Her face deflated slightly, and she nodded. "How have things been since Toni's accident? Have you talked anymore with Buzz?"

I paused a moment.

Most people ask questions like that as currency—"How are your grandparents?" actually means, *Where are the cracks in your armor? Where can we press?*

It was always calculated. Their curiosity came with an edge, a purpose. If my grandfather's mental health was faltering, that meant a power vacuum. If my grandmother was struggling, it meant we might be distracted.

Weak. Vulnerable.

But with Sophia… it didn't feel like an interrogation. It felt like *care.*

I cleared my throat, focusing on a particularly sticky spot on the booth. "Toni's home now. Buzz is still… quieter than usual. Different."

"Are you okay?" she asked softly, gently brushing my shoulder with her hand.

I wasn't. Not entirely. But it wasn't just my grandparents weighing on me. It was the way her touch still undid me, the way my blood pumped when she looked at me like that.

"Corbin, come over here!" Trevor called from behind the bar.

Sophia gave me an excited smile before nodding her head toward the bar. "C'mon, these rascals won't stop until we *toast to Turkey Day*. It's tradition."

Devyn quickly jumped up onto one of the bar stools. "You know the drill, Sammy, pour me something strong."

"Your wish is my command." Sam grabbed her hand, kissing the back of it.

I stopped Sophia before she made it behind the bar, placing my hand on her shoulder and pressing her into a barstool. No way I was going to allow her to make her own drink. She worked her ass off tonight.

"I got you, Sophia," I whispered in her ear.

Her breath hitched, and she turned slightly to me, her lips near mine.

Her friends exchanged a look again, the same one from earlier. There was no hiding things from this group. They knew Sophia too well.

Sophia watched me intently as I pulled down a bottle of Hendrick's gin, a couple bottles of Vermouth, and a martini shaker. I knew she liked martinis and found myself wanting to prove I could make one as good—if not better—than her little bartender friend from the gala.

Lana requested white wine, which Brent seemed eager to make for her—probably because it only involved pouring one liquid into a glass.

Trevor got Cassie a whiskey, to which he tried to bribe her to pay him in an over-the-shirt boob squeeze.

Brent punched Trevor on the arm, telling him to find someone else's sister to hit on.

Sam made a beeline for the margarita machine, which was spinning the premade slush on the bar behind him. He plucked a glass and started pouring.

Sophia watched me intently as I shook the martini shaker, her eyes skimming down my arms. I had discarded my jacket and rolled up my sleeves, and I may have flexed a little more than necessary as I mixed the drink. I strained the liquid into a martini glass and set it on the bar in front of her.

Her hands brushed mine as she grabbed it, and I slowly traced her hand with my fingertips as I let go.

I watched her sapphire-blue eyes intently as she took a sip.

Her tongue darted out to lick the remnants from her pink lips, lips I could still taste on mine, lips I enjoyed seeing wrapped around me, all the way to the base.

Suddenly, that was all I could think about.

"What the hell is this?" Devyn's voice cut through my lust-fueled thoughts.

All heads turned to her, and she held up a plastic straw with a margarita-soaked diamond ring dangling from the end.

Confusion flickered across her face as she looked around for answers—until she noticed Sam wasn't standing behind her anymore.

He was kneeling on the floor.

A collective gasp rippled through the group as Sam took Devyn's free hand.

"Devyn," Sam began, his voice steady but thick with emotion. "Two years ago, I met you in this bar, and you've owned my heart every day since."

Sophia slid from her barstool, stepping toward Lana and Cassie, their arms wrapping around each other as they squealed in unison, an almost choreographed burst of excitement.

"These floorboards," he continued, gesturing toward them with a wry smile, "they've seen a lot—our first date, some stale beer, and… if I'm not mistaken, the aftermath of your first Jägerbomb."

The group chuckled, though Brent muttered, "You're losing her."

Cassie groaned something about leaving out the vomit.

Sam exhaled a shaky breath. "Devyn Flores, will you marry me?"

"Yes!" Devyn squeaked, her voice breaking with emotion.

Sam rose to his feet, lifting her off the barstool in one swift move and spinning her in an exuberant hug before pressing his lips firmly to hers.

The girls huddled together, jumping up and down and squealing, while Trevor and Brent exchanged grins, glasses clinking.

I stayed where I was, a whiskey glass in hand, watching the scene unfold from behind the bar.

Sophia, Lana, and Cassie rushed to Devyn, their voices a flurry of high-pitched squeals about how beautiful the ring was—until Devyn laughed, holding up her hand. "It's sticky."

Sam ambled over to the guys, chest puffed like he'd just hit a game-winning shot. Trevor and Brent greeted him with rough hugs, back pats, and teasing grins.

"That was probably the worst proposal I've ever seen," Brent said with a smirk.

"Was it?" Sam asked, unbothered, still beaming with excitement.

"You could've left out the Jäger-induced puking," Trevor quipped.

"She still said yes." Sam's grin stretched ear to ear as he winked at me.

I joined them, stepping out from behind the bar.

"I thought it was perfect." I clinked glasses with Sam.

And I meant it—I'd seen proposals orchestrated to perfection, complete with flash mobs, champagne fountains, and designer rings.

But this? This was something else entirely.

Unpolished, quirky, and raw.

I looked around at this tight-knit group of friends, their lives interwoven with laughter, teasing, and loyalty that bound them together. They were a chosen family, weathering life's highs and lows in tandem.

Even more profoundly, I felt like I wasn't just a silent observer of their world—I was part of it.

Chapter 50

I LOVE MY JOB

Sophia

My skull pounded as I gently sipped water and hunched behind Elijah's front desk. I rested my head on the cold laminate counter to ease some of the throbbing tension.

I could kill Cassie for putting me on the schedule this morning, but I also knew she had no choice. I was the only one without family around to celebrate Thanksgiving with.

Last night, we had closed out the bar, then stayed for hours after celebrating Sam and Devyn's engagement.

I didn't want the night to end, but eventually, Hank arrived in the wee morning hours with his roomy van, allowing all of us to pile in and raking in extra cash and tips from the whole group.

Corbin rode shotgun, surprisingly chatting with Hank the entire time.

Corbin's presence last night had a way of making every moment feel bigger—elevated somehow. When he made me that martini, I felt the unavoidable tension build between us.

I stole glances his way all night—melting a little, at how his eyes lit up when he laughed with the guys and the carefree smile that sprang across his face, like he'd been a part of our group forever.

Sometimes, when I let my eyes linger on him too long, he'd catch me. A quick wink, a playful flick of connection before he looked away. I'd drop my gaze, cheeks warm, hiding behind a shy smile.

But once—just once—neither of us looked away. Our eyes held, suspended in a quiet, aching moment. No words passed between us, but everything we'd tried not to say lived in that look.

The wanting. The hope. The ache of knowing we couldn't. And when it got too heavy, too real, we both turned away.

No smiles that time.

In the harsh light of the morning, I heard someone approaching and peeled my face off the counter. I wiped the tiny bead of drool from my mouth and quickly straightened when I realized it was Corbin.

"Sexy," he smirked.

Despite his obvious sarcasm, I felt my heart lift at his comment.

He pulled coconut water and a tiny bottle of ibuprofen from a bag. He also set some crackers and a banana on the counter. "Figured you could use some essentials."

He looked impeccable despite being up as late as the rest of us. His green ribbed sweater clung to his chest and arms, and a neatly pressed collar stuck out of the top. His dark tan pants fit him like they were made just for his body, which, knowing him, they probably were.

"Thank you," I croaked with a dry mouth. "How'd you get back to your car this morning?" I added, realizing he'd left it at Boomer's last night.

He leaned on the counter, eyes meeting my level. "Believe it or not, there is more than one Uber driver in Misty Springs."

"How dare you," I gasped. "Hank is not an Uber driver. He's an entrepreneur. He's a brand all his own."

Corbin chuckled. "That he is."

We stared at each other for a few heartbeats. Words lingered on my tongue, but none of them would change a damn thing.

"I have to head back," he said, breaking the silence as his brows knitted together.

This was it—the last time we'd see each other before we became Assistant Editor and boss's boss's boss... maybe one more boss was somewhere in there, I couldn't remember.

He had his dream. I had mine.

And they didn't intersect.

"Goodbye, Corbin." I managed to choke out, the finality of the words weighing on me.

He rapped his fingers on the desk. "Goodbye, Sophia."

***

"I'm so happy it worked out. It sounds like the perfect opportunity for you." My sister Penny's voice was overly enthusiastic as we talked on the phone after I left Elijah's later that day.

"Oh, and I spoke to David, and we decided to come to Misty Springs for Christmas this year. Luke is young enough, he doesn't question Santa's ability to track us down—he just knows he gets presents."

My heart lifted. Penny hadn't come back home since Luke was born. "That's amazing news!"

I couldn't wait to introduce Luke to my friends and show him where Penny and I grew up. My heart plummeted as I realized I couldn't show him around our childhood home. The brick building, which held so many memories, was infuriatingly unoccupied but locked up tight.

"Oh, and Luke wanted me to ask you about some guy named Bruce? Are you seeing someone?"

I laughed, even hundreds of miles away, Luke could lighten my mood. "Tell him I haven't found Bruce yet, but I'll keep looking."

***

Monday arrived quickly, and my nerves were on edge as I got dressed for my first day.

I lucked out. Cassie and Brent's grandparents were spending the winter in Florida, and they let me borrow their car while they were away. I planned to have enough for a down payment by the time they got back.

When I walked into the chic, eclectic office of Buescher-Jones Publishing, I practically had to pinch myself to believe it was real.

Andi wasted no time jumping right in. She introduced me to Susan, bypassing any introduction to Ned, and showed me to my very own—albeit tiny—corner office.

I settled in, setting up my email and access to the Buescher-Jones server. By mid-morning, she'd asked about the manuscript she had handed me during my interview.

"So?" she asked, leaning against my desk with that signature Andi confidence. "What'd you think?"

I'd been nervous, but I told her the truth. "It needs a lot of work—spelling, grammar, sentence structure—but the story's solid. The characters are well-developed, and the plot has a great flow."

Her grin was instant. "Exactly what I thought."

Then she told me it had been Monica McKenzie's first submission to the company—their best-selling author and a cornerstone of their success. "If we'd passed on her, it would've been a multi-million-dollar mistake. Trust your gut, Sophia. It's better than you realize."

A few hours later, I was pouring creamer into my coffee in the common area. My confidence was soaring, like nothing could pull me down—until the lobby door creaked on its hinges.

And in strode Corbin.

For a moment, my breath caught. A sharp twist of excitement pulsed through me, followed by a stab to my gut as I settled into the acceptance that he was completely off-limits.

To everyone here, Corbin and I barely knew each other, having only met briefly during my interview and again at the gala. None of them were aware of how well we got to know each other after said gala.

Corbin stood in the entry, eyes locked on me, silently assessing.

"Hey, Bossman!" Andi exclaimed as she barreled down the small hallway. "I assume your flight was good?"

Corbin reluctantly drew his attention away from me. "I assume my office is unoccupied?"

I haven't seen Corbin in this element before.

Was this his business persona? Arrogant, no-nonsense, direct.

"I didn't set foot in there today." Andi came to stand near me and grabbed a coffee cup. "Do yourself a favor and ignore him, okay, Sophia?" she whispered loudly.

I grinned sheepishly before focusing my attention back on my coffee. I wrapped my hands around the mug and blew on the steaming liquid before retreating to my office.

Corbin spent much of the day behind the closed door of his office, not that I was keeping tabs on him or anything. Not that I didn't make one too many trips to the coffee pot to see if his door was still closed.

Andi treated the office to lunch, and we gathered at a large table in the common area—everyone except Corbin.

"He never leaves that office," Susan commented as she chewed over her salad. "I don't know if I've ever seen someone work as hard as he does."

"His dad was always like that too, until it killed him," Ned said with a cold sneer.

It felt wrong to sit here, reducing Corbin's pain to flippant workplace gossip. I opened my mouth to say something, but my nerves kicked in—sealing my mouth shut.

"I heard his dad ran around with nearly every woman at the company—that's why they don't want coworkers hooking up," Ned continued shoveling a bite of pasta in his mouth.

This ignited something in me. Hearing Corbin talk about his father's past—what it did to his family, how hurt he was as a boy— lit a fuse that quickly exploded.

"I don't think it's appropriate to talk about that kind of stuff," I stated firmly.

Not quite the f-you that I wanted to say, but it still felt good.

"Yeah, Ned, do us all a favor and choke on your pasta, will you?" Andi commented, shutting Ned down quickly.

Ned's face turned red as he chewed the alfredo in his mouth, his eyes simmering toward Andi as she passively ignored him.

"You know." Ned swallowed loudly. "I don't know who you think made you in charge here. I've been with the company longer than you, so maybe you should watch your tone, young lady."

"Maybe you should watch your cholesterol, old fuck," Andi jeered. "Feel free to talk to Mr. Buescher if you feel you are being treated unfairly."

I gulped as I swallowed my water. Wishing I had an ounce of the steel Andi carried around.

If Andi and Devyn ever got together, they could decimate a major city.

Ned gathered his takeout container and stormed into his office, slamming his door.

"Andi, you shouldn't goad him like that," Susan warned calmly. "I know he's an ass, but he's got connections high up at this company. You don't want him to be an enemy."

"He shouldn't want me as an enemy," Andi clipped back, twirling spaghetti on her fork like a stage magician. "Sophia's right—he shouldn't be out here talking shit about Corbin when he's two feet away, working his ass off for this company."

Despite the minor workplace drama, I couldn't stop smiling as I packed up my desk that evening. I'd always imagined loving my job, but I hadn't expected it to feel like this—like I was on a path to something so perfectly—*me*.

As I left, I noticed the light spilling out from beneath the door of Corbin's office. Nightfall came earlier as we inched closer and closer to the end of the year, and the horizon nearly engulfed the final scraps of sunlight.

Against my better judgment, I stood outside his door, my hand raised to knock.

My pulse raced, and I swallowed the nervous lump in my throat. This was a bad idea.

I turned and left like the coward I was.

Chapter 51

NOT SAFE FOR WORK

Sophia

My days began to fall into a comfortable pattern. I gleefully threw myself into work. Andi's confidence in me fueled my own, and every manuscript I reviewed felt like a chance to prove myself.

Andi and I clicked instantly. We'd spend our lunches together, chatting about books and life. Last Friday, we even ate a Titanic-themed sushi dinner at Elijah's together.

Andi and Ned continuously clashed while Susan worked to keep the peace. Surprisingly, Corbin stuck around my entire first week, and strolled in again on Monday. He stayed tucked away in his office. If he spoke to anyone, it was Andi.

I decided to swing by Lana's shop on my way in on Wednesday, juggling a tray of coffees to drop off at everyone's desk. It was a subtle way to build goodwill.

Ned practically trapped me in his office with small talk so bad it bordered on painful, but I managed to excuse myself with a polite smile and headed for Corbin's door—the one that had remained firmly shut, a silent, unapproachable barrier.

I paused outside, balancing his coffee in one hand, my knuckles hovering over the polished wood.

Finally, I found my resolve and knocked.

"Come in," his gruff voice called from inside.

Steeling myself, I pushed the door open and stepped inside. Papers and files were neatly stacked on the desk, but the faint scent of leather and the cedar notes of Corbin filled the space.

Corbin looked up from his laptop, his sharp eyes locking onto mine, and for a second, I forgot why I was there.

"I brought coffee." My voice cracked slightly as I set the cup on his desk.

"From Lana's?" His expression softened.

"Of course. She remembered your drink, half-sweet maple bourbon cappuccino."

He smirked, the slightest flicker of amusement crossing his face. "Thanks."

I lingered for a moment too long, the silence between us pressing against my skin.

"Anything else?" he asked, his voice casual, dismissive.

"Nope, that's all." I awkwardly tapped my fingers on his desk and slipped out of his office, shutting the door behind me.

My heart raced the whole way back to my desk.

By the end of my second week, I had begun to settle into this new life. The office was quiet and still, like the cold December air had stiffened the pace.

Today, no amount of tea or coffee seemed to chase away the chill inside me. For what felt like the hundredth time that day, I stood at the coffee station, fumbling around for tea bags. My fingers brushed over packets of sugar and creamer as I searched absentmindedly.

A cough sounded behind me.

I froze, nervous energy zapped through me. Turning slowly, I found myself face-to-face—or rather, face-to-chest—with Corbin.

He was so close that I could see the faint shadow of stubble along his jawline, smell the sweet citrus as it danced in my nose.

My throat dried instantly.

"Excuse me," he thrummed, his voice low and smooth.

I shuffled to the side, my heart racing as he reached past me, his arm brushing mine.

The contact was brief—innocent by anyone's standards—but it set every nerve ending in my body on edge.

His hand hovered near mine for a split second, close enough to feel the heat radiating from his skin, and then he plucked a packet of sugar from the tray.

"You drink tea?" he asked, glancing down at the mug in my hand with the paper tag hanging from a string draped over the side.

I fumbled for words, my cheeks heating as I tried to keep my composure. "I, uh, already maxed out my coffee quota for the day. Tea seemed safer."

A small, almost imperceptible smile tugged at his lips. "Safe. That's a good choice." The way he said it made the word feel anything but.

"A little late in the day for you to be drinking coffee," I said, nodding to the steaming cup in his hand. "Big night tonight?"

I knew he was heading back to New York for the weekend. What I didn't know was when he'd be coming back to Misty Springs again. I had already seen him more than I expected to.

According to Andi—and Corbin—he wouldn't be spending much time here, especially not as the year ended—too many important board meetings and "societal posturing disguised as holiday parties."

"Well, yes. That, and the fact that I didn't have a gorgeous brunette stop by my office this morning to bring me a cup—has left me wanting," he murmured deeply, leaning in close.

A spark lit beneath my skin. My gaze fell to his mouth, then to the smoldering embers flickering behind his whiskey-colored eyes.

"Did you like it when this *gorgeous brunette* gave you coffee, Mr. Buescher?"

The fire in his eyes raged, but my gaze didn't falter.

The countertop was at my back, his hard body inches away—close enough for me to feel the tingly closeness of his proximity.

Flirting with Corbin was dangerous—a reckless indulgence I knew I should avoid.

"I liked a lot of things this *gorgeous brunette* gave me," he murmured, lowering his mouth to my ear.

Liquid heat rushed low in my belly. My hips rolled forward, barely grazing his thigh underneath the expensive suit he wore. I lifted my fingers, aching to trail them along the firm muscle of his chest where it clung to his soft shirt.

The sharp click of Andi's heels broke the moment, and I straightened, fisting my fingers at my side as Corbin took a casual step back.

"Good, there you are," Andi said, breezing into the room, oblivious to the static still crackling in the air. "Want to catch up before you leave?" she asked, glancing at Corbin.

"Sure. Let's go to my office," he replied, lifting his coffee cup to his lips and taking a slow, deliberate sip.

I watched them walk away, my knees weak as the tension ebbed, leaving me to melt into a figurative puddle by the coffee pot.

***

Later that evening, I was at Boomer's, tying on my apron and falling into the familiar rhythm of weekend shifts.

Despite my new job, I couldn't let this one go just yet. I told myself only a few more weekends—just enough to pad my savings for a down payment on a car.

My phone buzzed in my pocket. I froze when I saw Corbin's name flash on the screen.

Corbin: At Lucali's tonight. I took your advice and ordered something different this time.

A smile tugged at my lips. Lucali's—the restaurant he and I ate at when I spent the night with him in New York. I gave him grief for being there dozens of times and always ordering the same thing off the menu.

Me: I loved that place. Best risotto I've ever had.

His reply came almost immediately.

Corbin: Me too. It's been promoted to my first favorite restaurant.

I saw three dots appear and then disappear in rapid succession. I watched with quiet anticipation, curious about what words he was typing and deleting on his end.

Corbin: And I was right. Every time the elevator opens to my apartment, it's… disappointing.

An unbridled smile formed on my face, recalling what he said while we were getting dressed that morning: "You realize now, every time I come up that elevator, I'm going to imagine that it'll open up to you topless.

Before I could type a reply, my cell phone screen went black. A byproduct of its advanced age and the absolute abuse I put it through by dropping it, smothering it in strangers' coffee, and never installing updates.

As a customer flagged me down, I shoved my phone back into my pocket. My gut sank as I considered the possibility of needing to buy a new one, but then I remembered that I could actually afford a new one.

My walk to the customer had a little more bounce to it than usual.

***

Monday arrived too quickly, pulling me back into the hum of office life.

The morning was quiet. Corbin wasn't here, and despite my desperate desire to know if he was coming to Misty Springs this week, I didn't have the opportunity to ask anyone without feeling like I sounded fifty shades of desperate.

We had a group meeting in the common area in the afternoon, and I had just settled into my seat when the heavy door of the lobby creaked open, answering my question.

All eyes turned toward Corbin as he let the door slam loudly behind him.

His gaze addressed the rest of the group huddled around the table before landing on me, curious and heavy. The air pressed in around me, filling with the presence of him.

"Mr. Buescher," Andi said, her tone bristling. "We weren't expecting you."

Corbin smoothed his wool coat as he strode toward his office. "Something came up."

I watched Andi's expression sharpen toward Corbin before turning back to the group.

"Okay, let's just get started," Andi said, flustered.

Moments later, Corbin came back into the room and sat down at the table with us.

Once again, Andi paused to glare at him, but quickly resumed the meeting with Corbin observing.

It was near-impossible to keep my eyes on my laptop screen and not on Corbin.

The way his light blue button-down shirt clung to his chest. The stubble that formed along his sharp jaw, longer than usual, and somehow even sexier—if that was possible.

Every time he noticed me staring, he raised an eyebrow or gave a small smirk—it was torture.

Corbin participated in some of the discussions. Every time he spoke, I felt his voice vibrate over my skin, settling into me and heating my blood.

I barely heard the conversation, something about a new author, but when the word *"greedy"* came off his smoldering lips, my imagination went into overdrive.

Memories of his naked body hovering above me, my hands on his hips urging him to sink into me.

So greedy, Sophia.

"Right, Sophia?" Ned's voice broke through my steamy memory.

My eyes snapped to his across the table. Then they roamed to see that everyone was looking at me, waiting for a response.

I looked at Corbin, his nostrils flaring like he was inside my head with me, reliving the very moment I was.

I almost whimpered, but somehow turned it into a "hmmm?"

"You've almost finished that manuscript? *The Mask of Philonius?"* Ned repeated.

"Oh, yes. Yep. I'll be done today." I reached for my water, suddenly parched, and choked on it when I noticed Corbin wiggling his eyebrows at me.

Did he say greedy on purpose?

Andi patted my back.

Did everyone notice me unraveling here in this meeting?

"I think we're done here. Good work." Corbin ordered as he closed his laptop.

The rest of the table gathered their papers and laptops before quickly dispersing back to their offices.

My body felt like I'd just run a marathon.

Who am I kidding? I've never run a marathon.

My muscles ached from the tension I'd held, trying to keep my traitorous body from responding to Corbin.

This was supposed to get easier.

Corbin had said he'd be in New York most of the time—not here, not down the hall, not in these meetings, not everywhere I turned.

Corbin's presence was volatile. Dangerous.

And yet, it was tempting—like a new line had been drawn, one I couldn't wait to press against.

Chapter 52

CAUGHT?

Corbin

Every day spent in Misty Springs was a test. When I left the sanctuary of my office, I was hit by her smell, tempted by the sway of her step, or lured by the sound of her laugh.

Texting her was idiotic—an amateur mistake for someone like me.

What was I even thinking?

I was dancing with danger during that meeting.

Whenever her deep blue eyes locked on mine underneath those thick lashes, I felt my resolve waver. I knew she'd lock onto my words, knew the air would stiffen around us as we both drew our time together in our imaginations.

The meeting went on around us as if we weren't both drowning in our desires.

A distraction, that's what I had deemed Sophia to be when she sat next to me in first class.

She was proving to be more than that.

She was a need.

A craving.

I was a junkie—plotting, planning, focusing solely on how to get my next fix. Everything else in life was diminished, overshadowed by the urge to get closer to her.

And this damn charming crap town—I spent the last two weeks here, and here I was again. Another week in Misty Springs, another week I was supposed to spend in New York.

Andi strutted into my office, looking like she was about to rip into me for something—I knew that look too well.

"You're… here again. Why?" She raised an eyebrow over her thick purple glasses.

I put on an impassive face and shrugged. "I am just making sure things are staying the course here."

Wrong answer, it seemed.

"You don't trust me to keep things *on course?*" Andi's eyes narrowed at me.

I sighed, resisting the urge to glare at her—the key was treading lightly here. I was too tired from my early morning decision to come to Misty Springs to start a fight.

"No, seriously. You hand-picked Susan, who's fine, but also that loser Ned, despite telling me I would be in charge of hiring here. You *barely* let me hire Sophia. You said having eyes and ears here would be a relief, so you didn't have to spend time in Misty Springs, and that you planned to hand the branch over to me. But you've been here nearly every damn day. What changed? What did I do wrong here?"

"Andi," I said, releasing a breath. "This has nothing to do with you."

"Then what is the problem?" Andi's arms flew in the air dramatically.

Footsteps sounded in the hallway outside my office.

Andi glanced outside my open door and gave a soft smile.

"Hey, Sophia," she said with a wave. Her anger ebbed when she faced Sophia, before she looked back at me with a scowl. "Sophia and I have a meeting. But this isn't over," she seethed before storming out of my office.

Toward the end of the day, I scratched needlessly at the overgrown stubble on my chin as I fought my inner plans. I told myself I wasn't going to do this.

I had work to do, deadlines to hit, and a presentation to clean up before the board meeting next week. But none of it stuck in my head—not with her so close.

Sophia was down the hall, tucked away in her office. I'd walked past it three times today already.

Once pretending to check the thermostat, another under the guise of looking for Andi.

The third? No excuse.

Just weakness.

I didn't like that I felt my control slipping more and more. But I also couldn't find the strength to reel it back in. The question of why she didn't text me back over the weekend loomed in my head.

Before I could think again, I found myself standing from my desk, already making the walk before I had a plan.

She looked up as I approached the doorway to her open office, her brows lifting slightly.

"Hey," I said, casual, light. I had nothing. No script, no cover. "Got a second?"

She hesitated, then nodded once. "Sure."

I gestured for her to follow me down the hall toward the proofing room. Neutral territory. Quiet… and windowless.

The door clicked shut behind us, sealing us into something smaller, heavier.

"I just…" I rubbed a hand over the back of my neck. "I wanted to check in. I didn't hear back from you this weekend."

And I worried about it so much, I flew hundreds of miles to check on you.

"Right, sorry." She placed her palm on her forehead. "My phone officially bit the dust while I was working at Boomer's. I ordered a new one. It's coming today."

"You're still working there?" I asked, the memory of a sea of large men watching her with rapt attention gnawing at me.

"For now." She shrugged. "I want to save up for a down payment on a car."

"Ah," I replied.

Our eyes locked as the room fell quiet. I was out of excuses for bringing her on this makeshift excursion to the proofing room.

She tilted her head slightly, her voice a murmur. "Did you need anything else, Mr. Buescher?"

My eyes dropped to her lips the moment my name rolled off of them.

She tracked my movement.

The air somehow grew even heavier, thickening like the Jell-O surrounding those stupid gummy bugs the day I cornered Sophia in my hotel room.

"Just one more thing." I stepped in before I could stop myself, the space between us disappearing one breath at a time.

Her lips parted, her breath hitching just enough for me to hear it. But she didn't back away. Didn't blink.

Our mouths met in a kiss that unraveled every stitch of discipline I'd tried to sew up over the last few weeks.

It was heated—unplanned, and untamed.

Her hands dug into my hair. Mine gripped her waist.

The tension in my muscles eased, and the restraint I held from resisting Sophia finally loosened.

I felt like a starved man finally getting his fill, my hunger strike over, relishing my reward.

And then—

"Just let me grab this off the printer—"

We jolted apart.

Ned stood in the doorway.

He stopped in his tracks. Blinked.

"Oh... didn't realize anyone was in here. I just need to uh..." He motioned toward the printer and quickly stepped inside, grabbing a few sheets of paper before leaving, not acknowledging us again.

Sophia stared at me, breathless, lips swollen.

My pulse thundered in my ears.

"Do you think he saw—" she started.

"I don't know."

"I should go," Sophia whispered, not giving me time to respond before she hurried out of the room.

I ran my fingers through my hair and cursed under my breath, the taste of her still lingering on my lips.

This—this was exactly why I didn't want her hired in the first place. The tension, the pull, the way she looked at me like she didn't just want me—she saw me.

I'd told myself I could keep it professional—that I could manage it.

My pulse still hadn't slowed. I leaned back against a table, jaw clenched, trying to figure out what the hell I was doing.

I couldn't tell if the knot in my chest was fear—for my position, the board's opinion—or if it was her—the constant push and pull of her surrounding me every damn day.

Couldn't tell if I was more afraid of losing my future with Buescher... or losing her.

But I could feel the answer creeping in, quiet and undeniable.

And that terrified me most of all.

Chapter 53

JUST THE TWO OF US

Sophia

My hands were chapped with how much I had been wringing them. Ever since Ned walked in on Corbin and me. I was on high alert—overanalyzing every move Ned made as I fell into a sea of dizzy spells.

Did he pause at my door?

Did he just glance at me for too long?

What did he see?

I spent the rest of the week avoiding Corbin like it was a job requirement. But despite all my efforts to keep my distance, there was one moment I couldn't avoid.

Passing each other in the hallway—Corbin walking one way—me the other. I looked up at the same time he did.

Just a glance. An unspoken exchange.

But it was everything.

Heat. Regret. Longing. Conflict.

All of it tangled between us in the space of a second. Like neither of us had fully come down from what happened.

Like maybe, we never would.

I blinked first, dropped my gaze, and kept walking, pushing every emotion down.

My insides warred with the desire to find the new boundaries set within the confines of this office and the fear of crossing them—and risking it all.

If anyone found out—if this imploded like I knew it could—we'd both lose everything.

So whatever that was, I had to bury it.

We had to bury it.

Friday rolled around, and my mood was slightly lifted after spending last night raiding Devyn's closet. I was running low on outfits, but I felt a shopping trip would be on the horizon soon.

My heels clicked on the polished floors of the office as I eyed Andi, who held a Styrofoam takeout container with Ned's name sprawled across it. I watched as she tossed it in the trash without a second thought.

I grinned.

I was *not* getting in the middle of the Andi-Ned workplace drama.

"Cute outfit!" Andi beamed at me, pulling her attention briefly away from her scheming.

"You think so?" I asked as I did a little twirl. "You sure it's not too short?"

I had a few inches on Devyn, so the green plaid skirt was a tad on the short side, hitting somewhere between my knee and thigh.

"Absolutely not! I mean, maybe don't bend over in front of Ned, but it's perfectly fine by me." She dumped coffee grounds in the trash can, making sure to empty every last granule over the discarded takeout.

I shook my head and walked toward my office, ready to bury myself in beautiful, raw stories unseen by the world.

This job felt like a privilege—like I had access to a private screening of premier stories, just for my eyes.

I nearly had to pinch myself that this was my life now.

At lunch, I clumsily spilled sauce on my white button-down. Without hesitation, I walked into Andi's open office.

Her desk was like a well-stocked pharmacy. She always had ibuprofen or Kleenex, so I knew she'd have something to remove this stain.

"Andi, I got sauce on my shirt. Can I use your…" My voice trailed off as I noticed she wasn't alone.

Corbin was sitting in one of her spare chairs, his ankle resting casually on his knee, leaning back like he had just finished posing for a cologne ad.

And I was palming my sauce-covered button-down over my boob.

He ever so briefly cast a glance down at my hand.

I quickly removed it and pressed my hand nervously against my skirt.

His eyes dropped to my legs before he cleared his throat and excused himself.

I stepped back into the hallway to give him room to exit, holding my breath the whole time.

"I am so sorry for interrupting," I whispered to Andi as I rushed into her office.

"Don't worry, he was just pouting about some dinner he has to attend tonight."

"Oh." I did my best to feign indifference.

"*Obligations*, when you're a big important guy. Sometimes you must wine and dine people you can't stand."

"Well, this is what I get for eating without you," I joked, pointing to my shirt.

She handed me a Tide pen while we chatted about the latest manuscript I reviewed.

"Thank you." She grinned as she looked at me with a strange expression.

"Thank me for what? You're the one who saved my shirt."

"I did nothing. You can thank Procter and Gamble for making Tide pens. Thank *you*," she repeated. "I'm thrilled to have validation that I'm always just so right."

I laughed. "Oh yeah? What were you *so right* about?"

"You." She pushed her cobalt-blue frames up on her nose. "You're brilliant, Sophia. An absolute diamond in the rough. We're lucky to have you. Well... we're lucky to have me too, since I found you."

Her words settled deep within me, wrapping around that insecure part of me that always told myself I wasn't smart enough or good enough—the one that thought I'd never achieve the dreams I once held.

"Thank you," I choked out. "That means a lot, Andi."

She waved a hand. "Don't mention it. And if you want to leave early today, go ahead. I'm getting ready to leave. Susan's gone, and I think Ned just slithered out of here as well. It's such a nice day out. Go enjoy the break from the cold."

"Okay, I just might do that, thanks." I turned and walked out of her office, still beaming from her words.

Not only did I love this job, but I was *good* at it, too.

As I walked past the closed door of Corbin's office, my mind dangerously wandered. If Ned wasn't here, Susan had left, and Andi was about to leave, did that mean Corbin and I would be here alone?

Despite my best efforts, Corbin remained stubbornly lodged in my brain.

He was the first thing I thought about when I woke up and the last thing on my mind before I fell asleep.

My days were filled with meaningful work and beautiful stories, and my evenings and weekends were spent laughing with my incredible friends.

But the moment I was alone, it was always Corbin—filling the quiet, stealing my thoughts.

Thoughts that swirled with lustful memories of the way our bodies fit together. Thoughts I desperately needed to push away, but couldn't stop from infiltrating my mind.

I fell into my desk chair and took a deep breath, wishing I could pop in my earbuds and blare whatever the sound trigger was for libido-away right now.

Chapter 54

FRESH OUT OF RESTRAINT

Corbin

I had to excuse myself when Sophia walked into Andi's office. Her bare legs asked for my fingers to skim along the surface of her smooth skin.

To find out what she wore under that skirt.

My fingers tapped wildly on my desk as I tried to focus on the month-end review of November actuals.

My computer let out a systematic beep—the sound of the server booting me out for the umpteenth time. I nearly tossed my laptop across the room.

Between the system issues and my pent-up *frustration*s, I was about to snap.

I stormed down the hall looking for Susan or Andi, but neither of them were in their offices.

Come to think of it, the entire floor was oddly quiet.

"They all left." Sophia's voice cut through the silence. She sat in her office, eyeing me through the tiny glass window near her door.

I casually strode over and leaned in her doorway, eyeing her neatly organized stacks of papers and pastel-colored sticky notes. She had a cup of perfectly color-coordinated highlighters and pens tidily arranged.

"It's two o'clock, where are they?" I asked, disgruntled.

She shrugged. "I guess they wanted to go enjoy the sunshine."

I made a fist and rested it on the doorframe. "I'm kicked out of the server. Andi usually helps me get back in."

"Oh, I can help." She walked from behind her desk toward a tiny filing cabinet in the corner of her office.

I noticed she was barefoot, her heels discarded in the corner. The sight of the light pink polish on her toes reminded me of the hours together in my apartment—our agreement to wear scraps of clothing, the way my hoodie barely covered her ass, and how I felt seeing her in it.

I waved the memory away like a cloud of smoke.

That was then, and this is now. Though I hadn't washed that hoodie since.

She handed me a Post-it with a series of letters and symbols written on it.

"What do I do with this?" I asked.

She lifted her brows and grinned in amusement. "That's the password. You type it in for the server access."

"What do I do with this?" I asked again.

She laughed and crossed her arms. "I thought you were some bigshot executive. You're telling me you don't know how to log into the server?"

"What does one thing have to do with the other?"

"C'mon. I'll help you." She took the sticky note from me and motioned for me to follow—her bare feet padding on the tiled floor.

It was highly unprofessional, but it was just her and me here, and I enjoyed seeing as much of her skin as possible, so I let it slide.

I trailed behind her, basking in the relief that no one was here to see me stare at her ass.

She pulled my chair from the desk and leaned over, clicking my mouse and then typing on the keyboard.

I slid onto the chair beside her, rolling close, my shoulder grazing hers.

She stiffened and glanced at me. A playful smile formed on her lips, accompanied by a lecturing look in her eyes.

"What? I need to see how you do it." I shrugged innocently.

"Hm," she huffed, unconvinced, but she continued typing anyway.

She was right to be skeptical. I wasn't paying any attention to the server access. Her scent pulled me in, her body too tempting to ignore.

I had been restless without her, my mind drifting to thoughts of her constantly. My apartment was off balance without her in it—

cold, lonely, quiet. Phantom memories of her clung to every surface, making the weekends feel hollow and lonely without her presence.

I spent week after week in Misty Springs, away from my responsibilities back in New York, despite the board circling like sharks. The pull to be here—near her—was too great.

I leaned back in my leather chair, my eyes skimming the back of her legs, roaming over the smooth skin until my gaze reached the hem of her skirt.

When she was bent over like that, it fell just inches below her ass. My fingers twitched at the desire to slide underneath the plaid pattern.

After weeks of telling myself no—of pushing against her like waves crashing against a crumbling wall—my resolve finally eroded.

And I gave in.

Chapter 55

INEVITABLE

Sophia

The moment Corbin's fingers met my skin, something detonated—hot, blinding, all-consuming.

This wasn't just chemistry. It was nuclear, and it was breaking me down one slow, aching touch at a time.

His touch trailed higher, rotating to the inside of my thigh, slipping underneath the hem of my skirt.

"Do you ever think about me?" he asked in a deep whisper.

I nodded, the words *every second of every day* lodged in my throat.

He straightened in his chair, his hand fully buried beneath my skirt, his fingers trailing my soaked scraps of lace.

"You're so wet for me," he whispered in my ear.

"Always," I breathed in response.

I hadn't moved, still bent at my waist with my fingers hovering above his keyboard.

"Tell me to stop," he said, almost pleading as if his resolve was too weak to resist without me ending it.

Rules. Policies. The reasons why we couldn't do *this* circled my mind.

Those reasons vanished into thin air when his fingers pushed my panties aside and plunged inside of me.

I let out a breathy moan, my eyes flicking to the open door of his office. No one was here, but this still felt reckless—and *thrilling*.

"What if someone sees?" I asked with a sharp breath.

"No one is here," he promised as his fingers moved slowly in and out of me.

I rocked into his palm, my body coiling tighter with every stroke.

The feel of his hands on me, finally bringing to life the dripping-wet fantasies I'd imagined every time I stepped into this office, was beyond anything I could describe.

I was sure we were already crossing a line—but I didn't want to stop here.

I wanted to run past the line.

No, I wanted to erase the line completely.

"I don't want you to stop, Corbin," I panted. "I want more."

He pulled his fingers out of me and, in one swift motion, he caught me by my waist and spun me around.

Gazing up at me from his leather chair, his amber eyes turned ravenous. He looked like temptation barely holding itself together—tortured, beautiful, and impossible to resist.

His hands slid back under my skirt, one of them leaving a trail of moisture from my arousal along my thigh, before forcing my thong down my legs.

After stepping out of the underwear, we exchanged one last heated glance before Corbin shot out of his chair, forcefully wheeling it into the wall.

His lips crashed into mine, and it felt like that split-second before a roller coaster plunges—pure anticipation turning into a rush that stole my breath.

I reached for his belt, hastily working the buckle. Our mouths met in frantic kisses, breaking just long enough for him to shove his pants down—then coming together again, harder, hungrier.

His cock sprang free, rigid and heavy. I wrapped my hand around its base, and his breath shot into my mouth. I began to stroke him, using beads of his precum to wet his shaft, letting me glide effortlessly up and down.

He broke our kiss, resting his forehead against mine.

"I fucking missed you, Sophia," he breathed, his voice heavy with want.

"I missed you, too," I confessed.

He hiked my skirt around my hips and pushed me down on his desk. My legs opened, allowing him to settle in between them.

I lined his hardened cock up to my entrance. Just the proximity of him—not yet inside of me, his head nudging me—left me in a frenzy.

I was wild and untamed, desperate to feel him inside of me. I no longer cared that we were in his office or that the door was wide open.

I didn't care that we shouldn't be doing this.

His hands settled on my hips, locking me in place as he buried himself fully.

We both let out moans of pleasure—of relief.

This felt *inevitable*.

We were two stars on a crash course, barreling toward each other. It was only a matter of time before we collided.

My legs spread wider, and Corbin pressed in closer, burying himself deeper.

Our breaths came out hot and fast, the silence of the office filled with nothing but our moans, exhales, and the rattling of the desk drawers.

I leaned back, my palms resting on the cool wooden desktop.

With one large hand, Corbin wrapped his fingers around my shoulder, his thumb pressing into the column of my throat—holding me in place so he could bury himself even further.

His other hand gripped my hip as he slammed into me again and again. Strong fingers dug into my skin, the pressure igniting every inch of my body.

Harder. Tighter. I wanted *more*—more of him, more of this. I wanted to feel him in every inch of me, to carry the ache of him even after it was over.

I wanted to wear this moment like a bruise.

His name ripped from my throat, no longer able to worry about getting caught—my mind as locked up as my body as the tension mounted.

I moved out of Corbin's grip, pressing my chest to his and wrapping my arms around his shoulders.

His arms curled around my back, and he buried himself deeper, reaching a previously undiscovered part of me.

Then I imploded.

Every inch of my body lit up as my orgasm ripped through me—cresting with each thrust of Corbin's hips.

I let out a slew of words, sighs, and moans.

I was mindless, unable to control what tumbled out of my mouth. I buried my teeth into his shoulder, feeling untamed and primal as I came completely undone.

Corbin moaned my name, his thrusts slowing as I felt him fill me from deep inside.

We stayed locked in place, our shallow breaths filling the space. Wrapped around each other, clothed except for where our bodies connected—our need too imminent to waste time removing anything more.

My muscles felt liquid, and my body was hot as I slowly clawed my way back to reality.

I'd never, *never* felt a need so dire.

Never been so desperate, so driven with need.

It was like something in me broke away, and suddenly, I couldn't think past the need to have him—like a ship snapping free of its moorings and being swallowed by a raging sea.

Corbin slid out of me, his absence leaving me feeling empty, and I watched as he tucked himself away.

I stayed in place, too full from Corbin's release to move.

The room was thick with the remnants of what we'd done—our combined scent lingering in the air as the flushed skin of my thighs cooled against the edge of his desk.

Corbin's eyes found mine, something in them warring—like he was trying to win a battle inside himself.

For a moment, I thought he might actually say what I wanted to hear.

That there was something here to fight for. That he'd find a way around the no-relationship policy.

That we were worth it.

Instead, he said, "I'll get you something to clean up with."

I nodded, putting on a false smile, pretending the unsaid words didn't sting. Pretending I wasn't an idiot for expecting words to come out of his mouth that didn't exist in his head.

We fit together so well, like two corresponding puzzle pieces— pieces you might have to spin a few times to get them to lock correctly, but they belonged together all the same.

When he walked away, I tried to find the right words to say, to express how I felt. Maybe all it took was one of us to speak up, to admit that we wanted more from each other.

His phone buzzed on the desk next to me. It wasn't intentional—I didn't mean to look—but the screen lit up, and my eyes betrayed me before I could stop them.

Cindy: *See you tonight, babe ;)*

My world tilted slightly, twisting my stomach into knots.
Babe?

I stared at the screen, my pulse hammering in my ears—the text message delivering a slap of clarifying reality.

That I'd convinced myself this was more than it was. That there was something bigger between us.

Even if he had feelings for me—whatever those feelings were—he wouldn't stick around once this branch was off the ground.

He had his life in New York.

His *real* life.

I was just… a temporary escape—a small-town fling.

Nothing special. Nothing more.

I couldn't even be mad. Corbin and I never defined our relationship.

In fact, we spent most of our time discussing why this *wouldn't* work.

But that didn't stop the ache from spreading through my chest, the feeling of betrayal that he could look at me the way he did—make me feel the way I did—while he had someone else.

I almost had to laugh at myself for allowing it to happen again—falling so hard for someone who didn't feel the same way. At least Corbin was upfront about not wanting to be with me.

I forced my eyes to dry and hardened my heart.

By the time he returned—two glasses of water and towels from the breakroom in hand—I'd built a wall around myself.

I cleaned myself up with a shy, polite smile, straightened my skirt, and smoothed my hair, tucking it behind my ears—all the while pretending nothing had happened, pretending my heart wasn't shattering, pretending Cindy didn't exist.

"Thanks," I said, taking a sip of the water. It was cold, but it did nothing to cool the heat of my humiliation.

"This was… " he began, his voice trailing off as his fingers brushed a stray strand of hair from my face. The touch was gentle, almost tender, making my resolve waver for a moment.

"Yeah," I interrupted, forcing another tight smile and pushing his hand away. "We should try harder to avoid these *situations* in the future." My voice came out cold, disconnected.

He paused, and a look of confusion filled his features.

"This *can't* happen again," I clarified, my words seemingly throwing him off guard.

He looked pained—or maybe he was just a good actor.

But I wasn't losing my focus here. I refused to open my heart to someone who didn't even want it.

"I guess, I thought—"

"We always knew what this was," I interrupted with a light shrug.

His head recoiled slightly, his brows drawing together like my words had struck him. "I guess we did."

I bent to retrieve my discarded thong, fisting it in my hand as I padded toward the door. I refused to look back, afraid of what I'd say and the weaknesses I'd expose if I did. I would not allow myself to be the pathetic girl, romanticizing a relationship only to get tossed aside again.

I closed the door behind me with quiet finality, leaving him and whatever happened between us firmly on the other side.

This had to end anyway—I just made it easier for both of us.

Chapter 56

A LITTLE LIGHT BROOM HUMPING

Sophia

I sighed and clicked my pen as I stood behind the bar at Boomer's.

It was Sunday night, so I'd had nearly 48 hours to cry over my delusional romance-novel-level unrealistic expectation of love.

The clicking echoed in the quiet barroom. Devyn lifted her head from where she sat across the bar top, giving me a pointed look.

"Will you stop that?" she snapped before dropping her head back down.

I shoved the pen into my apron and began tapping the bar with my fingers instead.

"I'm so bored," she groaned, her voice muffling into the crook of her arm. "Why can't a couple of teams of hot hockey players walk in right now and leave me hundreds of dollars in tips?"

I barked a laugh.

"Well... since we've got all this quiet time to reflect on things, and since you brought up hot guys—" Devyn lifted her head again, her expression serious.

"Hold up, you brought that up just now. That was you," I interrupted.

"Can I finish?" Devyn waved her finger in the air at me. "You got any new news regarding a tall, dark, and handsome boss guy who held you hostage in New York, bought you fancy clothes, whisked you home on his private jet, fought your ex, took you to pound town, and then gave you a dream job?"

I spent Sunday brunches with the girls trying to carefully downplay everything with Corbin—for my sake and theirs. There was no reason to get excited about a fling or express feelings that shouldn't exist.

Instead, I fed them mimosas and redirected the conversation towards Devyn's upcoming wedding, Lana's shop, and Cassie's latest gossip from the hotel—anything to take the attention off me.

They were my best friends—I *wanted* to spill everything, to let them in the way I always had. But this time, I couldn't. Not when it wasn't only my secret to tell.

They knew Corbin and I had been together in New York. Devyn's "you totally had sex" radar was apparently on high alert—and there was no dodging it. But that was it, that was where the line was initially drawn between us, before I started working for him. That's where I kept it with my friends. They didn't know about our hotel room encounter, and they didn't know that just a few days ago, I was splayed out on his desk underneath him.

Devyn's eyes narrowed on me before softening. "We used to tell each other everything, Soph. Why does it feel like you're blocking us out again?"

I leaned over the bar, my hands falling on her hands. "I promise I'm not blocking you out, Dev. I just.... there isn't much to tell. Corbin and I aren't anything more than Assistant Editor and COO."

"Really? Nothing?" Disappointment filled her voice.

"Really. Nothing. He made it very clear." I tried to hide my disappointment by wiping at an already cleaned spot on the bar.

"Well, then, what are you doing? Landon's gone. You're not with anyone. Let's get you out there!" she howled as she twirled around on the barstool. "I need time to vet this guy if you want to bring him to the wedding. So, chop, chop."

Devyn and Sam settled on their wedding date: next September. Devyn had asked me to be a bridesmaid, along with Cassie and Lana, of course.

One of my best friends was going to be married, and I couldn't be happier for her.

I sighed, trying to release the stupid part inside of me that was clinging to Corbin. "I agree with you. However, we can't do anything about it right now. It's not like Mr. Perfect will walk right through that door. So until then... tequila shot?" I asked with a grin.

"Oh God, yes." She beamed back.

It was a tradition we'd done anytime it was toward the end of the night, and we had nothing better to do. My time working together with Devyn would be ending soon—though I hadn't officially decided when I would quit Boomer's—we may as well enjoy these fleeting moments together.

Though it almost felt like there was a tether tying me here, like this was my last lifeline, *just in case*. I tried not to dwell on that thought.

I poured each shot and grabbed the saltshaker and two slices of lime. We let out synchronized gasps after downing them, sucking the juices from our limes.

Paul peered his head out of the kitchen door. "I'm cleaning up. If anyone walks through that door, they don't get any food. Do you hear me?"

"Gotcha, Paulie D," Devyn said with a fake Jersey accent.

He batted the air with his hand before disappearing behind the swinging door.

"One more?" I asked, my eyebrows wiggling.

Devyn nodded enthusiastically.

I felt slightly buzzed as closing time drew nearer.

Devyn swept the floor, and I was cleaning glasses when the door opened, the bells breaking the quiet with a sharp clang. Our heads snapped toward the door.

I didn't know who to expect. Landon? Corbin? A couple of football teams?

But it was just one person—someone I faintly recognized from a few weeks ago. He smiled at me when he walked up to the bar, and his dimples sparked a memory.

"Hey," the stranger said casually as he sat at the bar.

"Hello. Can I get you a drink?" I asked.

"No, thank you. I um—I didn't come for a drink." He caught his lower lip between his teeth, his eyes searching my face.

My eyes shot to Devyn as she stood behind him, pointing at his back and fake-humping the broom she was holding.

I tried to shake my head nonchalantly, my eyes widening at her to stop.

"You never called," Dimples said, returning my focus to his face.

"Called?" I asked, confused.

"Yeah," he said through a shy smile. "A few weeks ago, I left my number. You never called."

His walnut eyes were warm, like an inviting mug of hot chocolate, precisely what a frigid day like today called for.

Flurries danced on strong gusts—the first snow of the year. Too light to stick, they swirled through the air, a sure sign winter was closing in.

Just a few days ago, we'd been basking in an unusually warm afternoon—classic Midwestern weather, always keeping you on your toes.

I thought for a moment, recalling the night the hockey teams invaded the bar—the night Landon got the jump on me and almost drove Corbin to assault him.

"Oh, right."

Like I was ever going to call. I was a mess. My life was a million different ways from fucked. The last thing I needed was to introduce a new person into the fray.

"I thought I'd come in here, hope you were working again, and give it another shot."

I was thinking about how to say no—running through the excuses in my mind, trying to pull out the one that seemed the least pathetic.

"She'd love to!" Devyn interjected before I had a chance to respond.

My wide eyes shot toward her.

What the hell was she doing?

Dimples turned to Devyn, then back to me. "She thinks you should," he teased, tossing his thumb behind his shoulder at her.

"I do. I really do think you should." Devyn giggled, then proceeded to fake make-out with the broom behind his back.

My throat tightened, and I cleared it nervously. "I don't... I don't know if that's a good idea."

"Just one drink," he offered, his sweet smile nearly melting my heart.

"Yeah, just one drink," Devyn mimicked from behind him.

I gave her a death stare.

"I'm going to go clean the bathrooms now, toodles!" She scurried down the hallway, dancing with her broom along the way.

"I don't even know your name."

"I'm Will," he said, holding his hand out for mine.

"Hi Will, I'm—"

"Sophia, I remember."

I placed my hand in his.

His hand felt nice—warm and gentle—nothing like the charged electricity that amped through my veins when Corbin touched me.

I didn't know if I should consider that a good or bad thing.

"Look, I'm going to say that I won't take no for an answer, even though I will very much take no for an answer." His soft eyes sparkled in the dull bar. "I just want to get to know you."

"So sweet, Will. She's in. She'll meet you on Wednesday. Here at six, early date, no weekend commitments," Devyn yelled from a distance, her head sticking out from the hallway along with the broom bristles.

Will stood up, wrote something on a napkin, and slid it over to me. "Here is my number again. I'm going to leave while you pseudo-agreed to come. Text me if you change your mind though, and I'll leave you alone from here on out." He walked away with a wink and a dimpled grin.

As soon as he left through the door, I turned to face Devyn.

She yelped as I chased her down the hallway—shutting herself in the bathroom and throwing her weight against the door, holding it closed.

"I'm just doing what's best for you! He's super cute!" she yelled through the wooden door.

I stopped pushing and rested my back against the slab with a sigh. Maybe she was right. What reason did I have to say no?

Devyn didn't realize I was still there and pulled open the door, causing me to crash to the floor, taking her with me.

We laughed as we lay there, semi-buzzed on the bathroom floor and struggling to get back up.

"I'm going to kill you, Dev," I threatened through my laughing tears.

"You love me. Besides, you need this. You seem sad again. I don't want sad Sophia back." She jutted her lip out as we faced each other, still sprawled out on the bathroom floor.

Gross, sure. But the room was starting to spin, so it felt safer to stay put.

Devyn stood up, extending a hand to help me. "Besides Soph, the best way to get over someone is to reverse-cowgirl someone else."

I accepted her help, standing in front of her, I placed my hands on her tiny shoulders. "There will be no reverse-cowgirling."

She shrugged, and we both fell into another fit of laughter before walking back to the barroom to finish cleaning.

I felt a little uneasy about this date, considering just a couple of days ago, my boss was inside me while we had forbidden-but-incredibly-hot sex in his office.

But reality came crashing back, the way it always did whenever I let myself think about Corbin and me—cold and unforgiving, like the tile floor in the ladies' room at Boomer's.

I swallowed hard, like forcing spit down my throat could act as a balm to my aching heart.

The thought was quiet and still in my mind, but the weight of the truth sliced through me like tiny, piercing daggers.

Corbin and I just weren't meant to be.

Chapter 57

A WOLF IN SHEEP'S CLOTHING?

Corbin

I sat on the jet Monday morning, anxious to return to Misty Springs.

I had an exhausting weekend, starting Friday with a four-hour-long dinner at the Governor's mansion—ninety of those minutes spent deflecting Cindy's not-so-subtle advances.

She dangled the promise of new information regarding my company like bait, but it became clear she had nothing of value.

I wanted to tell her off in front of the crowd—to cut ties and make it clear I wanted nothing to do with her—professionally or personally. But she wasn't even worth the effort of making a scene.

My leg bounced with restless energy as nerves tightened in my chest at the thought of seeing Sophia again.

Another impromptu trip back to Misty Springs, another one that felt mandatory—an invisible tug pulling me by my insides—back to the middle of the country.

My heart twisted when I thought back to that moment on my desk—the way everything had crystallized between us.

I was certain we both felt it. That whatever had been building between us wasn't just attraction—it was something bigger.

Something neither of us could keep denying.

I couldn't find the right words, the right way to tell her. The path we could walk together was riddled with landmines and potholes, but I wanted to walk it—with her.

But when I returned to my office, something in her eyes had shifted.

And her voice—cool, composed—framed this thing between us like it was nothing. Like she flipped some switch and turned *us* off.

That moment gutted me.

I was deep in thought, sipping a maple bourbon cappuccino that was not nearly as good as Lana's, when Davis marched onto the jet.

"Morning," he said briskly, sliding into the seat across from me.

"This is a surprise," I remarked, setting my cup down and putting my defenses up.

"I heard you were heading back to the wild Midwest. I thought I'd hitch a ride and finally check out the financial viability of the Misty Springs branch. Plus, the board has been interested to see what's been keeping our COO so *occupied.*"

His words triggered an alarm inside me, but I kept my composure. There have been quiet rumblings about the board's unease with Buzz's leadership, but nothing overt was reported in the meeting notes—notes I've only been skimming lately because my trips to Misty Springs have caused me to miss those meetings.

But Davis could've assessed the financial viability of the branch from his corner office.

Hell, I'm sure he already had.

And I'm sure he found the numbers were promising, stronger than expected.

There was no reason to question the branch's performance—unless he was questioning *mine.*

"Fair enough." I schooled my expression into polite neutrality. "I suppose it's always best to see things in person."

"Exactly," he said, a ghost of a smile tugging at the corners of his mouth.

He picked up his phone and began scrolling through it, but I could feel every time his eyes flicked toward me.

Measuring. Calculating.

Whether he was coming as an objective observer or if he was gathering reconnaissance for the board, I was going to make sure it fit *my* narrative.

I shot Andi a quick heads-up text as the plane lifted off the ground.

***

Once we arrived, I led Davis through the office, introducing him to Susan and Andi.

We were early. No sign of Ned or Sophia yet.

I left Davis in an unclaimed office and stepped into my own to make a few calls. When I emerged about fifteen minutes later, I spotted Davis in a corner near the proofing room, speaking quietly with Ned.

The sight gave me pause, and I instinctively retreated into my office, watching them from just inside the doorway.

Ned wasn't exactly the type to draw Davis's attention, yet there they were—heads bent together in deep conversation.

The sharp clink of ceramic broke through the low hum of the office. I glanced over as Sophia reached for a mug near the coffee station.

Davis turned, too.

His attention peeled away from Ned. Without hesitation, he moved—cutting across the room with that casual confidence that always rubbed me the wrong way.

Straight to Sophia.

His body eclipsed my view of her, his back facing me, leaving me unable to read either one of their faces. I couldn't hear a word he said to her—just the faint rumbling of his low voice.

What was he saying?

Was he pressing her for intel on me?

Could Ned have said something about what he saw—or thought he saw—between Sophia and me in the proofing room?

Or was he just flirting? That smug, easy way he had—too casual, too damn confident.

Davis had a talent for turning charm into opportunity. I'd never seen a woman turn him down.

Then she laughed.

Short. Light. Easy.

Something in my jaw locked.

I had no idea what he'd said to earn that laugh—and I didn't like that he'd earned one from her at all.

I stalked over to them, suddenly in the mood for coffee myself.

As I drew closer, my eyes landed on Sophia nodding at something Davis said through a sip of her coffee. Her smile was polite, but I could see the flicker of uncertainty in her eyes as they darted toward me.

I wished I knew what that look meant. I hated that I didn't.

Davis noticed my approach, his voice trailing off mid-sentence—like someone had pressed mute. He didn't rush to greet me, didn't offer a word to fill the silence—just watched me approach with that unreadable expression of his.

It was a Davis tactic I knew too well, but was still falling for—how to wield silence like a weapon. It was the kind of move designed to rattle people.

Let them imagine the worst. Let them fill in the blanks.

"Corbin," Davis said finally, his tone laced with irritation as if I was somehow intruding. "Show me the first floor? You have space for a tenant there, right?"

Before I could respond, he added to Sophia, "Thanks for the chat. Always good to hear things from someone who knows where the pressure points are."

Pressure points?

She gave a slight nod.

"Come with me," I said to Davis, my voice level, stepping toward the door as heat rose beneath my collar.

Davis had a talent for getting under people's skin—especially mine. My rational brain knew he wasn't getting near Sophia. The no-relationship policy would topple him just as easily as it would me.

But that didn't matter.

What bothered me—really bothered me—was the realization that her heart was still available, that someone else could reach for it and grab it.

And even though it wouldn't be Davis. It also wouldn't be me.

Davis followed me to the first floor, our footsteps echoing across the empty space before he broke the silence. "Look, Corbin, I want to be frank with you."

Here we go.

"Word is, you're on thin ice with the board. Your continued absence isn't doing you any favors." He placed a hand on my shoulder, a fake attempt at consoling me. "It doesn't look good."

My muscles tensed under his touch. "Kind of hard to be present when I'm exiled here to babysit Buzz's pet project."

"That's the thing," Davis continued, dropping his hand and sliding it into his pocket. "The board isn't a fan of this *project*—or your grandfather—right now."

I snorted. "Buzz appointed the board. If they're unhappy, he can deal with it. Or fire them."

"Not that you've been around at meetings to find out, but the board has been shifting. These days, more members are being voted in without your grandfather's vetting than with it."

His words landed heavily, but I kept my tone light. "Thanks for the heads-up."

"Just looking out for you. That's why I wanted to come here—to ensure we could speak face-to-face. You're so rarely in New York these days," he said, his teeth gleaming in a smile that was all show—predator-level polite.

Davis and I both craved power—it was one of the few things we had in common. As we climbed through the ranks at Buescher Enterprises, he'd never held his punches regarding my family name.

Was he trying to stake a claim to my seat?

I couldn't shake the unease settling in my chest. I always knew to trust my instincts, and they told me Davis wasn't here to warn me about the board.

He was looking for something.

And whatever it was, I had a sinking feeling it wasn't anything good.

Chapter 58

Don't Say Date

Sophia

I am *so glad* that sneaky little fox is slinking out of here today," Andi announced as she dropped dramatically into the purple chair in my office.

"Who? Davis?" I asked, setting my pen down. "I wasn't going to say anything, but I got a bad feeling about him, too."

Davis had been here for three days. His eyes always seemed to be scanning, assessing—and every time they landed on me, it felt like they were trying to claw through me, digging for something I wanted to keep buried.

I avoided him at all costs, offering only polite conversation when he cornered me near the coffee station or lingered in my office doorway.

"*A bad feeling?* No, no, he gives more than a bad feeling. He gives off whole body heebie jeebies."

I laughed.

"I'm serious. I don't trust him. And he kept talking to nasty Ned, which means I *double* don't trust him." Her voice was loud enough that Ned probably heard every word.

Not that she cared.

Since I started, Andi and I had spent a lot of time together, and I'd grown to adore her blunt, unfiltered personality. She was unapologetically herself, and I admired her for it—hopeful even, that some of her strong traits would rub off on me.

She sighed as she inspected her long, manicured nails. "Anyway, let's change gears. Tell me about this *Will* guy." She leaned in, propping her chin on her hand and wiggling her eyebrows underneath her black-and-white, checker-patterned glasses.

"There's not much to tell," I admitted. "My friend Devyn set it up. And it's not a *date*. It's just a drink. Mostly to get Devyn off my back."

Andi snorted. "You're lucky to have someone looking out for you."

"Speaking of dates, I have one this weekend with Stacy…"

I gasped, spinning my chair toward her. "Stacy? Who is Stacy? Dish! Please!"

Andi opened her mouth to respond, but a deep, familiar voice cut in.

"Andi, a moment?"

I tried to pretend that the sound of his voice didn't send a thrill through my body.

His eyes flicked briefly to me. "Morning," he acknowledged with an emotionless voice.

My stomach tightened. Had he heard us talking about Davis? Or worse—about Will?

"Morning," I managed to reply.

Corbin's attention moved back to Andi. "Meet me in my office."

He turned and left without another word.

Andi wrinkled her nose at me as she stood. "I don't want to face him right now. He's going to be *so cranky* today. I can feel it."

"Stay strong, Andi," I whispered with mock seriousness.

"Oh, you know it," she replied, flipping her hair dramatically over her shoulder. She strutted out in her flawlessly coordinated navy suede outfit.

As the office wound down for the day, I saw Ned wrestling with a stack of papers.

I curiously peeked at them, not thinking anything of it.

When he noticed me watching, his head snapped up, and he quickly shuffled the papers into a folder.

"Something I can help you with?" I asked, trying to sound casual.

"Nope. Just finishing up," he snapped, his eyes darting away as he tucked the folder under his arm and walked briskly toward his desk.

Ned's previous advances towards me, which were just slimy enough to make me feel uncomfortable but innocuous enough to be plausibly deniable if I presented anything to HR, had halted abruptly.

Now, he barely spoke to me or even looked in my direction. Not that I was complaining, but the sudden shift in behavior was... oddly timed.

I stuffed my laptop in my bag and grabbed my coat, stopping by Andi's open door on my way out.

She was leaning over her desk, scribbling furiously on a notepad, her ever-present coffee mug within reach.

"Hey," I said, stepping inside.

"You heading out?" she asked without looking up.

"Yeah... hey, have you noticed anything... weird about Ned?"

She straightened, her pen paused mid-air. "Weird, how? Other than his general Ned-ness?"

I let out a soft laugh, brushing it off with a shake of my head. "It's nothing. Probably just me reading too much into things."

I didn't feel like explaining that I'd been watching him closely after he walked in on Corbin and me in the proofing room a few weeks back.

"Keep your eyes open. Ned's been cozying up to Davis, and we know how to feel about Davis," she said, snapping her jaws shut.

I set my laptop bag on her chair and began pulling on my coat.

"Have fun on your *date*," she teased.

And because timing had a cruel sense of humor. Corbin chose that moment to walk through the door.

I froze, getting my coat only halfway on, catching the slight twitch in Corbin's jaw when he placed a stack of papers on Andi's desk.

His eyes flicked to mine, sharp and unreadable, before returning to Andi.

"I need you to package these and mail them to the New York branch. Stephanie's attention," he ordered firmly.

"You got it, boss," Andi said, unaware of the silent storm crashing around her.

Then he turned and left. No words, no more glances my way.

The breath caught in my chest finally loosened—the entire exchange only lasted a few seconds, but it left my heart pounding frantically, like I'd just sprinted up a flight of stairs.

I finished pulling on my coat, slung my bag over my shoulder, and waved goodbye to Andi as I strode out of her office.

I was a bundle of nerves as I walked down the hallway.

Why was I so worried?

I wasn't doing anything wrong. Corbin and I knew we wouldn't work. Besides, he had Cindy and who knows who else on rotation back in New York.

I steadied myself with each step, fortifying the walls I had tried to build around my heart.

"Have fun on your date." Corbin's voice stopped me dead in my tracks as I stepped into the lobby.

I spun to face him.

He was standing near the coffee maker, absently stirring a tiny straw through the steaming cup in his hands. His eyes were solely focused on the task—nowhere near me.

"Thanks," I answered, my voice cracking slightly.

His eyes snapped to mine, searching for something—what, I wasn't sure.

For a moment, I was caught in his gaze—warmth building beneath my heavy coat. I took a steadying breath, locking those walls around my heart into place.

"Have a good evening, Mr. Buescher," I said firmly before retreating with my head held high.

I thought I saw a flicker of hurt on his face, something that dug through my hardened heart, like roots digging into stone.

But I couldn't focus on that look or whatever I wished that look meant for me, for us.

Because no matter how hard I wanted it to happen, there was no *us*.

Chapter 59

DAVID HASSELHOFF'S DRUNKEN WHISKEY-SAUCE BURGER

Corbin

My fingers tapped impatiently on Andi's desk, barely registering her words—my mind focused on one subject.

Sophia was going on a date.

How long had she been seeing someone? Was it serious?

"Do you want to… I dunno, maybe knock that off?" Andi snarked at me.

I stopped and waved my hands innocently in the air before bringing my nails to my lips and gnawing anxiously at them—a nervous tick I hadn't done since college.

"Did you even hear a word I said?" She leaned back in her chair, crossing her arms. "I think Nasty Ned has it out for you, and I think your shady little buddy Davis is in on it, too."

"You're paranoid, Andi. No one *has it out for me.*" I dismissed her, though a part of me had already considered the same thing.

I've made plenty of enemies—the Norwood family being the latest added to the list.

But Ned? I wasn't worried about Ned in the slightest. And Davis was nothing but competition.

Besides, the last thing I needed was Andi poking her nose in my business.

"Fine, don't listen to me," she resigned. "But you can buy me some dinner, and I know just the place."

***

"David Hasselhoff's drunken whiskey-e burger?" I asked as Andi tore into the massive burger in her hands.

Baywatch played in the background in Elijah's dimly lit dining room. The room was packed with a steady crowd who had gathered to enjoy the movie and the food.

"I thought they only did theme nights on the weekend?" I grabbed the extra napkins on the table, covering my lap and half tempted to stuff them down my shirt like a baby's bib—this thing was a mess.

"They really do it up around the holidays. The hotel is fully booked," she garbled through a mouthful of food.

"You would at least think they would go with a Christmas-themed movie."

"That starts this weekend—Die Hard," she said as she shoved another huge bite in her mouth.

"Don't forget to swallow that," I joked.

She flipped me off.

I reluctantly took a bite, unwilling to accept that a small-town hotel in the middle of nowhere could churn out food that would draw such a crowd.

But as soon as the food hit my tongue, I realized just how wrong I could be.

It was gastro-heaven.

This nine-dollar burger was better than my favorite pub around the corner from my place—which charged me thirty.

I swallowed, not ready to admit that Andi was right. "You've gotten quite familiar with the ins and outs of this hotel, huh?"

She nodded as she finished chewing. "I didn't think I would, but I love it here. However, living in a single room for more than two months was starting to drive me crazy. I actually found an apartment in Sophia's building."

I tried not to let my mind wander at the mention of Sophia.

Where was she on this date? What were they doing? Would they go back to her place?

My insides twisted as images flashed in my brain of her with someone else.

I turned my direction to the big screen on the wall, hoping to distract myself with busty, slow-motion running in red swimsuits.

I devoured my burger until every last bite was gone, then licked my fingers.

Andi was right—

"Told you," Andi smirked as she watched me.

A flash of movement behind the bar caught my eye as Cassie wove around the bartender and toward the register.

I took the opportunity to refill mine and Andi's drink—a guise to corner Cassie instead.

"They'll come to us," Andi protested, but I was already on the move.

I made it to the bar just as Cassie was about to leave, clipboard in hand, checking off her managerial to-do list for the evening.

"Hey," I said, setting my empty cups on the bar top.

"Oh. Hey, *Zoolander*," she hurled the nickname like a slur.

I pinched the bridge of my nose. "I really hate that nickname." She shrugged and started walking again.

I took a few hurried steps to catch up with her. "Hey, hold on."

Cassie turned and raised her eyebrows at me, tilting her head in question.

"Sophia, she's on a... date?" I asked, trying to sound nonchalant.

Cassie rested the clipboard on her hip and gave me a sly grin. "Oh yeah, that *is* tonight."

She turned and continued walking like we were finished with this conversation.

I followed her out of the dining room—aware that Andi was probably watching the entire exchange, but I couldn't bring myself to care about that right now.

"Who is he?" I asked, my tone taking a half-degree turn toward desperate.

"Who? Will? Oh, he's just this super handsome, super built, super sexy hockey player. Great guy, *super hot*... did I mention that?" She scrunched her eyebrows before turning away from me again.

I followed her to the front desk. "How long has she... how many dates have they gone on?" I pressed, fully desperate now.

Cassie walked behind the front desk and set her clipboard down.

"Let's see." She puffed her cheeks with air, blowing a big breath out as she held up her fingers. "Carry the two..."

I growled in frustration.

She looked at me with a devious smile. "What's it to you anyway?"

I paused for half a second as I considered.

What is it to me anyway?

I didn't have an answer, but I didn't need one—Cassie wasn't a damn psychiatrist, and I didn't need analyzing.

I crossed my arms. "I'll buy you a bottle of Macallan."

Her eyes lit up at my bribe. "Okay. I suppose I *could* tell you it's their first date. And I suppose I *could* tell you they are just grabbing a drink at Boomer's. And I suppose I could also tell you that she didn't even want to do it, and it was all Devyn's master plan."

"Thanks," I grumbled, turning to leave.

"Corbin," she added with a serious tone.

I turned back to face her.

She tapped her fingers on the desk lightly. "I'm not telling you because of the whiskey. I'm telling you because... she's happier... with you around."

I was stunned into silence.

"I don't know what kind of corporate-y bullshit there is keeping you two apart, but I can tell you—she's worth it."

"I know she is," I agreed, my throat tight. I spun on my heels and headed toward the dining room, coming up with an excuse in my mind to tell Andi why I was leaving.

"I want the Eighteen, though!" Cassie yelled at my back—the woman knew her whiskey.

I walked into Elijah's dining room, weaving in and out of the little rectangular tables adorned with plastic beach-themed tablecloths.

My steps slowed as I approached my seat—the one I'd abruptly left without explanation was now occupied.

A woman who looked about Andi's age leaned in close, her posture relaxed and familiar as she spoke to Andi. Her dark hair fell over her shoulders, and her light skin was dotted with freckles.

For all her sharp edges and no-nonsense demeanor, Andi was... *softened*. Her face alight with a kind of ease I hadn't seen before.

I stepped closer, clearing my throat.

Both women turned their attention toward me, the newcomer's hazel eyes scanning me with polite curiosity.

"You're back." Andi's eyebrow arched as she reclined slightly in her chair. "Did Cassie have something *riveting* to share with you?"

"Just needed some... clarity on my hotel bill," I lied smoothly, adjusting my tie as I reached for my wallet. I pulled out a few bills and slid them across the table to Andi. "This should cover dinner."

Andi grabbed the money without a second thought.

I glanced back at the woman who stole my seat.

"Stacy, this is Corbin. Corbin, Stacy," Andi said sweetly.

"Nice to meet you finally." Stacy shook my hand gently, giving off a quiet demeanor, a lamb to Andi's lion.

"You look like you're in a rush to get somewhere." Andi smiled wide, a knowing look filled her eyes.

"Yeah, I have some things to finish up at the office."

As I stepped away, her voice followed me. "You're predictable, you know."

I didn't respond.

What could I say? She wasn't wrong.

I had no real plan as I left Elijah's, my shoes hitting the pavement with purpose despite my lack of direction.

All I knew was that Sophia was at Boomer's—on some *date*— with someone who wasn't me.

And no matter what.

I *had* to stop that date.

Chapter 60

The Calm Before the Storm

Sophia

Will was sweet. I learned he was an artist, had a studio in Kingston, and played amateur hockey in his spare time. He was also considerate, funny, and undeniably handsome.

But when his touch brushed against my hand, I felt his warmth, but nothing more. I saw kind eyes and a nice smile when he looked at me, but I didn't see much beyond that.

He wasn't Corbin.

"This isn't going well, is it?" Will's question broke my thoughts.

I straightened in the booth across from him, my hands nervously spinning the base of my martini glass—which didn't taste nearly as good as the one Corbin made for me a few weeks ago.

"I wouldn't say that." I smiled. "I'm enjoying your company, I just…"

His hand reached for mine, gently pulling it from the glass.

"It's okay," he said, his voice soft and reassuring. "This is what dating is all about—you try it, and sometimes, it doesn't work. But eventually, someone comes along who doesn't just fit into your life—they rewrite the definition of it."

His words startled me.

What if Corbin rewrote the definition of my life only to cast me as a footnote in the story we were meant to share?

I tried to wave off my depressing thoughts, focusing back on Will, staring at where our hands interlocked.

"That's a profound thought to be had in the corner of a dingy bar, Will."

"What can I say? I've got an artist's heart trapped in a hockey player's body."

I looked up and smiled at him. He gave me a dimpled smile back, his warmth spreading through me like a calming hug.

"You—well, your friend—agreed to have a drink, and we had it. I can close our tab."

"No, you drove all the way here, drinks are on me."

A movement near our booth caught my eye.

I broke away from Will's gaze to look, and my heart leaped into my throat.

Corbin towered over us like a storm cloud in a perfect wool coat. His midnight-black hair was tousled, but not from neglect—more like the wind outside had teased it into an effortless style that only made him look more achingly handsome.

His eyes—those piercing amber-whiskey eyes—locked on mine, unreadable but intense. The heat of his presence seemed to suck all the air from the room, and suddenly, I couldn't hear the soft murmur of conversations around us or the clinking of glasses.

Will shifted across the table, his hand slipping from mine.

"Uh, hi." His polite smile faltered as he glanced between us. "Can we help you?"

Corbin's gaze flicked briefly to Will, narrowing slightly.

"Will, this is… my boss, Corbin Buescher."

Will extended his hand. "Oh, nice to meet you."

Corbin stared at it for a moment—like he wanted to rip it from Will's body—before finally reaching out to shake it.

I caught a small wince that Will instantly wiped away, and when Corbin let go, Will gently massaged his palm with his other hand.

"Nice to meet you, *Will*. Sophia, I need to speak with you." Corbin's words were friendly, but they held a sharp edge.

He turned and walked toward the bar—I watched his retreating back the entire way.

"That guy is your boss?" Will asked once Corbin was out of earshot.

I nodded, my heart throbbing in my throat, leaving no room for words.

"Where do you work? Langley?"

I exhaled a shaky laugh, while my eyes drifted back to Corbin—his presence eclipsed everything, leaving no room for anyone else.

And suddenly, this entire night—this attempt at moving on—felt laughable.

"Listen, if you ever want to try this again, you have my number." Will stood up and grabbed his coat from the booth.

I stood up to say goodbye, and he pulled me into a hug, the scent of cloves and honey encircled me.

He was warm, comfortable, cozy—like rolling up in a blanket while cookies baked in the oven.

"Bye, Will. And thank you for a nice evening," I said into his chest.

"Bye, Sophia. Thanks for the drink." He unwrapped his arms from me and turned to leave.

After watching him walk out the door, I turned around to face the bar. Corbin's eyes were boring into me, penetrating me from across the dimly lit room.

Swallowing my nerves, I grabbed my things and strode over to him.

"Care to join me for a drink?" he asked, his voice like rolling thunder in my chest.

I nodded—aware that I had rolled out of the warm blanket and was now running right into the eye of the storm.

Chapter 61

THE NIGHT THAT CHANGED EVERYTHING

Corbin

Sophia took the empty barstool next to me as the bartender approached us.

The bartender's dirty blonde hair was pulled up high, and her face was meticulously made up—the kind of make-up where you couldn't distinguish which features actually belonged to her.

"Hey, handsome, can I get you a drink?" She used her breasts to point in my direction.

I suppose it was entrepreneurial of her to use her assets accordingly.

She leaned over, laying her *assets* on the bar in front of me. "You know, we don't get many guys like you in here. I'm happy to take care of you all night."

"Hi, Theresa," Sophia grumbled beside me.

A wave of recognition washed through me: Theresa, Sophia's boss—the one who slept with Landon.

Oh, this was awkward.

"Oh. Hey Sophia, I didn't notice you there. I thought you were still at table 27 with that adorable snack."

I felt my body stiffen at the mention of the curly-haired hockey boy Sophia was just with. I practically lunged across the barroom when he wrapped his arms around her.

"I'll have an Old Fashioned and whatever Sophia wants. We have a lot to discuss." I focused on Sophia as I placed the order.

Theresa stood still, assessing us, perhaps wondering how I knew Sophia's name and why she was sitting next to me now—or maybe just wondering what we were to each other.

A thought I wondered myself.

"Gin martini," Sophia ordered, her eyes locked with mine.

In my periphery, I noticed Theresa step away with a little less perk in her chest.

"What would you like to discuss, *Mr. Buescher?*" The way she said my name sounded accusatory.

My eyes narrowed on her.

"How was your *date?*" I asked, my tone sharp, laced with my own accusations.

She tilted her head. "I'm not sure why that matters."

Her expression was cool and unbothered, but something was telling in her eyes.

"I guess it doesn't," I admitted, though the words felt like ash on my tongue.

Because it did matter.

The problem was that Sophia did something to me.

She made me want to cross lines I'd spent years carving into stone. She was like wild ivy, creeping through the cracks, burrowing into every hidden weakness until she wasn't just breaking through— she was becoming part of the structure itself, fortifying it in ways I couldn't control.

Theresa set our drinks down and turned away without another word.

The silence between Sophia and me grew heavy, and before I could stop myself, the words tumbled out of me.

"I didn't realize we were seeing other people," I admitted, exposed, vulnerable.

I took a sip to hide my nerves.

"That's rich, coming from you." She picked up her drink and took a big gulp.

I paused mid-drink, certain that I had misheard her. I slowly lowered the glass back down on the sticky bar top.

"What is that supposed to mean?"

Sophia sighed. "Nothing, forget I said anything. I'm being…" She stared at her martini, spinning it slowly in front of her. "This is just harder than I thought it would be." She gestured between us.

We both admitted something, each of us losing ground slightly.

But it opened something.

"Screw the drinks. Come with me." A plan had formed in my head, and I wasn't going to waste time executing it.

Her brow furrowed, her lips parting slightly. "What?"

"Leave with me. Right now," I repeated, my pulse hammering against my ribs.

She blinked, stunned, but there was no hesitation in the way she grabbed her coat. That simple act told me everything I needed to know—we were in deeper than either of us wanted to admit.

"One sec." She held up a finger. "Hey, Theresa!"

Theresa eyed Sophia from behind the taps as she filled a beer glass with foamy liquid.

"I'm not coming in tomorrow. I quit!" Sophia yelled with a huge smile on her face.

I smirked as I threw a fifty down on the bar and grabbed her hand. We quickly escaped Boomer's and slipped into the freezing night air.

The drive out of Misty Springs was meant to be a relief, an escape from knowing looks and whispered judgments. There were too many prying eyes at Elijah's, so I left with a different destination in mind.

I knew a Hilton property was a few miles away because I considered staying there during several of my early visits to Misty Springs.

Whatever it took us to sort things out, whatever we needed to say to each other, we would do it tonight without any distractions.

The sky was inky-black, the stars and moon blotted out behind a thick layer of clouds, and the road ahead was illuminated only by the car's headlights. The hum of the tires on the asphalt was soothing, almost hypnotic, but I couldn't relax—not with her sitting so close, her scent lingering in the air, and the weight of unspoken words filling the car.

Sophia broke the silence first. "Where are we going?"

"To sort things out." The vague response was not telling, but it was honest. "I think we have a lot to discuss, and everywhere around here feels too... crowded."

Silence stretched between us for just a couple of beats.

"Who is Cindy?" she asked.

I barked out a laugh, the question catching me entirely off guard. "Cindy? She's a bit... hard to describe." I collected myself before continuing, the concern on Sophia's face urging me to clear the air quickly. "She was a mistake years ago, and now she is an incessant thorn in my side that I can't seem to extract."

Sophia's lips twitched. "Oh, God." She threw her head back against the headrest. "I admittedly saw she texted you the other day. She seemed pretty excited about your dinner together in New York."

I grimaced. "Cindy's excited about anyone who can help her climb another ladder rung. Trust me, she's nothing to me."

Without thinking, I reached over and took her hand. Her fingers were soft and hesitant at first, but then they curled around mine reassuringly.

"That dinner was with Cindy and about twenty other people. I sat as far away from her as possible all evening."

She let out a small huff of a laugh, but I could see doubt swirling in her features from the low light of the dashboard.

"Look, I don't know what you've heard or what you've thought, but I haven't been with anyone else after I met you. Not since that day you called me an asshole in first class."

That earned me a bellow of laughter, and my heart swelled at the sound.

"You're the only one who has been in my bed, in my mind, damn near everywhere I go. It's only been you," I admitted.

Her hand gave mine a soft squeeze, and I pulled it to my lips, brushing them against her smooth skin and inhaling her floral scent.

For a moment, everything felt right.

And then it didn't.

It started as a faint vibration in the steering wheel, a subtle tremor I might've ignored if it hadn't quickly escalated. The car lurched slightly, and I tightened my grip on the wheel.

"What's wrong?" Sophia asked, her voice tinged with worry.

"I don't know," I admitted, releasing her hand as I tried to keep the car steady.

The vibration worsened, becoming a violent shudder that made the steering wheel almost impossible to control. The car swerved, and I slammed on the brakes, but the pedal felt off—soft, spongy, and unresponsive.

"Hold on!" I shouted as the car veered toward the shoulder.

The car jerked violently as I fought to keep it on the road. The brakes were nearly useless, and the steering wheel felt like it was fighting against me. We were on a stretch of highway bordered by a steep embankment on one side and a dense line of trees on the other.

"Look out!" Sophia's voice was sharp and panicked as the car fishtailed.

The next seconds unfolded in chaotic fragments: the tires slipping, the car spinning out of control, the sickening sensation of weightlessness as we veered off the road.

A deafening crash erupted as the front of the car collided with the embankment. The force threw me forward, the seatbelt biting into my chest.

Glass shattered, and the airbags deployed with a suffocating *whoosh*.

Everything was silent and still except for the sound of the engine sputtering and the faint ticking of the cooling metal.

"Sophia?" I rasped.

She didn't answer.

Panic surged through me as I twisted to look at her.

Her head was lolled to the side, her face pale under the blood smeared across her temple.

My stomach dropped.

"Sophia!" I reached over, shaking her gently, scared to jostle her too much.

A groan escaped her lips, and relief coursed through me. Her eyes fluttered open, unfocused, before closing again.

"You're okay. Just stay still." My voice shook as my eyes raked over her.

I glanced down and saw the dark stain spreading across her tan coat—blood.

My hands trembled as I fumbled for my phone, dialing 911. The operator's voice was calm, but mine was anything but as I explained our location and Sophia's condition.

It felt like an eternity before I saw the flashing lights of an ambulance cutting through the darkness.

The paramedics worked quickly, stabilizing Sophia as I hovered nearby, helpless.

"She's losing a lot of blood," one of them said, their tone urgent.

"She's going to be okay, right?" My voice cracked with fear.

The paramedic didn't answer, which only tightened the knot in my chest.

As they loaded her into the back of the ambulance, I felt like my entire world had just crashed, along with that car.

Chapter 62

THE HITS KEEP COMING

Corbin

I hated these machines. The rhythmic beeping should provide a sense of comfort—at least they told me her heart was beating—a heart that had been through so much loss and pain. A heart caught, slammed to the ground, and then punted by Landon.

A heart I wanted to be mine.

That realization had settled deep within me the moment we headed out of Misty Springs together.

I was ready.

Ready to tell her how I felt. Ready to step down—hell, step away completely—if that's what it took.

But looking at Sophia now, banged up and bruised—it was hard not to think of the accident as a sign.

A warning.

Because love didn't belong to me.

It got sick. It left. It crashed and burned.

And some twisted part of me couldn't help but think that *my* love wasn't something you wanted—it was something you survived.

I tried and failed to check emails on my phone. My eyes blurred with tears I was too scared to let fall, and my mind was too distracted by the events that had landed us here.

Sophia suffered a laceration to her side and a mild concussion, but she'd recover, according to the doctor.

Devyn walked in with two coffees in hand, her expression soft. She was Sophia's emergency contact, and they called her right away.

I spent the night falling in and out of consciousness on a lumpy orange chair with a broken recline feature.

Devyn handed me a cup of lukewarm coffee, the small diamond on her ring catching the morning sun filtering through the window.

"How is she doing?" she asked me gently.

"She's fine," a familiar voice croaked.

"Gah!" I exclaimed, startled.

I turned to see Sophia's eyes fluttering open.

"How long have you been awake?"

"Long enough to hear you sigh about eighty-seven times," Sophia teased, sitting up slowly.

I hid a smile behind my cup.

The door to Sophia's room quickly burst open, and the space filled with the chaos of her friends.

Cassie came in first, clutching a giant stuffed bear. Trevor followed with at least a dozen balloons, Lana carried a pink pastry box, and Brent and Sam balanced drink carriers of coffee.

"Surprise," Trevor rasped as he shook the balloons.

"This isn't a party, Trevor," Cassie scolded.

"It feels like a party. There are people, balloons, drinks, cake." He gestured toward the room.

"They're muffins, dude. Already checked," Sam said, seemingly disappointed.

"See? I told you we should've texted Devyn," Lana said, glancing at Brent. "They already have coffee."

"This is nasty hospital coffee, though," Devyn declared, snapping her fingers for one of the new cups. "Gimme, gimme."

Devyn and I abandoned our half-finished hospital brews.

Lana handed Sophia a cup first, then one to Devyn. She held up another, squinting at the squiggled sharpie writing before passing it to me with a knowing wink.

Her friends crowded the small space, trading jokes and tossing around ideas to celebrate Sophia's survival. Their energy was infectious, and I found myself oddly at ease despite the hell I had just gone through.

Brent pulled me to the side. "Any idea what happened?" he whispered.

"Nothing. I'm waiting for the police to get back to me. Something was wrong with the car, Brent. It wasn't just a patch of black ice."

Brent looked at me with concern. "We're just glad you guys are okay," he said, wrapping his hand over my shoulder.

The buzzing of my phone on the arm of the orange chair broke through the chatter. Davis's name flashed on the screen, giving me pause. It was strange for him to call so early in the morning.

I excused myself, stepping into the hallway. The cold quiet of the corridor stood in stark contrast to the lively warmth of Sophia's room. I swiped to answer.

"Where were you last night?" Davis asked without preamble.

"What do you mean? I was here, in Misty Springs. You saw me here before you left."

"Did you forget about the board meeting?"

I either hit my head in the accident or was missing some vital piece of information. "Board meeting? What board meeting?"

"The one that neither you—nor Buzz—bothered to attend last night."

I put him on speaker and scoured my emails for the board meeting invite. Sure enough, there it was, received and accepted by me.

But why didn't I remember seeing or accepting it?

I don't admit either of those oversights to Davis.

I took the phone off speaker and pushed it firmly back against my ear. "What did we miss?"

"It's not good, Corbin. The board wants you and Buzz out. They think he's lost his mind, and you're too unstable."

"Look, I know Buzz had been making some seemingly rash decisions, but this branch was a great investment. And *unstable*? What gave the board the impression that I was unstable?"

Davis paused, his quiet adding to the tension in my chest. "Just make sure you don't miss the next meeting."

The line went dead, and I almost threw my phone against the concrete wall of the hospital hallway. My chest constricted as the walls felt like they were closing in around me.

I pocketed my phone and headed back toward Sophia's room. The muffled sounds of laughter reached me before I even opened the door.

"Corbin, catch!" Trevor said with a grin, tossing a muffin to me.

I caught it and stole a glance toward Sophia. Her radiant smile was bright.

I couldn't help but admire her. Tragic loss, cheating exes, working herself to the bone, and she still held on to so much beauty—hope.

She sat surrounded by her chosen family—friends who cared for her, supported her, and rallied around her with easy affection.

Sophia met my gaze, her laughter softening into something quieter, more intimate.

For a moment, the storm churning in New York seemed to disappear, the tightness in my chest began to ease.

This life was unguarded—easy, calm, and filled with laughter. A life where the weight of power struggles, boardroom alliances, and calculated moves didn't exist.

It was as far from my world as it could be, yet it felt like home.

The bright atmosphere shifted the moment the door swung open again, and two uniformed officers strode in.

Everyone turned to the new arrivals, a collective look of uncertainty settling on their faces.

"Do you have an update on what happened to my car?" I asked, assuming that was the reason for their visit and hopeful for answers—though the looks exchanged between the officers quickly doused that hope.

One of them, a stocky man with a stern jawline, stepped forward.

His partner, leaner but no less imposing, hung back by the door, his hand resting casually on his belt.

The first officer fixed me with a hard stare. "Corbin Buescher?" he asked assertively.

"Yes, that's me."

"You are under arrest. I need you to come with me." He pulled out a pair of handcuffs and began stepping closer.

"Wait. What?" I managed, shaking my head in disbelief.

Before I could process it, his hand clamped down on my arm, twisting it behind my back and stretching my muscles in an uncomfortable way. The cold steel of the cuffs bit into my wrists.

"Hey, what the hell?" Brent stepped forward.

The second officer moved swiftly, extending an arm to block Brent's approach.

"What am I being arrested for, officers?" I asked, my voice low and seething.

Still gripping my arm, the stocky officer replied assertively. "Driving while intoxicated, attempted kidnapping, and attempted manslaughter."

The room erupted into chaos.

"Are you kidding me?" Devyn practically yelled.

Sophia, despite her injuries, tried to push herself up. "Kidnapping? Manslaughter? I'm right here! That's not what happened!" Her voice cracked with urgency, her pale face flushed with the effort.

Lana immediately leaned over, coaxing Sophia back down.

"Sophia, don't hurt yourself," she said softly before turning a steely glare at the officers. "Surely there's been some mistake."

The stocky officer ignored her, yanking my other arm behind my back and tightening the cuffs until they cut into my skin.

His grip was ironclad, and his tone was as unyielding as his actions when he spoke. "Not our problem. We're just following orders."

The words settled in my gut, twisting with betrayal, but I kept my voice level. "Who gave those orders?"

He didn't answer. Instead, he gripped my arm harder, wrenching it enough that pain flared in my shoulder—a shoulder that was already on the verge of dislocating after the accident.

I let out a pained gasp.

The group surged forward, a wall of anger and desperation. "You can't just take him!" Trevor barked, while Cassie shouted, "This is unlawful, and you know it!"

The officer dragging me out didn't flinch, but his partner stepped between us and the group, one hand raised as if to ward them off.

"Enough!" he yelled at the rioting group.

I turned back as they shoved me toward the door, the sight of Sophia's pale face and worried eyes carving itself into my memory.

The officers hauled me down the hall, and as they shoved me into the backseat of their squad car, I caught the name on the stocky officer's uniform: **NORWOOD**

The name sent a flame of anger through me as I thought of the family I had just exiled—and the evidence I'd used to do so.

A sheriff's deputy, tied to the same web of lies and deceit Sullivan had uncovered.

This wasn't an arrest.
This was a retaliation.

Chapter 63

BEDRIDDEN

Sophia

"Guys, what the hell just happened?" Trevor asked, twisting his ball cap around backward.

His voice broke the quiet tension we held onto after the police escorted Corbin out in handcuffs.

My eyes flicked to the door Corbin had disappeared through. I hated the helplessness that gnawed at my chest.

I had to do something, *anything.*

Brent stopped his pacing by the window and spoke up. "I know the guy who owns the auto body shop the police towed Corbin's car to. He'll have some insight on what happened to it." He came to stand over me, a worried smile on his face. "We'll get it straightened out, Soph. I promise."

He kissed my forehead and walked out into the hallway, his phone glowing in his hand.

I felt a tingle in the back of my nose as tears stung my eyes.

Devyn came to stand by me. Her hand rested on my arm, the other wrapped around Sam's bicep. "Sam and I will go down to the station. His cousin works there. We'll try and find out what we can."

"Thank you." My eyes blurred with the beginning of tears.

"Corbin isn't alone in this, neither are you," Sam added as they turned to leave.

I felt a flicker of hope spring to life. I'd been down before. I'd fallen from grace and felt like my whole world was crumbling beneath me, and my friends were there for me.

And here they were again, but this time for Corbin.

I sat up, testing the pain in my side, hoping I could get out of bed to help. It felt like something was twisting my insides between my ribs. I slowly settled back down.

"I don't know what to do. I feel so helpless." A solitary tear broke free and streamed down my cheek as I looked at Lana, who hadn't left my side since she got here.

She wiped the tear away. "Hey, don't worry. We'll get some answers. In the meantime, you need to rest. The nurse said you have stitches—we don't want them to burst."

My breath rattled as I sighed.

Rest, how could I possibly rest?

One moment, I felt the happiest I had in a long time. It felt like Corbin and I were turning the corner on some monumental moment, something defining—a definition I needed to understand desperately.

The next, we were careening off the road, and I woke up here—with him beside me.

And now, he was being arrested?

The echoing sounds of loud, complicated shoes filled the air moments before Andi stormed into my room.

Her energy was as big as her hair, styled in a larger-than-life afro. She wore a bright yellow jumpsuit with matching chunky glasses, lighting up the small, dim hospital room.

A man walked behind her, someone I didn't recognize. He was polished with a bit more of a roguish exterior.

"Sophia!" Andi walked up to me and hugged me tightly.

"Ow," I croaked.

She stepped back and cupped her hands around her mouth. "Oh, I'm so sorry. I am just so glad you're okay!"

She looked around at my remaining friends, the tension in the air still palpable. "Where's Corbin?"

We quickly filled in Andi and Sullivan—I learned his name was—on everything we knew.

I remembered hearing Sullivan's name before. Corbin mentioned he was a friend of his and a lawyer for Buescher Enterprises. But after meeting Davis, I was slightly concerned about the kind of *friends* that Corbin kept.

"Sullivan is one of the best, Sophia. He'll make sure Corbin gets out of there," Andi assured me.

"Aww, Andi-wandi, I knew you liked me," Sullivan said with a coo.

Sullivan casually strode over to my bed. His navy-blue eyes locked with mine, and he flashed me a cocky grin.

"I knew Corby had a girl in Misty Springs. I just knew it," he said, shaking his sandy blonde hair back and forth.

"Yeah, they totally like each other," Trevor added.

"Shut it, Trevor," Cassie scolded as she stood from the chair that Corbin had stayed in all night. "I'll take lawyer guy to the police station now that he knows the details."

"Lawyer guy is my father. Call me lawyer boy," Sullivan said with mock authority, crossing his arms.

Cassie glared at Andi. "You sure about this guy?"

"Just wait until he's in action. He turns into a shark, trust me," Andi affirmed.

Cassie and Sullivan walked toward the door, meeting Brent in the doorway.

Cassie murmured something to Brent as Sullivan nodded along, the three of them in a strategic huddle.

"I'm going with them," Trevor quickly announced as he bounded after Cassie and Sullivan.

Everything was happening so fast that I had difficulty processing it all. Everything felt like a dream—or a nightmare.

I wish it were.

Andi's phone rang, and she quickly answered it, pacing the room with clipped one-word responses.

Her eyes grew wide as she paused mid-stride. She hung up the phone with a short *bye* and started mumbling to herself.

"What? What's going on?" I asked.

"There is another board meeting *tonight*. They are voting on a new CEO." She turned in a tight circle and began pacing again. "Fuck! Davis. It's Davis. It's got to be him. He's organizing the whole thing."

"What about Ned? Is he involved, too?" I asked.

"Who knows? Maybe." Andi stopped her pacing and then strode toward the door.

"Where are you going?" Lana asked.

"I'm gonna find that fucker Ned and make him sing." She stormed out of the room in a sunny yellow blaze of fury.

My heart sank at the thought of someone Corbin trusted turning against him. How many enemies was Corbin up against? How many knives waited for his back the moment he let it turn?

Brent stepped to my side. "My friend has Corbin's rental, but he didn't want to talk over the phone. I need to go to his shop."

He looked at Lana. "I don't have a car. Cassie drove me here. Can you take me?"

Lana looked down at me with concern.

"I'll be fine," I assured her.

She nodded toward Brent. "Let's go."

"We'll get answers, Soph," Brent assured me as he and Lana stepped away.

The once-crowded room was now empty—save for me—lying helpless in my hospital bed.

Corbin walked out of the hospital room with his head held high, like a soldier heading into battle. But I'd seen the tension in his jaw, the flicker of worry in his eyes.

I looked down at my trembling hands and willed them to steady, fists clenching in my lap.

If this was war, it was a war he wouldn't fight alone.

Chapter 64

SULLIVAN, MY HERO

Corbin

I sat in the cramped interrogation room, my hands clenched tightly on the metal table. The flickering fluorescent light above cast an eerie glow over the dull gray walls. This entire place smelled like piss.

Cuffs still bit into my wrists, but at least my arms weren't forced behind my back anymore. The ache in my shoulder eased, but it still burned.

My mind raced, sifting through every scenario, every possible reason why I was being held on such absurd charges.

Something didn't add up.

The false charges were one thing, but whatever happened to cause that accident was another. The two had to be connected, the link hiding somewhere.

The sound of footsteps in the hallway snapped my attention to the door.

It opened with a loud creak, and in walked Sullivan, looking like he just stepped off the show *Suits*.

His expression was one of calculated focus, but his familiar smirk lurked just beneath the surface.

"Well, isn't this a charming setup?" Sullivan drawled, closing the door behind him.

He pulled out the chair across from me and sank into it gracefully. His briefcase echoed in the tiny room as he hoisted it on the table and clicked it open.

"Let me guess, the coffee here is just as bad as the decor?"

"Sullivan," I said with a relieved smile. "What are you doing here?"

"I flew here immediately after leaving last night's board meeting. Davis is up to something, man. It's not pretty."

"As much as I hate to admit it, I get the feeling he is too—and he's not fighting fair."

Sullivan held my gaze.

My muscles tightened, and unease wormed its way into my chest. I wasn't sure where Sullivan stood—not really. The three of us had known each other for years, but Davis had a way of shifting loyalties, of turning people in his favor.

"Then we hit back harder," he said darkly.

The tension in my shoulders eased by a fraction.

I didn't know how deep this mess went, but at least I knew who stood beside me. And Sullivan was someone you definitely wanted in your corner.

Sullivan pulled some files from his briefcase.

"Anyway, I showed up this morning at the Misty Springs office, and you weren't there. Andi made some phone calls, we showed up at the hospital, and the Scooby Gang filled me in on the rest."

"Scooby Gang?" I smirked.

"Oh yeah, the overtly-attractive-but-snarky redhead, the smart-but-subtly-sexy nerdy girl, the goofy guy, the buff, handsome one."

"You missed a few of them, but it's strange. I know exactly who you are talking about."

"Great, you can introduce me to the rest of the gang later. For now, let's get you out of here." Sullivan leaned back in his chair, his eyes glinting with something cold and dangerous.

"I know that look. What's the plan?"

Sullivan loved to joke but didn't mess around when laying down the law. He was a force to be reckoned with, and he could turn it on at the drop of a hat.

One minute, you're talking to a carefree goof—the next, you're being eaten alive.

"First, I deal with the buffoons running this show. Then, we walk out of here. Simple as that."

Before I could respond, the door swung open. The two officers who had arrested me entered, both looking considerably less confident than when I had first been brought in.

"Gentlemen," Sullivan greeted smoothly, standing and extending his hand—which neither of them took.

"Sheriff Norwood. Deputy Bates. My client and I were just discussing this unfortunate misunderstanding." Sullivan buttoned his suit coat as he strode over to me.

"This ain't a misunderstanding," Norwood shot back, though his voice wavered. "Mr. Buescher here has been charged—"

"Ah, yes, the fabricated charges," Sullivan interrupted, his voice like silk over a blade.

He slid a crisp stack of documents across the table.

"This is your problem, Sheriff. Lack of evidence, procedural errors, and, most importantly, the lovely little detail that you falsified an affidavit three years ago. You remember that, don't you, Norwood?"

The Sheriff's face darkened, his jaw tightening as Sullivan's words sank in.

"We're not here to play games," Sullivan continued. "You'll release my client immediately, or I'll have a field day exposing every skeleton in your department's closet. And trust me, you've got plenty."

The tension was palpable.

Norwood glared at Sullivan, his jaw ticking under his double chin, but eventually nodded to Bates. "Let him go."

The deputy sidled over to me, unlocking the cuffs around my wrists. I rubbed at the red marks left behind by the rough metal.

The men wordlessly left the room, defeated and careful not to add more ammunition to Sullivan's arsenal.

Sullivan turned back to me, his menacing air evaporating. "That was fun, Corby. I like this town."

"Unbelievable," I muttered, shaking my head.

Then Sullivan and I walked right out of the station.

The crisp morning air smelled sweeter than usual, and the sight of Devyn, Trevor, and Cassie waiting on the curb filled me with an unexpected comfort.

They had to be freezing, but they stuck around, ensuring I got out.

I spied Sam off to the side, talking on the phone and pacing back and forth on the sidewalk.

"You alright, man?" Trevor asked, stepping forward.

I nodded and swallowed the rising lump in my throat. After years of fighting through life alone, having people rally around me was... overwhelming.

Sullivan sucked air through his teeth, giving the group his signature cocky grin. "You all ever considered getting a dog? Maybe a Great Dane."

"No need for dogs when these boys are barely housebroken," Cassie quipped, scratching Trevor's scruffy face.

Trevor fake-panted and leaned in to lick Cassie's face before she pushed him away in disgust.

"What was your name again? Daphne?" Sullivan asked, his interest piqued.

"It's Cassie." She placed her hand on her hips and shot him a glaring look—one I was glad to not be on the receiving end of for once.

"Cassie," Sullivan drawled, his eyes narrowing on the intimidating redhead. "You've got a sharp tongue. I like that."

Cassie smirked, cocking her head to the side to mimic Sullivan. "And you've got an inflated ego. I *hate* that."

Devyn snorted, trying to cover her laughter, while Sullivan's grin widened.

"Oh, I'm going to enjoy getting to know you," he said smoothly.

I would tell Sullivan later to stop wasting his time on Cassie, but for now, I needed to get back to Sophia.

Sam jogged over to us. "Holy shit, do I have updates. Cassie—can you and Trevor meet your brother and Lana at Yannie's Body Shop? They said to bring Sullivan... who I'm assuming is you." Sam said as he gestured his hand toward Sullivan.

"My reputation in this town is already spreading," Sullivan mused as he adjusted the cuffs of his sleeves.

Cassie rolled her eyes. "Sure, I can put extra newspaper down," she gibed, then turned and whistled for the two men to follow her.

"Bye, Corby," Sullivan said gleefully, before whispering over his shoulder, "Wish me luck."

I shook my head as I watched the three of them walk away.

"Let's get you back to the hospital. I'm sure Sophia wants to see you." Devyn placed her hand in the crook of my arm and pulled it.

My shoulder winced in protest at the slight jostle, and I let out a pained groan.

"Thought so. And we need to get your shoulder fixed," she scolded, storming toward her car in high-heeled boots.

"You ready for this, man?" Sam asked as we walked after Devyn. "It sounds like there's quite the storm coming."

"I'm ready. Whoever is behind all of this is going to pay," I promised. "I'll make sure of it."

"We'll make sure of it," Sam added, placing his hand on my non-dislocated shoulder.

I couldn't suppress the smile that formed on my lips. I may be a little worse for wear, but I had an arsenal of people rallying around me.

I was ready for whatever life threw at me next.

Or so I thought.

Chapter 65

Go

Sophia

The sterile smell of the hospital room clung to everything—the sheets, the air, even me. I sat propped up in bed, my legs stretched out beneath the thin blanket, my fingers nervously tapping against my lap.

The TV was on, but I wasn't watching it. The noise was just background—a failed attempt to drown out the anxious thrum in my chest.

The door creaked open, and my gaze shot toward it. My heart shriveled when a nurse walked in, her smile polite but perfunctory.

"How are you feeling, Ms. Carlson?" she asked, checking the monitor next to my bed.

"I'm fine," I said quickly, even though my head ached and my body felt like it had been hit by a freight train. "Do you know when I can leave?"

She frowned, glancing at the tablet in her hands. "Your temperature is still a little elevated. The doctor wants to keep you another day to rule out infection."

"Another day?" I repeated, the restless energy in me ramping up to a boil. "I'm fine. Really."

"We just want to be sure. Rest is the best thing you can do right now," she said, typing quickly on a nearby computer before giving me a soft smile. "Hit your call button if you need us."

I watched her leave, leaning my head back on the pillows. The thoughts swirling in my mind made it impossible to stay still.

What was happening with Corbin?
Was he okay?
Was Sullivan helping him?

The dizzy spell was gnawing at me.

The sound of the door opening again made me sit up straighter. This time, it was Devyn and Sam. Relief flooded through me at the sight of familiar faces.

"What's going on? Is Corbin okay?"

Devyn pulled up a chair and sat by my side.

Sam leaned against the wall. "He's fine. Sullivan got him out. He's a free man."

"What happened?" I pressed.

Sam and Devyn exchanged a look like they were protecting me from something.

"There's more to the story than just a faulty arrest," Devyn answered.

Sam pushed off the wall and lowered his voice, as if he didn't trust the walls of the hospital. "Sullivan's with the others at the auto body shop. They're trying to figure out what happened to the car. They don't know for sure, but it sounds like someone tampered with the brake lines, maybe the power steering, too."

I exhaled a shaky breath.

"Where's Corbin?" I asked.

"I forced him to get his shoulder checked out. He was wincing all morning, and when Deputy Diphead grabbed him, I heard it pop out of place. I knew he was in pain." Devyn said with a roll of her eyes.

As if on cue, the door opened again, and there he was.

Corbin stood in the doorway, a sling around his arm. His face was drawn, and he looked like he was on the verge of collapsing with exhaustion.

"We'll leave you two alone." Devyn winked at me before standing and grabbing Sam's arm.

Sam gave me a soft smile before following Devyn out.

The door clicked shut behind them, leaving Corbin and me in the quiet room. Now that I was awake, the monitors no longer beeped—nothing but our unsaid words filled the space between us.

Corbin stepped closer, sinking into the chair beside my bed with a wince.

"Do you have a ticket for that seat?" I asked, a small smile tugging at my lips despite everything.

"I'll show you mine if you show me yours," he quipped back.

We both laughed softly, the tension between us easing for a moment. Then his expression turned serious.

"Sophia, about last night—"

The door flew open, cutting him off. I was just about sick of people bursting through that damn door.

This time, it was Andi, her chest heaving as if she'd sprinted all the way here.

"We've got a problem," she announced, not even bothering to say hello. "Ned's not in Misty Springs. He's claiming to have something on you, Corbin—something big. He's in New York, and Davis called an emergency board meeting tonight. They're voting to name a new CEO, and if you're not there… Corbin, it's over."

Corbin stiffened, his jaw tightening. He looked at me with worried eyes.

"You have to go," I said immediately, the words tumbling out before I could stop them.

"Sophia—"

"No." I shook my head, reaching out to touch his good arm. "This is everything you've worked for. You can't lose it. Not like this."

I knew how deep his family's legacy ran and how important it was to him. Whoever was trying to destroy him would get exactly what they wanted if Corbin didn't go and fight for it.

Corbin's eyes searched mine—flecks of amber staring longingly, another look that spoke a thousand unsaid words.

"I can't just leave you here. The only reason you're in here is because of me."

"It's not your fault, Corbin," I assured him as my hand moved to cup his cheek. "You're not going to do me any good sitting here watching me sleep. But your grandfather's company—your company—needs you."

He sighed and kissed the palm of my hand, the heat from his lips blooming up my wrist and settling within me. He stood and used his free arm to smooth out his slightly blood-stained suit.

He turned to Andi.

"Let's get to that meeting," he ordered.

"I'll get our travel arranged." She nodded and hurried back out of the room.

Corbin looked down at me, his fingers found mine where they lay at my side, and he gave them a gentle squeeze.

"I didn't get to say…" He swallowed as his brows knit together.

I squeezed his hand, pulling our joined hands into my lap.

"Tell me when you get back," I whispered.

He had just been through so much.

We had just been through so much.

And even though part of me ached to hear whatever truth was pressing behind his eyes, I knew I couldn't let him say it.

Not now.

There was still a battle ahead—more enemies to vanquish before we could even dream of something more.

And if, after all that, there was still an *us* to return to.

If the damage wasn't permanent.

If the barrier between us hadn't grown too wide.

Maybe we'd find our way back here.

But I couldn't ask him for more right now—not while chaos swirled around us.

Not when love felt like both a promise and a price.

He lowered his head slowly down to mine, pressing a soft kiss on my forehead. "I'll be back as soon as I can," he said with a resounding sigh.

I responded with a tight-lipped smile and watched him walk out the door—tears filling my eyes as it closed behind him.

A sinking feeling settled into my already aching body—a sense that this was the end of our story, one that ended before it was ever written.

I felt like one of the authors I worked with, clinging to the spark of an idea, a story I could see so clearly in my mind but could never quite put to paper.

Too many plot holes. Too many obstacles. Too much *life* in the way.

I let my tears fall freely for the story of Corbin and Sophia—a story that would never see the light of day.

Chapter 66

LET'S TAKE A VOTE

Corbin

Lucky for us, Sullivan had arrived in Misty Springs using the company jet, and it was now parked in the hangar at the Misty Springs Regional Airport.

Andi secured a pilot, and within the hour, we were airborne, racing toward New York.

Andi had invited herself along, insisting she needed a front-row seat for whatever chaos was about to unfold.

Sullivan stayed behind in Misty Springs to help investigate whatever happened to my rental car.

Now that the adrenaline had worn off, I could feel every sore and torn muscle. I could also feel the fissure spreading through my chest as I waged an internal war with myself.

"So, you and Sophia, huh?" Andi sat across from me, legs crossed, a pen twirling like an unlit cigarette between her fingers.

I didn't answer—I just clenched my jaw and stared out the window at the bright, full moon staring back at me.

"You know," she continued, unfazed by my silence, "you two were so painfully obvious. I knew you had a thing for her when she came in for her first interview."

I chuckled at the night sky, then frowned as I continued my internal deliberation.

My mind drifted to Davis—smug, manipulative Davis, spinning my downfall into a polished narrative for the board.

How bad had he made me look? When had it all started to slip away? Could he have orchestrated whatever happened with my car, too?

My stomach churned as I thought about the unanswered questions.

And Buzz—where the hell was Buzz?

Every call to him went straight to voicemail, and his ghost act, with everything going on right now, felt more like a slight. Could he not even be trusted right now?

I swallowed the truth as it came lurching up in my throat.

Sophia didn't belong in this fucked up world of mine.

Andi leaned forward, her sharp gaze cutting into my thoughts.

"You're spiraling. Stop it. Whatever lies Davis has told, you're still Corbin Buescher. Walk in there and remind them who you are."

"What if I get everything I've worked for my entire life… but lose her?" I asked, surprising myself at the vulnerability I'd just exposed.

"Fuck that." Andi threw the pen at my chest.

I glanced down at it and then glared at her, eyebrow raised.

"You think success is worth shit if there's no one to come home to? Grow up, Corbin. Figure out how to have both—or get real about what you're actually willing to lose."

I stared at the pen resting against my chest, which landed like a grenade with the truth of her words.

Having someone eight years younger than me tell me to grow up was rather enlightening.

"I couldn't keep her from getting hurt." More vulnerability, more raw truth leaked from me.

"Corbin…" Andi gave me a disapproving glare.

I lifted the pen off my chest and handed it back to her, silently stewing in my guilt.

She grabbed my hand, forcing my eyes to meet hers.

"You think you're the only one with assholes coming after you? Look at her dumbass ex and his insane family."

She let go of me and leaned back in her seat, shoving her canary yellow frames up her nose. "You can't stop bad people from doing bad shit. But you *can* surround yourself with good people—people who'll help you face the flames others throw at you. Or say 'fuck it', and light a blowtorch to help you fight back."

Crude, crass—exactly what I needed to hear—as usual.

She turned back to her notebook casually, like dropping prophetic truth bombs were no big deal.

But something shifted. The cracks in my chest filled with something solid.

Resolve. Purpose.

Not enough to make me whole again, but enough to hold me together.

I was going to walk into that boardroom and take control. And I was going to take anyone down who dared to stand in my way.

Andi didn't look up again, but I saw the satisfied smirk tug at her mouth.

Once again, she'd managed to gut-check me into clarity. Once again, she'd proven she was the best damn hire I ever made.

***

When we arrived at Buescher Enterprises, the board meeting had already started. The building loomed over us, its steel and glass exterior reflecting the dull gray of the overcast sky.

Andi and I hurried inside, our steps echoing in the expansive, quiet lobby.

I was painfully aware of my appearance—bloodstains on my shirt, my arm in a sling, exhaustion etched into every line of my face.

But there was no time to change or play out the million potential outcomes. There was only time to follow my gut and implement my plan.

When we pushed open the doors to the boardroom, every conversation halted. All eyes turned to me, and the air seemed to grow heavier with the weight of their shock.

I quickly scanned their faces—no sign of Ned.

Andi took a seat in a chair propped against the wall, her expression challenging anyone in the room to question her presence.

Davis stood at the head of the table, mid-sentence, his expression frozen at my interruption. He'd been in the middle of a seemingly heartfelt monologue, one hand resting on the polished oak surface as if he were delivering a eulogy.

I didn't give him the satisfaction of showing any reaction. I walked to my seat at the table, meeting the wide-eyed stares of the board members with a calm, deliberate gaze. I sank into my chair, the springs groaning in the quiet boardroom.

I gestured with my good hand toward Davis. "Please, don't let me interrupt. Continue."

Davis's face paled slightly, but then he recovered, forcing the corners of his mouth upwards.

"Corbin," he said, his voice dripping with false concern. "We weren't expecting you. Given... *everything.*" He gestured vaguely at my disheveled state.

"Clearly," I countered, leaning back in my chair. "But don't let that stop you. I'm curious to hear what you've prepared."

His sharp jaw tightened, but he pressed on, his discomfort evident in how his fingers fidgeted against the table. He launched into a carefully rehearsed speech, weaving a narrative of declining oversight, Buzz's prolonged absence, and my so-called *reckless behavior.*

"And most recently," Davis continued, his voice tinged with righteous indignation, "Corbin was arrested on charges that could bring unnecessary scrutiny to this company. We cannot afford such risks, especially in today's market."

The room was silent, every pair of eyes flicking between Davis and me. I wasn't sure how Davis found out about my arrest or if he was responsible, but neither of those considerations surprised me.

I was prepared for Davis either way.

I leaned forward, the weight of the moment pressing down on me. "Are you finished?"

Davis faltered, his bravado cracking under the pressure of my unwavering stare.

"I—yes." He glanced at his watch. "That's the situation as it stands."

I nodded, letting the silence stretch just long enough to make him squirm. "Good. Then it's my turn."

I stood to address the room, holding in the groan at the strain it put on my aching muscles. I still had fight in me, and I wouldn't be able to look at myself again if I didn't do everything I could to keep this company out of Davis's clutches.

I opened my mouth to speak, but before I could get a word out, the doors to the boardroom opened—and in walked Ned.

My body had a visceral reaction to seeing his face.

How had I never realized how offensive it was before?

He slithered in like a timid mouse, blustering up to Davis's side and giving an almost undetectable nod.

"Ladies and gentlemen of the board, I'm afraid I have one more piece of information to share," Davis added, clicking on a remote and lowering the projection screen.

I lowered back into my seat, feigning a calm presence, though Ned's sudden appearance settled under my skin uncomfortably.

The screen glowed blue until Ned connected a cable to Davis' computer and inserted a USB stick into a port on the side. He tapped a few keys before a video started playing.

The board murmured as they awaited whatever bullshit Davis decided to drum up next.

A video appeared, and it took me a couple of seconds to recognize the scene.

My office.

Me in my office, an angle from a hidden camera perched somewhere in the corner.

A camera I didn't know existed.

Sophia stood near me, bent over my desk in a plaid skirt.

I knew what happened next.

We crossed a line.

Broke a rule that had toppled so many others before me.

Anything Davis brought up before was inconsequential—just opinions and unfounded accusations.

This? This was real—concrete evidence of me breaking company policy.

The entire board was about to watch me do it, and what was worse, I was about to take Sophia down with me.

"Turn it off!" I demanded as I bolted out of my chair, adrenaline and rage surging through me.

"Oh, but Corbin, it's just getting good," Ned sniveled as he shrank behind Davis.

I pulled Davis's laptop off the table, yanking it free of the cable and the feed that projected my transgression, and threw his computer against the wall with a forceful blow.

The image on the screen cracked and then turned blue.

Davis looked at me with a devious grin. "Now, Corbin, that was company property."

I used my good hand to grab Davis by the collar. The room gasped, pulling my attention away.

This is what Davis wanted: to paint me as unstable, the loose cannon, unfit to lead.

And I played right into his hands.

I released him, backing up a couple of paces.

Andi stepped to my side, surveying the room. Her gaze lingered on each board member as if trying to gauge their reactions— measuring the damage Davis had done.

"You guys can't be serious," she gaffed. "You're going to listen to this conniving snake and this weaselly little pervert?"

The board murmured amongst themselves again, and I watched their faces as they flicked between Davis—calm, polished, perfectly put together—and me—disheveled, wild, bloodstains and bruises.

Every second that ticked by without a word only made the difference between Davis and me more stark.

I read it on their faces.

Davis looked like the future of the company.

I looked like a cautionary tale playing out in real time.

I looked just like my father.

"This is clearly a very emotional decision," one of the members I didn't recognize said as he stood to command the room.

His face was long, with harsh lines, his features seemingly painted on—fake as a Ken doll. He wore a quarter-zipped pullover with a collared shirt and tie poking underneath, his slicked-back hair gave off used car salesman vibes.

"But it's one we shouldn't take lightly," he added as he paced the room, his hands behind his back.

"Corbin, I've been a member of this board for months and haven't met you once. It's evident that you are disconnected, disengaged, and flaunting like the rules don't apply to you."

Andi stepped forward and started to speak, but I put my hand on her arm to quiet her.

I knew whatever she added wouldn't help the snowball that had already begun its descent.

There was no stopping it now.

"I've seen this before. Nepotism makes way for poor leadership, and before we know it, everyone is out of a job. The company goes under while the millionaire playboy keeps his money and flits off to the next thing."

Davis crossed his arms in quiet satisfaction, and I wondered if this guy was a plant. I wouldn't put it past Davis to have his bases well covered.

"We came together to make a decision. We have all the information we need," the man continued, eyes scanning me hostilely. "Let's vote."

My heart sank as the board conversed.

The future of my family's company was in their hands, and there was nothing I could do about it.

Chapter 67

No News is Good News, Right?

Sophia

I was out of the hospital, but I felt anything but relieved. After I was discharged, Devyn drove me back to my apartment, and the familiar routine of her carting me around was almost a comforting scene.

She followed me up the stairs and ensured I was settled before leaving to taste wedding cake samples with Sam.

I promised her I would be fine eight times before she reluctantly left, leaving my door unlocked behind her.

Brent would be coming soon to check on me.

I appreciated their concern, but didn't need them to check on me. Physically, I was fine—just a little sore and slow-moving.

Emotionally? I was a mess.

I hadn't heard from Corbin or Andi. I wasn't sure what the verdict was after last night's board meeting, and I wasn't getting any information from my very limited contact list at Buescher-Jones Publishing.

I sat in my quiet apartment, feeling unsettled. All the shattered pieces of my life I had just started to glue back together were rattling—about to break again.

I pulled out my phone and texted Corbin, adding to the dozen I already sent him.

```
Please call me.
```

The soft whoosh of the sent message barely registered before my front door opened.

"Devyn just left. You guys could leave me alone for more than five minutes, you know," I joked to Brent.

I looked up from my phone screen, and my blood ran cold.

Not Brent.

Landon.

He strode in, shutting the door behind him with a hasty slam.

He looked terrible—pale, disheveled, dark circles etched beneath his eyes like bruises.

Before I could say a word, he rushed toward me, crashing to his knees by me on the couch.

"Thank God you're okay," he choked out, his hands hovering near me, as if he wanted to touch me but didn't dare.

I stiffened, fumbling with my phone, fingers clumsy as I tried to unlock it to call for help.

"I'm so sorry, Sophia," he sobbed, the rawness in his voice catching me off guard. "You weren't supposed to be with him. It was never supposed to be you."

His words sent a shockwave through my system, my heart pounding as the pieces clicked into place.

Slowly, I set my phone down, not yet dialing but not letting it out of reach.

"You... you tampered with Corbin's car." The words weren't a question. They were a verdict.

Landon nodded, his face contorted with guilt. "It wasn't my idea," he stammered, his words tumbling out in a rush. "We just wanted to scare him, to make him pay for what he did to my family. To get him out of town."

"You could have killed him!" I shouted, the force of my voice pulling at my stitches, making me wince. "You *almost killed me!*"

"I know!" he cried, his hands clenching into fists. "I know, Sophia. It wasn't supposed to be you. I'd never hurt you—I love—"

"You already did!" I snapped, cutting him off. My voice trembled, but it was no less fierce. "You hurt me, Landon. Every time you made me feel like I wasn't enough. Every time, you used your words to beat me down. You shattered my self-confidence, then you cheated on me like I didn't even matter."

I locked away words my whole life—let them burn me from the inside rather than risk lashing out at someone else. But now, I felt raw, cut open by everything life had thrown my way, and the words I usually kept buried started spewing from my lips like lava.

"You and your family take and use. You leech and destroy, with no regard for anything other than yourselves. You never loved me. You don't even know how to love."

"Sophia," he pleaded, his voice desperate. "You don't mean that. I just—"

"I mean every word," I seethed. "Hear me loud and clear, Landon. You mean nothing to me now. Nothing. And you never will again."

He stared at me for a moment, his face a canvas of pain and disbelief. Then he reached out again, but I recoiled, unlocking my phone screen to call for help.

The door flew open again, startling both Landon and me.

Brent stepped inside, his expression incensed, but he wasn't alone.

Two officers followed, their uniforms crisp and official—not the corrupt puppets on the Norwood's payroll. They didn't waste a moment, pulling Landon off the floor, wrenching his arms behind his back as they slapped handcuffs on him.

Landon didn't struggle. He didn't say a word. His gaze, however, stayed fixed on me, searching for something—sympathy, forgiveness, anything.

But he'd find nothing.

I met his stare with icy resolve, letting him see that whatever part of me had once cared for him was long gone.

Brent rushed to my side, his calloused hands carefully helping me off the couch. He wrapped me in a gentle hug, mindful of my stitches. His familiar scent—soap and something faintly earthy—was grounding.

"You okay?"

I nodded, feeling a renewed sense of calm despite the chaos.

Brent squeezed my shoulder lightly as we watched Landon walk out of my life once more.

This time, it felt final.

One of the officers approached me and handed me a card. "We have some statements we'll need when you feel up for coming down to the station."

I nodded and thanked him.

Once we were alone, Brent blew out a long breath and turned to me.

"How'd you know he was here?" I asked.

He ran a hand through his deep red hair. "I found out at the body shop that the brake lines, the power steering, and a bunch of other shit were tampered with. Sullivan and I rushed over to Boomer's to get our hands on the security footage. That guy's smoother than I thought—Theresa gave us the footage from last night without blinking."

A flicker of admiration tugged at Brent's mouth as he got me a glass of water.

"We spent all night combing through hours of footage until we saw it—Landon under Corbin's car." He paused, jaw clenched.

"Watching you both get in afterward... I nearly lost it. We brought the tape straight to the station—avoided the idiots who arrested Corbin. When I pulled up and saw Landon's car out front..."

His face contorted into a pained look, his eyes heavy with worry.

"I called the police immediately. They told me to wait outside. Said I could blow the case if I didn't. But sitting in that truck, knowing you were in here with him—I couldn't do it."

"I was fine," I said, managing a smile. "Actually... it felt kind of good to tell Landon off finally."

Brent smirked and gave my chin a light tap. "Atta girl."

"The Norwoods orchestrated Corbin's arrest, too. Sullivan was able to expose everything." Brent chugged his water in a few large gulps and clanged the glass loudly on the counter.

A moment of quiet passed between us before he spoke again.

"So, what now?" he asked, wiping his trimmed beard with his sleeve.

I let out a breath. "I don't know. I guess we wait and hope Corbin gets control of the company."

"Sophia." He dropped his chin and glared at me under furrowed brows.

"What?"

"We all see the way you two look at each other."

"Yeah, but it's... complicated." My voice broke off into a whisper.

"Corbin is a good guy. You both deserve to be happy. If you want to make it work, you will. Screw the rules." He pushed off the counter and walked around to wrap me in another hug.

"It has been good to see you smile again, Soph. No matter what happens, please keep that up," he said into my hair.

I nodded as he backed away.

"I've gotta run Sullivan to the airport. Want me to give him your number?"

"Please. Ask him to keep me posted?"

"You got it," Brent said, locking the doorknob before closing the door behind him.

I sank back onto the couch, picking up my phone. My last message to Corbin still sat unanswered.

A sinking feeling settled in my gut as I stared at my blank screen.

Something that told me I wasn't ready to hear the truth about what happened in New York—and what it might mean for our future together.

Chapter 68

SPY GAMES

Corbin

My phone chimed, waking me from my alcohol-induced dreamless sleep. I slowly lifted off my pillow, my head throbbing from the slight movement.

After the board meeting took its devastating turn, I stormed out of Buescher Enterprises' offices and into the blistering cold streets of Manhattan. The sharp wind bit at my face, and I welcomed it, letting the chill seep into my bones to match the numbness inside.

I left Andi behind, adding insult to injury to the fact that she chose the wrong person to hitch her wagon to.

I'd lost the position I'd worked my entire life for—and in the process, I'd managed to crush Sophia's dream, too. The board decided that I wasn't fit to be CEO and that the Buescher-Jones Publishing branch in Misty Springs must be closed *effective immediately*.

I walked into a little bar around the block from my apartment and went to work on drowning my sorrows.

My phone died, and I embraced the quiet.

Just me, my problems, and a bottomless supply of liquor.

I stumbled back to my apartment, tossed my phone on the wireless charger, and fell into bed.

I missed shutting the shades, a regrettable mistake at this moment, as the sun barreled into my bedroom—through my eyelids, and right into my sensitive skull.

Prying my eyes open, the sun seared into my brain, and I reached hastily for my phone. I had thirty-two missed calls and ninety-nine text messages.

My phone dinged again.

Make that one hundred text messages.

The latest text preview popped up and my heart sank. It was from Sophia. Just three words.

`Please call me.`

I groaned and set my phone back down.

I couldn't call her. What could I possibly say?

As my head throbbed and I reflected on the recent crumbling of my once-promising life, a singular nagging thought pulsed over and over in my skull.

Where the hell was Buzz?

I stood up, gave the room some time to stop spinning, and went to the shower.

I was going to drop in on the bastard, and he was going to give me answers.

***

My shoes pounded on the polished marble floor of the foyer as I walked through my grandparents' apartment, fueled by visceral anger—and likely a slightly elevated blood alcohol level from the night before.

I paused at the beautiful bouquet of pink peonies on the dark oak entry table. The sight tempered my anger slightly—Gram always liked to keep the peace between Buzz and me.

But I didn't have time for peace.

I made a beeline for Buzz's office. Considering he spent ninety percent of his time there, it was a good place to start.

My steps slowed as the muffled sound of music hit my ears.

I approached the closed door of the parlor, a room where Toni and Buzz hosted many a soirée. Where, as a kid, I'd sit outside the door and listen to the muffled sounds of laughter and music, while women dressed in designer cocktail gowns and men in tailored suits flitted in and out.

A room that had sat silent for years, like a museum of the past.

I slowly turned the handle, the hinges groaning as the door opened. The faint smell of cigar smoke still lingered in the walls, preserved in this room with the memories of Gram and Buzz's youth. The scent and the swelling wave of nostalgia both hit me when I pushed my head inside.

Then I saw him.

Buzz, dressed in his silk pajamas, held tight to Gram in her floor-length nightdress and robe as they slowly spun to Nat King Cole's song "Unforgettable."

It was the middle of the morning on a Friday. His inbox was likely overflowing. There were always at least a dozen meetings on his calendar on any given day—he was undoubtedly missing one right now.

But he was here, in his pajamas, dancing with his wife to a fifties love song in the museum of their youth.

Buzz's eyes landed on me as I stood frozen in the doorway. My shriveled and dehydrated brain was still trying to make sense of the scene unfolding before me.

A soft hand landed on my shoulder, startling me.

I turned to see Louise's tear-filled eyes looking into mine. She nodded her head toward the kitchen.

I gave my grandparents one last look before begrudgingly following her.

"What was that in there?" I asked as we walked into the kitchen.

"She's been slipping a lot lately, Corbin. Today, she thinks it's their wedding day. She is sad no one showed up, so he's trying to comfort her." Louise grabbed a carton of eggs from the fridge. "He hasn't left her side in weeks."

I marinated in that statement as Louise quietly worked. My mind drummed up memories of the life I watched Buzz and Toni Buescher live together: the joy on his face that only showed when she was around, the light she added to his dark, the way she held all the patience in the world, and support for a man who worked tirelessly, who spent more time in the office than at home, and who prioritized work over anniversaries and birthdays.

The door to the kitchen opened, and Buzz walked in. His typical larger-than-life persona shriveled to reveal a broken man clinging to the last moments he had with the love of his life.

"I suppose you want to talk." His gruff voice tore into my aching skull.

Louise wrapped an egg sandwich in a paper towel and set it in front of me with a cup of coffee, two aspirins, and water.

I downed the little white pills and water, then scooped up the coffee and sandwich before following Buzz to his office.

The room was a chaotic mess. Papers were scattered all over the desk and floor, and file drawers were partially opened. There were empty coffee cups with ring stains and half-smoked cigars heaped in an ashtray.

Louise obviously had not been allowed in here for some time. She would lose her mind if she saw this place.

"What do you want, Corbin?" Buzz asked.

He sat in the leather chair behind his desk, clearing his throat and shuffling some loose papers.

"What do I want?" I asked incredulously.

The words hung in the air, and for a moment, I didn't know how to answer.

What *did* I want?

I wanted answers—about where he'd been, why he'd vanished when everything was falling apart, why he'd abandoned the company he'd spent his life building, the empire he'd once expected me to carry on.

But after seeing that moment, the quiet moment between two people who chose each other and built a life together, Andi's sage wisdom echoed in my head: "You think success is worth shit if there's no one to come home to?"

What did I *want?*

I wanted a life that had nothing to do with boardrooms or power struggles. I wanted to go back to Misty Springs—not as an outsider trying to claw my way back to New York—but as a man who'd found something worth staying for.

I wanted dart leagues at Boomer's on Tuesday nights, and not just to listen to, but to be a part of the inside jokes.

I wanted to earn a new nickname besides *Zoolander*.

I wanted quiet mornings, waking up to the smell of Sophia's flowery scent and the sight of her messy hair spilling over my pillow.

I wanted to spend Sunday afternoons with her curled up on my chest with an unhurried pace that allowed us to stay like that all day if we wanted to.

I wanted a life that didn't revolve around deals, mergers, or board votes.

I wanted a life that revolved around her.

I wanted Sophia.

"I fucked up." The words burned like bile as they spilled from my mouth. But they were the truth.

Buzz's eyebrows lifted in question.

"I… I let Davis." I ran my good hand through my disheveled hair. "He bested me. We fought, and he won. It's over. I lost the company. *We* lost the company."

Buzz leaned back in his chair, his head tilted to the side, his silent expression urging me to continue.

"The board looks at me and sees my father," I admitted, the words nearly choking me.

I thought of Sophia and how I didn't choose her at first. I didn't tell her how I felt about her. I didn't lay it all out on the line.

Instead, I acted like the rules didn't apply and that I wouldn't get caught toying with both of our fates.

"Maybe I am just like him," I whispered, defeated.

I lost everything.

Lost my reputation. Lost the job. Lost the girl.

"Your father." He clicked his tongue between his teeth as he paused. "I made so many mistakes with him."

I swallowed hard at his admission. If I thought shedding a tear and skipping work was another side of Buzz—him admitting he was wrong proved he was a completely changed man.

"You are not like him, Corbin. He was selfish and reckless. He didn't care how his actions reflected on him, on me, on *you*."

"Well, I'm certainly nothing like you. You built this company." The words started pouring out of me before I could scoop them back in. "Do you have any idea how hard it was to grow up in both of your shadows? To have people wonder which Buescher torch I was going to carry? The constant pressure to be great—or the suffocating fear of being a failure?"

This felt like uncharted territory. Buzz and I never talked about things as trivial as emotions or feelings.

"I know," Buzz said softly.

He stood up from his chair with a slight groan. "It took me a long time—too long—to realize something."

He began pacing slightly, his march steady and disciplined, like the soldier he was.

"Life is about the people you love and who love you back. It's about giving, not taking. It's something to embrace, to enjoy, not a

343

competition," he paused, looking at me more deeply. "If I could go back and do it all differently, I would."

He stopped in front of a framed one-dollar bill, the first one he earned when he opened his publishing company, or so the story goes.

"Publishing was my passion project. It was what started it all. It was your grandmother and I, our love of literature, and our ambition to share stories with the world, together. That's how it was always supposed to be. Then money and power took over, and before I knew it, I lost sight of my original plan and the significant things in life, like her, like your father, like you."

I stilled for a moment, absorbing his words, the lessons learned after a lifetime of poor decisions.

"It's all for nothing now. You missed the board meeting. Everything is lost. The company is out of both of our hands."

"Yes, I'm aware. I do still have friends on the board, so I was informed of the events of yesterday's pity party," he said smugly as he continued his slow march. "It's too bad none of it counts."

My heart lifted, and my eyes snapped to him. "What do you mean, none of it counts?"

"Well... there are a couple of problems with their little vote. The main being, Buescher Enterprises has no legal control over Buescher-Jones Publishing," he remarked, pulling a manila envelope from atop one of the filing cabinets and flinging it onto the desk.

I opened it, pulling out a large stack of documents.

Divestiture of Buescher-Jones Publishing

"You... you split the companies?" My jaw felt like it was practically on the floor.

"Turns out, Buescher Enterprises isn't quite as profitable as Davis may have been led to believe."

I scanned the documents: P&L statements, asset listings, key clients, patents, trademarks, and other intellectual property, all of which belonged to Buescher-Jones Publishing.

"So you stripped Buescher Enterprises of all of these assets, and now," I paused as realization set in.

"Let Davis and the board have the shell of what remains. The real company—the company that started all of it has been transferred to you."

A knock sounded at the door.

"Ah, he's here, perfect timing," Buzz declared as he opened the door to welcome the new arrival.

I turned to see Sullivan standing in the doorway, wearing his trademark mischievous grin.

"Sullivan?" I asked with the same surprised tone I had when he swooped in to rescue me at the Sheriff's station.

"Who do you think helped me with all this?" Buzz asked, retreating and leaning to rest on his disheveled desk.

"See, I make a great spy, Corby," Sullivan whispered to me as he stepped inside the office and mussed my hair.

"Sullivan and I have been spending a lot of late nights working on this. It hasn't been easy prying the two companies apart without anyone noticing. And I've been working hard to ensure Davis was as comfortable as possible as we pulled this off. Keep your friends close and all that," Buzz added.

"We just have a few more loose ends to tie up, and Davis will be stuck holding the bag of an empty company." Buzz straightened, moving to once again stand before me.

His dark eyes met mine, assertive and dominant, but something new gleamed in them—caring, fatherly.

"Are you in?" he asked.

I nodded, eliciting sly grins from Sullivan and Buzz.

And with that, the three of us got to work.

Chapter 69

Libido-Away

Sophia

"It's called libido-away, and it works like a Pavlovian response, but instead of making you want something, it makes you *not* want something." I pitched my invention to my friends as we sipped cosmos in the dining room at Elijah's.

I wish I had some of this patented product when I first met Corbin. I would have blasted the noise in my earbuds on the plane. The sound trigger would have made me resist his lure, and I would have never allowed myself to dream this ridiculous dream that smashed to pieces before me.

I only had parts of the story, but from what I gathered, Davis had taken over as CEO, and my job at Buescher-Jones Publishing was officially terminated since the Misty Springs branch was shutting down.

"Okay, I like it, but what would the noise be?" Cassie asked. "Ohh, maybe I could record Trevor's snoring," she added deviously.

"Hey, I have a deviated septum," Trevor responded, placing his hand on his heart.

"So, how would you train the non-sexual response? Would they have to come into some sort of therapy session?" Lana asked.

"Maybe you could make an at-home version, like a do-it-yourself kit," Devyn chimed. "I bet Amazon would sell it."

"You know what I love about you all the most?" I asked with a lazy smile as I lifted my glass toward the center of the table. "This, right here. Your unwavering support. For all my terrible ideas and decisions."

We clinked our glasses and sipped on our hot pink cosmopolitans while *Legally Blonde* played in the background.

Cassie informed us that the idea for this theme was born when Julio said he wanted to make something simple, like hot dogs, for once. She said she gave him his best Jennifer Coolidge impression, saying she wanted a hot dog real bad—a reference that flew over his head—but he took it as a green light to do so.

A week later, a shipment of hot dogs arrived, and thus, *Legally Blonde* movie theme night was born.

Of course, Julio didn't know how to do simple things, so these hot dogs were anything but plain. Mine had a pickled jalapeno relish adorned atop a smoked cream cheese. It was heavenly.

The dessert was a Boston cream pie because Harvard was in Massachusetts. It was a bit of a stretch, but there are no rules when it comes to Elijah's movie-themed nights.

"We love you too, Soph," Brent said, sipping his water.

He had volunteered to drive us home tonight. "And take it easy on the drinks," he added, his big brother tone slipping through.

"C'mon, the doctor said she could have one," Devyn argued.

"The doctor said she could have none, actually," Brent corrected.

"One is basically none if you drink it slowly enough and have some water in between," she countered.

I laughed at Devyn's logic.

"I feel fine guys. I just need to figure out how to start over… again." I took another sip of my pink drink.

"You're welcome back here anytime, you know. Elijah literally cried when I told him you quit." Cassie squeezed my hand over the table.

"Yeah, come back to Boomer's, too," Devyn chimed in, sticking her lip out in an exaggerated pout. "Theresa will let you come back even though you yell-quit. She still owes you that much."

I forced a smile, though a pang of sadness lingered beneath it. My dream job had imploded, and my latest attempt at romance had seemingly turned into yet another spectacular disaster.

But despite it all, I couldn't call this a failure. I wasn't the same person I was a few months ago. I may have taken three steps forward and two steps back, but I was still new and improved.

"Actually," I said, the words forming like a sudden epiphany as I watched Elle Woods strut around the hallways of Harvard, "I think I might go back to school—finally finish that degree. I might have to spend the rest of my life paying off my loans, but at least I'll have doors open for me that have been sealed shut previously."

Lana placed her hand on mine. "That's a great plan, Soph."

"Then what?" Sam asked, sipping on his pink drink with a distinguished pinkie raised in the air.

"I don't know exactly, something in publishing." I felt a spark of excitement. "Turns out, I have a knack for it. Maybe with a degree and a solid month of experience, someone besides Andi will give me a chance next time."

Devyn raised her glass. "To Sophia, the next literary queen!"

We clinked our glasses together and celebrated the occasion of just being together, of being there for each other through all life's highs and lows.

In that moment, I realized Corbin was right—I was rich. And this crew was worth more than all the glitzy gold in the world.

"Another round?" Lana asked, already signaling to the bartender.

Before anyone could respond, a familiar voice came from behind me, deep and achingly resonant. "This one's on me."

My breath caught, my lungs seemingly forgetting how to inflate. Heat flamed across my skin, tightening every muscle as it coursed through my body.

Every face at the table snapped toward the voice above my head.

"And just where have you been?" Trevor spoke first, his tone mock-accusatory. "Waltzing in here like the prodigal son—"

Devyn slapped his arm, forcing him to stop.

"Ow!" he cried.

I pushed my chair back, nearly colliding with Corbin. His scent—that familiar citrus and pine—enveloped me, and I felt dizzy for reasons that had nothing to do with the vodka.

Without thinking, I wrapped my hand around Corbin's arm— the one that wasn't still in a sling—and pulled him away from the table.

As we left, I heard Trevor whining about wanting to know what was going on and Cassie scolding him.

My mind was spinning, and my legs were unsteady as I led Corbin into the quiet privacy of the breakroom. The sign on the door read "Employees Only," but I decided that former employees counted as well.

The fluorescent lights buzzed faintly, casting a sterile glow over the mismatched furniture and the trusty Mr. Coffee machine.

Corbin looked so out of place here, his tailored suit pristine, his tie slightly loosened. The sling around his arm was the only sign he'd just come from battle—literal and metaphorical.

He looked at me, and I met his gaze with a steely glare. I let my silence do the heavy lifting, willing him to come up with what had better be a hell of an excuse for dodging me these past few days.

"I'm sorry," he said, smoothing out an invisible wrinkle on his jacket. "I should've texted you. The past forty-eight hours have been... overwhelming."

I swallowed, my throat tight. "What happened, Corbin?"

"A lot... too much." His eyes softened, and I took a small step toward him, still keeping my distance.

"Are you okay?" I asked.

A faint smile played on his lips, tinged with exhaustion. "I'm okay. A little broken, a little bruised, and a lot pissed at Davis. But things are finally going down the right path."

I crossed my arms, frustration mingling with worry. "What path is that? Because from where I'm standing, everything feels like it's fallen off a cliff. Your company was stolen from you. I got fired. The Misty Springs branch is shut down. Everything is destroyed. The path isn't even visible anymore."

"Not the way I see it," he said softly, stepping closer.

The air around us thickened, humming with tension. His gaze, fierce and unrelenting, rooted me to the spot. The warmth radiating from his body teased my senses, making it hard to hold on to my anger.

"The way I see it," he continued, "is that my grandfather's company needed to cut some dead weight."

He moved closer, his fingers brushing my cheek, still slightly bruised from the accident.

"And it's not his company anymore." His breath was warm against my ear as he dipped closer. "It's mine."

My heart raced, hammering against my ribs as I struggled to make sense of the sudden shift. "So... you're in charge now?"

"Fully," he confirmed, a flicker of pride in his tone. "Of both branches, New York and Misty Springs."

"New York *and* Misty Springs? So, the branch here will stay open?" My heart lifted. I thought my opportunity to work in publishing meant leaving the town and the people I loved.

"The woman running the day-to-day in Misty Springs is tough but fair. And she needs an editor. Don't question her style choices, though—she'll tear you apart," Corbin added.

"Andi is in charge of the Misty Springs branch?"

He nodded, dropping his hand to my waist.

The feel of his fingers made my insides tighten with anticipation. I swallowed it down, still trying to process everything he said.

"So, will you be staying in New York? Or..." My skin tingled under the graze of his fingers as they slowly slid under my shirt.

He grinned with a lazy, confident curve of his lips. "I have a guy who will be helping me oversee the New York Branch. He's now the 'Vice President of Operations, Overcomplicated Legalese, and Bad Moods.' Sullivan insisted on the title."

A laugh escaped me before I could stop it. "Sullivan seems to be quite the character."

"He's definitely something else." Corbin's smile at the mention of Sullivan was youthful and genuine. "So I plan on having a lot more theme nights at Elijah's—since I plan to spend every moment I can trying to woo a brilliant, sexy, well-read brunette."

My breath caught, heat blooming in my chest at his acclaim. "You're assuming this brunette wants to be wooed?"

"I'm an optimist," he said with a devilish grin.

"What about the no-relationship policy?" I challenged, tilting my head.

He licked his lips as mischief flickered in his gaze. "I own the company now. And I say you can kiss me—or do whatever you want with me—whenever you want."

I didn't wait.

I closed the gap between us, my lips finding his in a fierce and claiming kiss.

His hand slid into my hair, pulling me closer as the weight of uncertainty melted away.

Someone doesn't just fit into your life—they rewrite the definition of it.
And Corbin did.

Every kiss, every conversation, every moment of reckless hope—it all changed how I saw myself, my future, *us*.

This wasn't the start of something—it was a redefinition. A slow remaking of the woman I'd hidden beneath fear and doubt.

And for the first time in a long time, she felt like someone I could believe in.

Epilogue

3 MONTHS LATER

Sophia

"It came!" I exclaimed as I burst into the bright, bustling office of Buescher-Jones Publishing, holding the envelope aloft like a trophy.

Andi stood in the common area, instantly attuned to my excitement. "Yay! Congrats!"

"Wait. I don't know what it says yet," I admitted, though my grin probably gave away my rising hope.

"Well, open it already!" she demanded, practically bouncing in place.

I ripped open the seal, my eyes scanning the bolded first line.

My heart skipped, then soared. "Thank you for your application…" I quickly rattled off the rest of the sentence in my head.

"I got in!" I screamed, my voice echoing through the office.

Andi and I jumped up and down in an uncoordinated but exuberant hug.

"Could you ladies maybe go squeal somewhere else?" Corbin's voice cut through the celebration as he poked his head out of his office, mock annoyance etched on his handsome features. "What's the excitement this time? Andi get another new purse?"

"That wasn't *just* a new purse—it was a Hermès. And I got an amazing deal on it," Andi shot back, hands on her hips. "Also, your girlfriend just got into Brown."

The shift in Corbin's expression was immediate. His teasing smirk melted into pure joy. "You got in?"

I nodded, unable to suppress my grin as he strode toward me.

Before I could say anything else, he wrapped me in his arms, spinning me in a full circle.

"I'm so proud of you. I *knew* you could do it," he said, his voice warm and genuine. Then his lips found mine in a kiss that made the world fade into the background.

Andi cleared her throat dramatically. "I miss the no-relationship policy," she muttered as she sauntered toward her office.

Corbin and I both smiled into the kiss, pulling apart just enough to exchange a shared laugh, our foreheads touching briefly before he pulled away.

The past three months had been nothing short of transformative.

After that day in the breakroom at Elijah's, Corbin whisked me off to New York, where I met Monica McKenzie—my idol. She was everything I dreamed and more, writing me a custom inscription on my latest copy of *Spilled Martini,* encouraging me to follow my dreams.

Corbin also took the opportunity to introduce me to his grandparents. His grandmother was lucid, according to Buzz—a rare sight these days. I shared photos of Misty Springs. We found common connections—friends and places she remembered from decades ago—and spent hours reminiscing about how things had changed.

Corbin's relationship with his grandfather, once strained, seemed to mend before my eyes. The two of them would lean close, talking in whispers, exchanging smiles that spoke of a bond finally repaired.

Meeting the Manhattan branch of Buescher-Jones was a whirlwind. New faces, new opportunities, and connections I hadn't dreamed of making.

Corbin beamed with pride as he introduced me to his team, and for the first time, I felt like I truly belonged in his world—our world.

I stayed until the day before Christmas Eve, marveling at the city's lights and decorations. But when the holidays came, we parted ways briefly. I spent time with Penny and her family when they visited Misty Springs, while Corbin stayed behind with his grandparents.

Luke teased me endlessly, asking if I'd met Bruce Wayne yet.

I laughed, telling him I kind of had. I mean, after all, Corbin was rich, hot, and had a knack for fighting the bad guys in my life.

Corbin pulled me into his office and handed me a thick black gift bag.

I eyed the white gift tag attached to it, huffing a laugh when I read the names he wrote in the pre-printed fields.

To: 1C

From: 1B

Corbin watched me closely, grinning his playful Corbin grin (my favorite).

I couldn't wipe the smile off my face as I dipped my hands into the bag, shuffling through layers of soft white tissue paper until my fingers brushed against something smooth, firm, and unmistakably luxurious.

Lifting it out, I uncovered a deep black leather backpack, the fine material supple beneath my touch. The iconic Louis Vuitton logo was subtly embossed into the grain, a brand even I could recognize as expensive.

"This is... beautiful."

"You needed a new backpack for your laptop—yours is literally held together with staples," he said into my hair as he wrapped his arms around me.

"Thank you, I love it. But I told you that just because we were together, I didn't want you buying me things," I warned, pressing a soft kiss to his lips.

He pulled away, a coy look on his face. "Oh, you're really not going to be happy with me when you find out what else I did."

***

"Where are we going?" I asked as Corbin drove down a familiar road, his expression unreadable.

"You'll see."

When we pulled up to the house, my breath hitched. The sight of it was like a ghost from my past, but instead of fear, it brought a wave of bittersweet nostalgia. The wraparound porch where I'd spent countless summers reading books. The flower beds my mom used to tend with care—now overgrown but still holding traces of her touch.

My old home. The one I'd sold when Landon convinced me I had no choice.

I looked at Corbin, confused as to why he had brought me here—or how he even knew what this place was to me.

I barely noticed the car coming to a stop before Corbin's voice broke through my thoughts.

"I bought it... *for you*," he whispered softly, his gaze fixed on me, waiting to gauge my reaction.

A jolt shot through my body as my head swirled back toward my childhood home. A home I thought I would never see the inside of again.

Tears misted my eyes as I turned back to him. "You... what?" My voice cracked, teetering between shock and disbelief.

"It's yours," he repeated.

I climbed out of the car, the spring air cool on my skin as I looked up at the beautiful brick two-story. My head started to feel a little woozy.

"Don't be upset," Corbin said quickly, following me to the curb.

"It was on the market, and I couldn't stand the thought of someone else getting it. It's in your name—fully yours. No strings, no loopholes," he paused, his voice lowering with a tenderness that made my chest ache. "I just... I wanted you to have it."

With Landon, I'd been conditioned to see every gift, every offer of help, as a trap. He had wielded favors like weapons, wrapping them in chains disguised as generosity. The fear of letting someone hold something over me was a reflex I couldn't shake.

But Corbin wasn't Landon.

Corbin didn't take. He gave. Not because he wanted leverage but because he wanted *me*—happy, whole.

I stared at him, overwhelmed by the magnitude of what he'd done. It wasn't just a house. It was a piece of my history, a reminder of where I came from.

My voice cracked as a tear ran down my cheek. "Thank you."

Corbin's smile beamed in the bright afternoon sun. He gently wiped away the lone tear before wrapping his hand around mine and pulling me toward the front door.

He plucked a single key from his pocket and let it dangle from his finger.

"You know," he said, his voice teasing as he unlocked the front door, pushing it open, "if you need help bringing your bag inside..."

"I don't know if that trick will work on me twice, Mr. Buescher," I teased, my cheeks heating as I remembered our hotel room encounter.

I turned to face him, and he settled his hands on my hips. I leaned in, kissing him, every emotion falling into my lips.

His strong hands pulled me close, and his fingers dug gently into my sides until there was no space left between us.

The spring air mingled with the scent of fresh blooms, hinting at new beginnings.

When we finally broke apart, he was grinning, his eyebrows wiggling in a way that told me he was thinking about our hotel encounter, too.

I laughed, the sound bubbling up with the memories we shared that were so preciously *ours*.

Without hesitating, I jumped into his arms, my legs wrapping around his waist as he caught me effortlessly.

"You're unbelievable," I murmured against his ear.

He carried me across the threshold into the house where so many chapters of my life had unfolded. A familiar smell greeted me, one that existed years later, woven so deep in the grains of the wood frame that it would linger forever.

It combined with Corbin's scent, mixing with the air and making it smell so inexplicably like *home*.

Corbin set me down, his arms lingering around my waist. He looked deep into my eyes.

"Can I tell you something?" he asked, licking his lips and catching his bottom lip with his teeth nervously.

"I love you, Sophia Carlson. I loved you ever since you stole my seat in first class."

My heart swelled. In front of me stood the most mesmerizingly handsome, ambitious, and generous man I'd ever met—and he loved me.

"Can I tell you something?" I asked, biting my lip too. "I wasn't even supposed to be in first class."

His jaw dropped, and his eyes widened in playful shock. "I knew—"

My kiss cut him off, and as it deepened, the final suture needed to mend my broken heart stitched itself up tight.

Everything finally felt right.

It was as if the pieces of my life had to be shattered first to form the rich mosaic that glowed like a stained-glass window lit by brilliant sunlight.

I pulled away and nestled my head into his chest.

"I love you, too, Corbin," I whispered.

This house had always been filled with stories—laughter echoing through its halls, love tucked into every corner.

Our moment imprinted itself on the next page, the start of a new chapter—one of many we'd build together, beginning with our first *I love yous*.

Building a story that would mean more to me than any love story ever written.

A love that was more than fiction.

The End.

ACKNOWLEDGMENTS

I will be forever grateful to my husband, who has put up with me saying, "one more chapter," for two decades now. Josh, thank you for doing fun things with the kids and taking care of the house while I tinker around with this hobby of mine. Thank you for being the first to read this book, and for giving me some very necessary insight into the inner workings of the male mind when it came to Corbin's POV.

Hillary—mentioned second only because Josh fathered my children, and it's hard to compete with that—I simply would not have **ever** written this if you weren't in my life. Thanks for all the reading (and re-reading), for the advice, and for always talking me down when I hated my draft and encouraging me to keep at it. Our friendship is truly magical.

Jae. Your unwavering support, amazing editing skills, design skills, and the sheer amount of talent you possess are nothing short of astounding. Look out, world, Jae Shadowlance will be filling up your bookshelf soon—she will do remarkable things, just you wait!

Ashley, Danielle, and Lydia. My girls. My Beta Beauties. My Framily. Thank you for being the inspiration behind the unbelievably close friendships in this book—my chosen family that supports me no matter what, even when I get a wild idea to write a book. I like to think the Misty Springs gang will have kids that grow up together assuming they are cousins, just like our kids.

Shelly. Thank you for taking the jumbled thoughts of mine and turning them into an adorable cover. You are pure creative talent and have such an amazing heart. I appreciate the months of back and forth you put up with my wishy-washy brain!

AND YOU, dear reader. Thank you for taking a chance on a no-name author like me. I hope you enjoyed reading this story as much as I did writing it.

If you liked this book, please consider leaving a review on goodreads or Amazon. Your review will help get this story in the hands of other amazing readers like you. ♡

ABOUT THE AUTHOR

Juniper Nicole is an emerging indie author. She lives in a small Missouri town with her husband, children, and crazy GSP doggo.

When she isn't working on her novels or spending time with her family, she writes stories and does bookish things with her dear friend Jae.

Together, they are Juniper & Jae.

Juniper believes that middle America is more than a flyover country, that you can measure the distance of a storm by counting the seconds between lightning and thunder, and that love conquers all.

SCAN ME!

Stay up to date on all things Misty Springs!
Join the Juniverse today: www.junipernicole.com